Romantic Times BOOKclub **loves**

ELIZABETH
LOWELL

"It is not hard to see why Lowell's novels have enjoyed
their superior success over the years."
—on *This Time Love*

"The masterful storytelling skills of perennial favorite
Elizabeth Lowell place her in a rarified class of authors
who never disappoint."
—on *Running Scared*

"The powerful storytelling that is a hallmark of Elizabeth Lowell's
work makes each of her books a riveting journey."
—on *Moving Target*

"...an emotionally driven and sensually
charged book that is vintage Lowell."
—on *Eden Burning*

"When it comes to delivering epic romance and suspense,
Ms. Lowell is in a class by herself."
—on *Midnight in Ruby Bayou*

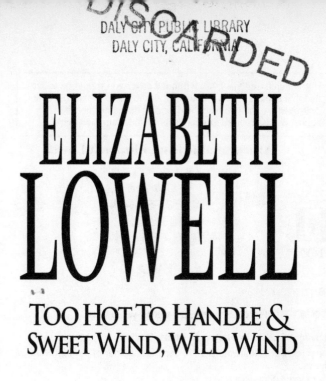

ELIZABETH LOWELL

TOO HOT TO HANDLE &
SWEET WIND, WILD WIND

HQN™

W

HQN™

ISBN 0-373-77173-8

TOO HOT TO HANDLE & SWEET WIND, WILD WIND

Copyright © 2006 by Harlequin Books S.A.

The publisher acknowledges the copyright holder of the individual works as
follows:

TOO HOT TO HANDLE
Copyright © 1986 by Ann Maxwell
SWEET WIND, WILD WIND
Copyright © 1987 by Ann Maxwell

This edition published by arrangement with Harlequin Books S.A.

® and TM are trademarks of the publisher. Trademarks indicated with
® are registered in the United States Patent and Trademark Office, the
Canadian Trade Marks Office and in other countries.

www.HQNBooks.com

Printed in U.S.A.

CONTENTS

TOO HOT TO HANDLE   9

SWEET WIND, WILD WIND   221

TOO HOT TO HANDLE

For Susan Kyle,
whose books are ardent,
amusing and addictive

Chapter One

TORY WELLS HUNG ON TO HER battered luggage with both hands. She felt as though the earth had been ripped from beneath her feet. It wasn't the earth being ripped, however. It was the letter that she had brought with her from Ethan Reever's cousin, a letter promising her employment on the Sundance Ranch.

"But I was told that—" she began, her voice low, urgent.

"You were told wrong," Ethan Reever interrupted ruthlessly, dropping the shredded, unread letter into an exquisitely woven Pima basket that held other paper debris. He gave the slender young blonde in front of him a hard glance. "There's no swimming pool on the Sundance so there's no need for a 'swimming counselor.'" His lips thinned in disgust over the last two words. "And unlike my dear cousin Payton, I have no use for bleached blondes who can't do two licks of work without whining about their nails."

"My hair isn't bleached, my nails are short and the day I whine you can fire me," retorted Tory, setting her luggage down with a thump.

Reever laughed. The sound was as hard as the large hands that slapped the desk in an impatient movement as he came to his feet. "Honey, I haven't hired you, and I'm not going to. I need you like a sidewinder needs ice skates."

Tory stared in silence at the man looming behind a desk that was as scarred as her luggage. Reever was nothing like his cousin, Payton Sundance. Payton's hair was straight and sandy, he was clean shaven, his eyes were a sparkling blue and his body was as thin as it was tall. Reever's hair was thick, blue-black and shaggy. So was his mustache. His blunt, angular face showed a shadow of beard, even though it was barely eleven o'clock. His eyes were the color of winter rain and were emphasized by heavy black eyebrows. He had the long, powerful bone structure of a natural athlete and the muscular development to go with it. He was at least six foot three—a dark, intimidating presence watching her with eyes that gave away nothing.

Reever's intense masculinity would have made Tory nervous if she hadn't been so desperate for the job. She was accustomed to being around men with flawless bodies, swimmers and divers whose lives were dedicated to physical perfection, yet never had she met a man whose very presence could send frissons of heat searching through her. Reever threatened her in ways that she couldn't describe. But even more than he threatened her, he fascinated her. She found herself wondering what it would be like to be held in those powerful arms. Did that beautifully shaped mouth ever smile gently, and were his hands capable of tenderness as well as strength?

Tory shook herself mentally, wondering if she had lost her mind. Reever was very unlike his cousin. She could well believe Payton's warning about Reever's "devil temper." Payton was charming, kind and known for his generosity throughout the Southern California amateur athletic community. Tory doubted that anyone would use the adjectives generous, charming or kind to describe Ethan Reever.

The thought didn't make Tory back down. She had spent her life working with male coaches who could most politely be described as "difficult." Besides, she had to have the Sundance job whether Reever was devil incarnate or angel in disguise. At the moment she had exactly two dollars and sixty-three cents to her name. She couldn't afford a bus trip back to town, much less a cab—not that either bus or cab was available, even if she had money. The Sundance Ranch was in the wild country of northern Arizona, a place where the roads were empty and the land was full of sunlight and silence.

"Mr. Reever," Tory said carefully, trying to show neither her desperation nor her fear, much less the very feminine curiosity that he aroused in her. She had learned early in life than any sign of weakness would be used against her.

"Reever," he said, his voice harsh. "Just plain Reever. You're not in the city anymore, Miss Victoria Wells."

"No kidding?" shot back Tory. Her glance went pointedly around the office, where a collection of spurs was tacked to the wall and a half-braided horsehair rope waited in one corner to be completed. "Call me Tory, Reever," she said, smiling. "Everybody does."

His eyes narrowed. Tory decided that all the books were wrong. The devil's eyes were gray, not black. She took a deep breath and tried again to get past Reever's hard exterior. Somewhere inside that man was something more than harshness and the glacial cold of his eyes. She knew that with an instinct so deep that she didn't question it.

"Mr. Sundance assured me that there would be work for me here," Tory said honestly. "I came a long way at my own expense on that assurance. If the Sundance Retreat isn't open yet, there must be something else I could do on the ranch until the retreat opens."

Reever stood silently for a moment, giving Tory the same kind of thorough, cataloging glance that she had given to him a moment earlier. Tory knew exactly what he would see. She had short blond hair streaked by the Southern California sun, green eyes that were too light to be called emerald and five feet seven inches of tan body conditioned by a lifetime of swimming and diving.

If Reever was hoping to make Tory uncomfortable with his stare, she had a surprise for him. She was used to being stared at while wearing a good deal less than beige cotton slacks and a T-shirt proclaiming "Be Kind to Endangered Species—Adopt a Mermaid." Competition swimsuits were designed to be a second skin, and they achieved that purpose with admirable thoroughness, especially when wet. As Tory stood on a diving platform high above a pool, poised for her second dive, the spectators knew just about everything there was to know about her physically.

Yet standing still for Reever's slow scrutiny became more difficult for Tory with each passing second. When he looked at her, it was as though his hands were moving over her body while his fingertips learned every feminine curve and hollow. The thought both shocked and intrigued her, making her breath shorten and her eyes darken as the pupils expanded with sensual curiosity. Deep inside Tory a gentle heat began to uncurl, making her mouth soften in unconscious invitation. She was too inexperienced to realize what was happening to her; she only knew that the longer she watched Reever, the more she became curious about him as a man.

"Please," Tory said, her voice husky. "If you had read the letter before you tore it up, you'd know that I'm a very hard worker."

Reever hadn't finished his leisurely appraisal of Tory's body. When he finally did, his mouth turned down and his voice shifted into a sardonic drawl that could have etched steel.

"No, thanks," he said. "I like my playmates small, stacked and sexy. You flunk on all three counts."

For a moment Tory was too stunned to respond. Her breath came in with a rushing sound as her temper flared. "I wasn't offering to—" she began angrily.

"The hell you weren't," interrupted Reever, his eyes as contemptuous as his tone. "You were begging for it."

Tory flushed, then went very pale. "Go to the devil, Ethan Reever," she said, trembling.

"Didn't Payton tell you, honey? I *am* the devil."

Tory looked at Reever and wished suddenly, violently, that she had spent her years learning karate rather than the gentle art of diving. Without a word she picked up her luggage, turned her back on the devil's cruel smile and walked out of the room. Before she had gone three steps, she heard the desk chair creak as it once again took Reever's formidable weight. The sound of the big leather ledger sliding across the desk was loud in the silence. She didn't need to look over her shoulder to know that she had already been wiped from Reever's mind as completely as though she had never stood in front of him and pleaded for a job.

Without hesitating, Tory walked through the living room, opened the front door and pulled it shut behind her, using her foot. She would have slammed the door until the house shook but had no wish to call attention to herself again. Just the thought of facing Reever's contempt brought a sweeping humiliation that was as great as her anger. She would crawl on her hands and knees all nineteen miles back to town before she suffered his contemptuous appraisal again.

Although the ranch house was thousands of feet above the desert floor, the June day was hot enough to bring a mist of perspiration to Tory's face as she stood on the porch and looked at the long, dusty ranch road that eventually led to a narrow county road and from there to Massacre Creek, the only town within ninety miles of the Sundance Ranch.

Tory knew from experience that the most exciting thing about Massacre Creek was the name. The sign outside the town had proudly proclaimed Population 401, but unless they were counting the litter of fat puppies that she had seen chasing flies and each other in front of the Sunup Café, Tory couldn't imagine where Massacre Creek's citizens were. After the relentless concentration of people in coastal Southern California, northern Arizona's empty reaches seemed alien and...oddly inviting.

At the moment, though, Tory could have done with a little less scenery and a lot more cheap public transportation. Abruptly she shifted her duffel bag over one shoulder, took a better grasp of the cracked, abrasive handle of her suitcase and stepped off the porch onto the dusty gravel drive. If she wanted to be in town before dark, there was no time to waste on wishful thinking.

Tory pushed aside the thought that there was almost no chance that she would be able to walk nineteen miles before sundown. Without luggage she would have done well enough. There had been some days when she had driven herself to swim nearly that many miles under the sarcastic goading of her coach. She hadn't been carrying a suitcase, however.

And then there was her knee.

Slowly Tory walked over the treacherous gravel, alert to each movement of stone beneath her right foot. She didn't want to think about the knee injury that had finally resulted in surgery three weeks ago. She didn't want to think about the doctor's final frightening words, words that had sent her rushing to Arizona with no more than a few dollars and Payton Sundance's letter in her purse. She had come back from an injury before. She would do it again. All she needed was the time to heal and the money to survive until she could take up the physical demands of her swim club scholarship again.

Tory was relieved when the gravel gave way to dirt road, but the relief was premature. She soon discovered that the rutted, washboard surface of the road was as tricky to walk on as the gravel had been. Trial and error taught her that the best walking was on the very edge of the road, where tires had passed often enough to make a flat trail but not often enough to leave ruts and ripples in the dirt. Her luggage tended to hang up on roadside bushes, but there weren't many rocks to bruise her feet through the worn soles of her shoes. Where her little toes had poked through the canvas, pebbles worked into the holes and from there to her tender feet.

At first Tory stopped and emptied her shoe every time a pebble got inside. She soon gave that up. She was spending more time hopping around on one foot and dumping out the other shoe than she was walking. So she just kept going until the first pebble was joined by a second and then a third, or until her arms and shoulders sent threatening messages to her brain. Then she would stop, dump her luggage in the dirt, stretch and empty her shoes.

The carefully rationed rest stops were far too short, but Tory knew that she didn't dare extend them. She really didn't want to be walking through the countryside after dark. Her best chance of a safe ride into town was to catch the mail carrier somewhere along the county road. She wished that she had listened more closely to the woman's friendly chatter as she had delivered Tory—and a generous supply of junk mail—right to the Sundance Ranch's front door. Had the woman said that she made a loop that led back to town after a circuit of ranch roads, or had she said that she went out the south end of town and came in the north?

If it were the latter, there was no hope of getting a ride back into town. Nor did Tory want to take her chances on hitching a ride with a stranger. Living in cosmopolitan Southern California had taught her not to trust strangers. If she kept walking, she would get to town eventually. She had no such assurance if she hitchhiked.

By the time the Sundance Ranch's dirt road met the two-lane blacktop of the county road, Tory was bathed in sweat and aching in every limb. She hoped that the road's dark, even surface would ease the throb in her right knee. She had no such hope for the burning of her blistered palms. Swimming might have strengthened her body, but it had done nothing to toughen her hands or feet.

With a stifled groan Tory remembered the mail carrier's words to the effect that it was five miles to the Sundance ranch house from the county road. She couldn't believe it. She had to have walked more than five miles. It couldn't be fourteen more miles to town.

"Stop whining," she muttered to herself. "Whining takes energy. Think about something pleasant—like drowning that arrogant son of Satan in the deep end of a pool."

Stretching, smiling, Tory thought of having Reever gasping and begging for mercy at her hands. It was a fantasy she had often had about her coaches in the past when they pushed her beyond what she thought she could endure. But each time she was pushed she had learned that she *could* endure. Not only that, she had learned that she could strengthen and improve until workouts that once would have left her gasping became nothing more than invigorating exercise. Until their bodies were conditioned, though, she and her teammates had spent many hours planning complicated and satisfying vengeance on their various coaches.

But when Tory thought of revenge on Reever, the picture of him apologizing for not giving her a job kept going out of focus. In its place came a sudden, searing image of him bending down to her and his large, hard hands cupping her face gently as he whispered against her lips that now that he had found her, he would never let her go. The image shocked her. It made her realize that in a few minutes Reever had had more impact on her than other men in the same amount of years. She had never been in love, never wanted to be in love— but now she wondered what it would be like to love and be loved by Ethan Reever.

"Sidewinders will be ice-skating in Reever's birthplace before that happens," Tory informed herself sarcastically, feeling a flush climb up her face. "He couldn't

have been clearer that he thought your attractions…
weren't. Face it. His eyesight is as sharp as his tongue."

*Small, stacked and sexy. You flunk on all three
counts.*

Tory wished that she could disagree with his assess-
ment, but she could not. She was tall, gently rounded,
and in all considered herself about as sexy as an ironing board. Although her hair was a shiny, many-hued
blond, it was also a short, softly curling cap. The first
rule of being a sexy blonde was that your hair had to
be a long, ravishing, silky mass slithering down between your shoulder blades. The second rule of a sexy
blonde was that your chest had to be a double handful
for any man, and your heart-shaped bottom had to
swing like a bell when you walked. The third rule was
that a sexy blonde was always ready, willing and able
to trip a man and beat him to the floor.

"Face it, Tory. Even if you could trip that devil, you
wouldn't know what to do next."

The thought shook Tory. She had grown up watching the sudden passions and equally sudden separations
of her teammates. The pressures of competition and
endless, grinding workouts were often relieved in brief,
volatile affairs. She had seen that usually it was the girl
who was hurt. It was the girl who paid the price emotionally, competitively and in terms of her reputation.
There were exceptions, of course—boys whose competitive edge was dulled by a failed love affair or girls
who changed partners as casually and frequently as they
changed swimsuits—but those exceptions were very few.

Tory had decided before puberty that the dubious rewards of "love" really weren't worth the costs. Life had taught her that men simply weren't capable of caring. Her father hadn't even noticed her when he was still living with her mother, no matter how many medals Tory had won in competitive swimming. After the divorce her father had simply vanished, sending nothing to his daughter, not even a card at Christmas. Nor had her stepfather been much better. He had begrudged every penny spent on Tory, pointing out to her many times that her father was a selfish jerk who had never sent a dime on child support and never would. Her mother had rarely interceded; she was too grateful to find a man to support her. Later Tory had realized that she had been born three months after her mother's first marriage, when her mother had been barely seventeen.

When Tory's stepfather had been transferred to Wisconsin, she had stayed in California and moved into an apartment with three other girls from the swim club. Within days she had a job working from 8:00 p.m. to 2:00 a.m., five days a week, at a nearby fast-food restaurant. Three months later she was promoted to cook when the boss found her filling in for a man who was more interested in partying than in working.

The hours were awful, the work was hard and the money was barely enough to survive on. Yet Tory wouldn't have traded one minute of it for life with her stepfather. Her boss agreed to schedule her around her swim meets and school, and in return Tory worked even harder. When the doctor had told her to take a minimum of three months off from diving, it had been a great temptation for her to stay in Mission Viejo and work double shifts and save money.

In the end Tory had reluctantly decided against it. The doctor had been determined that she remove herself from the "narrow, unnatural, short-lived, hothouse atmosphere of Olympic athletics." He had flatly told her that she was to get out, all the way out, to see something more of the world than an Olympic swimming pool and then to decide if going back to diving was worth the risk of a permanent crippling injury.

Hastily Tory bent and picked up her luggage again. She didn't want to think about the doctor. He was wrong. He had to be wrong. Her knee would heal again and be stronger than ever. She was sure of it. It would be like everything else in her life had been: if she just worked hard enough, long enough, and depended only on herself, she could do anything. Anything at all. Including walk nineteen miles through a hot Arizona afternoon and find a place to stay in a town so small that it hand-lettered changes on the population sign. Then she had to earn enough to pay for the room and to buy a bus ticket back to California.

"One thing at a time," Tory said aloud, stilling the rush of her thoughts. "It's like a competition. You can't worry about any dive but the one in front of you or you'll fall apart. So first you walk to town. Then you can worry about the rest, one thing at a time. Just like diving."

As Tory thought of standing on tiptoe on a platform more than thirty feet above the aquamarine perfection of an Olympic pool, she unconsciously licked her lips.

At the moment, even pool water would have tasted good, chlorine and all. And to arc up and out, to turn over and over before entering the water's stillness, to have her tired body embraced and supported by the cool water...ah, that would be heaven itself.

Head down, her duffel bag slung across her back and her blistered hand grasping the broken handle of her suitcase, Tory set off down the two-lane county road, limping slightly. As far as she could see, she was the only thing moving beneath the incredible blue of the sky. She was relieved to be so alone. She had been in cities for too long to relish the idea of meeting a stranger on that desolate road.

REEVER RODE ALONG THE SOUTHEAST boundary of the ranch, checking the range. It had been a good winter, a wet winter. Snow had lain thickly in the steep-sided mountain valleys and had melted slowly on the slopes, providing continuous natural irrigation for the meadows. Grass and wildflowers grew in profusion, brushing his stirrups, for Reever hadn't permitted this part of the ranch to be grazed for five years. He had wanted just one part of the Sundance to look as it had in his great-grandfather's time.

Sundance, Jawbone and Wolf creeks were brimming with bright water, as were the sloughs where birds gathered in wheeling clouds to raise their young. Despite the raucous birds, it was Wolf Creek itself that drew Reever's eye. It had been a long time since he had tasted fresh trout. Although the water was still quite cold with the runoff of barely melted snow, the fish should be shaking off their winter torpor and gliding through the green pools in search of the season's first insect hatch. Cold, clean water and winter-hungry trout—a fisherman's dream.

Reever's mouth turned down as he admitted that, even if he managed to tempt one of the wily trout onto a hook, it was unlikely that Cookie would turn the fish into an edible dinner. Cookie had been restless lately, which meant that one day soon the hands would show up for dinner only to find that there wasn't any. Then the men would comb out the bunkhouse or the barn and find Cookie, drunk beyond sobering. He would stay that way for two days, two weeks, whatever it took to temporarily appease the demons within. Lately it seemed as if Cookie's demons came more often and stayed longer.

Swearing under his breath, Reever told himself that he really had to find another cook. He'd been telling himself that for two years. He would have done it, too, but finding a cook who didn't mind the Sundance's isolation wasn't easy. With another muttered curse, Reever pulled the buckskin to a stop at the crest of a bank overlooking a series of pools joined by brilliant white ribbons of tumbling water.

One of the pools was directly in the sun. The color of the water was a green so luminous that it seemed to quiver with life. He had seen nothing to compare with that green—until this morning when a girl as slender and supple as a streamside willow had watched him with sensual curiosity darkening her big eyes.

"Payton Sundance, you charming, blue-eyed son of a bitch, if you ever send me another of your cast-off playmates, I'll peel your soft city hide and nail it to the barn."

The horse twitched a black-tipped ear at the harsh sound of Reever's voice. Stamping uneasily, the animal registered its awareness of the sudden tension sweeping its rider.

"For God's sake, she couldn't have been more than sixteen," Reever continued in disgust. "City nymph with hungry green eyes and a body like a cat's. Sleek. Graceful. Made my hands itch just to look at her. And when she looked back at me…"

Reever shifted in the saddle as his body responded to the memory of that delicate face tilted slightly to the side, eyes wide and luminous and as sensually curious as the lips that had parted with a tiny rush of sound. The temptation to go right over the desk and slide his tongue into that sweet mouth had been so strong that it had first surprised and then angered Reever. As he had told Tory, he didn't need a pretty, useless female. He already had two of them, and he had been supporting them since he was sixteen. When he found a woman, she would be just that—a woman, not a girl. She would be quiet, enduring, and she would love the Sundance as much as he did.

He had been a long time looking for a woman like that.

With a snort and another stamp of its hoof, the buckskin settled into a lazy, three-legged stance. The horse was accustomed to its rider's peculiarities. One of them was to sit and look over the ranch while the wind curled around him, bringing the rich scents of a fertile land uncluttered by man.

After a final curse Reever forced himself to look away from the Wolf's radiant green pools. He congratulated himself for throwing Tory out on her tempting little fanny. The last thing he needed was a paternity suit or an arrest for contributing to the delinquency of a minor. Besides, once he had her, he would lose interest, she would pout and things around the ranch would go to hell in a hand basket. No matter how mature they thought they were, girls that young always believed at some level that sex with a man meant love everlasting. Yes, he definitely was well rid of little Miss Victoria Wells. Payton could damn well find another home for his former toy.

But God in heaven, what a walk she had. Smooth. Feline. Hot.

A thrust of desire went through Reever like raw lightning, making every muscle in his body suddenly tighten. Before he knew it, he was full, aching, ready. The speed and the force of his arousal surprised him. At thirty-three he was too old to go off like a teenager. But there it was, hard against his jeans, silently demanding release.

With a sound of disgust at his own unruly sex, Reever lifted the reins and urged the buckskin down the faint trail. Cold water climbed almost up to the animal's black hocks, and stones grumbled beneath steel-shod hooves as the horse plunged through the icy creek, sending up sheets of spray on either side. Drops of water more brilliant than diamonds flashed in the air, shattering sunlight into a thousand tiny rainbows. Reever laughed suddenly, a different laugh than he had used on Tory earlier. This laugh was vital, rich, alive, a sound of pure sensual pleasure.

"You do love crossing that creek, don't you, Blackjack?" asked Reever, giving the horse's neck an affectionate slap. "Your mammy must have been part beaver."

The horse snorted and pranced, tugging at the bit, plainly asking for the freedom to run.

"Sorry, boy," said Reever dryly. "At the moment I'm in no shape to oblige you."

With a disgruntled swish of its black tail, the horse settled into a gliding, ground-eating single-foot that was part walk, part pace, as smooth as water, fast and much easier on its rider than a gallop. Before long Reever reached the top of a fold of land that overlooked the southeastern part of Sundance Ranch. Without waiting for a command, Blackjack slowed and then stopped, for this was one of Reever's favorite places. The country stretched away before him to the far blue horizon, a land unencumbered by man but for the dark ribbon of the county road winding between green meadows.

A tiny movement at the corner of his vision caught Reever's attention. The motion would have been overlooked by most people, but he was accustomed to the land. He knew the difference between the pale flash of a hawk stooping on its prey and the languid movement of a white-faced cow cropping lush grass. What had caught his attention was neither hawk nor cow nor startled rabbit. It was someone walking along the county road. The figure looked no bigger than Reever's thumb at this distance, but he had no doubt that it was two-legged rather than four.

"Well, Blackjack, someone's truck must have broken down. We'd better see if they need help."

Even as Reever reined the horse in the new direction, he saw a bright red car slowing. He expected the car to stop, take on a passenger and pull out again. When the car stopped but no one got in or out, Reever was surprised. When the car raced off, made a U-turn, then raced past the pedestrian, made another U-turn and stopped suddenly again, Reever reached into his saddlebags for the binoculars he always carried.

"Looks like the Metlock car," he muttered, focusing the glasses. "Wonder who Billy's hurrahing today. Damn that kid. Eighteen years old and more coyote than man. Somebody should have taught him manners by—"

Reever's words broke off. With a single vicious curse he spurred Blackjack into a dead run.

Chapter Two

TORY HEARD THE CAR SCREECH TO A stop for the second time and tried to still the frantic beating of her heart.

Three of them are just kids, she told herself firmly. *Not even old enough to drive.* Then helplessly, *God, but they grow them big out here!*

"C'mon, baby," called the redhead, hanging out the window of the dusty Ford. "We don't bite. Well, not where it shows anyways, if you get what I mean."

That witticism brought a chorus of raucous cheers and whistles from the boys in the back seat.

Tory ignored them. She'd heard a lot worse the first time they went by. The driver in particular had yelled the kind of filth that she had rarely heard, even during the overnight shift at the restaurant when drunks had come in to drink coffee and grab at the waitresses. She had learned to ignore the obscenities; any other attitude only encouraged them.

Acting as though she were alone, Tory kept walking. She had already refused the driver's leering offer of a ride with a cheerful "Thanks, but I like walking." There was nothing more she could do except look straight ahead and keep on walking. Or run. She wouldn't do that yet, but she had decided that the instant a car door opened she was going to throw her luggage over the barbwire fence that ran alongside the road, and then go through the fence herself.

Tory hoped that wouldn't be necessary. Except for the driver, the carload of boys was more obnoxious than really threatening. She hoped that they would be satisfied with baiting and insulting her and would tire of the sport quickly when she refused to answer. Above all she hoped that if she went through the fence they wouldn't follow her. She had little doubt that she could outrun the rude, rawboned teenagers as long as her knee held out. That was what really worried her. Her knee. It was already tender from the long walk.

The bright red car stopped a few feet in front of Tory. The driver's door popped open. Tory didn't stop to argue or plead or find out how many boys were getting out. She threw her luggage over the fence and followed it, tearing her T-shirt and her skin on the wicked barbs. She didn't even notice the pain. She began to run, sprinting for fifty yards before she risked a look over her shoulder. Only the driver was still following her. The rest of the boys were through the fence but were using their breath on catcalls and laughter rather than running.

After that single quick look, Tory ran on at a headlong pace, breathing harshly, tearingly, her heart beating so fast that it frightened her. Suddenly she heard the rolling thunder of a horse running flat out over the land. From the corner of her eye, she caught a blur of movement as Ethan Reever flashed past her, bent low over the neck of a huge, hard-running horse.

The driver saw Reever, too. The big teenager turned and raced back toward the fence with more speed than he had shown in chasing Tory. She sank to the ground and tried to catch her breath. All at once she began crying and shaking. She held on to herself and fought for control, trying to force herself to breathe deeply, evenly, until the adrenaline-induced hysteria had passed.

Reever shook out a loop of the long rope that he always carried strapped to his saddle. Billy was close now and getting closer with each one of Blackjack's long-legged strides. Reever coolly waited until Billy was almost to the fence, almost free. Then Reever's arm shot out and a loop of rope settled sweetly around the teenager's broad shoulders. The instant the rope tightened, Blackjack stopped running and sat right down on his hocks, bracing himself as though Billy were a mean half-ton steer needing to be thrown.

Billy's feet flew up and he sat down so hard that his hat jumped off his head. As soon as he had caught his breath, he struggled to his feet. Blackjack surged backward, yanking Billy flat again. With a light touch on the reins, Reever spun Blackjack and trotted toward Tory. Billy bumped along behind like an oversize sack of potatoes.

"You all right?" Reever asked, stopping near Tory.

She looked up into the pale blaze of his eyes and felt almost sorry for the overgrown boy on the end of the rope. She nodded, knowing that her voice would shake if she tried to answer.

The buckskin spun on its heels and backed suddenly, yanking Billy flat once more. Reever dismounted in an easy, flowing motion and went to stand over the big teenager. He waited until Billy met his eyes.

"It's a good thing your daddy's dead, boy," said Reever flatly. "He'd have peeled you clean as a willow switch for a stunt like this. I've got a mind to do it myself."

Billy couldn't meet Reever's eyes any longer. The boy's glance fell on Tory. He saw her pale, dirt-streaked face and the hints of blood where barbwire had ripped through her T-shirt. He looked away quickly.

"What were you planning to do after you caught her?" continued Reever, his voice low, deadly.

Billy shrugged.

Reever bent, fastened his hand on the boy's shirt and hauled him to his feet and then beyond, dangling the raw-boned teenager from his fist and braced arm like a dirty, struggling fish.

"*What were you going to do?*"

"Not a damn thing! I swear it! I was just havin' some fun with the snotty little—ow! That hurts!"

"Fun." Reever's lip curled in disdain beneath the black slash of his mustache. "Then you must have enjoyed being dumped and dragged behind Blackjack, huh? Wasn't that fun?"

Billy looked away from Reever's pale, narrowed eyes.

"Answer me." Reever's voice was like a lash.

Billy shivered and said, "N-no."

With a single, vicious word Reever opened his hand and let Billy fall to the ground.

"Listen up, boy," said Reever, his tone conversational and his eyes like steel. "You've just hurrahed your last little girl. I kept hoping you'd grow up before I lost my patience, but—" Reever smiled and Billy went as pale as Tory. Reever nodded his head as he saw real fear dawning on Billy. "You're man-sized and snake mean," Reever said matter-of-factly. "I've had a gutful of your dirty mouth and cruel games. If I hear about any more of it, I'll give you the kind of lesson you'll spend a lifetime trying to forget. Hear me, boy?"

Billy nodded sullenly.

"I sure as hell hope you're smarter than you look," said Reever. "That's the only warning you'll get. Stand up."

Billy scrambled awkwardly to his feet. He was almost as tall as Reever but hadn't nearly the hard muscle of the older man. Nor the hard experience.

"I'd have you apologize to the lady," continued Reever, his voice still casual and his eyes utterly savage, "but you wouldn't mean it, and she doesn't want to hear any more of your filth. Now get out of here before I forget how much I liked your daddy and drag you behind old Blackjack until there's nothing left but rope."

With a flick of his wrist, Reever removed the lasso from Billy's shoulders. Reever waited until the teenager was about ten feet away and said, "Pick up her luggage and take it to the Sunup Café. And Billy—"

The big teenager turned around.

"Show me how bright you are," Reever said, coiling the rope again as he spoke. "Make sure that everything of hers is just the way she left it."

Reever watched Billy walk stiffly back to the fence, stopping only long enough to pick up Tory's luggage. While the car speeded away toward town, Reever fastened the lasso to the saddle again and turned to help Tory to her feet. It wasn't necessary. She was already up and walking toward the fence, favoring her right leg slightly.

"What do you think you're doing?" demanded Reever.

Tory wiped her forehead on her dusty arm. "About two miles an hour," she said, smiling crookedly, hoping that he wouldn't hear the faint quaver in her voice. She was over the worst of it now. She simply felt as if she'd spent an afternoon diving in front of hypercritical judges—tired, used up, unsure of herself, determined not to show any of it. She paused and looked over her shoulder. "Thanks. Those kids really had me going."

Reever watched in disbelief as Tory turned away again. He caught up with her in five long strides.

"Where did your car break down?"

"Nowhere. I don't have one."

"Aren't you old enough to drive?"

Tory's hair flashed in the sun as she turned toward Reever quickly, hardly believing what she had heard. A single glance told her that Reever was serious. "I'll be twenty-one this summer," she said tightly.

"Really?" he asked, amusement and relief deepening his voice. He had hated like hell being aroused by someone who appeared as young as Tory. He had always preferred his partners to be as experienced as he was.

Mentally Tory counted to ten and then to twenty. She didn't need Reever's amused glance to remind her that her body wasn't up to the mark for sexy blondes. Most of the time she didn't mind. After all, she didn't want to look like a whacking great milk cow when she dove off the platform. Yet it irritated her unreasonably to know that a man with the raw masculine appeal of Ethan Reever thought of her as a little girl.

"If you didn't drive, how did you get to the ranch?" he asked. His tone was deep, almost lazy, and the steely shade of his eyes warmed as he looked from the delicate curve of Tory's neck to her mouth and remembered how the full bow of her lips had looked when they had parted in silent invitation.

"I came in on the mail truck," she said curtly.

"Where are you meeting Melly for the return trip?"

"Melly?"

"The mail ma'am," said Reever, grinning.

"Oh. Will she be by later on?"

With a feeling of angry disbelief, Reever realized that Tory had not only walked the miles from the ranch house to the county road, but that she had planned to walk the rest of the way to Massacre Creek as well. His hand shot out and he grabbed her arm, stopping her right in her tracks.

"Do you have any idea how far it is to town?" he asked curtly.

"What time is it?"

He answered automatically, frowning. "About one o'clock."

"Then it's about twelve miles to town from here."

The look that passed over Reever's face was indescribable. "Are you crazy?"

"No," she said flatly, meeting his eyes.

What Tory didn't say was that she was hungry, thirsty to the point of spitting cotton and the burning of her raw hands was competing with the throbbing of her knee. She wouldn't say a word about any of it, either. She would quite cheerfully crawl the rest of the way into town rather than whine to the hard-faced cowboy who had taken one look at her, decided she was useless in every possible way and dismissed her with a contempt that still stung.

"Then you're a fool," Reever said harshly. "Or maybe you like swinging your ass down a public highway, just asking for it?"

"*Asking!*" Tory's eyes narrowed as her temper flashed. "You arrogant son of Satan!" she hissed, appalled at herself even as the words escaped her lips. She had taken far worse insults from her coaches, but none of them had been able to set off her temper like Ethan Reever. "I walked down that damned road because there was no other way for me to get into town!"

"If you had told me—" began Reever.

"When?" she interrupted sweetly. "Before or after you turned down my imagined offer of prostitution?"

Reever muttered a few savage words under his breath. Tory didn't bother to listen. She simply turned and marched toward the fence, her back as straight as the line of her mouth. She had heard all she wanted to and then some. It was bad enough to be taken advantage of by a carload of foulmouthed jerks. To be accused of asking for that kind of abuse simply because she was too poor to afford her own car made her furious.

"The next bus won't get to Massacre Creek for three days," said Reever matter-of-factly, catching up to Tory with ease.

She shrugged. Three days, three hours, three weeks. It didn't matter because she didn't have money for a ticket yet. She hoped that the Sunup Café needed a cook or waitress, a dishwasher or someone to clean out the grease trap over the stove. Whatever. She wasn't fussy about honest work.

Reever watched Tory from the corner of his eye. For the first time he saw past the fact that she was female, young and able to arouse his temper and his body with maddening ease. He saw that her thick blond hair was cut simply and that the sun-streaked effect, like her tan, was natural rather than purchased at an expensive salon or resort. She wore no jewelry—no necklace, no bracelet, not even an inexpensive silver ring. The T-shirt she had on was faded and baggy. The slacks were the same and frayed at the cuffs. Her tennis shoes had more holes than canvas and sported no logo from one of the makers of trendy, expensive leisure shoes.

"Wait," Reever said, catching Tory's arm again. His voice was rough, but his hand was gentle on her arm. He had been poor long enough in his youth to recognize the signs. "I'll have one of my men drive you into town."

Tory stared at Reever, her surprise plain. Quite clearly she hadn't expected any help from him.

"For the love of God!" snarled Reever suddenly. "What the hell kind of man do you think would let you walk down a lonely road rather than help you out?"

Before Tory could answer, Reever turned and whistled shrilly between his teeth. Blackjack's ears came up in twin black arcs as the horse trotted obediently to Reever. He mounted in a single flowing motion, kicked his boot out of the left stirrup and looked down at Tory. She was watching him with wide green eyes, looking for all the world like a wind-ruffled, curious cat. He shifted the roping rein to his right hand and held out his left to her.

"Come on."

"Come on what?" asked Tory, looking up at Reever. Way, way up. The horse was as big as a mountain, and Reever wasn't much smaller.

"Get on," he said impatiently.

"How?"

Reever stared at Tory for an instant, not sure that he had heard correctly. He made a sound of disgust, swung his right leg in front of him and over the saddle horn, and slid down to land lightly on his feet in front of her.

"City girl," he muttered. "Useless as teats on a boar hog."

With no more warning than that, Reever picked Tory up and set her down behind the saddle as though she weighed less than a shadow. He put his left foot in the stirrup, swung his right leg up and over the saddle horn and settled securely into the saddle in less time than it took for Tory to realize what was going on. It was obvious that Reever was supremely at home on a horse's back. Despite his size and power he had yet to make a move that wasn't both sure and graceful.

"Hang on."

Tory tried. She grabbed the smooth, raised back of the western saddle with both hands as Blackjack moved off at a pace that seemed terrifyingly fast but was actually no more than a sprightly walk. With each unexpected motion her hands slipped more. The task of hanging on wasn't made any easier by the fact that her blisters had long since broken, leaving her palms raw and oozing a clear fluid mixed with blood. No matter how hard she gripped, her hands kept slipping.

After a few minutes she mastered the rhythm of Blackjack's walk to the point that every movement didn't take her by surprise. She began to breathe more easily. The distance to the ground didn't bother her because she was accustomed to heights, having spent most of her life diving from one kind of platform or another. She would have felt a great deal better, however, if it had been water rather than dirt waiting to catch her if she fell.

Reever sensed Tory's distress and kept the big horse down to a walk. He could have told her to hang on to him but didn't. His hands still burned from their brief contact with her. He had expected her to be soft, and she was. She was also surprisingly firm. If there was any city flab on that young body, he hadn't felt it.

Besides, he was still irritated by her surprise when he had offered to give her a ride into town. If she had decided that he was such a rude bastard that she refused to touch him even to keep her seat, then she could just fall off.

For a long time there was only the muted sound of hoofbeats and the occasional wild cry of a soaring hawk. Blackjack chewed resentfully on the bit that held him to a walk. Reever chewed resentfully on everything that had happened since he had looked up and found a girl-woman standing quietly in front of his desk, setting off his temper and his body with a single look from her faintly tilted green eyes.

When Reever reined Blackjack down the trail to Wolf Creek, the horse shied at nothing more than the shadow of a hawk skimming over the land. Reever moved with the horse like a second skin. Tory didn't. One instant the horse was supporting her bottom and the next instant there was nothing beneath her but air. She grabbed frantically at the saddle, only to feel it sliding out from between her raw palms.

"Reever!"

Even as Tory called out, Reever made a lightning movement, turning and scooping her up in one arm. With a strength that shocked her, he put her back into position behind the saddle using nothing more than a shrug of his shoulders. Blackjack snorted and minced sideways. Tory gasped and grabbed frantically for the saddle again.

"Damn it," snarled Reever, "settle down."

Tory didn't know whether he meant her or the horse. She didn't want to know, either. She bit her lip and tried to guess which way the frisky beast would jump next. Blackjack snorted, then turned and lipped the stirrup as though to ask why they were standing around in the middle of the trail. At a nudge from Reever's heels, the big horse began to trot. Reever didn't need to turn around to know that Tory was losing her balance again.

"Of all the clumsy—" He bit off a curse. "If you can't stand the thought of putting your arms around my waist, hang on to my belt."

Tory looked at the broad spread of Reever's shoulders and the powerful back that tapered down to a lean waist. The thought of touching him made both weakness and a curious heat course through her. Tentatively she lifted her right hand, only to realize that if she held on to him as he suggested, she would get blood all over him. Her frantic attempts to hang on to the saddle had finished the work that carrying her suitcase had begun. Her palms were scraped raw.

"I can't," Tory said in a low voice. "I'll get you—dirty."

"Dirty?" Reever snorted. "Honeybunch, in case you haven't noticed, I'm a rancher, not a damned drugstore cowboy. I'm not going to faint at a little dirt."

Tory's only answer was a choked sound as Blackjack's broad, muscular rump skipped sideways. The horse was just trying to balance Tory's weight more evenly on his back, but she didn't know that. She only knew that she was falling again.

With an exasperated curse Reever dropped the roping rein, reached behind his back with both hands and
jerked Tory's arms around him. When he saw the
smears of blood across her palms, he knew why she was
having so much trouble hanging on to the saddle and
why she was afraid of getting him "dirty."

"For the love of God, don't you have any sense at
all?" he asked harshly, grabbing Tory's hands and
looking at them more closely. Ragged circles of broken blisters showed clearly. The tender flesh was
smeared with a mixture of dirt and blood. "Why didn't
you say something?"

Tory made a sound that could have been a laugh or
a curse. "Then you could yell at me for whining, right?"
she said raggedly, furious that everything she did only
made Reever more angry with her. "Sorry to spoil your
rustic entertainment, but I've been worked over by men
who make you look like the tooth fairy. I don't whine
or beg or 'swing my ass' for any man, even you. Especially you!"

Reever's whole body tightened as he turned and
looked over his shoulder at Tory. Her face was dirt
streaked, pale beneath the tan and defiant despite the
white lines of fatigue etched around her mouth. Her
eyes were a blaze of green fury that was more
provocative than any practiced swaying of a
woman's hips. Whether she knew it or not, she was
crying out to be taken down onto the soft green
grass and rolled around until her claws were
trimmed and her spitting snarls turned into husky
purrs. She would bite and scream at first—and at the

end, too. Differently. He knew it, and it made blood gather heavily, hotly, making him bigger with each slamming heartbeat.

"It's bad enough to be so soft, little girl," said Reever in a low voice, "but to be so stupid is dangerous. Don't push me into doing something we'll both regret."

"*Me?* Pushing *you?*" asked Tory, outrage in every syllable. "You—" Her teeth clicked as she snapped her jaw shut. She badly wanted to describe Reever's genetic heritage, most personal habits and certain destination after death, but the only words she could think of had already been used by Billy and his friends. She had no intention of joining their sordid ranks.

"You. Pushing me," Reever agreed flatly.

Lips still parted over words she wouldn't speak and quivering to tell him just what she thought of him, Tory looked straight into Reever's eyes.

It was like diving off a platform as high as the moon. She was falling, twisting, turning, but she wasn't moving at all, everything around her was spinning, and she was motionless, suspended, held absolutely still within his gray glance as heat exploded through her.

The soft, unconscious sound that came from Tory's throat made Reever feel as though he had walked naked into an electric fence. Every muscle in his big body tightened violently. He dragged at breath, aching. The effort it took to control himself shocked him.

"Stop it," grated Reever, unable to look away from Tory's wide green eyes.

"Stop...what?" she asked, her voice husky, her expression dazed.

For a long, seething moment Reever glared at Tory. Gradually he realized that he had been wrong in his assumption that she was one of Payton's pretty toys. Tory wasn't experienced. She didn't understand what was happening between them, what her soft mouth was promising, what her sweet, wild whimper had revealed. She had gotten to him faster and deeper than any woman he'd ever known—and the longer Reever was around her, the more he was afraid that she was a virgin.

"You really don't know, do you?" he whispered, touching the pulse beating rapidly beneath the smooth skin of Tory's throat.

Her only answer was the visible quiver of her lips as she responded to his fingertips caressing her throat. Knowing he shouldn't, unable to stop himself, Reever bent and brushed his mouth over Tory's, breathing in her sweetness, tracing her trembling lips with the tip of his tongue, feeling her pulse go wild beneath his fingertip.

Slowly, very slowly, Reever lifted his mouth from hers, feeling as though he were pulling off his own skin. Her half-closed eyes were a smoldering green, her breath was uneven and her mouth followed his like a compass needle following a lodestone. His breath hissed out in a single savage word as he turned away from her.

"R-Reever?"

"Forget it, honey," he said roughly. "I'm too experienced for a city innocent like you to cut your teeth on."

Tory flinched as though she had been slapped. She wanted to scream at Reever's broad back, to tell him that he was as conceited as he was big, that she wouldn't touch him if he were the last man in the universe. But his single gentle caress had gone through her like lightning, burning away her breath, burning away her thoughts, burning away inhibitions, freeing a surging wildness that frightened her.

Reever held Blackjack to a slow walk, not wanting Tory to have to throw her arms around his hips in order to stay on because what she would find in his lap would have shocked her to her innocent core. He clenched his teeth at the thought of her slender arms sliding around his waist, her fingers testing the power of his thighs and then finding another kind of male power, testing it with her soft hands, measuring the hunger he had for her.

Blackjack tossed his head and minced sideways against the sudden hard pressure of the bit. With a startled sound Tory grabbed Reever. He felt her fingers inside his waistband like a brand. Raging at his own lack of control, he pulled Blackjack up short and dismounted, knowing that he'd never make it back to the ranch at this rate.

"Is that as clean as it looks?" asked Tory.

Reever's head snapped up. "What?"

Tory bit her lip to keep it from trembling, regretting that she had spoken. Everything she did seemed to make Reever furious. Now his eyes were as cold and savage as a winter storm. She swallowed painfully. The dryness of her mouth was a goad, forcing her to speak against her better judgment.

"The water," Tory said huskily. "Is it safe to drink?"

Hard gray eyes glanced toward the creek as though it had just popped up out of the ground. "Yes."

Tory had no stirrup to aid her dismount. Nor did she trust her slippery hands to hang on to the saddle and allow her to ease down to the ground. In the end she did what she had done the first time she had been confronted by a high dive and had become so frightened that she had sat down astride the diving board and refused to move. But she had had to move eventually, just as she had to move now. So she swung her right leg over alongside her left and jumped.

The ground was harder than the water in a swimming pool, and her legs were wobbly from being stretched over Blackjack's powerful back. Favoring her injured knee threw her off balance. She knew that she had a choice between catching herself with her right leg or falling flat on her face. No choice, really. Even as she fell she turned, hoping to take the impact on her shoulder.

Hard hands grabbed Tory and yanked her back onto her feet.

"How anyone as sleek looking as you can be so damned clumsy is beyond me," Reever said in disgust, releasing her instantly. "Or is it just an act to get me to touch you? It won't get you a thing, little girl. I don't believe in on-the-job training."

The only possible answer to that was two words long, and one of those words was at the top of the list that Tory had already forbidden herself to use. Very carefully she walked around Reever and went to the stream. She found a flat, sun-warmed boulder at the edge of the creek, eased herself slowly onto her stomach and lowered her face to the water until she could sip from its silver surface. It was cold, sweet, perfect, like drinking a torrent of winter moonlight. With a husky sound of pleasure, Tory buried her raw hands in the crystal water and lowered her face again, turning it slowly from side to side, bathing away dust and sweat.

Reever watched and felt as though Blackjack had kicked him in the stomach. Tory's sensual pleasure in the water was as wild and pure as the creek itself. As he watched her, he could almost taste the water as she did, could almost feel its bright chill sliding down his throat and caressing his face, washing away dust and sweat, dissolving everything but the sensations of the instant. Without realizing that he had moved at all, he found himself kneeling on the bank just downstream from her, sinking his hands beneath the brilliant silver ripples, wanting simply to be touched by the water that had just flowed over her.

With a savage motion Reever came to his feet, flinging water in all directions, and strode to where Blackjack waited patiently. Tory didn't notice, for her face was still in the sweet water, her eyes closed as she gave her attention completely to the mountain stream that had both slaked her thirst and soothed her burning palms.

"For God's sake," Reever said finally, "what are you trying to do, drown yourself?"

Tory looked over her shoulder at him and laughed, a sound that was as rippling as the water itself. "Cowboy, the day I drown, those sidewinders you once mentioned will be ice-skating in the hottest part of hell."

A corner of Reever's mouth kicked up unwillingly at the image. "You're good in water, is that it?"

"I get by," she said, coming to her feet, wincing slightly as her right knee bumped against the stone. Unselfconsciously she wiped her face on the hem of her loose T-shirt. Even if she had known that the movement revealed a sleek, tanned strip of her skin from her waist to just below her breasts, she wouldn't have thought anything of it. She was accustomed to being wet and to drying herself on anything handy. She was also accustomed to being all but naked and utterly ignored by the males around her.

Reever frowned, unable to understand Tory's conflicting actions. He touched her and she went off hot enough to burn both of them to the bone, yet she seemed unaware of what she was doing. Although she seemed innocent, she was as unselfconscious as a cat around him. She wasn't immodest; it was just that she seemed unaware of the sensual possibilities of her own body and how easily, how violently, she could arouse men. She was...unawakened.

The thought of being the man to awaken her was a sweet agony in his loins.

Tory walked over to Blackjack, who snuffled gently at the damp tendrils curling around her face where her hair had fallen into the water. She laughed softly, delighted by the horse's velvet muzzle and tickling, grass-scented breath.

"What—?" she gasped as she felt herself snatched off her feet without warning.

"Spread your legs," said Reever impatiently.

Speechless, she stared over her shoulder at him.

"God save me from useless city girls," he grated.

His grip shifted. Even as he swung Tory up toward the saddle, his right hand slid down her back, over her buttocks and fastened on the inside of her right thigh, forcing her legs apart. An instant later she was dumped into Blackjack's saddle with about as much ceremony as a hog-tied calf.

"It's called riding stride," Reever bit out. "It's an old custom among us rustics."

Tory's startled, wildly flushed face confirmed Reever's worst fears. She definitely was not used to a man's hands on her sleek body. *Passionate as hell and innocent as heaven.*

A virgin who's too hot to handle. Why me, Lord? he asked bitterly. *Why me!*

"Try not to faint when I get up behind you," he said curtly.

Tory didn't know what Reever meant until he stepped into the stirrup and swung into the saddle as though she weren't already sitting there. With a startled sound she scooted forward, giving him as much room as she could.

The saddle was big—but so was Reever. The saddle was also higher at the front and back than in the middle, a design that helped to keep the rider in place. It also ensured that the only way Tory could rest her weight was smack up against Reever in an intimacy that made her cheeks burn. It made Reever burn, too. His only consolation was that Tory was probably too innocent to know that not all of the hard flesh pressing against her hips was muscle.

It was a small consolation for a problem that would get bigger with each rocking motion that Blackjack made.

"Do we have to—" began Tory, only to gasp as the horse stepped forward eagerly, sending her sliding down into the hot, hard cradle of Reever's thighs.

He heard her breath come in sharply. He saw the shiver of sensation that raced through her, goose bumps clear on her skin. He knew without seeing that her nipples would be rising and tightening, nuzzling against the soft cloth of her T-shirt, searching for a man's caress to ease their sensual ache.

Tory scooted forward again, only to slide back. Grimly she shifted her weight, trying to find a position that wouldn't surround her with Reever's male heat.

"Goddammit," growled Reever, putting his right arm around her hard, pinning her in place. "Stop wiggling!"

"Put me in back again!" Tory said desperately.

"You wouldn't last three seconds."

"But I rode all the way here without—"

Tory's protest ended in a yelp as Blackjack leaped into Wolf Creek with the abandon of a child, dividing the hock-deep water in glorious sheets that sprayed head high on either side of him. Tory clutched wildly at the saddle horn, but it was Reever's steel grip that kept her in the saddle.

Reever tried to be a gentleman and ignore the feel of Tory as his fingers spread wide to hold her in place. But before Blackjack had finished plunging through the creek and up the bank on the far side, Reever knew that Tory's loose T-shirt concealed lush, firm breasts. He also had searing confirmation of his earlier guess—her nipples were as hard as he was and every bit as eager to be touched. The tip of her breast had tightened violently as his fingers accidentally brushed over it when he had to shift his grip at Blackjack's first leap.

Desperately Tory hoped that Reever hadn't heard her gasp when his hand had held her so intimately for just an instant, but there was little hope that he wouldn't notice the flush of embarrassment climbing her neck and flooding her face. She stiffened and leaned away from him, an instinctive reaction that was utterly wrong for the time and the place. She heard him swear violently and wrap his other arm around her to keep her upright in the saddle.

With a combination of fascination and embarrassment, Tory saw Reever's muscular forearm slide beneath her breasts, taking their soft weight, pushing her tight nipples against her water-splashed shirt. Each of Blackjack's rhythmic movements made her breasts sway against Reever's supporting arm. She twisted helplessly, trying to retreat from the intimate contact, but only ended up rubbing against his body even more.

"For God's sake, relax," said Reever harshly. "You've got nothing up top that I haven't felt more of and better."

For an instant Tory couldn't believe what she had heard. Then she believed it. A bitter tide of humiliation washed all the color from her face. She finished the ride to the ranch in absolute silence, counting all the ways it was possible to drown an oversized, under-mannered cowboy.

Chapter Three

REEVER AND TORY RODE INTO THE ranch house yard
with identical, tight-lipped expressions on their faces.
Reever had the edge, though. His black hat, black hair
and the harshly masculine lines of his face gave him a
distinctly satanic look that Tory's wide-eyed, delicately
triangular face couldn't hope to equal. Her eyes, however, matched the devil's in the emotion that made them
burn like green flames. By the time the ranch came into
sight, Tory had counted sixty-three improbable ways
for her to drown a rude cowboy, but she hadn't yet decided how to manage even one of them without touching Reever.

That she refused to do. After she got off Blackjack,
she never intended to touch Ethan Reever again.

Tory's stomach growled miserably, audibly, beneath
Reever's muscular arm. He cursed under his breath as
he realized that she probably hadn't had time for break-

fast and certainly hadn't eaten lunch. Then there was always the possibility that, even if she had had the time, she hadn't had the money to buy food. Close up, her clothes were even more frayed than he had first thought.

And there were streaks of blood where barbs had bitten into her tender flesh.

Reever didn't know whether to yell at Tory for being so stupid or to gently lick her as clean as a mother cat would a kitten. One thing he did know—he didn't feel the least bit parental toward Victoria Wells. It had driven him crazy to feel her firm little rump rocking between his thighs. He didn't even feel guilty about her cuts and scrapes anymore. He might not look it, but he was in a lot worse shape than she was. He was steel hard and hot as hell, and his guts were tied in knots from wanting a soft, useless girl with scratches on her back and palms like hamburger. He'd suffered the tortures of the damned on the ride home and had no sympathy to spare for a sweet young thing who wreaked havoc on every male in sight.

Reever cursed softly, steadily, fluently, letting Tory know with each word how very happy he would be to get her off his lap and out of his hair. She ignored him. She had heard a lot of dark muttering during the ride and had promised herself that she would say nothing until she reached the dubious safety of the ranch. Then she would tell Reever just what she thought of him. As the ranch house drew near, she only wished that she had spent more of the ride choosing killing words rather than ways of killing, period.

Blackjack stopped in front of the main corral. Tory's stomach growled vigorously.

"God above," muttered Reever as Tory's stomach rumbled and rumbled and rumbled beneath his arm, "now I suppose you expect me to feed you before I send you to town."

Tory's mouth flattened even more. "Why shouldn't you feed me?" she asked curtly. "You owe me."

"Yeah? How do you figure that?" asked Reever as he dismounted.

The easy power of Reever's movements only made Tory more angry. She knew that her legs weren't going to support her. After she dismounted, she was going to go flat on her face in a sprawl that would only under-line Reever's opinion of her. *Clumsy. Useless. City girl.* She gritted her teeth. Why should she care what that muscle-bound, icy-eyed son of Satan thought? She should go down on her knees in the dust and give thanks that she wasn't his type!

"I figure you owe me lunch because you've taken enough bites out of me during the ride for a nine-course meal," Tory said, glaring down at Reever with slitted green eyes.

"Honey," he said coolly, giving her a slow, danger-ous, once-over kind of look, "if I'd been nibbling on you, you wouldn't be complaining now—and you sure as hell wouldn't be hungry."

The sensual impact of Reever's eyes and smile made Tory feel as though she were being stroked. She closed her eyes, swallowed hard and muttered, "I thought cowboys were shy, modest and had a vocabulary consisting of 'giddy up' and 'aw, shucks.' But not you, Ethan Reever. You're as proud as Lucifer, and your vocabulary is fully suited to hell."

Reever's mouth turned up in a smile that was very male and frankly threatening. "Keep pushing, green eyes," he said, his voice low, deep. "You'll find out just how hard a man I am."

Blackjack sighed loudly and shifted his weight, hinting that he would like to be in the corral and out from under the saddle.

At the horse's first motion Tory grabbed wildly at the saddle horn, only to wince as her raw palms met leather. Reever cursed softly at the sign of Tory's pain. He jerked off his hat and swept his fingers through his shaggy hair to keep from reaching for her. As she sat up shakily, he yanked his dusty black Stetson back into place, grateful that he wouldn't have to touch her again. The feel of her soft, supple body would tie so many knots in him that he'd be lucky to stand up straight for a week.

"Get off poor Blackjack so he can get some food," said Reever. "He's as tired as I am."

"I don't know what you're complaining about," retorted Tory, delaying the inevitable moment when she would dismount and land in an ungainly heap at Reever's big feet. "You don't ache from your knees to your, uh—"

"Honey, I ache in places you can't even imagine." He watched color climb up Tory's cheeks as his words registered. He laughed softly. "Penny for your thoughts," he offered with a slow smile.

"Go away," Tory said, spacing each word carefully.

"Can't," he said blandly, but beneath his mustache his lips quirked over a hidden smile. "You might need me."

"Like a sidewinder needs ice skates," she said succinctly.

"A sidewinder isn't going to get all rubber-legged from an hour on horseback."

"A sidewinder doesn't have—"

"Legs," interrupted Reever. "Real quick for a city girl, aren't you? Come on, honey. Get it over with. Or can't you even get down alone?"

Tory looked at Reever and brought her running total to sixty-four ways to drown a grinning cowboy. That made her feel better, but it didn't solve the problem of transferring her weight from Blackjack's back to her own feet. She shifted slowly, trying to dismount as Reever had by swinging her right leg over Blackjack's broad rump. As her leg came halfway over, she fished around with her left foot, trying to find the stirrup. It was a long reach because the stirrup length was set for Reever's six-feet-three-inch height.

Belatedly Tory realized that she should have secured her left foot in the stirrup before she started to dismount. It was too late now, though. Her right leg was bumping over Blackjack's rump, her left foot was treading air and saddle leather was racing through her slippery hands. Suddenly her left foot found the stirrup, only to slide right on through the opening as her hands slipped completely off the saddle. The world spun crazily as her left foot went all the way through the open stirrup. She landed flat on her back with enough force to knock out her breath.

Blackjack, who was used to a higher order of skill in his riders, was so surprised that he shied away. Tory was yanked with him because her foot was wedged through the stirrup. Even as the horse moved, Reever leaped for the bridle and hauled Blackjack up short.

"Easy, boy, easy," murmured Reever, calming the animal, for Tory lay half beneath those dancing steel-shod feet.

The thought of what a blow from those hooves would do to Tory's soft body made Reever's blood chill. Despite that his voice was as gentle and firm as his hands while he held the trembling Blackjack still. Tory lay dazed on her back and wondered if that was really Reever's voice, gentle and sweet, deep and soothing, a voice that verified her instinctive belief that there was much more to Reever than his harsh surface. She tried to sit up, to get closer to that reassuring voice.

"Don't move," snarled Reever. "If you spook Blackjack any more with your clumsiness, he'll forget his manners and step all over you."

That voice belonged to Reever, too. Tory had no doubt about it. She had felt its icy lash before. She closed her eyes because suddenly the sunlight was so bright it felt like hot sand beneath her eyelids. She blinked fiercely, wondering why a stupid little fall made her want to cry. It had never been like that in the pool when she was learning a new dive and landed wrong, knocking out her breath and raising livid welts on her skin. She hadn't cried then. Not once.

Maybe it was just that she was so hungry. Maybe that was why she felt as though everything familiar was falling away from her, a row of dominoes kicked over by the doctor's calm description of what had happened to her knee, what might happen again, the future she had worked so hard for toppling in front of her.

Tory didn't bother to look up when she felt Reever's hands easing her foot from the stirrup. She didn't even open her eyes when he swung her up into his arms and began carrying her to the house.

"Are you all right?" he asked roughly.

She nodded and turned her face away from him, hoping he wouldn't see the tears that she felt scalding her eyelids. She wasn't like this. She hadn't cried since she was seven and her father had looked at the first swimming ribbon she had ever won and asked her if third place was the best she could do.

"You sure, honey?"

It was the voice Reever had used to calm Blackjack, warm and gentle and reassuring. It was Tory's undoing. She was accustomed to whip-cracking lectures when she fouled up, not compassion. A shudder went through her.

"Poor little green-eyed cat," Reever murmured, shifting Tory in his arms until her face was tucked against his neck. "This just hasn't been your day, has it?"

Her only answer was the trembling of her body and the hot, silent slide of her tears down his neck.

Reever carried Tory into the ranch house and set her gently in a big oak kitchen chair. "Got your breath back now?" he asked.

"Y-yes."

"Can you sit up without help?"

Tory nodded and leaned back, her eyes still closed. The tears had gone, but she was too embarrassed to look at Reever. He already thought her a clumsy little girl, and she had just proved that he was right in the most humiliating way possible. One corner of her mouth turned down in a bitter smile. It really hadn't been her day.

Yet it had been magic to be held like that, to be cherished by him, if only for a moment.

While Reever ran hot water into a pan, he watched Tory out of the corner of his eye. Beneath her tan she was as pale as a morning glory in moonlight. Her pallor didn't disturb him as much as the sudden quenching of the life in Tory's body that told him she was just about at the end of her rope. Watching her, he knew that he couldn't drive her in to town, dump her at the Sunup Café and drive off. Hell, he didn't even know if she had enough money for the crummy motel at the edge of town. How would she live for the next three days until the bus came in?

Frowning, Reever wrung out a clean cloth in the water, added a mild disinfectant to the pan and carried it over to the table.

"Here," he said, lifting Tory's hands gently. "Soak them in this."

The water was hot without being painful, and the familiar smell of denatured iodine rose from it. It was a favorite disinfectant around the pool because it didn't stain, sting or leave grease floating on top of the water. Tory sighed and sat back again, only to make a startled sound when she felt a warm, moist cloth moving over her face.

"Easy now," Reever said, holding her still. "The war's over, little girl. You're in no shape for any more fighting."

Tory felt both Reever's strength and his gentleness as he cleaned her dusty, tear-streaked face. After the first surprise passed, she made a tiny, inarticulate sound of pleasure and relaxed, giving herself to the unfamiliar luxury of being cared for. Without thinking, she rubbed her face slowly against the cloth and his hand, moving as she had while she bent over the stream.

The hunger that hadn't left Reever since he had first seen Tory sat up and howled. He watched her through narrowed eyes, reassuring himself that she wasn't playing a teasing game with him. She wasn't. Nothing showed on her face but simple, sensual pleasure. She didn't look nearly twenty-one right now. She looked like fifteen, and she made him feel like a lecherous sixty. The longer he looked, the more he became convinced that she had lied about her age.

"I think you better call them," Reever said finally, tossing the wet cloth into the sink and leaning back against the table with his arms crossed, watching her.

"Who?"

"Your parents."

Tory's eyes flew open. "What do you suggest I call them?" she asked flatly.

"Hell, honey, nobody gets along with their parents," Reever said, shrugging. "It's not the end of the world. Call them and tell them you're sorry. They'll be glad to send you bus money to get home."

"How did you know I—"

The words stopped abruptly as Tory realized that
Reever had decided she was some kind of teenage runaway. She didn't know whether to laugh or try to
drown him in the pan of water. After a few electric seconds she decided to do neither. She reached with a dripping hand into the frayed pocket of her slacks and drew
out a cloth wallet that was even more worn than her
tennis shoes. The wallet landed on the table with a soft
plop and fell open, revealing a California driving license.

"Read it and weep, cowboy. I may have all the sex
appeal of an ironing board, but I'll be twenty-one on
my next birthday. I've been on my own since I was sixteen. I haven't asked my parents or anyone else for a
dime since then."

Reever's eyes narrowed as he measured the change
in Tory. She looked twenty-one now, and then some.
He didn't need to ask if the years had been easy. The
threadbare, empty wallet told its own story. Yet he
knew if he offered to buy her a bus ticket home she
would refuse with the same determined independence
that had sent her on a nineteen-mile walk to town
without a whimper.

"An ironing board," he repeated neutrally, raising his
dark eyebrows as he remembered the soft, firm weight
of her breasts nuzzling his forearm. "Honey, they must
make some damned unusual ironing boards where you
come from."

Tory looked at Reever's sexy, off-center smile and
wondered if he were remembering the long ride to the
ranch or the plunge through Wolf Creek when her

nipples had tightened suddenly beneath his hand. He had touched her only for an instant, but even the memory of it sent heat coursing through the pit of her stomach.

Tory's breath came in with a soft sound as she saw the focus of Reever's gray eyes shift from her face to her breasts. It was happening again, now, right now. She could feel it, the sudden soft burst of sensation in her nipples as they rose into hard peaks, stretching and teasing nerves that went straight to the wild, secret core of her.

"We'd better get them wrapped up," Reever said curtly, turning away before Tory could see his body's reaction to her taut breasts.

Tory stared after him, wondering if he had meant what she thought he meant. As she watched him walk out of the room, she wouldn't have been surprised if he had come back and thrown a bra in her lap. She wasn't wearing one because she didn't own any. For one thing she didn't sag. For another, she was usually in a swimming suit. The overriding factor, however, in her decision to go without that particular piece of clothing had been money. She could appear in public without a bra. She couldn't say the same for a T-shirt or jeans.

When Tory turned and put her hands back into the soothing water, she looked down at her breasts. Instantly she realized Reever must have seen her nipples clearly outlined against the soft T-shirt. She groaned and wondered if she had lost her mind since she had walked out of that doctor's office three days ago. She had been numb since then, an automaton going through the motions of eating and sleeping, and all during the long bus ride here, she had hung on to Payton's letter like a lifeline.

Then the letter, too, had toppled at a touch, one more in a long row of falling dominoes.

A sigh compounded of tiredness, hunger and determination shuddered through Tory. She would find a way to take the months off from diving that the doctor had recommended. She didn't need much in the way of money. There was nothing wrong with her knee that would prevent her from working. If the knee hurt too much, the doctor had told her to take that miracle drug called aspirin.

Strong, gentle fingers lifted one of Tory's hands from the water. Her eyes opened wide, startled. For a big man wearing cowboy boots Reever moved very softly. Eyes that were as clear as rain studied her. She studied him in return, fascinated by the uncompromisingly masculine lines of his face, the high, blunt cheekbones, rugged nose and heavy, wickedly arched eyebrows. Beneath the slightly shaggy mustache his lips were distinctly curved, a sensual contrast with the strong white teeth that showed in his rare smiles.

"See anything you like?" asked Reever dryly, not even looking up from his work on her hand.

Tory realized that she had been staring openly at Reever. She didn't even have the energy to blush or to think of a snappy retort. "You're very handsome," she said simply.

Reever's head jerked up, surprise clear in his eyes. He looked at Tory's expression and realized that she meant exactly what she had said. "That's a first," he muttered and returned to dabbing carefully at her hand.

"Surely women have told you that you're good-looking before," said Tory, feeling uncomfortable.

"Yeah, but never out of bed."

Reever glanced up in time to see the shock on Tory's face. He laughed softly. "You sure you didn't forge that driver's license, honey?"

"You're a—"

"Devil," he finished smoothly. "Yeah, you've pointed that out about once a minute since I hoisted you up on Blackjack."

"I didn't say a word the whole ride."

"You didn't have to. I could feel the anger vibrating through you. Such a passionate little cat. I'm surprised some man hasn't trimmed your claws and tasted all that wild honey by now." Abruptly Reever stopped talking. The direction of his thoughts was having a pronounced effect on the fit of his jeans, not to mention the color of Tory's face. "Don't look so hopeful. I'm not volunteering for the job."

"Listen, you big—" began Tory in a hot voice.

Reever covered her lips with his long, hard fingers, cutting off her tirade. "No, you listen. I'm a man, honey, and I'm used to having women. Women, not girls. If you keep tempting and teasing me, I'm going to grab you and teach you things that will make you blush all the way down to your toenails."

Tory's breath came in and wedged hard in her throat. She wanted to rage against Reever, against what he was saying, to deny every word. But there was truth in what he said, even though she hadn't realized it until that moment. She had taken one look at him and had wanted to get beneath that hard surface to...what? What did she want from him? Why did he have an uncanny ability to set off her temper? Why did just the simple act of being touched by him as he dried her hands and smoothed ointment into her blistered palms make her feel both safe and threatened?

And why was she so certain that in some deep, unknowable way she had been born for the moment when she had opened the Sundance's gate and walked into Ethan Reever's life?

When Tory spoke, her voice was husky, almost ragged. "Normally I'm one of the most even-tempered people you'll ever meet. Ask any of my coaches. But lately..." She shrugged and smiled weakly. "Well, last week was one of the worst I've ever had and having you treat me like a cross between a pushy tart and a juvenile delinquent was adding insult to injury."

"And you were depending on this job, weren't you?" Reever asked gently. "Let me buy you that bus ticket home, honey."

Tory shook her head in a curt negative. "Thanks, but I earn my own way. Always."

"It will be a loan. You can repay it when—"

"No," she interrupted flatly. "It's my problem, not yours. Despite what you believe, I'm a big girl. I've survived much worse disappointments than not being hired by the Sundance Ranch."

There was a taut silence while Reever tried to think of a way to get Tory to accept money. Even as he did, he knew that it was futile. Beneath that smooth, delicate surface she was both proud and determined to make it on her own. He admired those qualities too much to want to fight her over them.

"What happened last week?" asked Reever finally, knowing that he shouldn't. Whatever had driven Tory from Payton's civilized, moneyed circles to the untamed north of Arizona was none of Reever's business, and he knew it. Yet when he had seen the bleakness that had claimed Tory in the instant before she hid it beneath a determined smile, he had wanted to take her into his arms and promise to make everything better. "A man?"

"As in lover?"

"Yes."

"No fair, cowboy," Tory said wearily. "If you want me to stop digging at you, you'll have to stop digging at me. As you've taken pains to point out at every opportunity, I'm not the stuff passionate male fantasies are made of."

"Fishing for compliments?"

"No more than you're fishing for a pan of dirty water in your face," she retorted, anger giving color to her cheeks again. "I know what I am and what I'm not. I'm not sexy."

Reever looked at Tory for a long, long moment and decided that she was telling the truth as she saw it. She didn't believe that she was sexy, period. She was innocent to the last husky breath. And as long as she was that innocent, she could drive him or any other man right over the edge and never know it.

Deliberately Reever lifted his hand and brushed the back of his fingers over Tory's breast. She made a startled sound deep in her throat as her nipple rose tautly. She stopped breathing entirely as his big hand smoothed out the folds of her T-shirt until her hard nipple stood out clearly against the thin cloth. She shivered and made another soft sound.

"That," he said, watching, listening, his expression dark, intense, "is what male fantasies are made of. You respond to a look, a touch, and you make me wonder what would happen if I really looked at you, really touched you."

"Reever, I—" Tory's voice broke as Reever touched her again, softly, so softly, and turned her nerves to lightning.

"Yes," he said. "I know. You want to find out, too. But you're a virgin."

Her eyes widened to reveal a green so pure it made him ache.

"How did you know?" she whispered.

Reever closed his eyes and said something terrible beneath his breath. "I was hoping I was wrong."

He turned away from Tory, traded the tube of ointment for the roll of gauze he had left on the table and began winding the delicate white cloth around one of her palms.

"I'm going to wrap your hands for now," he said, his voice flat. "Tonight, though, be sure to take off the bandages. You'll heal faster in the air."

"Reever," said Tory softly.

"No, honey," he said, not even looking up. "You're too damned young. You'd have to tell yourself that you loved me, and then you'd want me to talk about love, too. That wouldn't happen." He glanced up, pinning her with his hard gray gaze. "I don't lie to women, in or out of bed. I know what kind of woman I'll need before I start talking about love, and I know you're not it."

Tory couldn't believe the sharpness of the pain that went through her at Reever's matter-of-fact words. With a feeling close to fear, she realized how much she cared about him and how many dreams had come into focus at his gentle touch. She could have loved him. She knew it, and it was like dying to know that he couldn't love her in return. She tried to hide her agonized response beneath the flippancy that had allowed her to survive so much in the past.

"Because I'm not small, stacked and sexy?" Tory asked, repeating what he had told her when he had thrown her out of his office.

"Those are qualifications for a roll in the hay, not a gold ring," said Reever matter-of-factly, tying off one ribbon of gauze and going to work on Tory's other hand. "For a wife I want a grown woman who will love me and who will want to have my children, even if I can't promise her city frills and fancies. I want a woman who won't fade the first time the going gets rough. I want a woman who will work beside me on the ranch because she loves the land as much as I do." He shrugged. "I want a woman, not a girl."

Tory closed her eyes and knew that Reever's words shouldn't hurt so much. There was no reason for her to feel as though she were being sliced apart by a razor made of ice. He wasn't deliberately being cruel.

And that was why it hurt so much. He wasn't trying to bait her. He was simply, calmly, telling her the truth. She could turn him on, but that was all she would ever be to him—a roll in the hay, not a woman to love.

For the second time Reever saw the life drain out of Tory and knew that he had caused it. He heard the echoes of his own words in his mind and winced. He had told the truth, but he hadn't thought how it might sound to her, a belittling of her possibilities as a woman.

"Little green-eyed cat," he murmured, touching Tory's cheek with his finger. "I didn't mean that the way you took it. I'm too old for you, that's all. There's nothing wrong with you. You'll find a nice boy who will teach you what it's all about."

"I know all I want to know about boys grabbing and pawing," Tory said in a thin, tired voice.

"That's not what it's all about," said Reever, smiling slightly to himself.

"Yes, I know," she whispered, closing her eyes so that she wouldn't have to see Reever's gentle, very male smile. "But you're the one who taught me that, Reever. Just now, here, in this kitchen." She opened her eyes. "And you're not a boy."

"I'm not going to—" he began tightly.

"I'm not asking you to," Tory shot back. "And I'm not going to ask you. But if you pat me on the head again, I swear I'll bite you."

"I bite back, honey. And you know it, don't you? You like the idea." Abruptly Reever made a disgusted sound. "Hell, here we go again, teasing and baiting and throwing kerosene on the fire. I should know better, even if you don't. Did you ever ask yourself why I keep harping on how damned young you are?"

Eyes wide, the edge of her teeth buried firmly in her lower lip to hold back a hot rush of words, Tory shook her head. Silently Reever pushed back his chair and stood up, no longer trying to conceal what she did to him. Her eyes widened even more as she saw the blunt length of his arousal beneath his jeans. She might be in-experienced, but she was neither blind nor stupid. She knew exactly what that hard bulge of flesh meant.

"My conscience keeps telling me that I shouldn't take you," Reever said flatly. "I don't want to hear a young girl who doesn't know better whispering undy-ing love in my ear. But I want you, honey. I want you like hell on fire. Now do you know what I mean when I tell you not to push me?"

Mutely Tory nodded, trying not to stare at the po-tent evidence of Reever's masculinity. It was impossi-ble. The thought that she could affect him to that extent made her melt and run like hot, sweet honey.

Reever had expected Tory to be frightened or re-pelled by his body's frank hunger. He had not expected her to make a swift, soft sound that was halfway be-tween a whimper and a moan, and to look at him as though he were a hidden spring and she was shaking with thirst.

"Sweet God," he said hoarsely. "How the hell did you stay a virgin this long?"

Tory closed her eyes. "It was easy. I hadn't met you." She laughed almost helplessly, and then the laughter faded. She opened her eyes and looked straight into

Reever's. "I have too much self-respect to chase a man who wants nothing from me but a roll in the hay. So relax, cowboy. I wouldn't rip your clothes off you, even—" she eyed her trussed palms wryly "—even if my soft little city hands were up to it."

"You're just naturally sassy, aren't you?" Reever asked, smiling against his will.

She laughed slightly, then with genuine humor. "Yeah, I guess so. It's how I stayed sane when the coaches yelled at me. I'd smile and tell them how wonderful they were. Some of them believed me."

Reever laughed out loud, shaking his head. "Coaches, huh? What are you, some kind of tennis baby?"

"Nope. Some kind of water baby. That's how I met your cousin. He's one of the swim club's biggest supporters. He finds jobs for—" Tory bit off the rush of words as she heard Reever's name being called from the yard between the house and the barn.

"In here, Jed," called Tory.

The back door to the kitchen opened, and a man's disgusted voice said, "That lazy son of a bitch Cookie is off on another goddamned toot. If you ask me, when we find him, we ought to string him up by his useless, pea-sized—" There was an instant of shocked silence as Jed spotted Tory. "Er, sorry, miss. I didn't know anyone but the boss was in here."

"No problem," Tory said, smiling at the lean, blond cowhand who looked barely as old as she was. "Where I come from, cussing is one of the favorite outdoor sports."

Jed slanted her a sideways smile. "Yeah? Where you from, pretty lady?"

"Sin City," she said in a husky, theatrical voice, winking at Jed, falling quickly into the kind of kidding that had been a way of life at the swim club.

With narrowed eyes Reever watched the instant, easy camaraderie between Tory and the young cowhand as they introduced themselves. Reever knew that he should be relieved to have those wide green eyes looking anywhere else but at him. He also knew that he wanted to pick up the handsome young Jed by the scruff of his neck and heave him out the back door.

"You bring the cards?" asked Reever curtly.

The buried anger in Reever's voice gave it a crackle that made Jed's head snap around instantly. "No, sir."

"Get a pack while I unsaddle Blackjack and round up the rest of the boys. We'll draw to see who replaces Cookie and who drives him into town."

"Town?"

"Town," Reever said flatly. "This is Cookie's last toot on my ranch. We'll cook for ourselves until I find someone else."

"The boys won't be happy."

Reever grunted.

Tory saw both the distaste and the acceptance in Jed's face. Apparently none of the cowboys liked to cook. Her conclusion was underlined by the banging of the screen door behind Reever on his way out and by the outraged howls of various men as Reever gave them the news.

She hesitated, then turned away from the back door and began rummaging in the kitchen. It was obvious that if she were going to eat anytime soon, she'd have to fix something herself. Humming quietly, she began piling ingredients on the counter by the stove. She looked up from time to time as heated outbursts from the men outside told her that the draw had either been inconclusive or was being hotly contested.

By the time Reever stalked back into the kitchen with the men at his heels, savory aromas were arising from the meat and onions browning in a huge pan on the stove. Tory was working at the counter grating cheese, pausing only long enough to stir the meat from time to time. In a second frying pan, thumbnail-sized chunks of bread were cooking in garlic butter. As Reever walked up behind her, she stretched over the big old stove and shook the pan, making the cubes of bread dance.

"What the hell do you think you're doing?" demanded Reever.

The huge cast-iron pan clattered to the burner, sending chunks of bread flying in all directions.

"Of all the clumsy—" began Reever angrily.

"You're supposed to be a cowboy, not a darned Indian," snapped Tory, cutting off Reever's words. "Why are you always sneaking up on me?"

There were snickers from the six men behind Reever, but nobody said a word. Tory noticed the men for the first time.

"Oh," she said. "Hi." She licked the side of her index finger absently, where garlic butter had run down. "Who lost the draw?"

"Reever," said Jed, unable to hide his smile.

"Oh."

Reever barely heard. His eyes were riveted on Tory's pink tongue licking so delicately over equally delicate skin. He couldn't help but wonder how it would feel to have that hot, sweet tongue caressing him.

Little green-eyed cat. God, she's tying me in knots.

Tory glanced at Reever and saw darkness and anger. "I figured you'd be all day arguing the draw," she said quickly. "I was hungry. So I started cooking."

Reever picked up one of the errant bread cubes, popped it into his mouth and chewed. One black eyebrow lifted in surprise at the unexpected crunch and flavor. He took the spoon and stirred the meat before running his fingertip over the spoon's shallow metal bowl.

"Not bad," he said grudgingly.

"You're too kind," said Tory, her voice as sweet and empty as spun sugar.

As one the cowhands began to fade from the kitchen, sensing with great certainty that the poor fool of a girl was going to set the match to their boss's famous temper.

"Probably," agreed Reever sardonically. He ate several big bites of the meat, apparently impervious to the steamy heat. With a sigh he tossed the spoon back into the skillet. "If I don't die by dinner, you've got a job until you earn enough for a bus ticket home."

"How did you know I was broke?" asked Tory in the instant before she realized that she had been suckered again. As with her virginity Reever had guessed, but he hadn't known until she confirmed it.

"How much money do you have?" he demanded, grabbing her chin when she would have turned away.

"A few dollars."

"A few dollars," he repeated, taking in and letting out a long breath. Then in a deadly voice he asked, "Just how the hell did you expect to get home after you left the Sundance—walk and eat sagebrush?"

"There's always the oldest profession, isn't there?" Tory said flippantly.

Reever's lips flattened. "Honey, you're so clumsy you'd have to give your tricks combat pay."

For the second time that day Tory felt tears clawing at her eyes. She knew that her lips were trembling and hated Reever for seeing it, for shredding her pride until she couldn't conceal her hurt. She hated herself for being so endlessly vulnerable to him. She jerked free of his grasp and turned away before he could see her tears.

Reever swore bitterly. "I told you, little girl. Don't push me."

Numbly Tory nodded, grating cheese blindly.

"If you want the job, I'll have Dutch pick up your stuff when he dumps Cookie," Reever said, his voice harsh.

Tory knew that Reever wanted her to refuse. She wanted to refuse, too. But she had no choice. She hadn't seen a Help Wanted sign anywhere in Massacre Creek. Today, like so many times in the past, she couldn't afford the luxury of pride. She had to take what was offered and smile and make the best of it. Normally it didn't bother her. It did now.

She took a deep breath before she spoke, afraid that her voice would shake. She didn't want that. She would

die before she showed Ethan Reever any weakness
again.

"Yes," she said finally, quietly. "I want the job."

Reever watched the slender, proud line of Tory's back
for a long time, cursing silently. He had seen the too-
brilliant green of her eyes and the betraying quiver of
her hands as she worked. He stalked out of the kitchen,
yanking his hat into place and letting the screen door
bang loudly behind him, cursing himself thoroughly—
and hoping to God that he could keep his hands off
Tory until she earned a bus ticket back to the city,
where she belonged.

Chapter Four

"I'LL DO IT, JED," SAID TORY, reaching for the egg basket that the young cowboy was holding.

"You sure?" he asked. "That one-eyed hen is as mean as a snake. She's pecked Reever more than once."

"And survived to lay another egg?" Tory asked dryly. "You should cast that feathered phenomenon in bronze."

Jed laughed and looked at Tory with lively blue eyes. During the three weeks that she had been on the ranch, the men had come to enjoy her quick tongue as much as her cooking. All except Reever, of course. Jed didn't know what had happened in the kitchen that day when the hands had slunk out, leaving Tory to face the boss in the full flare of his devil temper. But Jed knew that since that day Tory hadn't done anything in Reever's presence except be cheerful, prompt with meals and a very hard worker.

"Sure I can't talk you into a movie tonight?" asked Jed wistfully. "That old kitchen will come apart if you clean it one more time."

"I'm sure. But thanks, Jed," she said, winking at him. "It's nice of you to ask a senior citizen."

Jed winced and then laughed, shaking his head. "Hell, Tory, I'm only two years younger than you." He looked at her suddenly. "You got a guy back home?"

"No." Tory hesitated and then said simply, "I don't want one here, either. I'll go to a movie with a bunch of the hands, but not with just one. I'm a friend, not a date."

Jed sighed. "Okay," he said finally, "if that's the way you want it."

"Thanks for understanding," she said, smiling in return.

"You watch out for that old hen," Jed repeated, walking off toward the corral. "She's been a real terror lately."

Tory walked out to the henhouse, swinging the basket from her arm, grateful that Jed had decided to look for romance elsewhere. With the Sundance hands, Tory had quickly established the easy, humorous camaraderie that had been the hallmark of her relationship with the various boys and men who had shared the swim club's huge pools. The inevitable sexual innuendos of the cowhands were either ignored or topped with a deadpan innocence that had caused more than one man to choke into his napkin with disbelief and laughter. Invitations for dates were turned down quickly, firmly and with a pleasant smile. Tory didn't want to be a challenge to the men. She wanted to be a sister.

Reever was the only exception to that rule. Tory wanted to be more to him, but she knew that it wasn't going to happen. She tried to accept the bittersweetness of finding for the first time in her life a man she could have loved and then losing him before she ever had a chance, simply because she had been born in the wrong place and years too late to attract him. It wasn't fair to lose that way, through circumstances that she had never controlled, but that kind of loss didn't surprise her. Life simply wasn't fair. She had learned that the hard way in the past, when judges were capricious or outright biased in choosing the best divers. Win some. Lose some. Some never had a chance. Maybe next time luck would break her way.

At least, that's how she had always consoled herself in the past.

All around Tory sunshine poured down from a sky so blue that it almost hurt to look at it. There were a few fluffy clouds skidding about, chased by a wind that never touched the ground. The smell of new growth and damp earth swirled invisibly around Tory. She took a deep breath, savoring the sweetness of the air, feeling herself expand into the limitless land. She loved the early mornings when the world was fresh and the Sundance's sweeping vistas brought a feeling of peace to her that she had never experienced before she had come to the ranch. Nerve endings and muscles that she hadn't known were tight had slowly relaxed through the weeks, leaving her with a feeling of contentment that was like coming home.

Even Ethan Reever's satanic temper and razor tongue hadn't been able to spoil that.

After a lifetime of buying perfectly matched eggs in cold, sterile plastic cartons, Tory found the gathering of various sizes of eggs still warm from the nest to be satisfying in a way that she couldn't describe. She couldn't have enjoyed collecting the eggs more if they had been brightly colored and full of Easter chocolate.

"Morning, you ugly, one-eyed witch," said Tory cheerfully, pouring feed into the small troughs that ran along the exterior of the henhouse.

The hen in question gave Tory an evil look before going to work pecking at the feed through the fence. The other hens followed suit with only a small flurry of clucking and flapping. They were getting used to Tory as she slowly took over the lighter chores, freeing Jed for other work. When she was sure that the hens were busy, Tory climbed up the rickety old stepladder leaning against the coop's outside wall. She opened the small door that would give her hands access to the raised nests and wedged her upper body into the henhouse while she patted through the warm straw in search of eggs. She couldn't see much inside the dark coop, but she didn't need to. Her fingers could find the eggs faster than her eyes.

As Tory pulled out eggs one by one and put them into the basket she had braced between her feet, she thought covetously of the small patch of land just in back of the house. Sometime in the past that patch had been a kitchen garden. She was sure of it. The suggestion of neat furrows was subtle yet distinct, and she had found the remains of a compost pile behind the chicken house. She had never had any time to garden as a child, yet the thought had always tempted her. Growing seeds into whole plants, eating the fruits or vegetables that unfurled so miraculously from such vulnerable beginnings, taking part herself in the advancing of the seasons across the earth—she wanted to do that. She wanted to touch the land and feel it warm and fertile beneath her hands.

Tory was so caught up in dreaming about a garden that she was slow to collect the eggs. The first warning she had that something was wrong was a sharp pain, as though someone had rammed a thick thorn into her finger. With a gasp she jerked her hand away, upsetting her precarious balance as she leaned into the coop. Her feet kicked over the basket of eggs as she tried to right herself without using her hands, which were shielding her face from the one-eyed hen.

Tory succeeded in protecting her eyes but only at the cost of getting her hands severely pecked. She tried to back out but couldn't without uncovering her face. Frantically, blindly, she braced her weight on her elbows and tried to grab the mean hen. The wild battle stirred up the rest of the chickens. Some of them joined in the effort to repel the intruder. Others simply rushed around clucking and screeching as though a coyote had slipped into the coop and was eating them one by one.

Reever heard the noise, came out of the barn where he had been checking on a lame horse and saw Tory struggling half in and half out of the henhouse. With five running strides he was there. His big, leather-gloved hand shot over Tory's shoulder, covering her face as he yanked her out of the one-eyed hen's reach and slammed shut the high, narrow opening.

"You clumsy little city idiot," he said roughly, setting Tory on her feet amidst the broken eggs. "Look at that mess! I should take a whip to Jed for not warning you about that one-eyed hen!"

Tory tried not to flinch from the icy contempt in Reever's eyes. "Jed warned me. I was just slow getting the eggs."

She took a step backward, then another, retreating from Reever's black presence. She had managed to get along with everyone at the ranch but its big, harsh-faced boss. No matter what she did, how well she did it or how careful she was to be cheerful and respectful of Reever at all times, he had ridden her mercilessly about her youth, her softness and her unfamiliarity with the ranch. She didn't want to give him another verbal stick to beat her with. She had to reach the kitchen and get her hands cleaned up before he noticed them.

"It was my fault," Tory said quickly. "You're right. I'm clumsy. I'm sorry. You can take the eggs out of my pay. I'd better get back to the kitchen," she continued as she turned, trying to use her body to shield her painful hands from Reever's glance as she moved. "I don't want the beans to burn."

Tory knew the exact instant when Reever saw her fingers. His body went absolutely still, then his hands shot out and fastened around her wrists. The words he said made her wish that she could fall right through the ground. She tried not to show it. She had decided to treat Reever like the hardest coach she had ever had. No matter how sarcastic, how cutting, how cruel he was, she would be unfailingly agreeable, never argue and never, ever show how badly she was being cut up.

"Where the hell are the leather gloves I told you to get?" finished Reever with a snarl.

Mentally Tory braced herself and said quietly, "I didn't buy them."

"What?"

"I didn't buy them."

"Why not?"

For a long moment Tory said nothing, knowing that her next words would set off Reever's famous temper but good. The job as cook wasn't high-paying work. There was no reason for it to be; room, board, laundry, almost everything was paid for by the ranch. She was given a small—very small—weekly salary. Out of that she had already bought shoes, socks, a new T-shirt and a pair of jeans to replace the clothes that had been ruined the day she had tried to walk to town.

Nor did the expenditures end there. She had had to buy anti-inflammatory medicine and elastic bandages for her knee, soap, lotion, shampoo, toothpaste and intimate feminine items. By the time she had bought the necessities, there was nothing left, not even enough to pay her way in to a movie in town. The leather gloves that Reever had ordered her to buy would cost the equivalent of half a week's pay.

"I'll look for gloves the next time I'm in town," said Tory, knowing that "look" was all she would be able to do. She could barely afford to renew her prescription for her knee. Then there was the second set of weights she had ordered to allow her to continue strengthening her knee. They were coming COD. She had to be able to pay for them. She couldn't do that if she bought the gloves.

"I didn't tell you to buy them next week," retorted Reever. "I told you to buy them two weeks ago when you started stumbling around after the men in the barn and the corral. Remember?"

"Yes, sir."

The formality wasn't sarcastic, it was a reflex left from years of being coached by overbearing males. Reever didn't know that, however. His eyes narrowed as though Tory had slapped him.

"Just plain Reever, city girl. Think you can remember it, or should I have that hen tattoo it on the back of your soft, useless hands?"

"I'm sorry, Reever," said Tory tightly, struggling to keep her voice from breaking.

He stared at Tory's downcast eyes, but she neither moved nor looked up at him. She had been like this since that first day in the kitchen—polite, respectful, trying very hard to please. And the harder she tried, the more angry he became.

Tory realized it but didn't know what she could do. The verbal punishment Reever had given her for her flip remark about taking up the oldest profession still made her pale with humiliation every time she thought about it. So she stayed polite and cheerful and prayed that sooner or later he would get tired of peeling strips off her, or she would be able to save enough for that bus ticket home.

Only it wasn't home she would be going toward, and Tory knew it. It was simply the only place she had left to go.

"Wash your hands," Reever said in disgust. "I'll have one of the men drive you into town so a doctor can look at them."

Tory stared at Reever. "But when Jed got that wicked rope burn, you didn't make him go to town. Why should I go for a few lousy pinpricks?"

Reever's mouth flattened until there was nothing but a tight line beneath his black mustache. He held Tory's hand up to her face as though the fingers were separate condemnations. Blood trickled from the various small wounds the hen had inflicted. "Jed isn't a soft little girl."

"Neither am I," Tory said, fighting to keep her voice even.

"I said go and you'll go."

"I can't," she said. "I'm sorry. I can't afford a doctor."

In silence Reever examined the thoroughly pecked flesh on Tory's hands. "Is that why you didn't buy gloves?" he asked finally.

She hesitated, then nodded.

When Reever's eyes shifted up to Tory's face, she couldn't help flinching. Seeing that didn't make his temper any softer. Or his tongue. "Then maybe you should have spent less money painting the town red with the boys," he said harshly.

Tory stared, her green eyes wide with disbelief. "What?"

"Do you think that I didn't notice all of you piling into Smitty's car on Saturday afternoon and not coming back until early Sunday morning?"

Tory closed her eyes, telling herself that she could not, simply could *not,* let her temper slide out from under her control. "It was Dutch's birthday."

"Yeah, I heard. Was it a Dutch treat all around," continued Reever sardonically, "with you doing the treating and the boys doing the paying?"

All the words Tory couldn't say crowded her throat. She pulled her hands free of Reever's grasp and said, "I'll buy gloves as soon as I can afford them."

"Better buy a face mask, too, city girl. That old hen will peck your eyes out next time," retorted Reever.

He watched Tory's retreat with narrow, steel-colored eyes. When he looked down at his scarred leather gloves and saw her blood on them, he swore savagely. Abruptly he kicked aside the egg basket, climbed the stepladder and opened the henhouse door.

As Tory soaked her hands in a pan of warm, iodine-tinted water, she heard another wild squawking from the henhouse. It ended before she could see what was happening. An hour later Jed came into the kitchen, carrying the egg basket.

"Boss says he wants chicken and dumplings for dinner."

"I'll check the freezer," said Tory, "but I think I fried the last chickens for Sunday lunch."

"No problem," said Jed, reaching into the basket and tossing the plucked, cleaned and rather lean body of a chicken on the counter.

Tory gave him a startled look.

Jed grinned. "Guess the 'feathered phenomenon' pecked the boss once too often. He wrung her neck and cleaned her himself." Jed spotted Tory's hands. "Holy cow, Tory. What—oh, Lord! It wasn't Reever the hen got, was it?"

She smiled crookedly. "Like Reever says, I'm clumsy."

"Clumsy?" said Jed with an incredulous look at her. "You're about as clumsy as the cat when she's prowling for mice in the barn."

"Yeah, sure," Tory said, grimacing.

Her mouth turned down as she remembered all the times she had made a fool of herself in front of Reever—most recently at the henhouse. She had no illusions as to how graceful she had looked with her fanny hanging out of the chicken coop and her legs kicking air. Sighing, she picked up the big hen gingerly. It was one thing to gather eggs that were still warm. It was quite another to confront a barely cooled chicken carcass.

"Pretend you just unwrapped it from the store," offered Jed, grinning at Tory's obvious discomfort.

She smiled weakly and began filling a big pot with water as Jed closed the screen door behind him. While the hen simmered on the stove, Tory found the old ranch cookbook that had become her bible in the last few weeks. Being a short-order cook hadn't given her a very large list of specialties. While her pancakes had been wonderful, her biscuits could have been used to shoe horses, as Reever had pointed out. She had kept trying, working when no one was around, until she had learned how to make a tender, savory biscuit. The men had complimented her extravagantly. Reever had said nothing but "Pass the butter."

It had been that way with everything. If she did it badly, he let her know in no soft terms. If she did it well, he ignored her. Dutch had told her that it was nothing personal—Reever was like that with everybody. But even Dutch had to admit that Reever gave Tory less slack and more spur than anyone else in the outfit.

Tory's solution had been to work longer and harder, just as she had done at the swim club, hoping that sooner or later Reever would let up. In the past even her toughest coach had acknowledged it when she had done a good job.

But not Reever. It seemed that the harder she worked, the more sarcastically critical he became.

Nothing personal.

Tory wished that she could believe it. She wished that she could forget all the times that Reever had cut her to the bone with his caustic appraisals of her as a cook, egg collector, dishwasher—and woman. That most of all. The memory of how her breasts had risen eagerly to his touch humiliated her to her core. Even now he had only to look at her and she felt it starting all over again, the shivering, melting fire.

Honey, you're so clumsy you'd have to give your tricks combat pay.

Nothing personal? Yeah. Sure.

Gloomily Tory began to read the recipe for chicken and dumplings. For once she had all the ingredients on hand, including an old, tough hen.

Throughout the day Tory hovered over the stew pot, tasting, poking, adjusting herbs and salt as the cooking progressed. The chicken itself had a fine flavor that kept improving as the hours passed. When it was time for the dumplings, Tory did everything according to the book, bit into a dumpling and knew she was in for the cutting edge of Reever's sarcastic tongue.

With a sinking heart she threw out the first batch and made more dumplings, measuring the flour so scrupulously that she all but counted each particle. The result looked and tasted like what it was. Boiled dough. Unfortunately the dumplings were the backbone of the meal, for one chicken divided among nine mouths didn't go very far, even when that chicken was formerly the biggest, meanest hen in all of Arizona.

As Tory set the table, she braced herself for the ordeal to come. The chicken was tender and flavorful, quite the best that Tory had ever tasted, although she had to admit that revenge might have been part of the savor—her hands still hurt from the punctures and bruises the hen had inflicted. The vegetables she had cooked were just right, firm rather than mushy, with a scattering of herbs to bring out their natural flavor.

But the dumplings still tasted like boiled dough.

The men piled into the kitchen as Tory was pouring the thick, lethal coffee that they all loved and she could barely swallow.

"Evening, Tory," said Dutch, hanging his battered hat on a knob projecting from one of the old oak chairs that surrounded the scarred wooden dining table. He slid into his chair eagerly. "Been smelling this all day. Driving me crazy, it smells so good."

The others were right on Dutch's heels. Within moments the big kitchen was full of hungry men. One of them was Reever. He gave Tory's hands a long glance as she poured his coffee. His eyes narrowed at the sight of the small, livid wounds dotting her fine-grained skin.

"Jed," said Dutch, "you better check the henhouse after dinner. When I went by on the way in, that one-eyed hen didn't come out to peck at my boots through the wire. She might be sick."

"Nope," Jed said confidently, helping himself to chicken and dumplings. "That crazy old biddy done pecked her last," he drawled.

"Yeah?" asked Dutch, forking a chunk of chicken into his mouth. "Lord, Tory, you're gonna spoil us," he said, closing his eyes and chewing slowly. "Best chicken I ever had." He sighed and turned his attention back to Jed. "What happened?"

"Reever wrung her neck," said Jed succinctly.

Dutch looked at his dinner plate with new interest. "I'll be damned." He looked at Reever. "Hell, boss, I thought you said you'd never touch one feather on that mean old—"

"Are you going to talk or eat?" interrupted Reever.

Tory stared at Reever, wondering if that really could be a dull red climbing up his blunt cheekbones. Quickly she glanced away, concentrating on pouring Dutch's coffee without spilling a drop. She didn't need another of Reever's cutting lectures on her clumsiness.

"I can eat and talk at the same time," Dutch said, grinning. "What changed your mind about that crazy old hen? Did she peck your favorite horse? Did she—" Dutch's baiting words stopped abruptly when he saw Tory's hands hovering over his coffee cup. He muttered something under his breath and shot Reever an approving glance before looking back at Tory. "The boys and I will take turns on the dishes until you're healed. Ma always said there's nothing worse than dirty dishwater for infecting cuts."

"That's all right, Dutch," said Tory quickly. "I'll just put iodine on my hands afterward."

"Hell, girl, don't be silly," Dutch said, his voice gruff. "Who sewed up the rip in my new shirt so good I couldn't even see the mend? Who spent half the night writing letters to the government for Teague and Miller so they wouldn't be shamed by their spelling in front of city folks? Who's been changing the dressing on Smitty's best horse so that the cut heals twice as quick? Who's been—"

"Pass the dumplings," Reever said coolly, cutting across Dutch's words.

Tory heard the anger vibrating in Reever's curt command and wondered what was wrong now. As she handed him the dumplings, she realized that whatever was riding him would soon be supplanted by the uninteresting taste of her dumplings. She watched his strong white teeth bite into a creamy lump of cooked flour and braced herself for the worst.

Reever grunted, heaped more dumplings on his plate and resumed eating.

Tory almost dropped the coffeepot in her astonishment. She watched the other men from the corner of her eye as she finished pouring coffee. They attacked the dumplings with every evidence of pleasure, complimenting her between bites. With a soundless sigh, she took her place at the table and ate a bite of dumpling herself, wondering if it had somehow been miraculously transformed by the trip from the stove to the table. A single bite told her that nothing about the dumpling had changed. She'd eaten tastier library paste.

Thank God that Reever hadn't.

Tory ate slowly, ignoring the dumpling, listening to the men talk about how the range was greening at the higher elevations as spring progressed up the steep slopes of Blue Wolf Mountain, which comprised the northwestern half of the Sundance. All the talk of spring and growing things reminded her of the garden she wanted.

"Jed?" she asked quietly, catching his eye. "Are you going into town soon?"

"Early tomorrow morning. Need something?"

"Seeds."

Although Tory had tried to keep her voice down, she sensed Reever's sudden interest.

"Sure. What kind of flowers you want?"

"Beans, tomatoes, peas, squash, parsley, onions, carrots." Tory paused for breath. "Corn, too. Do you think I can grow corn out back?"

Jed shrugged, smiling. "Beats me. I couldn't grow a toadstool if I tried."

Tory didn't really hear him. She was remembering the last time she had stood in a supermarket in South California, slowly turning a rack of seed packets with her hand, watching the brightly colored pictures flow by with a hunger that she was just now understanding.

"Zinnias," she murmured. "And sweet peas and marigolds and daisies and—" She laughed suddenly. "Oh, all of them, Jed. Every seed you can buy. I want to plant them all, watch those first tiny shoots push up from the ground, see all the different shapes of leaves and flowers." Abruptly Tory remembered that seeds weren't free. Some of the vivid pleasure faded from her expression. "Well, not all at once, of course." She smiled crookedly. "About three dollars' worth to start, okay?"

"You got it," said Jed.

"Where are you going to plant all that?" asked Reever, looking at Tory with an expression that she didn't understand.

"Out back where the kitchen garden was."

"'Was' is right," Reever retorted sardonically. "That ground hasn't been touched since my grandmother Abby Reever died a half century ago. After her the Reever and Sundance wives lived in the city. They sucked the ranch dry buying store beef and fancy clothes, and they wouldn't have dirtied their fingernails in a kitchen garden to save their lives. City girls every one of them."

Contempt resonated in Reever's voice. Every year he managed the ranch for his aunts and his cousins, dividing the hard-won profits with them. Fifty-five percent to the Sundance family, including Payton, who had earned a fortune investing the money elsewhere. Forty-five percent to Reever, who reinvested every penny in the ranch itself, even though his was not the deciding vote in how the ranch was run. Payton could, and had, forced Reever to build the Sundance Retreat up on Wolf Lake. Reever had given in finally because he knew that Payton would lose interest in the retreat after a few years. Then the beautiful cedar lodge and outbuildings would make a perfect center for the ranch, miles closer to the road than the present ranch house.

One day the Sundance would be Reever's, all of it. Until then Reever's "pay" every year for managing the ranch for his aunts and cousins was another one percent ownership of the ranch that nobody else in his family wanted. They wanted the money that the ranch yielded beneath Reever's sweat and skill, though. His aunts wanted to be carried on Reever's broad back so that they'd never have to work. And it had happened just that way.

"City girls," muttered Reever, forking chicken and dumpling into his mouth. "Useless."

Tory had to bite her lip to keep from pointing out that being from the city didn't ensure that a woman was lazy any more than being from the country ensured that a man was a hard worker.

"Tell me, city girl," Reever continued, pinning Tory with a metallic glance. "How are you going to prepare the ground for all those seeds?"

"I saw a shovel in the barn," she said neutrally.

"You'll have to do a hell of a lot more than *look* at a shovel to get a garden," he retorted. "Or did you just expect to plug the shovel in and watch it dig all by itself?"

Tory swallowed a crack about not being able to find an extension cord that long. "No," she said quietly. "I expected to get it done one foot at a time."

"Left or right foot?" asked Jed innocently.

Tory tried not to smile but didn't succeed. "Whatever works," she said, giving Jed a sideways glance out of eyes as green as gems.

Reever caught the look, and his mouth flattened until there was nothing except a thin, hard line. But whatever he was going to say was lost beneath the genial argument over whether it was better to shovel with the left or the right foot. Tory listened to the men with relief, hoping that Reever had been deflected from another scathing speech about useless city girls. She didn't know how much longer she could hold her tongue, especially when being polite was a one-way street. She couldn't bait Reever or even respond to his baiting, but he was under no such restraints with her. If he wanted a bite out of her, he just took it and dared her to bite back.

And she was terrified that she would. Then she would lose, and lose hard. She could all but taste the scalding humiliation that would come if she crossed Reever.

Quietly Tory pushed back her chair and began to clean the kitchen while the men finished dinner. Normally she enjoyed sitting around the table with them, listening and learning as they talked about horses and cows, grass and creeks, storm and sunshine. She didn't want to stay around tonight. Reever was in a savage mood, his features bleak and unforgiving. Sooner or later she would bear the brunt of his temper unless she got out of his sight.

When Dutch started to object as Tory took his plate, she bent closer and whispered, "Don't get up. Please, Dutch. Reever will skin me alive. My hands are okay. Really."

Dutch muttered something fully suited to Reever in his worst mood, but the wiry little cowhand didn't get up and help Tory with the dishes. Dutch, too, had seen the black signs of Reever's temper. So had the rest of the hands. Within minutes the kitchen was empty but for Tory and Reever. To her relief he got up and went into his office to work on the books. Tory sighed unconsciously and wondered if Reever's temper would be any better the following morning.

It wasn't. None of the hands escaped the caustic effects of Reever's tongue. Tory waited until he had ridden off before she went out to the barn, found an old shovel and went to work on the garden.

And work it was. The ground was rich but stubborn. The shovel was heavy and better suited to boots than tennis shoes. Dutch came by with a pair of his old work gloves in his hand. They were big on Tory, but they made it much easier to handle the splintery old shovel. Even so, she had done only one short furrow by the time she had to go inside and begin lunch. The ragged line of earth glistened with fertile promise each time she looked out the window.

One time when she looked out, the line of turned earth had suddenly, impossibly widened. She blinked, shook her head and stared. From the back porch came the sound of Jed's and Dutch's voices. Then came Miller's. She raced to the other window and saw the three cowhands making short work of the earth. Two of them used spades that sliced easily through the ground. The third broke up the big clods with the shovel.

"Reever's gonna tan our hides," said Jed casually.

Miller grunted, rubbed a weathered leather glove over his equally weathered jeans and spat a stream of tobacco juice off to one side.

Dutch shrugged. "I figure it this way, son," said the cowhand, leaning on the spade. "Reever told us to shovel out the corral. Now, if we want to shovel them sunbaked turds into this patch of ground instead of off behind the barn, that's our business." There was a pause, then, "Move it, Miller. Here comes Teague with another wheelbarrow of Blackjack's best."

Tory watched until tears blurred the men into shadows. Slowly she turned back to the chili that was simmering on the stove. She wiped her eyes impatiently as she opened the flour bin. She had been practicing piecrusts for two weeks. Now was as good a time as any to see if she had learned to make a crust that tasted better than it looked.

By lunchtime the smell of apple pie was competing with the spicy fragrance of chili. As she pulled the second pie out to cool, she looked at the crust critically. Not gorgeous, but acceptable. And she knew the pie itself would taste good because she had eaten a spoonful of filling when she cleaned the bowl. Now all she had to do was find out if the hands liked cheese or ice cream with their hot apple pie.

Tory went to the back door. As she reached for the handle, the sound of Reever's voice came clearly through the screen.

"What do you think you're doing?"

"Shifting turds," Dutch said succinctly.

Reever's ice-pale glance went from man to man. Without a word he turned Blackjack and went back to the corral. Tory let out a long breath and crept silently back to the kitchen. When the table was set, she went out to the metal triangle that hung from the porch roof. She banged enthusiastically with a steel wand, calling the hands in to lunch.

No one came running. Frowning, she banged some more. Still no one. She walked out into the yard, looked around, but saw no one. Slowly she climbed the steps onto the back porch and walked into the kitchen, wondering where all the men were.

Everyone was in place around the table but Reever. All of the men were trying so hard not to smile that their faces must have ached. Bewildered, Tory looked from one to the other, wondering what was going on. Then she spotted the mound of small, colorful packets heaped to overflowing on her plate. Seeds and more seeds, a cascade of possibilities calling to her. There were so many—far more than three dollars could have bought.

"They're all yours, Tory," said Jed, grinning and sliding three dollar bills under her plate. "And if you try to pay us back, we'll pour cement in your garden."

With an excited sound Tory hurried to the table, feeling like a kid on Christmas morning. She didn't see Reever silently close the porch door behind him. He leaned a hard shoulder against the doorframe, stuck his thumbs through the loops of his jeans and watched while surprise and pleasure transformed Tory's face. She ran her fingers through the piled packages of seeds as though they were gold and jewels, reading off the names while her voice got more and more husky until it shivered into silence over her words of thanks.

"City girl," said Reever curtly, "I think you and the boys have forgotten something."

Tory started, scattering bright packages over the table. She looked over her shoulder almost fearfully. "Oh, Reever, please," she said, her voice husky. "Let me use that little bit of land. I won't let it get in the way of my cooking."

"Hell," Reever said roughly, hating to hear the catch in Tory's voice, "you can have the damned garden, for what good it will do you."

"What do you mean? Isn't the ground good?"

"The ground's fine. You're the problem, city girl," he said, looking straight into Tory's pleading green eyes. "You're not going to be around long enough to see any of those seeds bloom, are you?"

Tory looked at the bright faces of the packets scattered across the table and knew that Reever was right. She had forgotten that the Sundance wasn't her home and that Reever had made no secret of the fact that he wanted her out of there at the earliest possible moment.

"I guess not," she said sadly, blinking back tears. "So I'll just have to enjoy as much of it as I can, won't I?"

There was no answer but that of Reever's hungry, steel-colored eyes watching Tory's fingertip trace the bursting ripeness of the tomato pictured on a package of seeds.

Chapter Five

FLEXING HER HANDS, TORY LOOKED down at the supple yet sturdy work gloves she wore. They had appeared by her breakfast plate two weeks ago. The cowhands had all denied any knowledge of how the gloves had gotten there. When she had put the price of the gloves in cash on the dinner table the following week, the money had stayed there for three days before she gave up and put it back in her wallet.

The golden-brown, rough suede surface of the gloves was already stained by dirt from the garden and scratched here and there by angry hens, baling wire and barbwire. Tory was spending more and more time in the barn and around the corrals. Despite her rather hard initiation into riding, she found herself fascinated by the horses. Dutch and Jed swore that she had a knack for handling the big animals. The hands had taught her how to groom, bridle and saddle horses, as well as how to rake out a stall. She had gradually taken over the care of the horses that turned up lame or cut, as well as the calves that had been injured in one way or another.

If Reever objected to Tory caring for the animals, he had said nothing to her about it. That was what had given her the courage to wheedle riding lessons out of Jed. She was no longer satisfied with just being around horses. She wanted to be able to ride out over the land and feel the wind in her hair. She wanted to know again the pleasure of a horse's easy rocking motions, a pleasure that she had tasted a few times during that long ride to the ranch with Reever. She needed to be outside, moving; she was accustomed to more strenuous exercise than being cook for the Sundance's eight men. She was…restless.

Jed rode into the yard, spotted Tory in the garden and smiled. "Soon as you're finished fooling around in the dirt, come to the main corral."

"Are you sure you have time?" asked Tory eagerly, almost afraid to hope. Every time they had planned a riding lesson, Reever had piled more work on Jed.

"I got a head start on my work today," Jed said, yawning. "I've been riding fence since first light."

Suddenly Tory realized why the young cowhand hadn't been at the breakfast table or in for lunch, either. "Oh, Jed, I didn't mean for you to—"

"I'll forgive you if you bring a sandwich with you," interrupted Jed. "And you might bring a carrot for Twinkletoes. That fool mare thinks she's half rabbit."

Tory turned and gathered her gardening tools quickly. She washed them off at the outside faucet and

wiped them on her already fraying jeans. With a grimace she looked down at the thin denim. Next time she
would have to buy rugged jeans rather than the fash-
ionable imitations that fell apart under real use.

The thought of buying anything made Tory frown.
Money, which she had never had trouble hanging on
to before, just kept sliding through her fingers on the
Sundance. She had quickly discovered that the tender
new plants coming up couldn't be cared for with a
shovel or a spade so she had bought gardening tools.
While there were plenty of natural fertilizers on the
ranch, the gardening book she had bought—another
unexpected expense—had mentioned that certain kinds
of fertilizers were needed at certain times in the growing cycle. In the end she had bought some commercial
fertilizer to be sure that her eager little plants didn't go
hungry.

Fertilizer in bags was very expensive. Her anti-
inflammation medicine cost even more, but she didn't
dare go without it. The repetitious exercises that she did
for an hour each night were bad enough without having to cope with a swollen knee as well.

She also needed, and hadn't yet bought, some kind
of denim jacket for the cool mornings and nights. The
swim club windbreaker she had brought with her just
wasn't heavy enough. Then there were the hands'
birthdays; it seemed they all came in the summertime.
Rather than risk Reever's wrath by taking money out
of the kitchen budget, Tory had simply bought candles
and funny cards and cake decorations out of her own
money. Plus, when she went into Massacre Creek with

the hands on ranch business or for pleasure, she refused to let anyone buy her so much as a soda. If everyone ate lunch at the Sunup Café, then so did she, although the food was both relatively expensive and decidedly ordinary.

As a result Tory's bus ticket fund hovered at the halfway mark. No matter how many private vows she made, the fund seemed to stay there. Lately she had expected Reever to ask if she had enough for her bus ticket yet. After all, he hadn't agreed to hire her for all the months she was taking off from diving. He had simply told her that she could cook until she earned enough to buy a bus ticket home. She would just have to pray that Reever wouldn't lose patience with her and kick her off the ranch before she managed to plug the million leaks in her budget.

Besides, Tory didn't really think that Reever would physically throw her off the ranch. To do that he'd have to touch her. And that was something he had not done since the day he had bathed her raw palms so gently and then with equal tenderness had brushed her breasts into aching peaks.

Don't think about it, she told herself fiercely. *You promised yourself that you wouldn't think about it.*

But how do I control the dreams that bring me awake and shivering in the darkness, aching for—
Don't think about it!

Tory put the garden tools beneath the sink and began making Jed a thick sandwich using cheese and leftover roast. She moved quickly, anxious to finally begin her riding lessons and to have something to think about besides the hot male sensuality that seethed beneath Reever's cold exterior. She may have attracted him during the forced intimacy of the ride to the ranch, but he had made it very clear since then that he had no use for her as a woman.

City girl. Clumsy. Useless.

Too bad that she still wanted him. Too bad that every time she saw him gently handle an injured animal, or smile and tease Dutch's grandchildren when they visited the Sundance, or drive himself long past the time when another man would have given in to exhaustion, or stand quietly in the evening and look out over the land with love on his face—it was all she could do at those moments not to plead with Reever to look at her again, to see in her the woman of his dreams.

But it hadn't happened. It wasn't going to, either.

Don't think about it.

Tory slammed the screen door and ran out to the corral, clutching Jed's sandwich in one hand and a thermos of coffee in the other. A carrot stuck up out of one hip pocket and her gloves out of the other. She squinted at the brilliant sunlight pouring over the land and wished that she could afford a hat to shield her eyes.

"Here you are, Jed. I brought you some coffee, too."

Jed smiled down at her. "Thanks, Tory. You do spoil us, don't you?"

"I enjoy cooking for the hands," she said honestly. "You're all so appreciative."

"If you'd eaten Cookie's slop, you'd know why. Only thing he could do worth a damn was beans and biscuits. A man can get real tired of beans and biscuits three meals a day." Jed took a big bite out of the sandwich while he waved with his free hand at the corral where a placid old mare with the unlikely name of Twinkletoes stood dozing three-legged in the sun. "She's all yours."

Tory picked up the bridle that Jed had hung over one of the corral posts, ducked it through the cross poles and bridled the mare. While the horse chewed the carrot, Tory brushed her down, smoothed the saddle blanket into place and dragged the heavy saddle off the fence.

"Don't forget the stirrup," mumbled Jed around his last bite of sandwich. "If that chunk of wood comes slamming down on her ribs, even old Twinks here might cut up a bit."

Dutifully Tory hooked the right stirrup over the saddle horn before she swung the bulky saddle onto the mare's fat back. With a grunt and a few muttered words Tory got the saddle into place. Fastening the cinch came next. Twinkletoes knew it, too. Casually the mare took a breath that swelled her barrel to half again its usual size. Tory took a deep breath as well—she didn't like what she was going to do, but there was no other way. She brought her knee up smartly into the mare's barrel. With a disgusted whoosh the mare gave up and let out all the extra air. Quickly Tory tightened the cinch. Twinkletoes stood docilely, unruffled by the whole process.

"Good job," said Jed, sipping at the steaming coffee before setting it aside. "Now gather the reins in your left hand."

Tory did.

"Uh, better try that again," said Jed, walking over until he stood just behind Tory. "If you got on now, by the time you sat in the saddle, the left rein would be laid so hard across her neck that she'd be turning in little circles. Do it like this."

Jed reached over Tory's shoulders with both hands. Holding the reins in his left hand, he raised his hand until it was on the horse's mane just in front of the saddle horn. With his right hand Jed adjusted the reins until they were even on both sides.

"See?"

Tory nodded.

"Now you do it," said Jed, dropping the reins. They fell on either side of the mare's neck and dragged on the ground, for Twinkletoes's bridle didn't come equipped with the single loop of a roping rein.

Tory picked up the reins and did exactly as Jed had done.

"Good. Now," said Jed, putting his arms over Tory's shoulders again, "grab either some mane or the saddle horn in your left hand and—don't drop the reins!—stand by the mare's left shoulder. Take the stirrup in your right hand, turn it toward you, put your left foot in, step up like on a ladder and swing your right leg over the saddle at the same time. If you have to, you can haul yourself up with your right hand on the cantle—that's the back of the saddle that sticks up. Okay?"

Tory had watched the men often enough to have memorized the basic movements. She also had had a lot of practice doing unlikely maneuvers while moving through the air. Being able to use her left hand and foot as stable pivot points was a definite treat after some of the complex dives she had mastered. Besides, she knew that Jed wouldn't tear a piece off her if she didn't get it right the first time.

As though she were getting ready for a dive, Tory mentally reviewed all the moves she had to make. Then she turned the stirrup, stepped into it and swung her leg over the horse's fat rump.

"Hey, that was slick, Tory. You been practicing behind my back?" asked Jed, grinning up at her and casually swatting her leg in congratulations.

"That's just what I was going to ask," Reever said.

Tory froze. She looked from Jed's smiling face to Reever's unsmiling one.

"If I'd known you wanted something to pat and play with," Reever continued, giving Jed a cold stare, "I'd have found you a stray dog."

Jed took his hand off Tory's leg as though he had been burned. He turned to face Reever.

"Thought I told you to ride the east pasture," Reever said, giving Jed no chance to speak.

"I did. A few posts near the slough need work."

"Then get to it."

Although Reever's tone was calm, there was a chill in it that made the words bite like an ice-tipped wind. Jed didn't bother to point out that it was only two hours until dinner and he had already put in a full day. He just jerked his hat into place and left. Tory began to dismount.

"I thought you wanted to learn how to ride," Reever said to her in the same tone that he had used on Jed. "Or was that just an excuse to have Jed's hands all over you?"

"They weren't all—" began Tory hotly, only to be cut off by Reever's slicing words.

"Shut up or get down. But if you get down, you can be damned sure that you'll never learn to ride as long as I'm boss of the Sundance."

Tory closed her eyes and her mouth and took a deep breath. When she opened her eyes, Reever was watching her with an expression she didn't understand, as though he rather than she were being ripped apart. He walked over to the mare and stood looking up at Tory with winter-gray eyes. He was so close that she could feel the vital heat of his body. Except for yanking her out of the henhouse, he hadn't been this close to her in all the weeks since she had cooked her first meal for the Sundance hands.

"The stirrups are too long," Reever said, his voice calm as he stripped off his leather gloves and stuffed them into his hip pocket. He put his hand on Tory's calf and eased her leg away from the stirrup. With quick, clean motions he took up the leather before placing her foot back in the stirrup again. "Rest your weight on the ball of your foot, not the arch. Like this."

It took all of Tory's control not to shiver at the touch of Reever's hands on her leg. She felt chills all the way to her fingertips. She took a shaky breath as he went around the mare's rump and adjusted the right stirrup. When his hands closed over her right leg, she trembled.

Tory watched Reever's hard, sun-browned hands move almost caressingly over her leg as he placed her foot just so in the stirrup. She wanted to ask him if he had to stand so close, if his chest had to brush against her knee, if her leg had to be pressed so intimately down the length of his hard, warm torso as he adjusted the position of her leg in the stirrup. The bare flesh of her ankle felt as though it had been burned, and all he had done was touch her for just an instant with his fingertips.

"Now lift the reins and turn old Twinkletoes to the right."

Tory moved her left hand so that the left rein pressed against the mare's neck. Immediately the horse moved away from the pressure, turning right.

"Walk her around the corral."

Twinkletoes would really rather have stayed put. She let Tory know that be refusing to budge. Tory kicked the broad barrel gently with her heels. The mare didn't notice. Tory nudged her again. The mare stood firm.

"Honey," said Reever dryly, hiding a smile beneath his mustache, "Twinkletoes is so lazy and so fat she can't tell your cute little heels from a fly. If you want to go anywhere, you're going to have to use those long legs for something more than turning Jed on."

Tory pretended it was Reever that she was kicking. Her heels landed with a solid thump. The mare twitched her ears and began walking slowly along the inside of the corral.

"You just keep her headed around the corral while I get Blackjack," said Reever.

In a few minutes Reever returned with Blackjack and a long lead rein that he snapped to Twinkletoes's bit.

He saw Tory's mutinous expression and slanted her a hard glance.

"Little girl, I should be shot for letting you anywhere near a stirrup in those flat-heeled city shoes. I'm using the lead rein so that if your clumsiness scares the mare, I'll make sure she can't run away, dragging you behind. If that hurts your tender pride, get off."

Tory looked down at her hands. White showed clearly in the knuckles that grasped the reins. With an effort she forced herself to relax. At least with Reever up on Blackjack he wouldn't be able to touch her as easily.

He could look at her, though. He could make her feel as though he were touching her each time his glance shifted from her hands to her hips to her heels. As they rode side by side, he gave her a running commentary on how she sat wrong, held the reins wrong, held her feet wrong, her hands wrong, her head, her spine, her hips, everything was wrong. The harder she tried, the more clumsy her movements became. Every time his hand brushed over her fingers while he rearranged the reins in her hand, or positioned her leg or her arms correctly, or put his hand on the small of her back to change her posture, it was all she could do not to fall out of the saddle.

Before the ranch was out of sight, Tory decided that she had made a mistake in wanting to learn how to ride. By the time they were over the low rise leading to Wolf Creek, she was fighting not to show her feelings. No matter what she did, it was wrong. No matter how hard she tried, she only became worse. Finally she pulled back on the reins, stopping the mare.

"You win, Reever," Tory said, her voice achingly calm. "I'm convinced I'll never learn to ride."

Reever stopped Blackjack. "City girl, anyone as clumsy as you better learn to take a little criticism."

"Try giving me a *little* sometime," Tory said, fighting to keep her voice even, "and I'll see how I take it." She looked at him, her eyes silently asking for understanding, and added softly, "I'm only awkward around you, Reever."

"Tough. I'm the only teacher you're going to get on the Sundance," he retorted, his voice flat.

Tory closed her eyes for a moment before saying, "Then school's out."

As she spoke, she dismounted from Twinkletoes with a speed that surprised Reever. He came off Blackjack in a single swift motion that placed him only inches from Tory. Instantly she stepped backward, only to bump up against the mare's fat barrel.

"For God's sake," Reever said roughly. "Stop cringing like a whipped pup. I'm not going to touch you."

Being compared to a cringing dog was the last straw for Tory's pride and uncertain temper. "How was I supposed to know that?" she demanded. "You've done nothing but touch me since you came to the corral!"

Reever's face hardened into an expression that made Tory wish desperately that she had followed her original plan for avoiding conflict with him by keeping her mouth shut.

"You sure as hell didn't mind when it was Jed's hands all over you," snarled Reever.

The ice in his voice made Tory shiver. "It's not the same when Jed touches me," she said, her voice so tight that it ached.

"I'll bet. He's young, pretty and has nothing but smiles and soft words for you."

"That's not—" she began hotly.

Reever's hard hand closed over Tory's mouth, sealing in the words with surprising gentleness. He stepped closer, trapping her between his body and that of the docile mare. His thumbs traced the honey line of Tory's eyebrows, touched the outer corners of her faintly tilted eyes and smoothed the hollows beneath her cheekbones before he lifted his hand to caress the trembling bow of her lips.

"Little green-eyed cat," Reever said roughly as he bent down to Tory. "I've wanted to taste you since I looked up and saw you standing on the other side of my desk all those long weeks ago."

Reever's face came closer to Tory until all she could see of the world was the burning clarity of his gray eyes. Then his thick black lashes swept down, concealing the expanding darkness in the center of his eyes as desire exploded through him at just the touch of her breath on his mouth. With the hot, moist tip of his tongue, he traced the sensitive line of her lips until she shivered between his gentle hands.

"Open your mouth," he said, his voice dark, deep. "Don't you want to taste me, too?"

The warm glide of Reever's tongue over the interior softness of Tory's lips made her gasp. Instantly his tongue slid inside her mouth. His heat and salt-sweet taste and slow, caressing tongue sent currents of sensation radiating through her. She forgot to think, to breathe, to do anything except tremble between his hands. Heat claimed her, melting everything, even her bones, until all she could do was cling to his hard forearms when her legs refused to support her any longer.

Reever's hands shifted, no longer gently pinning Tory's head in place for his kiss. There was no more need. She wasn't going to refuse or withdraw from him. He had felt her trembling and the telltale sagging of her weight against his strength, and he knew that desire was claiming her as surely as it had already claimed him. He picked her up and carried her just off the trail to a hollow where grass and wildflowers grew waist-high. Slowly he sank to his knees, lowering Tory into the scented embrace of softly crushed grass and petals.

Tory opened her eyes and took a breath that shook her to her toes. Reever's wide shoulders blocked out the sky as he bent over her, easing his big, hard hands beneath her, arching her up to his hungry mouth. She wanted to say his name, to ask him why he was doing this and to tell him never to stop, but the look on his face froze the words in her throat. His eyes were narrowed, the pupils wide, the rim of iris a hot crystal glitter that made her tremble with answering fire.

Reever's mouth claimed Tory's with a power that made her cling to him. Her hands moved blindly up his arms, across the bunched strength of his shoulders and then swept up beneath his hat, knocking it aside. When she rubbed her palms against his full, thick hair and her fingers found the warmth of his scalp, she gave a husky sound of pleasure. The sound made him shudder against her. His tongue thrust deeply into her mouth, filling her until she arched up to him and her hands clenched in his hair, holding his mouth against hers with all the strength in her young body. She felt as much as heard his harsh groan as he deepened the kiss even more, flattening her beneath him, letting her know the muscular weight of his body all the way to the soles of her feet.

"Am I too heavy for you?" Reever asked, his voice almost rough. "I'd make two of Jed."

The glorious feeling of Reever's body caressing her drove everything from Tory's mind except the need to get even closer to him. She tried to tell him that, but when she opened her eyes, all she could focus on was the sensual line of his lips.

"Reever," she said, and then again, as though the word were being torn from her, "Reever—"

When he heard the passionate breaking of Tory's voice, his hands clenched suddenly and his whole body tightened as though he were being stretched on a rack. Slowly he lowered his head while he watched her eyes. Despite the sensual tension in his body, his lips barely brushed hers, inciting rather than soothing the fires of her hunger. When his tongue slid over the inner soft-ness of her lips, her honey-colored lashes quivered shut as she was overtaken by the sensations coursing through her. She knew nothing but his heat, his touch and the wild pleasure of his mouth slowly, completely, joining hers.

The sweet consummation of the kiss made Tory cry out. The sound was absorbed by Reever as surely as he was absorbing her taste and the touch of her tongue against his. Her response was both innocent and abandoned, unskilled and unaware, hungry and hesitant. For a long moment he moved slowly over her, caressing her with his hard body, claiming her mouth with the same deep rhythms that he wanted to claim her body.

When Reever shifted slightly aside, Tory followed him instinctively, trying to maintain the unexpected, consuming intimacy of the embrace. When he thrust into her mouth again, she whimpered softly and arched against him without realizing it. All she knew was that her breasts were full and her nipples were aching, and when she rubbed against him, it started fires inside her.

"What is it, little girl?" he said, biting her mouth gently, drinking her sudden gasp. "What do you want?"

"Touch me," she breathed in his mouth. "The way you did in the kitchen."

Tory didn't see Reever's triumphant smile or the maddeningly slow movement of his hand toward her breast. Her eyes were closed, and she couldn't breathe for wanting his touch. When his hand stopped just below her breast, she made a breathless sound of protest. She tried to turn, to nestle herself into his palm, but he held her in place. Slowly his hands went from her ribs, to her breastbone, to her collarbone and then back to her ribs. He repeated the caress but came no closer to the aching peaks of her breasts. When he began a third time, she opened her eyes and looked straight into his.

The pale glitter of Reever's eyes as he watched Tory was like lightning beneath the thick arch of his black brows. His face was taut, his lips slightly swollen from his passionate claiming of her mouth. She looked from his face to his teasing fingers. The weight of his hands had pulled the T-shirt tight, outlining her breasts clearly. There was neither loose cloth nor a bra to hide her arousal. The sight of her own nipples nuzzling against the thin cotton made color stain her cheeks.

"Reever?" she whispered.

His thumbs caressed the curves of Tory's breasts but stopped well short of the hungry peaks. "Yes?" he murmured, smiling narrowly as he watched her tighten and rise even more beneath the creamy cotton knit.

"Don't you want to—to touch me?"

"How bad do you want it, little girl?" he asked softly, moving his thumbs slowly, circling her breasts below the nipples. "Bad enough to help me?"

"H-how?"

"Pull up your shirt."

Tory's shock showed in the widening of her green eyes. "I'm not wearing—" Her voice broke as his thumbs barely skimmed the aching nipples.

"I know," Reever said, smiling and watching her helpless response. "Think how it will feel. Your skin and mine, nothing between us but heat and my fingers loving those sweet pink buds until you moan."

Slowly, her hands shaking, feeling awkward and shy and almost afraid, Tory brought up the hem of her T-shirt. The air felt cool against her heated skin as the cloth climbed higher and higher. The material bunched beneath the swell of her breasts and caught on the rigid points of her nipples, making her feel even more awkward. She twisted slowly beneath Reever's pinning weight, trying to remove the T-shirt entirely, only to end up with it tangled thickly under her arms. She twisted again, getting a firmer grip on the stubborn cloth—and then she forgot what she was doing as her whole body tightened in a wild rush. Reever's mouth had claimed her breast just as completely as he had once claimed her lips.

Tory's hands clenched on the T-shirt as Reever's tongue licked hotly at the captive nipple, ringing it in sensual fire. She began to shiver beneath his weight, and her breath came quickly. When he skillfully stroked the sensitive aureole with tongue and teeth, she cried out and wanted him closer, closer, needing the hard suckling of his mouth the way she needed breath itself. She arched against him helplessly, wholly lost. His hand captured her other breast, kneading it, rolling the tight peak between his fingertips, sending more sensual lightning through her body.

The twin assaults made Tory forget everything but the sweet, consuming wildness of Reever's touch. Blindly her hands sought his back and shoulders. She tugged futilely at his shirt, wanting to feel his naked skin against her palms. He shifted aside slightly, giving her access to the snaps on his work shirt, but her hands were shaking so hard that all she did was get tangled helplessly in the blue cloth.

Reever looked down into the innocence of Tory's flushed face. He closed his eyes for an instant, his face tormented. Then with a savage curse he pushed himself away from her. His smoky gray glance swept from her soft, passionately swollen lips to the T-shirt tangled just beneath her arms. Her breasts were full, firm, and their deep pink peaks glistened from the intimate touch of his tongue. Each short, shaky breath she took made her body tremble from her toes to her fingers still caught in the folds of his shirt.

"Did Jed make you want him like this?" Reever asked harshly, watching Tory with cold fire in his eyes.

"I never—wanted him." The words came out in shivering breaths, for Tory could breathe no other way. "Just you. Just *you*."

Reever looked at her for a long, aching minute, and then he closed his eyes.

"Too bad," he said, yanking Tory's hands free of his shirt and standing up swiftly. "I've spent all the time I can spare on a clumsy city girl."

For a moment Tory lay without moving, stunned. She looked up at Reever's hard face, unable to believe what she had heard. Suddenly she realized that she was half naked, her T-shirt shoved up beneath her arms. She flushed and then went pale. Awkwardly she tried to straighten her T-shirt, but her hands were shaking so hard that she couldn't manage even that. With a cry of shame she rolled over, concealing her naked breasts.

Cursing savagely, Reever bent down and pulled her T-shirt into place, covering the sensual temptation of Tory's tan flesh. "You have enough money for that bus ticket yet?" he asked, his voice harsh.

Tory shook her head, refusing to look at Reever.

"You better get it, little girl. You better get it fast."

Reever mounted his horse and looked down at Tory still lying curled around herself in a nest of grass and wildflowers. He closed his eyes and his hand clenched into a hard fist around the reins.

"Get up," he said quietly. "It's time to go home."

Again she shook her head.

"Tory, don't make me touch you."

Slowly she sat up and looked at him.

Reever's breath came in with a swift, harsh sound as he saw her eyes.

"I know the way back," Tory said, looking through Reever as though he weren't there at all. Her voice was like her eyes, dark, wounded.

"I can't let you ride alone."

"I'll walk."

"It's two miles."

Tory's lips curved in a travesty of a smile. "Walking is one thing even clumsy city girls can do, remember?"

Reever's breath came in with a harsh sound. "Be back by dinner," he said roughly, looking at the soft, honey-colored silk of Tory's hair lifting in the breeze above the vulnerable curve of her neck. "Don't make me come after you. We'll both regret it." He turned Blackjack, then looked back and said, "And stay away from Jed unless you want another lesson. You're too damned hungry to be so innocent. You'd get Jed so hot so fast that he'd hurt you and never even mean to."

"And you're different, right? You're cold so you hurt me—and you mean every bit of it." Tory shuddered with shame at the memory of how she must have looked as she pulled up her T-shirt and clumsily offered herself to Reever. "Go away," she said hoarsely, shaking. "Oh, God, please, go away!"

"Tory—"

Reever's voice was as raw as Tory's, but she didn't hear it. She wasn't even looking at him anymore. She had made him vanish in the only way left to her. She had hugged her legs to her chest until she could rest her forehead on her knees, closing out the world, closing out him.

Tory didn't move or open her eyes, even after the sound of shod hooves faded into silence.

Chapter Six

TORY MOVED AWKWARDLY AROUND the kitchen, trying to favor her right knee without being obvious about it. If Reever saw her limping he would just tear another strip off her for being a clumsy city girl. She couldn't take that right now. She was still too raw from the afternoon. She didn't know what she would do if he turned on her again. She didn't want to know. She had finally admitted that in defiance of common sense and her own usual clear-eyed approach to life, somehow she had managed to fall in love with Reever during the long, sweet, maddening weeks that she had spent side by side with him on the Sundance.

Every day she had spent on the ranch, every hour, every minute, had increased her initial attraction to Reever. She had come to deeply respect his skill and endurance and intelligence. He had taken a ruined ranch and transformed it into a land both productive and beautiful. Although she didn't know enough about ranching to understand all the thousands of hours of sweat and determination the Sundance's transformation had required, she did appreciate the results—fat cattle and sheep, clear streams and lakes, grass everywhere she looked, a land that was obviously cared for with an eye to the future as well as to the bottom line on a budget ledger.

Tory hadn't wanted to admit that her growing love for Reever was why she had been so endlessly vulnerable to his touch. She had told herself that she thought of him as just one more coach she had to please, but she could no longer keep up that pretense. No coach had ever reduced her to tears with a few cold words. No coach had ever made her breath shorten simply by walking past her. No coach had ever set her to secretly dreaming of what it would be like to be a woman with the man she loved, to have a home and children, a chance to build a lifetime of love.

As Tory had walked back to the ranch house, she had finally understood why she hadn't been able to save up enough money to leave the Sundance. She didn't want to leave. She had seen Reever watching her when he thought she wouldn't notice. She had seen and savored the gentleness that lay beneath his harsh exterior, a gentleness he fought against revealing to anyone, especially to her. She had seen him wanting her, and she had kept hoping that if he would only let her close, he would come to love her as she loved him.

Tory bent her head and leaned against the counter until the edge bit deeply into her palms. Silently she raged at herself. *You're a fool, Victoria Wells. You've let yourself in for a world of hurt. You'll never get close to Reever. He won't let you. He knows just the kind of woman he wants, and you are not that woman. The only thing left to do is leave. There sure as hell isn't any point in hanging around, waiting for the judge to explain why you were disqualified from the competition. This is just one of those times you never had a chance.*

City girl. Clumsy. Useless. Too young.

Abruptly Tory shoved away from the counter as though it were her unwelcome thoughts. The incautious movement made pain lance through her right knee. She bit her lip hard, cursing her clumsiness.

She shifted her weight and resumed slicing potatoes into a huge frying pan. Onions followed. She had discovered that the men loved fried potatoes and onions with everything up to and including ice cream. But that wasn't the reason she was cooking them tonight. She had stayed out so long trying to make sense of herself and Reever and her own life that it was nearly dinnertime before she had gotten back. Hamburger steak and fried potatoes were both fast and simple. Even so, dinner would be late. Already the hands were coming in from the range and looking hopefully toward the kitchen.

"Coffee's ready," Tory said, glancing up from the frying pan as Dutch came in. "Dinner in a few minutes."

"Don't hurry," Dutch said, looking curiously at the grass stains visible across the back of Tory's T-shirt.

Jed came in afterward, along with three other hands. The rest were on his heels. Jed, too, saw the grass stains.

"Don't tell me that old Twinkletoes threw you," he said, astonished.

"What?" asked Tory, turning quickly, incautiously, toward Jed. She braced herself on the counter before her right knee could give way beneath the twisting stress.

"The grass stains on your back," Jed explained, picking up the coffeepot and pouring coffee for everyone. "Did you get thrown?"

Tory flushed and nearly dropped the spatula she was using to turn the potatoes. She hadn't even thought that she might have stained her T-shirt rolling around on the grass with Reever. "Yes, I guess you could say I got thrown," she said, her voice raw.

"Hell, Tory," said Jed, setting down the coffeepot and going quickly to the stove. He put his hand on her shoulder. "Don't feel bad. Everyone that rides gets thrown. Even Reever."

"I'd like to congratulate the horse," Tory said, emotion crackling in every word.

The rest of the hands laughed and chimed in, offering comfort and recounting their own experiences "riding air." With her back turned to the table, Tory blindly stirred the potatoes while Dutch finished recounting an unlikely story about Reever riding a mare that was blind, crippled in one leg and the meanest bucker any cowhand had ever straddled. When Dutch told about Reever being unloaded into the manure pile, Tory started smiling, then laughed, shaking her head, not believing a word of it but enjoying the story just the same.

She was still smiling when she turned around with a big dish of steaming fried potatoes and onions in her hand. She hadn't heard Reever come in, but there he was, sitting in his place at the head of the table, watching her with a dark, unreadable expression. Instinctively she flinched from him, only to have her knee protest sharply at the sudden movement. For one awful instant she knew that she was going to fall full-length across the table, scattering potatoes to every corner of the kitchen.

Dutch made a lightning grab and saved the potatoes just as Jed dropped his coffee cup and caught Tory.

"You okay?" asked Jed, ignoring the coffee dripping down his shirt as he set her back on her feet. "You looked like your right leg gave way. Did you hurt it when Twinkletoes dumped you?"

Tory saw only the sudden, harsh look on Reever's face as he loomed over Jed's shoulder. Instantly she remembered Reever's warning about leaving Jed alone.

"I'm fine," she said, pushing away from Jed almost frantically. "Just—" Her voice broke. "Clumsy. Ask Reever. He'll tell you how awfully clumsy I am."

Tory's smile was a travesty of reassurance or humor, but it was the best she could do. She turned away too quickly to see the lines of pain that suddenly bracketed Reever's mouth. In silence she served up the rest of the dinner, not meeting anyone's eyes.

Normally she would have sat down to eat as soon as the food was on the table, but she knew that she couldn't do it that night. She couldn't sit with Reever's long legs not two inches away from hers and his icy gray eyes looking at her and remembering how she had offered herself to him so clumsily that he had been repelled. She couldn't even pretend to push food around on her plate. She knew that she would drop her fork or her coffee cup and further disgrace herself in front of the man she loved.

"I made some cake for dessert. It's in the pie cupboard," Tory said quietly, walking out of the kitchen. "Just leave the dishes on the table when you're finished."

"Aren't you going to eat?" asked Reever. His voice was like his face, aching with the savagery of the restraint that he had imposed on himself.

"I—I ate while I cooked."

"Like hell. You didn't have time. Come back here and eat, Tory," he added almost gently. "You're too thin as it is."

"No, thank you," she said politely, balancing her voice as carefully as she was balancing her body. She hurried around the corner, saying, "I'm really not hungry. Maybe later, after I pack."

Reever ignored the sudden stir as heads turned toward him when the cowhands realized that Tory intended to leave the ranch. One look at Reever's savage expression warned the men that anyone asking a question would probably be invited to drive Tory into Massacre Creek—and stay there.

Tory wasn't sure that she had escaped until she shut her bedroom door behind her. With a shaky sigh she leaned against the heavy wood and bowed her head. To her horror tears began to well silently from her eyes. She wiped impatiently, afraid of being caught crying. After a moment she realized that it didn't matter. There was no father or stepfather or coach to call her a cry-baby and no roommate to give her half-sympathetic, half-curious glances. In that, at least, Tory's stay at Sundance had been a success—it had given her a privacy she had never before known.

Ignoring the tears that fell very slowly, Tory peeled off her clothes and pulled on a knee-length green nightshirt. She wouldn't think about Reever and the Sundance and the love that turned in her like a razor with each breath. She couldn't do anything about those things except endure the pain.

Her knee was a different matter. It was within her power to hurt or help her knee. So she ignored her tears, adjusted the elastic support around the knee, sat on the edge of the bed, strapped weights onto her right ankle and began the hour of tedious, repetitious exercises.

She tried not to think as she worked, but it was impossible, just as it was impossible to stop the tears from running down her face in two slow, thin streams.

After so many weeks of exercises, Tory had expected her knee to be much stronger than it was. Even as the doctor had been cautioning her that the healing and rebuilding process would be slow, she had believed that he was wrong. She had believed that if she just worked harder and then harder still, she would be able to achieve her goal of finding a place for herself in the world as an Olympic athlete.

She had believed that it would be the same now as it had always been in the past when she had counted on no one but herself to get what she wanted from life.

With her knee as with her diving career, she would ultimately win because of her own discipline and drive, her own ability to work harder than anyone else, to give up more than others would give up, because to her the goal was worth any sacrifice. Anything.

At least, that was how it had worked before. It had to work that way now, too. It simply had to. Nothing had changed. The only person she could lean on was herself.

Counting softly, ticking off exercises and the timed pauses between, Tory worked her knee, ignoring the pain. Eventually the knee would loosen, strengthen, and the pain would stop. Until then she would simply have to work harder.

Tory was softly counting aloud, timing the pause before the final exercise, when the bedroom door opened behind her. She didn't hear it. Nor did she see Reever shut the door behind him and lean against it even as she had. His icy gray eyes saw first her tears, then the white elastic support around her right knee.

"What in God's name have you done to yourself now?" Reever asked roughly.

Tory flinched, then slowly opened her eyes. She saw Reever's face reflected in the dresser mirror and knew that he wasn't going to go away this time if she ignored him.

"Nothing new," she said, closing her eyes again, still counting, hoping against hope that he would leave her alone. She was too vulnerable now, too shaken by the discovery that she was in love with him.

Reever crossed the room and knelt in front of Tory. Her eyes flew open as she felt his hands on her bare leg.

He ignored her startled exclamation, just as he ignored her hands futilely trying to push him away. Very gently he peeled down the elastic brace. His breath hissed in when he saw the twin surgical scars bracketing her kneecap. As softly as a sigh, his fingertips tested the slight puffiness of her knee. Then he noticed the weights strapped to her right ankle.

"What the hell are you trying to do to yourself?" Reever asked. His voice was hard, but the hands holding Tory's knee were almost caressing.

"It's called physical therapy," Tory said, trying to pull the elastic support back into place but running into the gentle, immovable barrier of Reever's hands. "I do it every night."

His eyes widened. He looked at the evidence of tears on her face. "Does it hurt like this every night?"

"Depends on how clumsy I've been during the day," Tory said curtly, not wanting to tell Reever that her tears had been as much from unhappiness at discovering herself in love with him as from any pain in her knee.

The lines of Reever's face became more harsh when he heard Tory call herself clumsy, but all he said was, "Have you tried ice?"

"That comes after I finish the last exercise, which you're making impossible."

"I think you've done enough for tonight," Reever said, running his thumbs very delicately over the scars.

Tory shivered at the caress, but her eyes when she met his were unflinching. "No. There's one more exercise I have to do."

Reever looked at Tory, seeing the determination in her that most people overlooked because they noticed only her youth and her lovely, gentle smile. But she wasn't smiling now. Her eyes were older, unwavering. Bleak. He wondered what had happened to make her accept pain without complaint, how she had injured her knee in the first place and what her life had been like before she had arrived on the Sundance and turned his own life upside down.

"What happened?" Reever asked, pulling the brace back into place on Tory's knee.

She wanted to laugh wildly, to release the bitterness of her discovery of a love that he would never return, but she knew she could not. He hadn't asked why she was hurting now. He only wanted to know how she had hurt herself in the past.

"You should have read your cousin's letter," she said.

With that Tory stood up and braced her hands against the bedroom wall. She brought her right heel up to her buttocks and then straightened the leg, repeating the motion in rhythmic sequence. Even though she was careful, she tended to bang her knee or her foot against the wall each time she bent and straightened her leg. Instead of a wall to brace her weight, she needed a fixed, overhead bar that would allow her full freedom to move her leg.

"Here," said Reever, picking Tory up and turning her sideways to him. He extended his long right arm across her breasts, bracing his hand against the wall. "Hold on to me."

She gave him a startled look as she felt currents of awareness course through her from his nearness.

Grimly she tore her thoughts away from what she could not have and did as he suggested, bracing herself on his arm.

It was like holding on to a sun-warmed tree branch. He didn't move at all as she flexed her knee and swung her leg with a freedom that hadn't been possible before.

"Better?" he asked quietly, watching her.

"Yes." Tory stared straight ahead, not trusting herself to look at him without giving away everything she was feeling. "Thank you," she added politely.

"What happened, honey?" asked Reever again, his voice as gentle as his hands had been. "I'll call Payton if I have to, but I'd rather you tell me. All of it. Starting when you were a child."

"Why?" Tory asked flatly. "I'm leaving tomorrow so it doesn't matter."

Reever looked at Tory, all of her, his eyes going from the sun-streaked silk of her hair to her slender, naked feet.

"I have to know," he said simply.

Tory's hands tightened on Reever's arm. Despite his gentle tone, she knew that he was every bit as determined as she had been about finishing her exercises. Reever meant to have his answers one way or another.

"Why?" she asked again, her voice soft, frightened.

"I don't know," Reever admitted, running his left thumb delicately across the slim, tanned fingers holding on to his arm, watching the swift rise of gooseflesh up Tory's arm as she responded helplessly to the caress. "Do you know why you come apart at my touch as though God had made you just for my hands, my mouth, my body?"

"Reever—" Tory's voice broke as he caressed her again. "Don't!"

With a rough word he lifted his fingers from hers. "Talk to me, green eyes. Maybe we'll both find some answers."

For a moment Tory bowed her head, not knowing how to handle the situation. It had always been like that with Reever, from the first time she had seen him. One look, one touch, and finally the kind of love she had never expected to feel. She shivered and her hands gripped the warm, braced power of Reever's arm, remembering when he had told her. *Hold on to me.*

Did she have any choice?

Tory took several deep breaths and let them out slowly, as though she were preparing herself for the most difficult dive of her life.

"I've been swimming since I was six," Tory said as she resumed working her knee, counting off time in her head like a metronome, concentrating on anything and everything but the warm, powerful man standing so close to her, "and diving competitively since I was ten. I'm a better diver than a swimmer. My specialty is platform diving."

Reever saw the jeweled green flash of Tory's sideways glance as she measured his reaction. "Go on," he said.

"Do you know what platform diving is?"

"There's a television in the living room," he said dryly. "We may be so far out in the sticks that the signals arrive a day late, but we do get them eventually."

Tory smiled crookedly. "That's not what I meant. When I say I'm a diver, most people think of springboards, not platforms. Of course, I use the springboard, too, but I like the platform much better."

"Why?"

She hesitated, trying to put into words a choice that had always been instinctive. Like her response to Reever. Instinctive. Irretrievable. "Because every springboard, no matter how carefully it's made to Olympic specifications, is different," she said finally. "The diver is at the mercy of the equipment. It's not that way with a platform. All that gives when you spring is your own body, your knees and your legs. That stays the same, no matter who builds the platform."

Reever glanced sharply at Tory's injured knee.

"Yes," she said, understanding the question he didn't ask. "I can't dive anymore. Not for a while. Not like I used to. And," she closed her eyes as her voice thinned to a whisper, "maybe not ever. I don't know."

For a moment there was silence as Reever thought of all the questions he wanted to ask. He didn't want to hurt Tory any more, but he had to have more answers. He had to.

"Were your parents swimmers?" he asked after a time, wondering how she had been drawn to the sport.

"No."

Reever hesitated. The only other time that Tory had ever mentioned her parents, it hadn't been with pleasure. He could understand that. His own family life hadn't been very pleasant, either.

"Did you always want to dive?" he asked, watching the taut lines of Tory's face as she exercised her knee, feeling himself ache. It seemed as though he had spent his life watching her green eyes darken with pain, pain that he had deliberately caused.

Tory shrugged. "I always had a good time at the pool," she said after a long silence. "Before my parents were divorced, home wasn't a happy place. My mother remarried very quickly. That made it better for her, but not for me. My stepfather—"

Reever felt Tory's hands tighten on his arm, then relax. "You didn't get along," he said.

"We didn't get along," agreed Tory, her voice clipped. "He was very jealous of mother, and I was living proof of the fact that he hadn't been her first lover."

"So you spent a lot of time at the pool," Reever said softly, remembering all the times he had ridden out alone over the land to get away from his father.

"The pool was the only real home I had," Tory said matter-of-factly. "I had a natural talent for diving, but not as much as some of the other kids," she continued. "As long as I worked harder than they did and won more competitions, I was seen as Olympic diving material. I could keep the work-scholarship that made my membership in the swim club possible. I could spend time at the pool instead of at home."

Reever looked at Tory's clean profile, the high forehead and slanting cheekbones, the soft mouth that was now held tightly against the possibility of revealing pain.

"Did you enjoy competing?" he asked, watching her closely, wanting to know, needing it with an intensity that he no longer questioned.

Tory hesitated, wondering how she could explain. She had taken so many things for granted before her injury, before the Sundance, before Reever. As he asked questions, she was finding answers that she hadn't even been aware of before.

"Not really," she admitted finally. "Competition was the price I had to pay for diving. Other kids didn't feel that way. They only truly came alive during a competition when people watched and cheered."

"But not you. It was the diving itself you loved," said Reever, not guessing anymore. Despite Tory's determination, he knew that she was basically too gentle a person to enjoy the kind of cutthroat competition that must have existed as she grew older and had to fight with other divers for footholds on the slippery climb to Olympic glory.

The lines of Tory's face softened as her eyes focused on something that only she could see. "Yes, I love diving. There's nothing like it. When I stand on that platform and gather myself for a dive, nothing else exists. No arguing parents. No unpaid bills. No loneliness. No pain. No exhaustion. Nothing but me and the platform and the pool shimmering below. I used to think that, if I did everything perfectly, I would hang in the air forever, wholly at peace, as graceful as a leaf floating on the wind."

Tory's face changed again, older now. She smiled sadly, lowered her right foot to the floor and let go of Reever's hard, warm forearm. "Thanks, I'm done," she murmured, wincing very slightly as she put her full weight on her right leg.

"Ice?" he asked.

She sank onto the bed, peeled down the elastic knee brace and prodded her knee a good deal less gently than Reever had. "It's not that bad, really. A little swelling, but it won't get in the way of my packing."

Reever's expression darkened. "I'll get you some ice."

Tory started to say that it wasn't necessary, she could get the ice herself or do without it, but Reever was already gone. With a sigh she unstrapped the weights, pulled off the brace and stretched out on the bed. Within a few minutes Reever was back with an ice bag. When she would have sat up again, he put his hand on her shoulder, holding her down gently.

"I'll take care of it," he said. "You look pale."

Tory opened her mouth to tell Reever that it wasn't because of her knee, but caught herself as she realized that he would want to know what was bothering her. He would ask questions, questions that she really didn't want to answer—questions he really wouldn't like the answers to.

In the end she simply moved over to make room for him to sit on the bed, afraid to argue and end the rare moment of peace. She wanted it to continue. She wanted to take from the Sundance more than memories of anger and humiliation. She wanted—too much.

The contrast between Reever's big, warm hand holding her leg and the healing chill of the ice bag was like nothing Tory had ever felt, almost disorienting in its intensity. Her breath came in sharply.

"Does that hurt?" Reever asked quickly, his eyes searching hers.

"No."

He looked at her for a moment longer.

"Really," Tory said, her voice soft. Almost helplessly she added, "You have very gentle hands."

An expression close to pain tightened Reever's face. "How did it happen?" he asked for the third time.

Tory grabbed the question like the lifeline it was. "Ten meters is a long way to fall," she said. "If you land wrong, you can hurt yourself. I wrenched my knee trying to do a triple somersault off the platform. That was a year ago. I came back from the injury, and then one night I slipped in the kitchen at the end of the late shift. I fell with my knee under me at a bad angle, tearing hell out of everything. I had surgery the next day."

"How long ago?" asked Reever, moving the ice bag to the other side of her knee.

"About two months."

Reever went very still. "Do you mean you were going to walk nineteen miles to town three weeks after your knee was operated on and not say a word to me about it?"

Tory smiled sadly. So much for Reever's gentleness; but it had been lovely while it lasted. "People have won marathons three *days* after knee surgery," she said calmly. "Besides, the doctor told me not to baby the knee. Walking is excellent, easy exercise."

"Sure, as long as you're not carrying thirty pounds of badly balanced junk that turns your hands into raw meat," retorted Reever. "And then Billy chasing you over rough country. I should have broken his neck."

Tory's eyes snapped open. The grim lines of Reever's face told her how deep his rage was. Yet when he spoke, it was only to ask another question.

"What did you mean about the late shift in the kitchen? Does the swim club cook for its members?"

She couldn't help laughing. "It wasn't quite that much of a home."

Reever waited impatiently, the flat line of his mouth a silent threat.

Tory closed her eyes again, feeling like crying. It had been so nice not to have Reever angry at her for just a few minutes. "As soon as I turned sixteen," she said tonelessly, "I moved in with three other girls. I got a job at a local coffee shop, first as a waitress, then also as a cook. I worked the late shift because it didn't interfere with my training."

"You worked nights when you were sixteen?" Reever asked roughly, hardly able to believe that her parents had allowed it.

"Believe me, the stove didn't care how old I was."

"God, the drunks must have—" Reever bit off a savage curse as he thought of Tory subjected to an endless string of drunken men trying to sober up for the drive home after the bars had closed.

Tory shrugged. She had hated the drunks, but there had been no help for it. She had needed the job.

"How long do you have to rest the knee before you go back to diving?" Reever tried to make the question calm rather than harsh, but he didn't succeed.

"The doctor said two or three months. If the knee isn't back to full strength by then, chances are it never will be."

Although Tory's voice was calm, Reever could feel the sudden tension in her body when she spoke about her knee. For a moment his hand tightened over the smooth flesh of Tory's upper thigh. Slowly his fingers relaxed, as though by a deliberate effort of will.

"Did you hurt your knee again today?" he asked, his voice strained.

"I zinged it once or twice," Tory said carefully, "but nothing—"

"You little fool!" Reever snarled, not letting her finish. "I would never have let you walk back if I had known that your knee was—"

"Whatever happens to the knee is my fault, not yours," Tory said quickly, cutting across Reever's angry words. "As you've pointed out a hundred times, I'm clumsy."

Reever's mouth flattened beneath the thick black of his mustache. His ice-gray eyes glittered fiercely at her. "You keep pushing, little cat, and you're finally going to make me mad."

"Really?" Tory asked bitterly. "How will I know the difference? Will you wear a sign?"

Reever uncoiled in a single swift movement that ended only when Tory was stretched full-length beneath him, pinned to the bed by his weight. Yet even then he avoided hurting her knee by settling his leg between hers so carefully that she didn't even know what had happened until she took a deep breath and felt him from her shoulders to the soles of her feet.

"You innocent little fool," Reever breathed, his voice ragged as he lowered his mouth to Tory's. "You just don't know when to stop, do you?"

"Reever—"

"Sorry, honey. I warned you. It's too late now."

"No!" Tory said, turning her face aside despite the emotion that had darkened her eyes to emerald. She wanted Reever's embrace with a wildness that frightened her. "I'll come apart when you touch me, and then you'll pull back and cut me to ribbons because I'm so clumsy that I turn you off. I can't take any more of that," she said desperately. "Please, Reever, I promise I'll never talk back to you again. I'll leave first thing in the morning. Please! I can't take any—"

Tory's frantic words ended in a gasp as Reever's teeth fastened lightly on her earlobe. He laughed softly at her response and traced the sensitive rim of her ear with his tongue until she shivered, and he laughed again, triumphantly.

"Sweet little virgin," he whispered, biting her ear with gentle care despite the hunger racing through him with each heartbeat. "I didn't stop making love to you this afternoon because you turned me off. God," he groaned, moving his hips slowly over hers, both easing and increasing the ache of his aroused flesh, "even when I was a kid, I never had a woman turn me on as fast and hard as you do."

Tory's eyes widened and she shivered helplessly as she felt the hard, strong, beautiful length of Reever's body caressing her. "I don't mean to," she said. "I don't even know how to. I just—"

The words ended in a throaty moan as Reever thrust the tip of his tongue into Tory's ear, sending a sunburst of sensation twisting through her.

"Yes," he gritted, feeling Tory's response as though it were his own. "You just come apart when I touch you, that's all. Knowing you're a virgin, knowing you would melt and run for me like hot, wild honey—" He stifled a groan. "It's killing me, little one. I should be shot for even kissing you, but I want to do more than just this. I want to slide that nightshirt up your beautiful, innocent body and let you feel my hands and mouth everywhere, all over you, every hot, sweet bit of you. Oh, God, green eyes, you can't even imagine the things I want to do to that untouched body!"

Reever heard the tiny, wild sound Tory made, felt the involuntary arching of her body beneath him as his words set fire to her.

"Don't," he said hoarsely, holding her still, forcing himself not to stroke her body with his own. "I can't sleep at night for wanting you, but I won't take your innocence and give you only experience in return. A girl should at least hear 'I love you' from her first man, whether it's true or not—but I can't lie to you that way, Tory. That's why I've done everything but beat you with a whip to drive you away from the Sundance. From me."

With an aching sound Reever brushed his open mouth over Tory's trembling lips, tasting her with tiny touches of his tongue even while he spoke. "I sat on that damned ridge this afternoon and I watched you through the glasses and I hated myself for hurting you like that. I watched you walk all the way back to the ranch, and I wanted you until I felt like knives were turning in me."

Reever's breath washed warmly over Tory's lips as his tongue dipped lightly into the corners of her mouth. "It tore me apart to watch, but I had to know you were all right. I wanted to go to you, help you, and I knew if I went any closer, I would take you down into that soft grass and love you until you didn't know where you were, who you were, until you could touch me and not know whether it was my skin or yours you were feeling, my body or yours, because we would be so deep in each other that it would be like dying and being born all over again. It's never been like that for me with a woman, but I know it would be like that with you. I know it, and it's tearing me apart."

The small, involuntary sound Tory made ate at Reever's control.

"Oh, God, don't," he said raggedly, caressing Tory's face with his lips, his tongue, his teeth. "Don't move. Don't make a sound. I thought I could trust myself, but I can't. Not with you. And I'll hate myself if I take you. You deserve a gold ring and sacred vows. I can't give you that, sweet little city girl. We're all wrong for each other that way. But I couldn't let you leave tomorrow thinking I was cruel. Every time I had to hurt you, I bled. I'm still bleeding."

A shudder went the length of Tory's body. She closed her eyes, releasing a bright shimmer of tears. She remembered with terrible clarity what Reever had told her—when he married a woman, she would be just that, a woman. Not a young, clumsy city girl.

The thought was a razor slicing through Tory, making her bleed in ways she couldn't name. She knew that she would never love another man as she loved Ethan Reever. She loved him, and she was leaving him. She would never know what it felt like to give herself to the man she loved.

"Have I ever asked you for anything but a job?" Tory asked with aching quiet, her voice shaking, her tear-bright gaze holding Reever's. "This afternoon, did I push your hands away and say that you couldn't touch me until you gave me a gold ring and told me that you'd love me until you died?"

"No. But you should have," Reever said tightly. "You should have made me promise you the moon. I would have. I wanted you so bad I was all but blind."

"Do you think that's why I'm still a virgin?" Tory asked suddenly, as anger curled along her nerves. "Is that how little you think of me? Do you believe that I want to drive a man out of his mind with desire and then hold out on him until I trap him into marriage? You're wrong, Ethan Reever," she said harshly, the words tumbling out in a heedless rush, driven by the three words she could not say: I love you. "I'm a virgin because I've never lov— I've never *wanted* a man enough to let him undress me and touch me until I can't breathe for wanting more. I've never wanted a man to know my body in ways that even I don't, to be moving inside me, a part of me. I'm nearly twenty-one years old, and I've never wanted a man in any way at all. Until you."

Reever's eyes narrowed until they were slits of glittering ice. "Haven't you been listening? I have nothing to give you but passion."

"Why should I want anything more?" Tory whispered raggedly, touching Reever's cheek with her fingertips. "I never expected to have even passion from you. I want you to be my first. I want you to be the one to teach me. I want it all to happen with you, even the things I can't imagine. Especially those things, Reever."

"Tory—" groaned Reever, fighting for control.

"No," she said quickly, interrupting him by putting her fingers over the lips that were barely half an inch from hers. "Listen to me, Reever. I know myself. I know that I'll never—want—another man the way I want you. Don't refuse me. I promise I won't ask or expect anything else from you except your hands, your mouth, your body teaching me how to worship you."

Tory trembled as Reever brushed aside her fingers and kissed her so deeply that she couldn't breathe. After a long, long time he lifted his head and spoke in a shaking voice.

"You sweet, sweet little fool, don't you know what it does to a man to be told that he's wanted like that?"

"What does it do?" she whispered huskily. "Teach me, Reever. Teach me everything."

Chapter Seven

REEVER CLOSED HIS EYES AND didn't breathe, didn't speak. From his clenched fists to the soles of his feet, his body was as hard as steel, as motionless, and his expression was almost agonized. Tory felt tears scald down her cheeks as the certainty grew in her that he was going to reject her again.

The thought made Tory want to cry out in protest, pleading with Reever not to turn away from the woman who loved him. Yet even as the words crowded her tongue, she knew that she must not say them. If she said *I love you,* she would drive Reever away from her. He would simply take her words as proof that she was too immature to give herself physically to a man without the fiction of love between them.

But it wasn't a fiction. She did love him. She hadn't wanted to fall in love with any man, had never really expected to, but she had come to love Reever just the same. Deeply. Passionately. That was why she hadn't been able to save enough money to leave the Sundance. She didn't want to leave. She had seen Reever watching her, wanting her, and she had kept hoping that he might be falling in love with her as she had fallen in love with him—one day at a time, one glance, one look, one touch.

It hadn't happened that way after all. She had fallen alone. She was still falling.

Tory shut her eyes and fought to control herself in the face of Reever's rejection, but it was impossible. She couldn't even turn away, for she was still pinned to the bed by the weight of his big body. Helplessly she began to cry, her body shaking with tearing, silent emotion.

Reever rolled aside and gathered Tory into his arms, holding her very gently.

"Don't be frightened," he murmured, stroking her back slowly, nuzzling her mouth with a tenderness that made her shiver. "I want you until I'm crazy with it, but I won't hurt you. I swear it. I'll tease and love that sweet body until you're shaking and wild, and when I finally take you…" Reever groaned and his hands tightened on her soft skin. "Oh, God, little cat, when I take you, it will be like falling into the sun. You can't feel pain when you're burning alive with pleasure."

Reever looked down into Tory's huge, tear-bright eyes. "I know it's a lot to ask for after the last few weeks," he said huskily, "but will you trust me not to hurt you?"

Tory tried to speak through trembling lips, couldn't, and nodded instead. When she could trust herself not to blurt out her love, she tried to ask him to be patient with her, not to cut her up for being clumsy. At first all she could say was his name, the word a question trembling on her lips. "R-Reever?"

"Yes?" he breathed, kissing the corner of Tory's mouth with exquisite care.

"I'll try not to—to be clumsy, but please don't—"

"Hush, little one," Reever said, licking up Tory's painful words with the warm tip of his tongue. "You aren't clumsy at all. You're as graceful as sunlight on water. Watching you used to make me ache until I felt like something was tying my guts in knots. I'd lash out at you, trying to keep you away, trying to make you hate me instead of want me, and then I'd have to watch the light in your eyes die as you turned away from me." He shuddered. "Innocent little green eyes," he whispered, sipping at Tory's mouth with tiny touches of his lips and tongue. "I've never seen anything half as graceful and lovely as you. Remember that. Forget the lies and remember that truth because it's the only one that matters."

Reever fitted his mouth exactly to Tory's trembling lips, cherishing her with a gentleness that brought more tears to her eyes. He rocked his head slowly back and forth, changing the feeling of the kiss with each small movement, sensitizing her lips until she felt as though she were on fire. She wanted to put her arms around him, to bury her fingers in his hair and hold his teasing, beautiful mouth against hers. But despite his assurances she was afraid that he would think her clumsy whether he said it aloud or not.

"So soft," Reever murmured, biting Tory's lips with tender care. "And even softer inside. Open for me, honey. I've been driving myself crazy remembering how sweet you taste, how soft you are, how warm and giving."

"Reever," she whispered.

"More," he said, nuzzling her mouth. "I want to see you ready for me, waiting. I have to know you want my mouth."

With a shudder Tory parted her lips. She watched Reever's eyes widen and darken to a smoky gray. She looked at the sensual lines of his mouth and remembered how it had felt when he had kissed her so deeply that she hadn't been able to breathe. She wanted that again. She wanted the hard, complete claiming of his mouth, the taste and scent of him filling her until she couldn't tell where she ended and he began.

"What are you thinking?" Reever asked huskily, watching Tory's eyes and her parted lips, wanting to taste and feel her tongue sliding over his.

"Your mouth," she said, her voice trembling. "It isn't fair that a man should have such a beautiful mouth. And what you can do with it—" Her breath came in sharply with another burst of memories, of the heat and intimacy of him cherishing her breasts. "That isn't fair, either."

Reever's laugh was low and very male, a sound both sensual and triumphant. "Do you want my mouth?" he asked, nuzzling her teasingly.

"Yes," Tory breathed, watching him.

"How? Like this?"

The gentle torment of his lips and tongue continued, but other than tracing the line of her teeth, he made no move to claim the parted lips that she offered him. Tory put her arms around Reever's neck and tried to pull him closer. He was too strong. No matter how she tugged, he kept on teasing her, pinning her gently to the bed, not allowing her to come closer.

"Reever," said Tory urgently.

As she said his name, he took her mouth with a hot, slow movement of his tongue, teasing and caressing her even as he absorbed her into himself. She shivered uncontrollably at the sweet consummation, giving him even more of herself as she sought to taste more of him. The impact of the kiss left her disoriented, shivering, able only to hold on to him as the rest of the world fell away.

Gradually she began to move her tongue as he did, caressing him as he was caressing her. He made a thick sound of pleasure and deepened the kiss even more, exploring every dark, soft curve of her mouth until the kiss became an act of intimacy that made her feel both ravished and cherished. When he lifted his mouth, she tried to follow him, wanting more of him, trembling with her wanting.

"Easy, little cat," Reever said, his voice ragged. He looked down at the sweet young mouth blindly seeking his and didn't know whether to swear or shout with triumph. "So innocent. So hot. *God.*"

Tory's eyes half opened, shadowed by a thick fringe of lashes. She ran the tip of her tongue over her lips, and her eyes widened in surprise. "I taste like you," she whispered.

With a low groan Reever arched his hips into Tory, trying to ease the pain that was also pleasure.

"Don't say things like that," he grated. Then he saw her face change, passion draining into hurt. "Tory," he said, kissing her swiftly, repeatedly, calling her name between kisses. "I didn't mean it like that. I'm trying to go slow with you, but you're so damned sexy and giving and honest that I—" He took a shuddering breath and slowly lowered his hips into the soft cradle of her thighs. "Tell me again," he whispered thickly, licking her lips with hot touches of his tongue.

"Reever—"

"Tell me, Tory. Feel what it does to me."

Hesitantly his tongue touched her lips. She shivered as the tip of his tongue met hers. "I was wrong," she whispered. "We taste like each other."

The words ended in a tiny cry as she felt his powerful body tighten like a drawn bow. The hard length of his arousal caressed her intimately, separated from her only by his clothes and the thin satin smoothness of her underwear.

"You're right, little cat," Reever groaned. "I taste like you and you taste like me." He bit Tory's mouth gently, hungrily. "Say whatever you like. Say it whenever you like. I want to hear you. I want everything you think, everything you feel, everything you are. I want—" Reever laughed shortly and shook his head. "The things I want would shock you now. But not in a while. In a while you'll want everything I have, all of it, all the way, and you'll want it until you scream."

Tory's fingers flexed on Reever's shoulders as she shivered at the hot words flowing over her, making her burn. She watched his mouth hungrily. She loved the feel of it, hard and resilient, warm and skilled, teaching her things about hunger and satisfaction that she had never suspected could be learned from a kiss.

Hesitantly she ran her fingertips over his lips, tracing their clean outline until she touched his teeth. The difference between his lips and the small serrations of his teeth fascinated her. She ran her fingertip over him again. When the tip of his tongue licked hotly over her, she made a small sound of surprise and pleasure. She dipped into his mouth again and then again, enjoying his changing textures, touching him slowly, rhythmically, not knowing that her whole body was moving beneath his in the same slow rhythms of discovery.

Reever took as much of the sweet torment as he could before he turned his head away sharply, fighting for control. He felt Tory flinch and snatch back her hand.

"Tory—" he began, trying to explain.

"No," she said in a raw voice, covering his mouth with her hand. "Don't say it. Please, don't say it. I know I'm clumsy. I'm sorry, it's just that I've never done this before. I don't know what I should or shouldn't do."

Reever saw the legacy of pain in Tory's eyes, pain echoing from his cruel remarks ever since he had first seen her, wanted her like he had never wanted another woman and known that he shouldn't even kiss her.

And the worst of it was realizing that he had savaged her more deeply than he had ever intended because he hadn't really believed that he could hurt her at all. Not like this, her humiliation strong enough to taste.

The realization that Tory had no defenses against him shocked Reever even as it humbled him. He felt the same with her and had from the first moment. No defenses. Just a need and a fire that transformed him, giving him a strength and gentleness that he had never dreamed was possible for him.

"Tory," Reever murmured, kissing her softly with each breath, each instant. "My sweet, sensuous little virgin. I accused you of being clumsy because I was afraid to have you know what your grace did to me. You made me—burn. No other woman has ever done that to me. A look. A smile. A word. You didn't have to touch me. All you had to do was be there and my body—changed. Oh, God, honey. I got so hard I thought I'd die unless I undressed you and eased into that slender, perfect body. I almost took you the first time I saw you. And then on the ride back to the ranch, all I wanted to do was turn you around on Blackjack and slide you down over me and—"

With a shudder Reever stopped the reckless words, afraid that he would frighten Tory. "You are not clumsy," he said, biting off each word. "I pulled away just now because your sweet, sexy little moves almost made me lose control. I want you so much I'm afraid I'll hurt you."

Tory's eyes widened as she saw the truth written in every hard line of Reever's face. She believed him. She believed that he wanted her so much it was an agony inside him.

"Take me," Tory whispered, holding his face with trembling hands. "Take me where you're touching me now, where you're making me ache. Please, Reever. You can't hurt me more than I already hurt right now."

A few moments ago Reever would have taken her right there, ending his torment within her soft, willing body. But now he knew that there was no end to her vulnerability to him. Knowing that, he found the strength to be gentle.

"I'll take you," he promised, kissing her slowly, joining their mouths as perfectly as he knew he would join their bodies. "Eventually. But I want to know you first. And I want you to know me."

Reever's hand went from Tory's back to her ribs. He hesitated there, savoring her suddenly taut body and the sound of breath wedging in her throat. Smiling, he watched her nipples harden until they thrust against the soft cotton nightshirt in silent pleading for his caress.

"They remember me, don't they?" he murmured. "Which do you want first, honey—my hands or my mouth?"

Tory blushed at Reever's sensual teasing even as her back arched reflexively, bringing her breasts closer to his mouth. He saw her helpless reaction and smiled.

"Wild little innocent. So sweet. God, I could die finding out how sweet you are, and how wild."

Reever nuzzled one of Tory's breasts, drawing a ragged sound from her. He smiled again and slowly caught her erect nipple between his lips, tugging rhythmically as he drew her deeper and deeper into his mouth, listening to her tiny cries. After a long time he lifted his head and looked down at her breast. Wet from his mouth, the cotton was nearly transparent. It clung faithfully to her taut nipple. The rose-tipped breast made a warm, inviting contrast with the cloth clinging to it.

Groaning softly, Reever kissed the sweet peak once more before he turned his head aside and found her other breast. He suckled her languidly, deeply, hotly, wringing soft cries from her as she twisted in slow motion against him, seeking release for the tension coiling more and more tightly within her with each movement of his mouth. After a long, long time he released her, only to bite lightly again and again at the sensitive nipple until he felt the unmistakable shudder of true arousal take her slender body.

Reever's hands moved to the hem of Tory's nightshirt, which had been drawn up above her hips by her movements. He brought the shirt up to Tory's breasts a little at a time, nuzzling and teasing her with his mouth every bit of the way until he found her nipples again. They were still aroused, still needing him. As his warm mouth closed over one, she shuddered and unconsciously rocked her hips against his as pleasure expanded through her.

The movement tore a low groan from him. His mouth changed, caressing her with a lover's fierce demand. He felt the fire rip through her, felt her body arch beneath his, felt her intimate heat penetrating the heavy cloth of his jeans as he stilled her wild movements by letting his weight sink into her, pinning her to the bed.

"Easy, little one, easy," Reever said again and again, gentling Tory even as he fought his own violent need to give her what she was silently, innocently, begging him for.

"Reever?" Tory's question ended in a moan as his teeth closed with exquisite delicacy on her breast.

"Am I too heavy for you?" he asked, tugging at her, watching ripples of sensation race over her skin.

Tory's only answer was a husky sound as she eased her legs farther apart, trying to get even closer to Reever. The innocent sensuality of the movement made him groan. His hand swept down her body to her thigh as he attempted to hold her still. He saw her eyes widen in surprise when his palm brushed over the apex of her thighs. He knew in that instant that she had never been touched, never known a man's hand caressing the softness of her inner thighs, never known the seeking and finding and caressing of even softer flesh.

"Oh, God, little one," Reever said huskily, biting at the shadow dimple of Tory's navel, feeling the wild response coursing through her. "I've got to touch you. It may shock you at first, but when you get past that, you'll know you want it as much as I do. You'll know that you belong to me everywhere, no matter how secret."

Reever's hand smoothed down Tory's body again. The heel of his palm pressed against the sensitive feminine nub hidden beneath her tangled hair, and then his caress moved on to the smoothness of her inner thighs. He watched her face, not wanting to frighten her by a touch that was too new, too intimate for her to accept. He sensed the instant of her uneasiness and hesitation as his hand settled between her thighs. His fingertips stroked delicately over even more delicate flesh.

"I won't hurt you," Reever promised. His voice broke as he looked down at Tory's flushed cheeks and passionate mouth. "You don't know what you do to me," he said hoarsely. "You make me want—everything. Look at me, sweet virgin. Tell me if I frighten you."

Tory's eyes opened, revealing a deep green rim around pupils dilated by sensual response. Reever's breath came in with a hiss as he saw the evidence of her arousal. He felt as though he were being licked by fire. His fingertips slid over the satin triangle of her underwear, barely touching her, yet she trembled violently. His hand caressed her thighs reassuringly as he bent and kissed her breasts and then her lips, tasting her with a consuming sensuality that made her shiver and moan.

"It's all right," he murmured. "I won't do anything you aren't ready for."

"I feel so—strange," she whispered, staring into his eyes.

"Frightened?" he asked softly.

Tory shook her head. "It's just that—I thought I knew everything about my own body. But I didn't. I didn't know that you could touch me and I would feel it all over, everywhere. Even—"

"Even?" he asked.

"Inside," she whispered, "where no one has ever touched me."

Reever's whole body tightened, but when he spoke, his tone was very gentle.

"I'm going to touch you there," he said, bending and kissing Tory's mouth. Gently his fingers smoothed over the thin, sheer cloth separating him from her hidden warmth. When she began to tremble, he lifted his head, looking at her. "Let me," he said quietly. "I won't hurt you. I'll be so gentle that all you'll feel will be pleasure. Just let yourself respond as honestly as you responded when I loved your breasts until you moaned. Remember how it felt for you then," he said, his voice husky, "because that's just the smallest beginning of the pleasure I can bring you."

While Reever spoke, his hand moved caressingly between Tory's thighs. At first she lay stiffly, but after a few moments she relaxed and let the shimmering pleasure of his touch spread through her. Without realizing it, she sighed and shifted, opening her legs a bit more. She wondered why his eyes narrowed then as he smiled down at her, but the sweetness of his touch drove all thoughts from her mind.

Slowly he bent over and kissed her navel, letting her feel his teeth and tongue until her hips lifted with the involuntary sensual response he had been waiting for. At that instant he slid the sheer panties down her legs with a sweep of his hand. Any objections she might have had were lost when his mouth locked over hers, and he consumed her with strokes of his tongue that made her moan and move sinuously, slowly.

By the time Tory realized that the wild sensations shivering through her were coming from Reever's palm moving slowly between her legs, it was too late to be shy or frightened. She could only do as he asked, as he urged, opening herself to his touch, watching his eyes darken with the same wild desire that was shaking her.

Delicately, gently, he traced her layered softness with his fingertips, watching her eyes change as she understood what was happening.

"Yes," Reever whispered, teasing the tiny, sensitive bud hidden in Tory's softness. "You can feel what it will be like, can't you? You can feel us coming closer and closer to the instant when you'll give yourself to me."

Tory's breath came in with a moan as she felt Reever begin to deepen the caress with a tenderness that made her forget to be afraid. She watched his eyes through half-closed lids while he gently took more and more of her secret softness, and she felt as though he were unraveling her bones. She moaned again, watching him, unconsciously moving in counterpart to his touch, wanting more of him.

"You're like a dancer, all grace and fire," Reever said, smiling, holding Tory's glance as his touch slid more deeply into her and she gasped with pleasure and surprise. "Yes," he grated, "let me know how much you like it. Let me know how—" His words ended in a groan as she melted at his touch. He watched her eyes, saw her surprise consumed by another burst of pleasure when he caressed her intimately. "You're so hot, so soft, so perfect," he breathed, bending down to her. "You make me want to come apart right here, right now, with you watching me." He shuddered and took her mouth with a thrust of his tongue. "Little virgin," he said huskily, biting her neck and shoulder with barely leashed hunger. "But not for long."

Reever's hand moved hotly, intimately, and Tory cried out again, melting again. His smile was a savage mixture of pleasure and the pain of not taking her. Tory saw the smile and felt lightning race through her, a sensual hunger that he was focusing with each searching caress. She reached for him, needing the consummation of his mouth, needing to feel his weight over her, moving, and her own body moving in return, needing something she had never known and could not even describe.

"Reever, I want—" Tory's voice broke as pleasure radiated through her at his touch, a slow, bursting heat that made her moan.

"What?" he murmured, slowly releasing her, letting his hand slide up to her navel, teasing the dimple with his warm, damp fingertip. "What do you want?"

Tory's hands closed on Reever's shirt as she tried to bring him closer. The metal snaps gave way in a ripple of sound. For the first time she felt his naked skin against her palms. She made a sound of satisfaction and discovery, excited by his heat and the sensual tension that brought each of his powerful muscles into hard relief. The wedge of blue-black hair enticed her, caressing the sensitive skin between her fingers as she rubbed against him.

"Tory—"

"No," she said huskily, flexing her fingers until her nails dug in lightly and he groaned. "Don't make me stop. You feel so good, Reever. Or don't you—don't you want me to touch you?"

His laugh was a ragged sound that was torn from him. She knew the answer to her question even before he spoke because he was moving with her touch, twisting slowly, increasing the pressure of her fingers exploring his chest.

"I want your hands all over me," Reever said, his voice as deep and ragged as his laughter had been. His eyes sought and held Tory's. "But if I let you undress me, touch me, your time as a virgin will be over. I don't want it to end that quickly. It's only going to happen for you once, green eyes. That's worth waiting for." He shuddered as he felt her nails skim over his nipples. "Besides, if you see how much I want you, it may just scare the hell out of you."

Reever tried to lighten his words with a smile, but he couldn't. Just the thought of Tory turning away from him in fear made him want to take her right there, right now, before she could change her mind.

Tory heard the truth and buried fear in Reever's words and wondered how she could tell him that she was no longer afraid. All the words she could think of began and ended in *I love you,* and those were the words she must not speak. Her hands slid down his chest to his hard waist. The involuntary, sudden movement of his abdomen surprised her until she remembered that she, too, had responded like that at the first touch of his fingers sliding down her body. And it had been pleasure, not surprise or distaste that had moved her.

"Did you like that?" she asked softly, watching the smoky glitter of his eyes.

"Yes," Reever said, his voice almost harsh.

"And this?"

Tory's hands slid lower, seeking and finding the hard length of him pressing stiffly against the confinement of his jeans. Reever's hips moved involuntarily, and a groan was ripped from him at the first sweet touch of her hands on his aching male flesh.

"Oh, God," he gritted, closing his eyes and shuddering heavily. He put his hands over Tory's as though to push her away, but he could not. His need was too great. He pressed her hands harder against him and moved slowly, shaking with hunger and pleasure.

Then Reever opened his eyes and saw Tory watching him, sharing his pleasure as he had shared hers. For a moment he thought he would lose control. Only his determination and deep need to be inside her allowed him to drag himself back from the brink. The realization surprised him. With other women it hadn't particularly mattered to him how he found satisfaction. Yet it mattered with Tory. He didn't know why; he only knew that it did. It was a truth that was even stronger than his blazing sexual need.

Gently Reever smoothed Tory's hands up the length of his body until he could bite her palms and fingertips with barely controlled force, wringing cries of sensual surprise and response from her trembling mouth.

"I think you've made your point," Reever said, giving Tory a smile that made her heart turn over. "You may be a virgin, but you won't faint or run screaming if you see me naked."

Reever kicked off his boots and stood up, making no attempt to conceal himself from Tory's curious eyes. He watched her face as he took off his shirt and tossed it aside. The sound of her indrawn breath was like a caress.

"I'd think you'd be used to seeing half-naked men," Reever said, smiling at her, his hands resting on his belt buckle. "Or do they swim in T-shirts where you come from?"

Tory smiled without looking away from Reever's powerful shoulders and the sleek black pelt curling down to his belt buckle. "Oh, I'm used to seeing men in a scrap of cloth that isn't even worth mentioning," she agreed. "But they shave all their body hair to cut down on drag in the water. And even if they didn't shave…" Tory shivered as her glance moved over Reever like a caress. "They aren't you, Reever. No man is. No man ever will be."

The words sank into Reever like sweet tiny claws, bringing a violent surge of desire. He wondered again how anyone as honestly passionate as Tory had managed to stay out of a man's bed for so many years—and then he remembered what she had told him: *It was easy. I hadn't met you.*

Watching Tory, Reever unbuckled his belt, unfastened his jeans and pulled off all his clothes with a few swift motions. As her glance traveled down his body, he saw her curiosity, her approval and then her surprise at the extent of his desire for her. He realized that, even though she had spent most of her life around nearly naked men, she was totally unused to seeing a man who was fully aroused.

"It's too late to change your mind and run screaming," said Reever, lying down next to Tory again, touching her with a hand that trembled.

"How about fainting?" she asked, her voice shaking, breathless. "Is that still an option?"

"Don't be afraid, little cat," Reever said, kissing Tory gently despite the violence of his own need. "I know it seems impossible to you right now, but you'll fit me like a satin glove, all hot and smooth and close."

Reever's hand kneaded gently down Tory's body until he found and caressed again the softness hidden between her legs. As his fingers teased her feminine bud, she shivered and melted again with a tiny gasp.

"All of a man's changes are obvious," he murmured, nuzzling against her breast. "Yours are subtle, almost secret, until I touch what's hidden and feel how very soft you've become for me. If you would touch yourself, you would feel how you've changed for me. You can hold me inside you now and have only pleasure, not pain."

Reever saw Tory's helpless blush at the thought of touching herself and he smiled. "Then you'll just have to take my word for it, won't you?"

Her only answer was a ragged intake of her breath as his hand slid caressingly between her thighs. His fingertips tormented her so delicately that after a few moments she forgot to be nervous or shy. Involuntarily her leg flexed as she shifted in response to his teasing, maddening, incredibly arousing touch. As he found once again her hidden heat and need, her eyelids fluttered shut and she lost herself in the sensations he drew from her.

Tory moved her hips gently, sinuously, beneath Reever's caress as she opened to him completely. His eyes darkened and narrowed at her wordless, unconscious invitation. Seeing her so vulnerable, so trusting, so generous with her virginal body made him ache to bend down to her and tease her softness with his tongue, to know every shivering bit of her in an intimacy that he had never shared with another woman. With a groan he forced himself to look away from her secrets lying open to his touch.

But Reever could not wholly refuse the invitation that Tory had so innocently and hotly given to him. Gently he covered her body with his own, easing himself into the cradle of her thighs. Her eyes flew open even as her body tightened.

"It's all right," Reever breathed, brushing Tory's lips with his open mouth, biting at her gently. "I won't take you by surprise, little one. You're going to have your eyes wide open—and so am I." He shuddered as his violently aroused flesh nudged against Tory's moist, vulnerable core. "I'm going to enjoy every instant of you every way I can. I've never wanted a woman like this. I want all of you, Tory. I want to watch your face as you change from virgin to lover with a single stroke of my body."

Tory shivered and moved beneath Reever while he teased her with his hands and the hungry, hot length of him rubbing over her. Always he stopped at the edge of taking her, barely penetrating, giving her just enough of himself to make her wild to have more. Finally she gave a ragged cry and arched herself against him, instinctively trying to capture and hold him within herself.

As Tory's hands gripped the hard muscles of Reever's buttocks, he jerked reflexively, sliding more deeply into her, stopping just short of the irrevocable instant when he would transform her. She twisted wildly as she tried to evade his restraint. Her body was like his, hot, shining with a mist of desire that increased the sensitivity of skin rubbing over skin. She twisted again, blindly seeking what he had prepared her for. His arm wrapped powerfully around her hips, stilling her movements. With a thick sound he bent and took her mouth, pinning her completely, letting the shaking wildness pass.

"Look at me," Reever said in a gritty voice. "Tell me how you want me. Slow or fast, tender or wild, whatever you want. I want it to be so good for you. I want it to be the best you'll ever have."

Tory's eyes, almost black with desire, opened. "How should it be? How is it best?" she asked, her voice trembling.

"Hot. Deep. Forever."

Tory's nails dug into the rigid muscles of Reever's body as the words burst through her. "Yes," she whispered, arching helplessly against him, repeating the word with each rapid breath she took.

Tory felt Reever going deeper into her and shivered as his heat became part of her. When he reached the fragile barrier he stopped. She opened her eyes, knowing that he was watching her, waiting for her.

"Am I hurting you?" he asked, and his whole body trembled with the effort of controlling his own violent need. "Tell me, green eyes. I'll never forgive myself if I hurt you."

The contrast between Reever's gentle words and the savage restraint of his body undid Tory. She shivered repeatedly as fire raced through her. All she could say was his name, but he felt the wild heat of her melting around him and knew that at that instant she could feel only pleasure. He thrust into her, sweeping aside the barrier, sheathing himself deeply in her welcoming softness. He saw her eyes widen with realization and heard her breath sigh out in a moan of sensual pleasure that was also his name.

"You're mine now, little cat," Reever gritted, bending to take Tory's mouth as completely as he had taken her body. "Oh, God, you feel good, hot and sweet and deep."

Reever's tongue thrust and withdrew slowly, matching his other movements within Tory. She trembled and washed over him in hot waves of pleasure. She sought to take more of him and give more of herself as she reached instinctively for the ecstasy that shimmered just beyond reach.

When Reever felt Tory twist beneath him, seeking him fully, his control slipped. He arched into her, filling her, wanting the same release that she was reaching for. Her tiny, wild cry ripped through him. Desperately he forced himself to lie still, afraid that his instant of uncontrolled need had hurt her. But when he would have withdrawn slightly in order to spare her, she grasped his hips, trying to get closer to him.

"Do you want more of me, little one? Is that it?" Reever asked, biting Tory's nipple with sensual restraint, shuddering when pleasure burst through her and melted over him in the same hot instant. "Wrap your legs around my hips," he urged huskily. "If it hurts, I'll—" His voice broke as she shifted, wrapping around him, taking all of him, and telling him of her pleasure with every movement of her slender body. He rocked slowly against her, feeling currents of fire gather with each hot, sliding instant. "Am I—hurting you?" he asked, barely able to breathe, moving in tight, tiny circles against her, inflaming both of them.

Tory's whole body stiffened suddenly as her breath unraveled into soft, fragmented cries. Reever felt it begin for her, felt the tiny convulsions deep inside her. She opened her eyes and looked right into his, and her voice shattered as she called his name in surprise at the fire consuming her until she couldn't breathe, couldn't see, could do nothing but come apart in his arms. He held her tightly, rocking against her slowly, sweetly, deeply, holding back his own release with all his strength because he wanted it never to stop for her or for him. He wanted always to be deep inside her, to feel ecstasy ripple through her body, to hear his name a broken cry on her lips, to have it last until he died.

Then Reever could hear Tory's cries no longer because he was calling her name as the world unraveled in slow motion, control slipping away from him in a series of soft, fierce explosions that were like nothing he had ever known.

Hot. Deep. Forever.

Chapter Eight

THE MEADOW WAS EXQUISITE, unexpected. On a stage
of green grass, wildflowers swayed like dancers in the
wind. Dense, nearly black pines ringed the meadow on
three sides. On the fourth, low granite cliffs rose in a
ragged stairway winding along the brilliant blue of
Wolf Lake. Wolf Creek swirled gracefully across the
meadow, murmuring and flashing through sunlight
and shadow alike. A small cedar lodge had been built
just below the crest of a ridge overlooking the meadow.
The lodge's windows shone with the same clear silver
light as the creek.

A new road snaked over the ridge and on out to the
county road two miles beyond. A faint trail led from
the lodge to the lakeshore. Other meadow trails were
being marked out by the ranch hands. The trails in the
surrounding forest required more work. The sound of
axes biting into wood rang through the silence, telling

of men hard at work clearing paths for dudes who had never been on a horse, much less in a forest that hadn't changed since Indians once glided through the shadowed silence in search of game.

"Payton was right about one thing," Tory said. She glanced sideways at Reever, who was standing next to her as they let their horses rest. "This is a beautiful place just to be alive in."

Reever smiled and ran his fingertip down Tory's cheek to her lips. "Yes," he said.

Tory's heart stopped, then beat more quickly. In the past two weeks Reever had been so gentle and loving with her that sometimes it was all she could do not to cry. Never once had he been harsh or impatient with her, no matter what the provocation. It was as though he were trying to erase even the memory of seeing her eyes darken at his cutting words. He had taught her to ride and had nothing but praise for her grace and quickness while she learned. It was the same when he worked with her in the garden. He had been almost as excited as she was by the exuberant growth of the plants.

A pair of cowboy boots had turned up next to her chair at breakfast a week ago, just as the work gloves once had. All the men denied any knowledge of how the boots had gotten there. This time she believed the men. She had seen Reever's face as he eased her feet into the polished leather as though the boots were crystal slippers left over from a fabulous ball. This morning it had been a hat that had appeared without warning, a soft, cream-colored Stetson that fit her perfectly.

Tory had tried to tell Reever that she couldn't let him give her anything else after the boots. He had smiled and stroked her hair and told her that it must have been the tooth fairy because he had never seen the hat before in his life. Then he had brushed her lips lightly with his thumb, stilling her words and caressing her in a single warm touch. She hadn't been able to prevent the two tears that had spilled down her cheeks, tears that he had caught on the edge of his thumb and then brought to his lips.

She had almost told him then. The words had ached in her throat as she loved him silently because he would not allow her to say the words aloud. But they were true just the same. She loved him until it was an agony and an ecstasy radiating through her silence, through her soul.

"Don't look at me like that," said Reever, his voice husky.

"Like what?"

"Like the sun rises and sets in my eyes."

"But it does," Tory said simply. Before Reever could voice the objections darkening his eyes, she smiled and added lightly, "That's what happens when you face east early in the morning and west late in the day. Even a city girl knows that much, cowboy."

Reever hesitated, then smiled, shaking his head. "Some city girl you turned out to be. I can't believe it— dinner was late last night because you were out in the barn helping a heifer have her first calf. Lord, little one, I've seen men turn pale and run rather than help pull a calf. Not you. You lay right down next to me in the straw and pulled for all you were worth. By the time we got back in the house, you were wringing wet and covered with stuff from head to toe."

"I'd do it again in a minute," Tory said, her face softening as she remembered the big-eyed, incredibly long-lashed, wobbly little calf butting at its mother's belly in an instinctive search for milk. "To walk into a stall where there's only one cow and to walk out later and leave two cows behind—that's as close to a miracle as I've ever come." Her face changed as she focused on him again. "Except with you, Reever," she whispered. "When you make love to me, it's not just the sun rising and setting in your eyes, it's the whole world burning."

For a moment Reever was very still. He searched Tory's eyes as though trying to see right through to her soul. After a long silence he said, "It's like that for me. Every time is better than the last until I can hardly wait to wrap myself around you again and wrap you around me until—" He shuddered and his eyes darkened as the familiar wild heat began to sweep through him again. "Oh, God, little one. You're in me hotter and deeper than my own blood."

Abruptly Reever turned and mounted Blackjack. "I'd better see if Jed has managed to gnaw through that big pine yet," he said, reining around until he could look at Tory. "And I'd better do it now before I pull you down in the grass and love you until you cry and scream and come apart in my arms."

"Reever," Tory said shakily, her breath shortening. "I want that. No. I want *you* like—like—"

"Hell on fire," he finished, his voice almost harsh. "I know. It's the same way I've wanted you since the first time I saw you. Close your eyes, little cat."

"Why?" she asked, closing her eyes.

Reever bent over in the saddle, lifted Tory in his powerful arms and kissed her with a thoroughness that left both of them aching.

"Keep those beautiful green eyes closed," he said hoarsely. "It's the only way I'll be able to leave you."

Slowly Reever eased Tory back onto her feet, took one more quick, biting kiss and spun Blackjack around. Tory didn't open her eyes until the sound of the horse's hooves had faded. Then she let out a long, tremulous breath and mounted Twinkletoes. She guided the gentle mare along a path leading to the beach that the hands had cleared along the lake.

"Hi, Dutch. How's the fire ring doing?"

The wiry cowboy dropped a water-smoothed stone as big as a basketball into the ring he was building. "Slow, Tory. Real slow. Been trying to figure how to do it from the back of a horse."

Tory smiled. She had learned that all the hands wanted only the work that could be done from horseback. "Are you going to be here for a while?"

"Yep. Going swimming again?"

"Sure am."

Dutch shook his head. "How something as sweet as you don't melt in all that water is beyond me. Ain't natural."

"I think someone I know is angling for peach cobbler again," muttered Tory.

He smiled innocently. "Cobbler? You making cobbler tonight? Did I ever tell you that peach is my favorite?"

"Really?" she asked, feigning astonishment.

Dutch chuckled, winked and went back to sorting rocks for the fire ring. Tory tied Twinkletoes to a handy bush, pulled a rolled-up towel from her saddle bag and went toward a long tongue of granite that ran out into the lake. There she peeled down to the swimsuit she wore beneath her riding clothes.

Twelve days ago, when Reever had decided it was time to put the finishing touches on "Payton's Folly," Tory had discovered that one of the springs beneath Wolf Lake was hot. That, and the lure of clean, deep water, had been too great to ignore after months of abstinence. The first time Tory had gone swimming there had been a line of appreciative cowhands watching her. While Reever hadn't wanted her to swim alone, he didn't figure that she needed every man within fifty miles as a lifeguard. When he couldn't do the job himself, he had assigned Dutch to beach, fire ring and lifeguard duty because Reever knew that Dutch's interest in Tory was strictly avuncular.

The water along the cobbled shoreline was decidedly brisk. The hot spring's influence didn't reach that far, and it was too early in the season for the sun to have made much impression on the overall temperature of the lake. Only at the base of the lower cliff was the water warmed by the hidden spring far beneath the surface of the lake.

Tory entered the water in a long, running dive and then swam toward the cliffs fifty yards away. The color of the water beneath her changed as the bottom dropped steeply away. Close to the cliffs she had no idea how deep the water was. That was one of the things she was going to find out today.

With the ease of someone to whom water is a second home, Tory jackknifed her body and dove straight down. The pressure around her built swiftly. Automatically she swallowed, letting her ears adjust. All around her was clear, very blue water. There were no rocks, no dead trees, no obstacles of any kind. She continued down until she was sure that she was beyond thirty feet, then she flip turned and headed back for the shimmering silver surface.

Tory slung hair out of her face with a casual motion of her head, pulled up her swim goggles and saw that Dutch was watching intently. She waved, swam about twenty feet, pulled her goggles into place and dove again. Methodically she quartered the area beneath the lowest cliff, looking for any surprises that might be hidden by the water. She didn't expect to find any. Yesterday she had stood on the lower cliff and looked over the water very, very carefully, coming at different times of day to take advantage of different angles of sunlight penetrating the unusually clear water. She had seen nothing to suggest any danger to someone diving from the granite shelf that overhung the deep water.

Nor did Tory find anything dangerous as she physically inspected the area below the base of the cliff. The granite wall was smooth all the way down. It had a slight overhang, ensuring that no matter how badly botched a dive might be, there was no way of landing on rock. The water beneath the overhang was deep, clean and as free of obstructions as a diving pool.

Tory swam back to shore, pulled on the beach walkers she had carried in her towel and picked her way along the shoreline as it gradually humped up into the first of a series of steplike cliffs. The way to the top of the lowest cliff that she had found was short and quite safe, for the path didn't come near the edge of the rock. She stepped out onto the smooth, nearly flat granite platform.

Shivering slightly in the breeze, Tory stood at the knife-edge of the cliff. To her right more granite rose steeply, notching the sky. To her left the granite merged gently with the beach. Below her the lake shimmered and rippled in shades of blue, whispering to her. She knew that the cliff was almost exactly ten meters high. She knew because all her senses had been attuned to that height by thousands and thousands of dives off ten-meter platforms. It felt…right…standing there, looking down into the lake.

The temptation to dive was almost overwhelming. Tory had been working her knee for at least an hour every night, often more. Time went quickly as she braced herself against Reever's powerful arm and exercised while he talked about the ranch and his tangled family history. She had told him about her own family and her years spent around the swim club's Olympic pools. And sometimes there was a sweet silence while he watched her with clear gray eyes, smiling gently, approving of her without saying a word.

Yet despite all the exercises, all the care that Tory had taken not to stress the knee again, she was afraid that it wasn't as strong as her left knee. There was no way for her to be sure without diving.

For a long time Tory stood on the cliff looking into the depths of Wolf Lake as though it held the answers to her questions about the future. Wind ruffled the water's surface, making ghostly silver patterns. Gradually Tory realized that she was shivering with something more than cold. She turned her back on the sapphire depths and hurried down the trail.

"You sure do like that cliff, don't you?" asked Dutch, looking up as Tory went by dressed in her riding clothes again. "You can see everything from there, can't you?"

"Almost," she said quickly, shivering, not wanting to talk.

Once back at the lodge, Tory went to her room and changed into dry clothes. One wing of three bedrooms and the kitchen were the only parts of the lodge and cottages that were completely finished. The rest waited for carpenters and painters who always seemed to be busy elsewhere. Not that Reever was complaining; he wouldn't care if the Sundance Retreat never opened. Tory halfway suspected that he was paying the workers not to show up.

Tory hurried into the kitchen and stopped, astonished to find that Reever was there, calmly browning meat for chili on the lodge's big gas stove.

"If you make the biscuits," he said, looking up, "we can have supper all ready to go. Then we can sneak away for a ride to that tiny hidden meadow I told you about."

Tory's sudden smile made Reever wonder if he had ever seen anything half so beautiful. He smiled in return, holding out his hand to her, bringing her fingers to his lips. He rubbed his mustache against her inner wrist and traced the lines of her veins with the tip of his tongue.

"Can you make biscuits one-handed?" he asked in a low voice, biting the pad of flesh at the base of her thumb.

Slowly she shook her head.

"Damn." Reluctantly Reever released Tory's hand. "Show me how fast you can make biscuits, little cat."

As soon as Tory's heartbeat settled down, it took her very little time at all to get the rest of the dinner ready. Hand in hand, she and Reever walked down to the corral, which was little more than a series of ropes strung between pine trees. Twinkletoes was there, but not Blackjack.

"I told Teague that he could use Blackjack," Reever said casually. "We'll double up on Twinkletoes. It's about time you learned how to ride bareback anyway." He grinned down at Tory. "Don't look so worried. Twinkletoes is so placid you could hang upside down from her belly and she'd never notice. And you can hang on to me as much as you want."

Reever buried his left hand in Twinkletoes's mane, took one step and vaulted onto the mare's back in a single flowing movement, making no more fuss about mounting than if he had used a stirrup.

"Close your mouth, city girl. You'll catch flies," teased Reever.

"How did you do that?" demanded Tory.

"Practice. Strength doesn't hurt, either."

"No kidding," she said dryly. "Any other sugges-tions?"

"Hold out your left arm. Grab my left arm just above the elbow," he said, leaning down to her. "Step onto my boot just like it was a stirrup."

Tory did and found herself being lifted through the air and swung into place behind Reever. The first thing she noticed was the sensation of warmth radiating up from Twinkletoes through her jeans. The second thing was the ripple and play of powerful muscles as the mare shifted her weight.

The third thing was the fact that, short of actually mak-ing love, there was no greater physical intimacy possible for a man and a woman than riding double, bareback.

"Ready?" asked Reever.

"What a question," Tory muttered.

He looked over his shoulder, saw her dilating pupils and knew just what was happening to her. The same thing was happening to him. He had been looking for-ward to this ride for a long time. He smiled slowly, wickedly.

"Wrap your arms around me," Reever said. When Tory did, he twisted in slow motion, rubbing his back sensually across her breasts, caressing her. He heard her breath come in suddenly as her back arched, increas-ing the sweet pressure of his touch. "Ah, little cat," he said huskily, "I can feel your nipples asking for me. I'm going to make you wait, though. I'm going to make you as wild as my dreams."

Tory's breath shivered out as Reever's big, hard hand traced the length of her thigh nestled so intimately against his. "I'll get even with you," she said in a trembling voice. "I swear it."

"God, honey, I hope so. Hang on."

A touch of Reever's heels sent Twinkletoes walking out into the sunlight that was slanting down between the erect, fragrant bodies of the pines. After the first few minutes Tory found it surprisingly easy to adjust to being bareback. If anything, the lack of a saddle helped her to find and move to the horse's rhythms more quickly. Before a mile had gone by, she relaxed completely against Reever and let the warmth of the sun, of the placid horse and of the man she loved seep into her.

Reever sensed Tory's adjustment to the new style of riding in the easy, rhythmic swaying of her body against his. Smiling, knowing that he could safely distract her now, he brought one of her hands up to his mouth. Gently he sucked on each finger in turn, biting lightly at the most sensitive flesh, softly devouring her until he heard her whimper deep in her throat. Then his teeth closed less gently on her palm until she shivered and arched against him, clinging to his hard warmth.

With aching sensuality Reever rubbed Tory's hands over his chest, turning and twisting against her like a cat until her nails found his tiny, hard male nipples and scraped sweetly over them. A groan wedged deep in his throat. He released her fingers, but she didn't stop caressing him. Her hands moved in the same sensual rhythms of the horse walking, and her body stroked his with each motion.

Tory pressed closer to Reever's powerful back even as her fingers slid between the snaps of his shirt. At the first hot touch of his flesh, she made a low sound. Slowly her hands tugged in opposite directions, unfastening the snaps on his shirt one by one. Her palms rubbed over him restlessly, hungrily, and her fingers dug softly beneath the thick hair. He moved against her touch, stroking her with his own body while fire pooled hotly, heavily between his thighs. He felt her hand search each ridge and swell of muscle on his chest even as her mouth pressed against his spine. Her teeth tugged at his shirt while her fingers flexed and buried themselves in the warm black thatch of hair curling over his chest.

Reever let go of the reins he had knotted together and pulled his shirt free of his jeans. Even before he had finished, he felt a hot rain of kisses across his naked back. Then, with a catlike sound of contentment, Tory caressed his skin with her cheek, turning her face from side to side as though he were a warm river and she were bathing in him. Her mouth opened and she shivered as she tasted him.

Reever's breath shortened. He felt as though he were caught between two fires, Tory's hands on his chest and her mouth caressing his back. His own hands began a slow, sweet stroking of her thighs until she rocked against him with more than the horse's easy motions. Slowly, inevitably, her hands slid down his chest to the less sensually rewarding material of his jeans. She stroked his hard thighs once and then again and again, using her fingernails and sliding higher up his legs each time until she finally brushed against the rigid proof of his desire.

"Tory—" grated Reever.

Her hands returned, settling over him sweetly, hotly.

"Let me," she breathed, closing her teeth on his back with the slow, loving sensuality he had taught her. "Help me."

Reever looked down and saw Tory's delicate fingers against the faded blue fabric as she stroked him. He knew he should stop her, but it was too much what he had dreamed of since the first day she had ridden behind him and he had ached at the thought of having her hands on him. When she tugged blindly at the fastening on his jeans, he shuddered heavily.

"Reever," Tory said, her hands trembling, her breath hot against his back. "Please."

Slowly he guided her fingers over his jeans until the cloth parted. Her hands eased inside his clothes. She made a husky sound of discovery and pleasure as she found him. Reever felt her touch like sweet fire over his aroused flesh. He stifled a groan as he shifted position, bringing himself more fully into her hands.

"I love touching you," Tory said huskily, and her breath flowed hotly over Reever's skin. "I love feeling you change and knowing you want me more and more with each heartbeat. Your whole body gets hard. Everywhere, not just where I'm holding you now." Her teeth closed over a muscle that rippled beneath the taut, naked skin of his back. "You're so strong," she whispered. "I love your strength. I love the salty taste of your skin. I love your heat. I love—"

At the last instant Tory controlled the tumbling words, dragging herself back from the brink of admitting how much she loved Reever himself.

"Everything," she said finally, caressing him, measuring his potency, savoring the different textures that went from hot satin smoothness to the tight male flesh hidden within a thatch of hair. "I love everything about you, Reever."

"Oh, God," Reever groaned. The sight of Tory's slender fingers loving him was like being connected to an electric current. He shuddered convulsively, repeatedly, a man being softly, wildly devoured. "Stop," he said thickly. "You'll make me lose control."

"Then I'd just have to start all over again, wouldn't I?" Tory asked. She laughed softly and bit his back hard enough to leave a small mark. "I can hardly wait."

Reever endured it for a few moments longer, watching Tory's hands like sweet flames caressing him, burning him. And then he felt forerunners of the release to come shuddering through him. He called her name, trying to still her hands, but it was too much like his dream, sweet and wild, inevitable, and the knowledge that she was shaking almost as much as he was only made it hotter.

When he finally managed to ease her hands up his body and refastened his jeans, he kissed her palms lovingly and stroked her arms, trying to calm her. It was a long time before they both could breathe without air catching in their throats. Only then did Reever stop Twinkletoes, bring his right leg over her neck and slide off.

"Reever?" asked Tory.

"Scoot forward and lean to the right, little cat. It's your turn. And mine."

Tory didn't understand, but she did as Reever had asked. He swung up behind her in a single swift motion, reached around her and picked up the reins. A gentle nudge of his heels sent Twinkletoes ambling up the dim trail. He let go of the knotted reins, knowing that the mare would keep walking without his guidance.

"I was going to ride this way from the first," Reever said, pulling Tory even closer against his body, "but I didn't trust myself to get all the way to the meadow. Then I discovered that you're every bit as bad—and as good—as I am."

Tory gave Reever a puzzled look over her shoulder, still not understanding. He smiled down at her with such sensual promise that her lips parted on a sudden intake of breath. He caught her chin and licked her lips delicately, nibbling and tugging as though it were her breast rather than her mouth he was teasing. The promise implicit in his caress made Tory's nipples tingle and tighten in a rush that sent fire racing through her core.

"They know, don't they?" whispered Reever, biting the nape of Tory's neck as his hands settled around her ribs, pulling the T-shirt tight to reveal her hard nipples.

"What?" she asked.

"Your breasts," he said, rubbing his palms along her ribs. "See? They're changing for me." Just above the tight crowns his fingers traced circles that touched only air. Even so, she rose and tightened visibly, as though she had been stroked. "They know I'm going to love them with my hands and my mouth." His voice deepened as his fingers drifted down her body to her thighs. "Does the rest of you know that, honey? Are you changing for me where I can't see you?"

Tory shivered and Reever smiled.

"I'm going to find out," he said, tasting her neck as he caressed her thighs. "But not right away." His hands eased up to her ribs again, and this time he was beneath the soft cotton of her T-shirt. His touch skirted her breasts, defining them without touching them.

"Reever," she said huskily, turning toward him, trying to capture his elusive touch. "You're torturing me."

"No, I'm not," he said, laughing softly. "Not yet. But soon, little cat. Soon I'm going to hold your breasts in my hands. I'm going to stroke and tug on those pink buds until something flowers deep inside you. Then I'm going to undo your jeans and find another bud, another flowering, but this one won't be hidden inside you. This one I'll be able to tease and love until I have to hold you on Twinkletoes because you'll forget where you are, who you are, everything but my touch on your sweet, hungry body."

Tory tried to speak, could not and shivered instead. Reever smiled as he watched the march of sensation over his lover's smooth skin.

"I can't wait any longer," he said. His voice was very deep as his teeth caressed her neck with fierce restraint. "I've dreamed about this since I brought you back to the ranch on Blackjack weeks ago. But Blackjack isn't placid like Twinkletoes, and you couldn't ride worth a damn then. It's different now. Lift your arms for me, honey. Let me show you what a woman like you does to a man like me."

Slowly Tory lifted her arms over her head. Reever spread his big, warm fingers and eased the T-shirt up over her body without touching her skin. The sliding pressure of the cloth over her nipples made Tory's breath catch. Reever's left arm settled over her bare midriff while his right hand tucked her T-shirt safely inside the waistband of his jeans. He tightened his arm, bringing Tory fully against his body, giving him a view of the creamy curves and deep pink tips. His muscular forearm moved up to take the warm, soft weight of her breasts. The contrast between her pale, smooth skin and the tanned, black-haired power of his arm made Reever feel hot and very male.

"I feel like I've been waiting all my life to see you like this," Reever said, rubbing his forearm slowly against Tory. "All that long ride home I wanted to tear off that damned T-shirt and see those sweet buds against my skin. Then when my hand touched you like this—"

Tory's whole body stiffened as Reever's right hand skimmed over the aching peak of her breast.

"Yes," he said thickly. "You jerked just like that, like you'd been touched by a live wire. Is that how it feels when I touch you, honey? So good it almost hurts? It feels like that when you touch me."

"Reever," Tory moaned, seeing his hand so close to her but not giving her what she needed as much as she needed air. "Oh, Reever, please—"

"You get so hard," he said, his voice deep and dark. He shifted his hands until her breasts filled his palms and his fingers could capture the taut nipples. "I love seeing you, feeling you, knowing that I've done this to you. And then I love doing this." His fingers closed, tugging at her, rolling her between his sensitive fingertips until her hips began to move in the primal rhythms of passion.

"Tell me what it feels like," Reever said, his voice soft, hoarse.

"Wires—tightening," Tory said raggedly. "All through me. Hot—sweet—wires." She arched against his hands, silently asking for a harder touch.

"Put your hands over mine, honey. Show me how to make it feel even better for you. Don't be shy," he murmured when he saw the blush rising up her neck. He released her breasts, not touching her. "I want to know how to love you," he said huskily. "I want this to be your dream, too. Or didn't you want my hands on you all that long ride home? Didn't you ever dream about riding double with me, naked, and having me love you until you came apart? I dreamed about it, little cat. And every time I dreamed, I woke up shaking, sweating, wild."

Breath shuddered through Tory. The sunlight and air caressed her breasts, but that wasn't enough. She looked down and saw Reever's hard, tanned fingers on her thighs and saw the aching, rose-tipped hunger of her breasts. Slowly she pulled his hands up her body until they enveloped her. She turned from side to side, dragging her sensitive peaks across his palms, holding him close, hard. When his fingers caught her nipples, she shuddered and moaned her approval as she rubbed her cheek against his chest, needing the masculine textures of hair and hard muscle.

Reever watched Tory's eyes close while sensations shivered through her, making her whole body taut. He continued the sweet torment of her breasts until her cheeks were flushed and her breath came quickly, hotly. Then he tilted her face up to his and kissed her while his hand caressed the length of her body once and then again. The third time his hand moved over her jeans, they came undone. Long, lean fingers slid inside the tiny triangle of Tory's briefs.

The ragged cry Tory gave when Reever rhythmically stroked her was a sound from his dreams. His hands closed sweetly, fiercely, on her breast and between her thighs, holding her in a sensual vise while his teeth caressed the nape of her neck. Her hips lifted instinctively into his touch, giving more of herself to him. With a thick sound of satisfaction, he took her silky secrets while his thumb teased the hard bud concealed within her softness. She began to twist slowly, consumed by his touch. He whispered to her, asking her what she wanted, giving it to her even as she answered, feeling her melt and run like wild honey beneath the hot skill of his hands.

"Reever—" Tory's voice broke as his thumb moved slowly, smoothly, making her shiver, pleasure showering through her with each touch. "No more," she cried finally. "I can't—I'm going to—"

"Then I'll just have to start over again, won't I?" Reever said, repeating what she had told him a few minutes before. He smiled down at her, his eyes a silver blaze of passion and anticipation. "Only with you, little cat, it isn't a case of starting over like it is for me. The second time you'll start higher, and then I'll take you even higher, all the way to the other side of the sun."

Tory tried to speak but could not. Her body was no longer hers. Reever had stolen it one caress at a time until she could only twist in slow motion against him, covering his fingers with her own, teaching and learning at the same time until she gave a husky cry and arched like a drawn bow in his hands. He cradled her against his hot body, holding her in place on the horse's broad back. Slowly he kissed her flushed cheek and caressed her very gently, bringing her back to herself. When she gave a long, trembling sigh, he smiled and touched her hot skin with his open mouth.

"That's just the beginning," Reever murmured, tasting the warm mist that passion had brought to Tory's skin. "Look around you. We've reached the meadow."

Tory's eyes opened slowly. All around her grass grew thickly, and the air was heavy with the scent of flowers unraveled by the sun. Reever dismounted and lifted Tory from the mare's back into his own arms. He walked to a small rise and sank to his knees in the cool grass. Tory's eyes darkened until they were the intense summer green of the grass as she watched her lover bending down to her, his expression intent, dark, heavy with sensuality. Slowly he undressed her and then himself. Very gently he parted her legs, caressing their smooth length, watching her with eyes the color of tarnished silver, eyes that promised... everything.

"I'm going to make love to you the way I've dreamed of it," Reever said in a husky, caressing voice as his fingertips traced the curves of Tory's legs. "You couldn't have accepted it before now. And neither could I before I met you. This will be a first for me, too."

Tory watched Reever with eyes that were almost frightened. He was more aroused than she had ever seen him. The sight of his naked need was a live wire brushing her, sweetly shocking every nerve to life, promising a passion that she had never known. As he knelt between her legs, she began to shiver under the impact of the primal sensuality radiating from him. He lowered himself over her, stroking all of her with a single slow movement of his powerful body.

Reever's open mouth moved over Tory's face, tasting her, feeling her, caressing her, knowing her with teeth and tongue and lips. She caught and held him with her mouth for a long, sweet moment, and his tongue promised her things she had never dreamed of. When he tore his mouth from hers, she whimpered softly. His mouth closed on her neck in a fierce caress that left a loving mark and drew a sound of surprise and passion from her lips. He laved the mark with his tongue before his mouth moved lower. He found a breast and consumed it as slowly and completely as he had consumed her mouth. It was the same for her other breast, tugged and suckled to a hard peak while she shivered and twisted beneath the loving demands of his tongue.

Reever's open mouth traced the line of Tory's ribs as he eased further down her body. She felt the sudden, hard warmth of his rigid tongue flicking into her navel again and again, sending surprising bursts of heat through her with each touch. When she slid her fingers into his hair to hold him closer, he bit her shivering flesh gently and slid further down her flushed body. As she had done when she drank from the creek, he rubbed his face against her body repeatedly, turning from side to side, caressing the tangled triangle of dark gold hair until she moaned. His hands stroked her inner thighs with subtle demand. Instinctively she yielded, opening to him even more. And then her whole body tightened at the first intimate touch of his mouth.

"It's all right," Reever said gently, biting Tory with exquisite delicacy. "You're almost ready now."

"For what?" she whispered, and her voice, like her body, trembled.

"To die with me inside you, and then to be born again the same way. With me. We're going to be together all the way to our souls."

Tory didn't answer. She couldn't. Sensations she had never known were sweeping through her, dragging fire in their wake. She called Reever's name and was answered by a caress that made her cry out at the incandescent pleasure bursting through her. The world slid farther away from her with each wave of fire, each consuming caress, until she could neither think nor speak, only respond with an abandon that was like nothing she had ever experienced.

With a final, slow caress Reever moved over Tory, wrapping himself around her, catching her wild cries with his mouth at the same instant that he thrust into her, burying himself in the sweet heat and ecstatic fire he had created. He felt the fierce, delicate, overwhelming completion take her even as he did. He moved slowly, fully, increasing and savoring her release as though it were his own. When the last shivering tremors finally faded from her softness, he held himself perfectly still, waiting for her eyes to open.

"Tory," he murmured, biting her lower lip with exquisite sensuality.

Her eyes opened and she stared straight into the hot silver of barely leashed, soul-deep desire. "Reever?"

"Yes, little cat," he said huskily. "Now it begins."

The first powerful movement of Reever's body made Tory gasp. The second movement inflamed nerves still shivering in the aftermath of ecstasy. The pleasure was so intense that she had to bite her lip against a scream. Desire burst through her as she felt every muscle in Reever's body become rigid with sensual tension. She smelled the heady, musky heat of his skin and was deeply aware of every motion he made within her. He moved again and then again, harder, deeper, faster, ripping the world away from her with each potent motion of his body.

Tory didn't know that her nails raked down Reever's back as she wept and shuddered and cried her wild ecstasy. She knew only that she could feel no greater pleasure without dying. She tried to tell Reever that she could bear no more, but no words came to her in her need, only explosions of greater and greater ecstasy. She couldn't breathe, couldn't move. Dimly she heard her name torn from his throat in a harsh, broken cry as his control burst into a shattering release. With all his power he locked himself so deeply within her that each pulse of his pleasure was a live current touching her. Her whole body shook with the violence of the ecstasy sleeting through her. Wave after wave of pleasure transformed her, wringing sweet cries from her as each expanding ring of ecstasy swept through her and burst.

Slowly, slowly, the world condensed again around Tory. There was the untamed blue of sky and the rippling green of summer grass and the tan of Reever's face as he watched Tory darkly. He was holding her with bruising strength, still locked deeply within her. Somewhere a voice whispered, *I love you, I love you, I love you,* as though a breath could not be taken without that elemental truth being spoken.

At first Tory thought that she was dreaming—and then she realized that she was awake, that Reever was watching her with eyes that were the color of steel and that it was her own voice whispering the forbidden words to him.

I love you.

Chapter Nine

FOR THE HUNDREDTH TIME TORY relived the long, silent ride back to the ranch. Reever had been achingly tender with her, treating her as though she were made of the most fragile china. He had said nothing, done nothing to indicate that he had heard her helpless admission of love. But he had heard. She was sure of it.

He hadn't touched her since then.

Five days. Each day longer than the one before, shorter than the one to follow. It wasn't a return to the harshness of the time before they had become lovers. Reever continued to treat Tory with a gentleness that made her throat close around silent screams—because beneath that unfailing kindness she sensed him sliding away from her, retreating, easing apart from her so very carefully, not wanting to cause her any more pain.

He did not love her.

With each breath Tory took, that terrible certainty turned in her soul like a razor. She didn't even know if Reever desired her physically any more. He was so kind to her. Too kind. When he looked at her—if he looked at her at all—there was none of the leashed passion that once had turned his eyes to a smoky crystal blaze. There was only the kind of sorrow that made the razor of loss turn more deeply in her, her life bleeding away secretly, tears wept in darkness, unseen, unheard, untouched, unknown.

"Hi, Tory," said Dutch, shutting the lodge's kitchen door behind him and looking hopefully toward the huge, shining stove. "What's cooking?"

Tory blinked and looked down at her hands. She was cutting beef into cubes. That meant stew. Had she made stew last night or the night before? She couldn't remember. She hadn't even known what she was cooking until she looked down and saw the red chunks waiting to go into the seasoned flour.

"It looks like stew from here," she said.

"Great!" Dutch said enthusiastically. "We haven't had that for a week. Lots of gravy, okay?"

"Swimming in it," Tory promised, feeling as though she should make a note in the spilled flour on the counter before she forgot. She was living on automatic pilot. It had to stop. She had never been like this before, no matter how crushing a loss had seemed to her at the time.

Why won't Reever even talk to me? Why does he slide like water through my fingers every time I try to speak to him alone?

It would be different tonight. If there were no other way, she would wait until he went to bed, and then she would corner him in his bedroom. She would— "Watch it!" cautioned Dutch.

Even as he spoke, the knife that Tory was using slipped, drawing a red line over her finger. Without making a sound, she put down the knife, turned and went to the sink. She held her finger under the cold water streaming out of the faucet.

"Is it bad?" Dutch asked anxiously, hovering over her.

"Is what bad?" asked Reever from the doorway.

Tory's heart turned over just at the sound of Reever's voice. Her breath stopped, then came in harshly.

"She cut her finger," Dutch said.

"Let me see."

Tory shook her head, keeping her back turned to Reever, feeling hot and cold and dizzy, and her body shivered like a crystal glass struck by a careless hand. She was afraid. If Reever touched her, she would fall apart. She loved him. He had wanted her with a passion that had set them both afire. But now he didn't want her. She had waited, hoping with each hour, each minute, each second, that he would come to her. He had not. The longer she stayed close to him, the more unbearable her loss became. She was tearing herself apart, teetering on the instant of shattering.

The wild seething of Tory's emotions shocked her. In that moment she knew that she wouldn't corner Reever tonight or any other night. There was no reason to, except to hurt herself even more by refusing to accept the reality of her relationship with him. Reever had nothing to say to her that he hadn't already said—she had all the qualifications to be his lover and none of the ones to be his beloved. He had told her so the first day. She just hadn't believed him then.

She didn't want to believe him now. How could she love so deeply and not have it returned, even a little?

Dizzy, feeling the world slipping away from her grasp, Tory fought for self-control.

"Dutch, check on Blackjack, will you?" Reever said carefully, seeing the color drain completely from Tory's face. "I think his right foreleg might be swollen."

Dutch had just seen Blackjack, and the horse had never looked better. A glance at Reever's bleak eyes froze Dutch's protest in his throat. He turned and went out the back door without a word.

"Let me see it."

Reever's tone was gentle, coaxing, restrained...and somehow as distant as the moon.

"There's no need," Tory said, her voice thin. "It's just a scratch."

He didn't bother to argue. He simply took her hand from the stream of water and watched crimson blood well instantly from the cut. He also watched her helpless response to his touch, the shiver she couldn't control, and he heard the soft sound of her breath breaking. His eyes closed.

"Tory," Reever said achingly. "I didn't want it to be like this."

"Like what?" she asked faintly.

"You loving me."

"And you not loving me." Tory's eyes darkened as she looked out the kitchen window at the supple pines and the lake shimmering beneath the sun. "I believe you," she whispered. "I'll buy that bus ticket out of here, the one you've been telling me to get since the first time you saw me. You're free, Reever. Go find the perfect woman of your dreams. I'll go find the perfect platform, the perfect pool, the perfect dive, and then I'll step off into the air and float forever...." As the last word died away, she shivered violently. "But thank you," she added, her voice thinned almost to breaking. "You made it so very good for me. When you held me, it was more beautiful than anything I'd ever dreamed."

Tory pulled her trembling hand from Reever's grasp, ignoring the line of scarlet sliding down her finger. The cut was only superficial. The rest of her wounding was not.

"I should have driven you into town that first day," Reever said, his voice suddenly as harsh as though he had never held her, never felt her come apart in his arms. His eyes were dark, nearly wild, savage. "I didn't want your virginity. I didn't want the guilt of taking a young girl without words of love. But you burned like a fire in me all the way to my soul. So I seduced a city girl who was only marking time until she could go back to the bright lights. That's what you were doing at the Sundance, isn't it, city girl? Marking time until your knee healed, until you could make that perfect dive. God, I wish I'd never touched you!"

The little color that had been left in Tory's world faded away. "My fault, Reever," she said, her voice so frail that it was almost like silence. "I can't say you didn't warn me. I know that I'm a long way from the woman of your dreams. You told me often enough. I just didn't listen very well, did I?"

In the sudden, taut silence the sound of cowboy boots stamping off mud on the flagstone walkway beyond the kitchen was as loud as an exchange of gunshots. Jed's voice rose over the noise, as did Miller's. Both of them were speculating on whether any of Tory's cookies were available for starving cowhands.

"Tell them the cookies are in the blue jar," Tory said, her voice breaking as she slipped past Reever.

When Tory finally came back to the kitchen, the room was empty of cookies, cowhands and Reever. The remaining meat was cubed and neatly stacked to one side of the cutting board. She didn't have to be told that Reever had taken care of it for her. With trembling hands she dredged the big cubes in the seasoned flour, browned them and set them aside to simmer slowly while she made four cherry pies.

Tory tried not to think, not to feel, but it was impossible. By the time dinner was ready, it was all she could do to force herself to sit at the table with Reever only inches away.

God, I wish I'd never touched you!

But he had. Nothing could change that. All that remained was for Tory to find a way to survive loving a man who didn't love her in return, not even a little.

"Tory, are you on some kind of damn fool diet?" asked Dutch.

"What?" she asked, startled out of her thoughts.

"You're not eating enough to keep a kitten alive," Dutch said gruffly. "You haven't for five days. I just wondered if you was on some damn fool diet. None of my business, of course, but you sure don't need to get any skinnier."

Tory looked down at the stew she had been pushing from one side of her plate to the other, and at the biscuit she had shredded without eating. It had been the same for every meal since Reever had taken her to the small meadow and made love to her until the truth poured out of her in husky, heedless cries.

"I—I ate too many cookies earlier," lied Tory. "Ruined my appetite."

Dutch gave her a skeptical look but said nothing more.

"I checked on your garden today," Jed said, reaching for another biscuit. "The drip that Reever set up in the furrows is keeping everything green, but I think the beans need some more of that fancy fertilizer. Want me to pick up a bag when I go into town for supplies tomorrow?"

"That would be very—" Tory cleared her throat. "Could I go in with you?" she asked urgently. "I have to—do something."

For an instant Jed looked surprised, then he grinned. "Sure thing, Tory. Too bad I'm not twenty-one yet. I'd buy you your first legal drink."

Tory sensed Reever's sudden, intent scrutiny. "What?" she asked.

"Don't you turn twenty-one tomorrow?" continued Jed, oblivious to Reever's narrowed, icy eyes. "Or is that next month?"

"Is tomorrow the thirtieth?" Tory asked.

"As ever was," Jed said, heaping butter on the biscuit.

"Oh," she said, swallowing. "Yes. My birthday."

"Wear your best jeans," said Jed. "I'll spring for lunch." He winked at the other men. "You see, I've got this thing for older women."

Reever's fork rang heavily against his dinner plate. Tory carefully did not look at him. She looked only at the steaming, fragrant, beautifully prepared and utterly unappealing dinner that she was systematically rearranging on her plate. Around her the hands argued about the best way to celebrate her birthday. She ignored them because it would have been too painful to speak, to tell them that their argument was academic. Whenever they celebrated her birthday, the guest of honor would be absent.

"But don't worry, boys," Jed continued blithely, "I'll get Tory back in time to cook dinner, birthday or no birthday. Otherwise, you'd all skin me alive."

This time it was Tory's fork that rang loudly against her plate. She wasn't going to come back. She couldn't bear being on the Sundance any longer, so close to the man she loved, yet so very far away from being loved in return. With a brilliant, false smile she stood up.

"There's some pie in the oven," she announced, withdrawing quickly from the dining area.

"Tory?" called Dutch.

She answered without looking back. "Just leave the dishes on the table. I'll take care of them when I've finished my knee exercises."

Reever's chair scraped loudly against the unglazed tile floor as he pushed back with a force just short of violence.

"Boss?" asked Jed, looking surprised.

"I'm going to check on Blackjack," snarled Reever.

Dutch, who knew that there wasn't anything wrong with Reever's favorite horse, wisely kept his mouth shut.

Tory went to her room and did her exercises, trying very hard not to think of Reever as she braced herself awkwardly on the wall, bumping her knee or her foot with every motion. The knee, at least, seemed better. It was neither tender nor swollen, and it had been a long time since she had limped at all. In that way, if in no other, the Sundance had been just what the doctor had ordered.

As soon as the exercises were finished, Tory pulled out her duffel bag and began cramming clothes into it, wondering why she felt so lost. For the first time in months she knew exactly where she was going—back to Southern California and the swim club, back to the diving that she loved and the competition that she had come to realize she didn't like at all. But competition was part of the only world that remained to her. Diving.

Going back. Going home. Going away from the man she loved, the man who did not love her.

Halfway through the packing, Tory found herself standing motionless, staring out the window as the moon rose, full and round and silver, brilliant with promises that would never be kept.

Don't be ridiculous, she told herself. *It's the same moon that you'll see tomorrow and tomorrow and tomorrow. Same world. Same everything. Except Reever and the Sundance. They'll be gone. Tomorrow and tomorrow and tomorrow.*

Abruptly Tory turned away from the window. She realized that the lodge was utterly quiet. Making no noise, she walked out into the lodge's main room, which gave her a view of the dining area. The men had long since finished dinner and gone to the half-finished cottages where they slept. Reever was nowhere in sight.

Quickly Tory cleaned up the kitchen and returned to her room. She knew that she didn't need to hurry for fear of running into Reever. He would be with the men as he had been for the past five nights, playing poker and swapping lies until he thought she was asleep. Only then would he come quietly into the lodge, walking in his stockinged feet past her door, taking the bedroom at the end of the hall, as far away from her as he could get without causing a stir by sleeping out with the hands.

But Tory was never asleep when Reever came walking softly past her door. She was lying awake, afraid to breathe, praying with every bit of her strength that he would open the door and come to her, whispering words of love. It hadn't happened. It wouldn't happen tonight, either. He didn't love her. He didn't even want her anymore. Hanging around the ranch and hoping that he would change his mind was destroying her, and she knew it.

You've lost him, she told herself fiercely. *Accept it like you've accepted other losses. Accept it and get on with your life.*

It was late when Tory finished the last of her packing and crawled into bed. Suddenly, she knew that she couldn't go through it again. She couldn't lie awake until she heard Reever climb the lodge's front steps. She couldn't wait with her breath held and her body trembling while he ghosted toward her room. She couldn't bear to know again the terrible emptiness that came when he passed by her door as though she had never been born.

Nor could Tory tolerate being inside her room a moment longer. She threw aside the sheet and walked barefoot through the lodge. The screen door squeaked loudly in the absolute silence of the night, startling her for a moment before she shut the door and left the lodge behind. The path to the lake was a pale ribbon unwinding beneath a moon whose brilliance pressed sharp shadows from the trees. The air was warm, silky, so clear that the night was like an immense, transparent black bell whose ringing was expressed in the shattered brilliance of stars.

The cliffs rose in tones of gleaming pewter at the margin of the lake. Tory climbed the familiar trail easily, quickly, for she had come there many times and sat on the lowest cliff, looking down into the lake's thousand shades of blue. Tonight there was no breeze to disturb the pristine mystery of the lake's surface. It was like the night itself, deep, motionless, unknowable. It lay at her feet in a black-and-silver stillness that was uncanny. The moon's trail on the water was utterly sharp and so brilliant that it was painful to look upon for more than an instant.

Tory sat at the edge of the cliff's granite platform and looked down into the darkness and moonlight pooled beneath her feet. Shapes seemed to condense on the lake's surface as though on a shimmering black screen, shadows thrown by her mind as she thought about her life on the eve of her twenty-first birthday. Her years had been shaped by her yearnings to make a place for herself in the world, but to do that, it had been necessary to please men who couldn't be pleased. First her father, then her stepfather, then a succession of coaches. And finally Ethan Reever.

Ultimately she had failed in all cases, especially and most painfully with Reever.

Now she was going to buy a ticket back to a world that she no longer wanted, a world that might ruin her knee beyond recovery. Although she had exercised faithfully, sometimes painfully, every night in her room, the feeling had slowly grown in her that her right knee would never again be as strong as her left. Under most circumstances the difference wouldn't have been noticeable. Under the relentless stresses of world-class competition, it might be the margin between success and a crippling failure.

Narrow. Unnatural. Short-lived. Olympics. Get out and look at the world.

Fragments of the doctor's unwanted advice seemed to condense out of the night around Tory. She shivered and wrapped her arms around her knees, but it was her thoughts that chilled her, not the mild midnight air. The swim club had become home to her because she had no other and because she loved diving more than she had ever loved anything in her life.

Until Ethan Reever.

And the land. She had discovered that she loved the land, too, a love that had been eclipsed by her unexpected passion for a man. She loved being able to walk out into the night and to hear nothing but the sound of her own footsteps, her own breath, her own heartbeat. She loved standing on earth that had known the weight of millions of seasons and very few men. From the instant she had stepped down off the bus and seen distant, indigo mountains rising above a fertile land, something in her had uncurled from a tiny, hard seed and had begun to put down deep roots in the earth. Even now she could sense herself reaching toward the mountains, unfolding, growing, absorbing the beauty and the silence and the fragrant air.

She had been born in the city, but she had been born for the land.

With that certainty something eased inside Tory, dimming some of the pain that had paralyzed her. When she left in the morning, it wouldn't be to go back to the narrow world she no longer wanted. She would go to find a new world full of mountains and silence and tender grass swaying in the wind. There would be a place for her in that world—cook or waitress, cashier or baby-sitter, it didn't matter. There would be a way for her to eat and sleep and wake up surrounded by mountains and seasons. Part of her, at least, would finally have come home. As for the rest, it would either heal or she would adjust to living with pain. That, too, she had learned in the past.

But tonight, for a short time, for the last time, she would know again the beauty of being a leaf turning on a silver wind.

"THIS JUST ISN'T YOUR NIGHT, BOSS," offered Dutch, raking in a modest mound of chips. "Never knew you to try to fill an inside straight like that."

Reever grimaced. He hadn't meant to do anything so stupid, but since he had heard the lodge's screen door squeak open and shut, he hadn't been able to keep even part of his mind on the cards. He kept wondering what Tory was doing out in the night, if she were crying or simply walking, if the light had come back into her eyes or if she still looked far too old to be so young.

Twenty-one. How young is that? he asked himself harshly. *A hell of a lot older than it ought to be. Being seduced and dumped does that to a girl. What did she ever do to you but be the kind of lover you've always wanted and never had? For this crime you refuse to touch her? For this crime you're tearing her apart?*

And me, he thought bleakly. *I never knew how much it could hurt just to be alive. But then I never knew how much I could want a woman. City girl. Soft and sweet and just passing through the countryside. Too young to know what she really wants. Too young to know what love really is.*

But I know. It's like the land—enduring. It's a fire in the soul as well as the body. I know that, but she's too

*young to know it, no matter what soft words she says
when she comes apart in my arms.*

*I wish to Christ I'd never touched you, city girl. Let-
ting go of you is tearing me apart.*

With a soft, vicious curse that made the cowhands
look at each other uneasily, Reever picked up the cards
he had been dealt. Faces stared back at him, faces
laughing, crying, transformed by passion, pale with the
kind of pain that he had never wanted her to feel. Tory's
face repeated endlessly, her voice calling his name in all
the shades of longing and love as she gave herself to him
without reservation.

Too damned young!

Reever realized that the men were utterly silent,
watching him. He saw the cards crushed within his
fist. As he slowly opened his fingers, mutilated cards fell
to the tabletop. Without a word he got up and walked
out into the night.

Tory wasn't in the stable. She wasn't feeding carrots to Twinkletoes or leaning over the stall door
talking to Blackjack. She wasn't standing in the
small meadow behind the lodge. She wasn't anywhere in sight.

Without breaking stride, Reever took one of the three
paths down to the lake. He carried no flashlight because
he needed none. In the full moonlight it was bright
enough to read print. The path went through a stand
of pines and from there down the gentle slope to the
lake. At one point, just before the descent to the shore,
another trail snaked off toward the low granite cliffs.
Reever didn't even look that way. He expected to find

Tory along the moon-washed beach, watching tiny wavelets come apart.

There was no one along the shore. Reever felt a disappointment that was just short of pain. He searched the rocky beach again, unable to believe that Tory wasn't there. He had been so sure he would find her. He walked the shore with long strides, wondering if she might be hidden in the shadow of the cliffs.

As he reached the middle of the beach, a pale flash of movement caught Reever's eye. He looked up to his right, where a low granite cliff glowed like pewter in the moonlight. When he realized what he was seeing, he froze in disbelief.

Tory had been sitting so quietly that he had overlooked her. Then she had stood and thrown off her nightshirt. As naked as the moonlight itself, she walked with measured steps away from the edge of the cliff, turned as gracefully as a dancer and walked back toward the brink. With each step she moved faster, gathering herself, her intention clear in the elegant, poised tension of her body.

No! Stop!

The desperate cry went no farther than Reever's mind. It was too late. Tory had reached the brink and sprung up and outward. Arms spread wide, body perfectly arched, she floated on the air as though she were truly the swan from which her dive had taken its name. At the last possible instant her arms came together over her head, her body straightened and arrowed downward. She entered the midnight lake in a dive so perfectly executed that the water was barely disturbed.

The breath came out of Reever in a harsh rush when he saw Tory surface and swim cleanly toward the beach. Distantly he realized that he was trembling. When she rose naked from the lake and walked up the long tongue of granite leading to the shore, she didn't see him, for her eyes were turned back toward the cliff. Without hesitating, she climbed the trail to the top again.

Reever could have called out, could have stopped Tory, but he was frozen in the moment when she had dived into the lake with a grace and beauty that had literally taken his breath. He had not known that such a dive was possible.

Again Tory walked to the edge of the cliff, turned, paced a few steps away, then turned again, long legs eating up the distance to the brink. Her legs flexed and she arched up and out again. Her body bent at the hips, and she fell, turning and gleaming in the moonlight, describing a whole, incredibly slow circle that ended just in time for her to arrow cleanly into the water once more. Instants later she surfaced and swam for the ghostly tongue of granite.

Reever watched Tory leave the lake and climb the cliff trail again. She was like a condensation of moonlight, silent, shimmering with liquid silver, her feminine curves and hollows caressed by velvet touches of night. If he hadn't seen the dark, wet marks of her passage over the granite tongue, he would have thought he was dreaming.

Again the steps, the turn, the gathering speed, the leap into darkness. This time her arms came against her body at shoulder and hip, and she spun quickly, a gleaming whirlwind that became a woman only at the last possible instant, parting black waters with clean silence. Soon she was on the cliff again, leaping, soaring, spinning, falling, and then again and yet again, each dive more complex, more difficult, more beautiful than the one before.

Reever watched without moving, transfixed by Tory's skill. He had never known that the human body could be so elegant—and so ruthlessly disciplined in the search for perfection. He had never even imagined that such perfection was possible. Yet even as he silently celebrated Tory's extraordinary grace, he felt part of himself sliding down into a grim blackness that knew no end.

He had been wrong. No matter what her years were or were not, Victoria Wells was not a young girl. Not in any way that counted. She knew what was real and what was not, what was enduring and what was transient. That knowledge was shouted from every elegant movement, every difficult dive. He was watching the culmination of years of enormous discipline and effort. Few adults were capable of that kind of sustained sacrifice for a distant goal. Tory had been, even as a child. The truth of it was written in every beautiful line of her body turning and falling so perfectly through the night.

Another truth was written, too. As Reever stood and watched helplessly, he realized that he had come out tonight to find Tory, to hold her, to make love to her until pain was no longer possible.

Instead, he had lost her, and pain was all that was possible.

You never had her, cowboy, Reever told himself bleakly. *Look at her. You've never seen her equal. No one has. You might have made her sweet body sing, but you never could have competed with a lifetime of work and dreams. You finally found your woman—and it's too damned late. She has another life, other dreams. She's earned every one of them, too. All you can do is say goodbye.*

Reever lost count of the dives and the passage of time. He stood motionless, caught in a terrible net of beauty and despair until Tory stumbled slightly as she came out of the water, breaking Reever's bittersweet enchantment. He walked out of the shadows and lifted her into his arms. Her skin was wet, cool, as pale as moonlight. She was shivering. He held her and looked down at her face and knew that he had lost more than he could name.

"I just—" Tory's voice fragmented when she looked up into Reever's empty, tarnished eyes. "I just wanted to say goodbye," she whispered, almost frightened by the silence and the bleak emotions she sensed beneath his dark surface.

Reever's only answer was to hold Tory closer as he turned and walked back to the lodge, carrying her as though she weighed no more than his own shadow. Tory watched him silently, feeling caught within a dream. The sadness etched into Reever's expression made tears run like moonlight down her face. Only the warmth of his big body seeping into hers, driving away the lake's midnight chill, made her believe that the moment was real, that she wouldn't awaken and find herself alone, crying for him.

Without a word Reever carried Tory through the lodge to his own room. Moonlight poured in a silver torrent through the windows, transforming everything it touched. Tory trembled as she felt herself lowered to the bed.

"R-Reever?"

His mouth brushed darkly, warmly, over hers.

"Let me say goodbye, too," he said simply.

The words sliced into Tory like black crystal knives, but she did not cry out her protest. She loved Reever too much to turn away from him, from her impossible dream. Silently she watched him undress, loving him with every breath, every look. When he came down onto the bed beside her and gathered her against his warm body, tears welled from her eyes at the beauty of being held by him again.

Reever buried his face against Tory's neck and his arms locked powerfully, immovably around her, as though he would absorb her through his skin into his bones. Tremors went through him. As she felt the searing heat of tears sliding down her skin, Tory knew that it wasn't desire that was shaking Reever's powerful body. With a soundless cry she held him, sharing his pain without understanding its source.

After a long, long time Reever's grip loosened. He kissed Tory's eyelids softly, closing them, knowing that if he saw her watching him he would forget the promises he had made to himself and beg her to stay with him. He couldn't live with himself if he did that. She deserved the life she had trained so long to have.

Reever brushed his lips over Tory's, then dipped his tongue into her mouth for a single instant. The taste of her swept through him violently, almost overwhelming him. He wondered then how he had lived for five days without her...and how he would live for the rest of his days, days without number or end, a hell of his own making.

"When you told me you were leaving," Reever said, kissing the elegant line of Tory's neck and shoulder, her slanting cheekbone and soft lips, "I thought you had just used me to pass the time while your knee healed, and now you couldn't wait to get back." His mouth stilled the words he sensed forming on her lips. "No, little cat. Let me explain why I was so angry tonight. I don't want you to leave remembering only my devil temper."

Reever's mouth parted Tory's lips for the intimate caress of his tongue. He moved within her warmth slowly, loving and absorbing her until he felt her soften against him. Her tongue slid hotly over his, seeking to claim him in return. It was gentle agony to end the kiss, to withdraw his mouth by tiny increments until only the tip of his tongue could touch her.

"I didn't understand," Reever said huskily, kissing the smooth swell of Tory's breast. "I didn't realize what an incredibly good diver you are, what you must have given up to develop your skill and how passionately you must have wanted to be an Olympic diver to have achieved so much in so few years." He shuddered as his mouth tenderly traced the taut peak he had called out of her softness. "I didn't realize how beautiful the human body could be, either. You taught me that tonight. The memory of your diving will haunt me until I die. So elegant. So perfect." His voice dropped to a whisper. "You tore out my heart. That was when I knew what I had lost. You. My heart."

Tory's instinctive cry of protest was lost as Reever's hand gently covered her lips.

"Hush, little one," Reever said, trying to control the aching tumble of his words. "It's not your fault. You gave me only beauty, and I gave you—" His voice broke. For long moments there was only the soft, almost secret sound of Reever's hand smoothing over Tory's body. "It doesn't matter now," he said finally, his voice controlled again. "I just wanted you to know that I understand why you're leaving. There's nothing on the Sundance that can compare to what you've achieved. Nothing here can compete with your future as a diver. Not one thing. Certainly not the love of a man like me."

Tory shivered convulsively. She turned her face suddenly, eluding the hand that held her silent. "Reever— oh, God!" Her breath came in sharply. She was afraid even to hope. "Do you really care for me?" she whispered.

Reever's hands clenched on Tory's sweet body before he controlled himself. "You deserve more from life than I can give you. You've earned it, and then some. I'm going to see that you get it if I have to tie you on the bus myself. Otherwise, someday you'd hate me. You'd look at me and you'd see the man who stole your dream and called what he was doing 'love.' I couldn't take that, little cat. Anything, even losing you, but not stealing your dream the same way I stole your innocence."

Tory stared at the bleakness of Reever's eyes and knew that he meant every word.

"Do you know what I was saying goodbye to tonight?" she asked softly.

"To the summer," he said, turning his head from side to side against the softness of her breasts, caressing her as he spoke. "You were saying goodbye to your innocence, to the Sundance. To me."

"No!" Tory caught Reever's face between her hands and tilted it up to her, willed him to listen, to believe. "I was saying goodbye to diving, Reever, not to you!"

A shudder passed over him, but the lines on his face did not lighten.

"I don't believe you," he said gently. "You dove perfectly. Why would you give it up?"

"Because it's not worth the risk of crippling myself," she said, her voice urgent. "I didn't believe that a few months ago, but I believe it now. You can throw me off the Sundance, but you can't change this simple truth: I will never again enter a diving competition. That part of my life is over." She covered Reever's mouth quickly, as he had once covered hers. "No, let me finish. Diving was my way of finding a home. I don't need that anymore. I was born for the mountains and the tall grass, the pines and the wind. The Sundance is my home."

Reever searched Tory's face for long moments while the silence stretched until she called his name softly, moving against him as she whispered her love again and again. He shuddered and stilled the aching words with a kiss.

"You're wrong," Reever said finally, lifting his head until he could see Tory's eyes. "You were born for me, not the Sundance." Slowly he merged his body with hers, taking her even as he gave himself completely to her. He brought his lips to hers, worshipped her mouth, and said, "Just as I was born for you. I love you, Tory. I've loved you all my life and didn't even know it."

His whispers became hers, two voices joined in promises of love, two people discovering the beauty that would always be within their reach, a lifetime of love unfolding before them.

SWEET WIND, WILD WIND

Chapter One

RELAX, LARA CHANDLER TOLD herself silently. Carson has never set foot on the Chandler homestead—and he never will. He hates even the thought of you. You're safe here.

As Lara heard her own thoughts, she smiled ruefully. She really didn't need to worry about running into Carson Blackridge, on or off the small piece of land that was surrounded by the Rocking B's lush range. Carson had made it very plain the last time he was with Lara that he had seen more than enough of her. Even years afterward the memory of the moment when she had offered herself and he had turned away made her blush and then pale. She had tried to exorcise the memory, but she had failed. Every time a man had done more than hold her hand or kiss her gently, the memory rose, freezing her.

Lara forced herself to take one deep breath, then another, trying to shake off the tension that had come over her ever since she had agreed to return to the Rocking B to write an informal history of a century of life on a Montana cattle ranch. With hands that trembled, she turned toward her suitcase, opened it and began to unpack with the efficient motions of someone accustomed to shuttling between two homes.

At least, normally Lara was efficient. Today her fingers seemed numb. The third time she dropped the mascara applicator that she rarely used on her thick black eyelashes, she made an exasperated sound. It had been four years since that humiliating incident with Carson. She should have gotten over it by now. But she hadn't. Four years wasn't long enough. She came from a long line of people for whom the past was very much a part of the present. Nor was there a safe place in the future for her to hide from the past. Whether she liked it or not, the past would always be there, all around her, inside her.

She had grown up listening to her grandfather's tales of the Rocking B as it had been a century before. As a child, the years separating her from the past had seemed insurmountable, a barrier as high as the glacier-carved mountains that surrounded and defined the ranch itself. As she grew up, the years shrank until they became as understandable, and almost as tangible, as the progression of the seasons.

Finally Lara had come to love the turning and returning of the years, grandparents seeing the faces of the past reborn in their grandchildren, the family stories told and retold until they became an informal history. She loved the larger human history as well, history written across the land itself, the extended family of mankind with its own rituals, its own unique patterns of disappointments and dreams passed from generation to generation.

History was a living part of Lara's personal life, and the Blackridges' Rocking B ranch was the center of it. She hadn't "agreed" to come back to do research so much as she had been compelled by her own needs.

Lara stood with her hands full of brightly colored underwear and looked around the room that her great-grandfather had built for the birth of his first child. To Jedediah Chandler, a free hundred-year lease must have seemed like a permanent grant. A homestead, not a leasehold. Yet in the end the land was only leased from the Blackridge family, not owned by the Chandlers, and the lease had expired two years ago. Larry Blackridge had extended the lease for the lifetime of Cheyenne Chandler, Lara's grandfather.

But Cheyenne was gone, and the homestead had passed into Blackridge hands. No more Chandlers would live in the expanded, often-repaired and much-loved family home that lay in the center of the Black-ridges' Rocking B ranch. The name of the little valley would go on, however, passed from generation to generation as stories were told about the past. It had been called the Chandler homestead for the past century. It would be called that in a hundred years. The names of Blackridge and Chandler had become part of the Montana landscape itself.

Which meant that Carson Blackridge was very much a part of Lara Chandler, no matter how hard she tried to ignore him, especially there in the midst of the Rocking B. Every time she turned around, she would think of him, remember him, remember what he had done to her. He was part of her personal history—in many ways, the most important part.

"Fine," Laura muttered to herself. "So write a paper about Carson and file it under *M* for Mistake. Or Miserable. Misogynist, how about that?"

She sighed and gave up trying to characterize Carson in a single polite word. It would have been easier to forget him if he had made her unhappy while they were together. He hadn't. Having him close, seeing his rare smiles come more frequently while he was with her, talking with him, touching him, laughing with him... Miserable? Hardly. For a few short months she had lived in the center of rainbows, and sunlight had been a river of gold pouring into her outstretched hands.

"Sure," said Lara in a clipped tone. "Pigs flew then, too. Remember?"

Swiftly she emptied the suitcase, wondering with every movement if she had made a mistake coming back. There was nothing to tie her to the Rocking B but memories and a history that had no place for her. Her grandfather was dead. Her mother was dead. And the man who had never called her daughter was also dead.

Lara's hands hesitated as she remembered the call that had come to her aunt's house two months before. She had answered the phone. Carson's deep, gritty voice had told her that Larry Blackridge was dead. Hearing Carson's voice again after four years had been like being dropped into fire. She had barely heard the words he was saying for the sudden roar of blood in her ears. And then the words had penetrated. The man who had adopted Carson and never called him son, the man who had fathered Lara and never called her daughter, the man her mother had loved well but not wisely— Lawrence Blackridge was dead.

To this day Lara didn't remember what she had said to Carson, or if she had said anything at all. Her next memory was of standing in the thin March twilight staring at the phone in her hand. A wailing sound was coming from the receiver. For an instant she had wondered if the phone were mourning her dead father. Finally she realized that she had simply kept the phone off the hook too long.

Lara hadn't gone to the funeral. She had told herself that she had stayed away because it was too soon after her own grandfather's death to face the sadness of another loss. Yet even as she told herself that, she knew it wasn't true. Cheyenne Chandler had lived and died as he wanted to, in the center of the ranch he loved. After years of declining health, death had come to him as a friend, taking nothing from him that he hadn't wanted to give. She would miss Cheyenne for the rest of her life, but she wouldn't mourn him. He was still a part of her; his laughter and gentleness lived in her memories, and the love he had given to her was in every breath she took.

It was Carson she hadn't wanted to face, not sorrow. Lara still didn't want to face him.

"You don't have to," she reminded herself as she snapped the big suitcase shut and shoved it under the bed. "Your study covers 1860 to 1960. Carson's personal memories of the ranch are useless. He was too young."

The idea of Carson's being too young for anything made Lara pause. She had never thought of him as a child. To her, he had always been an adult and the nine years' difference in their ages an unbridgeable gulf. Even when they had dated, she had been more than a little in awe of Carson. That had faded gradually as her lifelong infatuation with him had deepened into love. She had thought that he returned her love.

M. For Mistake. File it.

Lara walked aimlessly around the room, grateful that Carson had left the homestead untouched after Cheyenne's death. As she quartered the room restlessly, her fingers brushed over odds and ends from her childhood. The ribbons she had won barrel racing in local rodeos were faded. The glittering sunburst of quartz crystals she had found years ago was dusty. The framed picture of her riding her first horse was also dusty. Absently she cleaned the glass with the long tail of her old red shirt. As she stared at the faded photo, she wondered if Carson had a similar picture of himself somewhere in the ranch house that lay in the big valley below, less than a mile and more than a world away from the Chandler homestead.

Though Lara tried, she couldn't form the picture of Carson as a young boy in her imagination. All her mind could see was Carson as he was now—taller than other men, stronger, tougher. The length of his bones made him look almost lean. It wasn't until she had stood close to him that she realized just how powerful he really was. His wrists were easily twice as thick as hers, his hands and shoulders half again as broad as hers, and his whole body was layered with the supple, cleanly moving muscles of a natural athlete. The closest he came to softness was in the long, thickly curling eyelashes framing eyes that shifted color without warning from green to amber. His mink-brown hair was also thick, with a tendency to curl at the ends when it was damp. The rest of his hair was thick, nearly black, warm and springy to the touch. She had loved to tangle her fingers softly in it.

Lara reined in her straying thoughts with the ease of too much practice. She buried her sensual response to the memories so automatically that she didn't even notice it. She had tried to date other men since Carson had rejected her so completely, but she had not been able to respond to them. Because she froze when they attempted to be intimate with their touches, she assumed that she was naturally cold. She hadn't been that way with Carson, but then, Carson had always been the exception to every rule. She had loved him before she had learned any defenses against love.

It was different now. She was very well defended. She had had the best teacher. Carson Blackridge.

Abruptly Lara decided that she couldn't yet face the cartons of family photos and mementos that awaited her in her grandfather's bedroom. Everything was just as it had been when the final heart attack had caught Cheyenne surrounded by the lifetime of memories he was sorting through and packing away. Eventually she would have to complete the job Cheyenne had begun, but she would do it as a scholar rather than as a granddaughter.

Eventually, but not right now. She wasn't ready to face her own personal history with a scholar's necessary detachment. There was no hurry. Carson had told her faculty advisor that the university's representative could live on the Chandler homestead for as long as necessary to complete the study; the Rocking B had no use for the old house. Whether Carson had regretted the open-ended offer when he learned that Lara Chandler was the university's representative—or whether he even knew that she was the historian who would do the study of the Rocking B—was never mentioned by her advisor.

In any case, Cheyenne's handwritten journals of his lifetime as the Rocking B's ramrod would just have to wait for Lara to sort through them. It was afternoon, the early summer wind was blowing silky and warm and she hadn't been riding in weeks. There were a few Chandler horses mixed in with Blackridge stock in the upper pasture. She would catch Shadow and ride over the long, rolling ridges and hidden side valleys that made up the Rocking B. She would say hello to the land she loved and would have to leave at the end of summer, when the oral histories had been collected and she had no further excuse to remain on the homestead.

Outside, Lara saw the small signs of disrepair that had come in the six months since Cheyenne had died. The barbwire was sagging in the boggy spot near the pasture seep. By spring calves would be able to wiggle out beneath the wire. The front gate, too, was sagging.

By spring it would drag on the muddy ground, making life difficult for everyone coming to and going from the homestead. The lowest step on the porch was also sagging. By spring the step would be a menace waiting to trip the unwary.

But that wouldn't be a problem. By spring no one would be living on the homestead.

The mare that came at Lara's whistle was a graceful, spirited half Arab whose coat was the same blue-black as Lara's hair. Cheyenne had often teased Lara by saying that he had bought the leggy mare because he missed Lara after she went away to school. It might have been true; certainly Cheyenne had spoiled the mare in a way that he had none of his other horses.

"So you remember me, Shadow," murmured Lara, rubbing the mare's ears.

The horse bumped her nose softly against Lara's shirt and blew warm streams of air over her neck. Agile lips caught a long streamer of Lara's hair and began chewing.

"Hey," Lara laughed, retrieving her hair. "That's mine."

Serenely Shadow found another strand and began mouthing it.

"Must be that lemon shampoo," muttered Lara, grabbing her hair and backing away.

She fished around in her pockets until she found the rawhide strings she always carried when on the ranch. With flying fingers she bound her hair into a single long braid, tied it and flipped it over her shoulder. Immediately strands started to work loose and curl softly around her face, making her look younger than her twenty-two years. Her eyes were as clear and blue as a high-mountain lake—and as shadowed by hidden depths and currents. Her eyes hinted at mysteries and emotions that rarely ruffled her surface, just as the curving lines of her breasts and hips hinted at a womanly sensuality that only one man had ever touched.

Lara bridled the mare and led her back to the small barn. As she walked, she looked around several times, feeling as though someone were nearby. It wasn't an uneasy or frightening feeling. It was simply there, like sunshine. Yet every time she looked around, the countryside was empty of all but horses and cattle.

Inside the barn the feeling of another person being nearby diminished somewhat. With a shrug Lara began to curry the mare. As she worked, she realized that someone must have been caring for Shadow since her grandfather's death. The mare's coat had the sleekness that comes only from careful grooming, her long tail was free of tangles and her hooves had been trimmed and shod recently.

"Which one of Cheyenne's old friends have you wound around your delicate little hoof?" asked Lara. "Is it Jim-Bob or Willie? How about Dusty? Murchison?"

Shadow snorted and shifted her weight. Her long tail swished, sending flies buzzing off to find a less lively target.

"Not telling, huh? I don't blame you. If I had one of those tough old sons eating out of my hand, I'd keep it a secret, too."

Lara cinched the saddle tight, then automatically checked all the straps for wear as she did at the beginning of every summer when she returned to the ranch. The cinch buckle on the off side was new, as was the stirrup buckle. The webbing of the cinch itself had been replaced. With a muffled sound of surprise, Lara went over every bit of Shadow's tack. The homestead might be fraying at the edges, but Shadow's gear was not. It had been carefully reconditioned, all of it, from headstall to saddlebags. Nothing would fall apart or give way under sudden stress, throwing Lara.

"Well, Shadow. We owe somebody a double batch of chocolate chip cookies."

The mare nudged Lara firmly with a velvet muzzle, plainly wanting an end to preparations and a beginning to the ride. Shadow liked roaming over the land as well as Lara did.

"All right, all right," said Lara, shoving the mare's nose away from her stomach. "I hear you."

Lara led the mare out of the barn and mounted her swiftly, settling deep into the saddle. She expected a few wild minutes while Shadow worked off the months of not being ridden. Instead of a friendly round of bucking, Shadow immediately settled into a ground-eating lope. Somebody had been doing more than grooming and shoeing the mare. Someone had ridden her, as well. Someone who had demanded good manners and responsiveness but had done so in such a way that the mare's soft mouth and eagerness to be ridden remained intact.

"That lets out Murchison," Lara said, stroking the mare's black neck. "He's a good man, but he's got a heavy hand on the bit and spurs."

Shadow flicked one ear back toward her rider's voice. Then both the mare's ears shot forward. Lara looked up and saw the silhouette of a rider on the ridgeline to her right, which overlooked both the Chandler homestead's small valley and the Rocking B's ranch house in the larger, lower river valley. As the mare caught the scent of horse and rider, she nickered a welcome.

Lara didn't feel nearly so welcoming. She didn't need to see the distinctive patterns of the Appaloosa that was Carson's favorite mount to recognize the rider as Carson Blackridge. No man rode quite like him, sitting easily on the horse as though he had been born there rather than in a distant city. No other man had Carson's combination of strength, quickness and male grace.

Without hesitation Lara guided Shadow onto the left fork of the trail, away from Carson. Simultaneously her legs tightened around the mare's sleek barrel, urging a faster pace. Lara's reactions were completely unconscious. She had come to terms with her life as the illegitimate daughter of Lawrence Blackridge. She had accepted her mother's death ten years before in one of the summer thunderstorms that Becky Chandler had loved so much. Lara had accepted her grandfather's death and the loss of the home and the land she loved.

But she had not come to terms with offering herself to a man who hadn't wanted her in any way at all.

Lara could tell by Shadow's actions that Carson was pacing them along the ridgeline. He knew the land as well as she did. Soon the valley would narrow to a ravine that opened into the Rocking B's home pasture. Another path intersected that ravine, the path that Carson was on. Long before the safety of the pasture was reached, she would be trapped. She would have to see Carson up close, talk to him, acknowledge him in some way—and she had promised herself that she wouldn't have to do any of those things until she was ready.

She was not ready. Not now, when she was seeing her home for the first time since Cheyenne's death. Not now, when she was having to say hello and goodbye to so much. Maybe tomorrow. Or the day after. Next week. Next month. But not now. She was too vulnerable. She had always been too vulnerable with Carson.

Although Lara gave no signal that the distant rider would be able to see, Shadow suddenly veered left, sliding on her hocks down the steep, grassy hillside with the agility that made her a great rough-country horse. Bear Creek was conquered in a long leap, and then the mare settled in for some serious running. Lara bent low over Shadow's neck, feeling her braid come apart until her long hair unfurled in the wind like a black silk flag. Although she never looked back, she could tell the exact instant when the fleet little mare took her out of Carson's sight because the feeling of being watched went away. Slowly, gently, Lara brought Shadow back to a lope, secure in her freedom from Carson's presence.

Only later did Lara wonder what Carson had been doing on Chandler land. As far as she knew, he had never so much as ridden across the homestead. Perhaps that was the explanation—he was getting acquainted with a part of the Rocking B that was now his to manage. That would be like Carson. Whatever she might think of him personally, there was no doubt about his qualifications to manage a ranch. During the years since his father's stroke, Carson had proven his ability to make the land and the business thrive. He was a Blackridge in everything but blood.

Unfortunately, blood had been all that mattered to the man who had adopted Carson. Blood hadn't mattered enough for Larry Blackridge to divorce his wife and marry the woman who had given him a daughter, though. Lara had often wondered why. Like her illegitimate birth, Larry's obsession with a blood heir was well-known. Lara had never asked her grandfather to explain the actions of her mother's lover, or to explain her mother's continuing love for a man who would father a child and then never acknowledge it. That subject was the one topic that had been guaranteed to make sadness replace laughter on Cheyenne's weathered face.

In the end Lara had stopped wondering and simply accepted her parents' mysteriously interwoven lives as she accepted the summer lightning or the crystalline patterns of ice forming at the edges of autumn creeks. The reality of ice and lightning she understood. The mystery of them remained untouched, untouchable.

By the time Lara reached the broad river valley that was the heart of the Rocking B, she felt calmer, almost ashamed of having fled Carson. He had probably been as surprised to come across her as she had been to see him. And he had probably been relieved when she chose another trail, making it unnecessary for either of them to have a travesty of polite conversation. Surely he could be no more eager to confront her than she was to confront him. In fact, she was certain that it was a tribute to her faculty advisor's persuasive charms that she was on the ranch at all. She could just imagine what Carson had had to say on the subject of an informal "family" history of the Rocking B done by Larry Blackridge's bastard.

The sound of a long "Yoooooo!" called Lara out of her thoughts. She turned and saw a man standing in his stirrups, waving his hat in wide sweeps to catch her attention. She recognized Willie and turned Shadow quickly toward the cowhand. As the horses came alongside, he bent over to give her a quick hug.

"You get prettier every time I see you, Lara. Got your mother's eyes, and God knows He never made nothing more blue. How's the city treating you?"

"I got a reprieve from concrete," Lara said, standing in the stirrups so she could reach Willie's dark cheek with a kiss. "I'm on the ranch until Carson's patience runs out or I pump the cowhands dry of Rocking B stories—whichever comes first."

"Hell's fire, gal, we ain't never gonna run out of tales, and that's a fact. Looks like you're here forever and a day. We're all champing and prancing in place, just waiting for you to unlimber your tape recorder and make us famous."

"I don't want to interfere with your work," Lara said quickly, voicing the same fear that she had to her advisor. She didn't want to do anything that would call down Carson's attention, much less his wrath.

"Now don't you get to worrying about Carson," Willie said, patting Lara's hand with his gnarled, work-scarred fingers. "He's already told the hands that he's all for helping to educate the dumb bas—er, city folks—that wouldn't know which end of a horse bit and which kicked. He told us to be right helpful to you. Not that we wouldn't have anyways. Cheyenne's granddaughter is solid gold in these parts, and Carson knows it."

Lara gave Willie a dubious look. "Carson told you to help me? Are we speaking of the same Carson Harrington Blackridge?"

"The exact same fellow," Willie said, nodding firmly.

Lara made a sound that could have meant anything and nothing.

"Now I ain't saying that he don't have a few blind spots, same as anyone," continued Willie, patting Lara's shoulder in silent understanding. "He's a hard man but a good one, and the best damn ramrod this outfit has seen since it registered the brand—and that includes your granddaddy Cheyenne."

Lara gave Willie a startled look.

He nodded firmly. "And what's more, Cheyenne was the first to say so. Cheyenne didn't have no patience for computers telling a man what to do when it rains, or for cows throwing calves by bulls they never, er, met. Carson's not crazy about them computers, neither, but he knows what the ranch needs, and he sees that it gets it."

For a moment Lara didn't know what to say. Then she spoke in a soft, husky voice. "I'm glad Carson is good for the ranch. This land deserves someone who knows and loves it for what it is. The Rocking B is alive, just like we are, and it needs care. If you care for it, it will take care of you. Granddad knew that, and he taught it to me."

Willie's narrowed, dark eyes searched Lara's face, seeing both truth and sadness in her expression. "If'n you were to ask, I'm sure Carson would let you stay on at the homestead as long as you want. Hell, he said as much to me after the Queen Bi—er, after his mother died."

Lara almost smiled at Willie's slip of the tongue. Sharon Harrington Blackridge—known to the hands as the Queen Bitch—had been a difficult woman to get along with. But then, she had had reason. It couldn't have been easy on her knowing that her husband's mistress and bastard were living on the ranch less than a mile away from her home. Lara didn't know why Mrs. Blackridge hadn't divorced her husband. Certainly there hadn't seemed to be much love lost between them, even after Becky Chandler had died. The Blackridges' enduring marriage was another mystery from Lara's childhood that she hadn't pursued as she grew up, another part of her personal history that was defined by silence rather than understanding.

"If'n you don't believe me," Willie continued earnestly, "just ask Carson."

"No," Lara said quickly. She smiled to take the edge off her refusal. "More than a hundred years ago, Jedediah Chandler saved Edward Blackridge from being mauled by a grizzly. The Chandlers have lived for a long time on that. The old debt has been more than repaid."

Willie grunted and pulled his hat lower, a gesture Lara knew well from her childhood. He disagreed, but he wasn't going to argue the point directly. "Mebbe," he muttered under his breath. "But that don't say spit about new debts, do it?"

Lara pretended she hadn't heard because she knew that Willie hadn't meant her to hear. None of the hands had ever spoken to her about the circumstances of her birth or the man who was her father. Willie might compliment Lara on having her mother's blue eyes, but he would never mention the source of Lara's black hair, widow's peak and full mouth.

"What I thought I'd do," Lara said, her voice cheerful and determined, "is talk to the hands in the evenings after dinner. During the day I can go through Cheyenne's journals and take pictures of the ranch and read various documents that are part of the ranch history. And transcribe tapes," she added, sighing. That was one thing she wasn't looking forward to. Hours and hours and hours of typing when she would rather be out riding.

"Sure glad that steer ain't wearing my brand," Willie said, shaking his head. "These fingers never got the hang of a pencil. A rope, now," he nodded, smiling. "In my day, I was the champion roper of eight counties. Roped anything that moved." He settled more comfortably in the saddle, dug out a twist of chewing tobacco and bit off a hunk. "Did I ever tell you about the time the boys bet me I couldn't rope Larry's spotted bull? That old bull was the fastest, meanest—" Willie looked up suddenly as he caught movement at the corner of his eye. "Wonder what Carson wants."

Lara had seen the movement, too, and had recognized the big Appaloosa cantering toward them. "He's probably going to chew on me for keeping you from your work. See you later, Willie. I'd better get back and get to work myself."

A nudge of Lara's heels sent Shadow loping off across the huge pasture. There were three gates between her and the homestead on the roundabout route she had hurriedly chosen to avoid Carson. The last gate was in an isolated draw above the homestead. The draw was little more than a crease in the land where the wind gathered until it bent the grass in supple waves, like a hand stroking thick fur. The sound of the wind was like fur, too, cool and smooth and soft.

The beauty of the place was lost on Lara as she rounded the shoulder of a hill at a canter and dropped into the hidden crease. When she saw the rider dismounted by the gate, waiting for her, her first impulse was to spin Shadow on her hocks and gallop off in another direction. Any other direction. She would have done just that, too, but her body wouldn't respond to the frantic messages of her mind.

Carson Blackridge was less than ten feet away from her. She hadn't been that close to him in years. Nearly four years, to be exact. She had been naked then. She felt naked now.

"Hello, Lara. Welcome home."

Chapter Two

FOR LONG MOMENTS LARA SIMPLY stared at Carson. His eyes looked very green as he watched her, but she knew that at night, in lamplight, his eyes would be nearly gold. And in passion, nearly black. Or had it been contempt rather than passion that had darkened his eyes when he looked at her, touched her, undressed her?

"Carson."

The word was forced past stiff lips. Lara said nothing more, for the only words she had for him were from the hurtful past, like the images swirling up out of the locked-away places in her mind, memories she had spent years trying to forget.

He hadn't changed. He was still big, still powerful, still able to make her heart turn inside out with a look. It had shocked her to see him standing there waiting for her. It was still shocking her, ripping away the careful layers of control built so painfully through the years, leaving nothing but naked vulnerability.

She had loved him. He had not loved her. She had told herself that she had gotten over that and him. She had been wrong. The scar tissue wasn't thick enough over the old wounds. He could still hurt her.

Carson's hand flashed out, grabbing Shadow's bridle in the instant before Lara would have spun the horse around and fled.

"Easy, baby, easy," he muttered.

At first Lara thought that Carson was speaking to her. Then she saw his big hand stroking Shadow's neck and realized that he was trying to soothe the mare, who had sensed the sudden race of fear in her rider. As Lara watched Carson, the years collapsed and she saw again that same hand so gentle on her own body, stroking away her fear as he had slowly unbuttoned her blouse and slid his hand inside. She had loved his hands then, so big, so warm, so unexpectedly tender.

With a shudder Lara looked away, fighting memories, fighting battles she thought she had already won— or at least had survived.

"Let go," she said, her voice little more than a harsh whisper.

"Look at me."

Lara's refusal was written in every tight line of her body.

Carson waited, then said quietly, "I made a mistake four years ago, Lara. I'm not going to let you make one now. Look at me."

Her head turned sharply. Wisps of black hair blew across her face, but they didn't conceal her surprise. "What?"

Carson's fingers closed over Lara's right hand. Gently he raised her palm to his mouth. His teeth pressed into the pad of flesh at the base of her thumb in a sweet, wild caress that sent a burst of sensation through her, igniting fires that had slept for years. When his tongue traced the tiny indentations in her skin left by his teeth, she forgot to breathe. Slowly his lips came to rest on her inner wrist, where her pulse beat frantically.

"That's what I'm talking about, little fox," Carson said deeply, looking at her.

Lara tried to pull her hand free.

"I want to start all over again," Carson said, holding on to her hand, his grip as gentle and implacable as his voice. "I wanted to do it nice and slow, but you wouldn't let me. You've done everything but dive down a prairie-dog hole to avoid me." He released her fingers, frowning as she snatched back her hand. "We're going to strike a bargain, Lara. If you stop running from me, I'll continue to give you the freedom of the Rocking B to work on your history. And that includes the documents and photos I have at the big house."

For a few seconds Lara could only stare. She had desperately wanted those family archives for her history but had been afraid to ask for them. The first Blackridge had been a photo buff at a time when photography was still an arcane art requiring a wagonload of equipment. Other Blackridges had been equally fascinated by photos. There were pictures up at the house that were literally priceless records of a time and a style of living that would never come again.

All of Lara's life she had wanted to be allowed to see those photos, but Larry Blackridge had kept the collection locked away from everyone, even his unacknowledged daughter, the last living Blackridge. The thought of being allowed access to that treasure trove was literally breathtaking to someone who loved history as much as Lara did.

Carson saw the look on Lara's face and smiled. "I thought that would do it. You really like the idea of getting your hands on those photos, don't you?"

She nodded slowly, knowing it was only the truth.

"Enough to stop running?"

Helplessly Lara nodded again.

"What happened four years ago won't happen again," Carson said, his voice deep, his eyes pinning her. "I never make the same mistake twice."

Lara didn't know which surprised her more—Carson's promise or the implication that she had just agreed to take up precisely where they had left off four years ago. She had not agreed to that at all. She would never permit herself to be that vulnerable again. The mere idea of it terrified her.

"Carson, I didn't agree to—to—" Lara made a helpless gesture with her hand as words failed her.

"Sleep with me?" Carson supplied smoothly, his smile a slash of white across his tanned face. "I know. I just wanted you to be certain that there's no reason to run from me anymore. That's all in the past, dead and buried. I'm going to make damn sure it stays that way."

"Why?" asked Lara, not understanding. For nearly four years she hadn't had any contact with Carson. Nor had he appeared to want any. Now he was offering to... Exactly what was he offering to do?

For a moment Carson's face shifted into a hard expression that warned of both his famous temper and his equally famous determination. "Like I said, I made a mistake. That's all I'm going to say about it. It's history, Lara, and unlike you, I never look back."

Carson's words were clipped, final. Lara knew that the subject was closed and it would stay that way, no matter what her wishes might be. Confused, more than a little angry, she watched as he turned and opened the gate for her.

"I'll be around in the evenings if you want to go through the photos," he said. "Anytime after dinner is fine."

The thought of spending evenings with Carson shocked Lara's tongue into action.

"Thank you, but that's not necessary. If you'll just point out the boxes, I'll take it from there."

Carson's head snapped up. Beneath the dark brim of his hat, his eyes were like pale green crystal viewed through an amber lens. "Running already?" he asked softly. "Is that how you plan on keeping your end of the bargain?"

Lara opened her mouth, but no words came out. She swallowed and said tightly, "I have no desire to be alone with you, Carson. Surely that can't come as a surprise to you."

For an instant Carson's eyes closed, and an expression that could have been either pain or anger tightened his face into grim lines. When his eyes opened, they were bleak.

"For God's sake, I'm not going to attack you," he said flatly. "What happened a minute ago was more of a warning than a seduction. I'm a hunter. If you run, I chase—and I catch what I chase. If you stop running, I'll stop cornering you." Carson's mouth shifted into a hard smile. "So relax. I'm not exactly starved for female companionship, if that's what's worrying you. There are more than enough women around who don't run the other way when they see me coming."

It was foolish, insane, but Lara couldn't help flinching at the idea of Carson with other women. She had no hold on him, she never had, yet the thought of his big hands caressing someone else made Lara's whole body clench in silent rejection. He hadn't wanted her, but he wanted other women.

And he had taught her to want no other man.

Carson saw the tiny, betraying flicker of Lara's eyelids when he mentioned other women. Surprise showed very briefly on his face, to be replaced by speculation. He watched her stiff back as Shadow walked through the gate. Before he could say anything, Lara kicked Shadow into a canter, leaving Carson alone with the gate and the grass and the soft wind blowing around him.

LARA LEFT THE LAST OF THE DINNER dishes to dry in the old plastic drainer that sat on the counter. Although it was seven o'clock, there was a lot of light and warmth left in the countryside. Montana was far enough north to have long summer days and equally long winter nights. Lara had always enjoyed both the light and the darkness, for each season had its special moments for her, its unique excitement.

As Lara dried her hands, she couldn't help thinking that the house seemed unnaturally quiet. She was accustomed to living alone but not to being alone in the old family home. She still expected to see her grandfather out of the corner of her eye, his legs stretched out on the old ottoman and smoke curling around his face from the pipe the doctor had forbidden and Cheyenne couldn't give up.

She didn't fight the tears that came suddenly to her eyes with the fresh realization that she would never see her grandfather again. She had known that coming back would be hard on her for a time. She also knew that occasional tears would help her to accept what could not be changed. There were so many good things to remember, so much of the past that deserved to be cherished and recorded. That was part of the reason she had come back to the ranch—to listen to the gentle ghosts of her childhood whispering to her, telling her about age and change and generations blending one into the other as naturally as summer blended into fall and winter into spring.

She might be alone, but she wasn't isolated, cut off from the rest of humanity. She was a part of history, both that of her family and that of the state she lived in, as well as of the nation and the larger international community of the world. Through that shared history, she was connected to life in countless ways that were both subtle and profound.

Lara's footsteps quickened as she went into the bedroom to change. The thought of being allowed to see the Blackridge archives had been bubbling through her all afternoon like a hidden spring. She didn't know what she would find. She did know that for a few hours she would live in another time, would see the land through the eyes of people long dead and would experience life in a new way. That was the endless fascination of studying history for her. History was her private time machine, letting her slide back through the years to share experiences and feelings and insights that would otherwise have been buried beneath the passing of generations.

It wasn't the conquerors or kings who moved Lara's mind and emotions. It was the ordinary people who worked and dreamed, cried and laughed and loved, bore children and finally died, leaving behind a legacy known only to the families who passed stories and more tangible mementos from hand to hand through the generations. It was those people Lara wanted to discover, those small histories she wanted to write, for they were the often unappreciated foundation upon which kings and conquerors and countries were built. For Lara, there was no excitement to equal the moment of discovery when a person long dead lived once again in her mind, teaching her the insights and dreams of another time.

"And if you stand around thinking about it any longer," Lara told herself crisply, "you're going to miss your chance to rummage through history tonight. This isn't the city. Folks around here go to bed early and get up the same way."

Her words drifted through the quiet house and dissipated in the larger silence of the land beyond.

"You're going to have to get yourself a cat or a dog to talk to."

Lara smiled wistfully to herself as she dressed. She loved animals, but the apartment where she lived didn't allow pets. She had tried goldfish. It just wasn't the same. There was life in a fish but no warmth, nothing to equal the gentle rasp of a hound's tongue or the purring contentment of a cat curled in her lap.

A critical look in the old, spotted mirror told Lara that everything was buttoned, zipped and clean. She had been tempted to wear something tonight other than her standard ranch uniform of jeans, boots and cotton shirt. All that had prevented her was the certainty that Carson would think she had dressed up for him—and he would have been right. She had been a girl rather than a woman when he had dated her. She wouldn't have minded wearing clothes that emphasized the difference four years had made in her body.

Unbidden came the thought that perhaps now he wouldn't turn away from her. Perhaps now she was woman enough to hold his attention when he undressed her and looked at her.

Even as the thought came, Lara felt fear burst through her in a freezing wave. Never again would she be naked in front of a clothed man. Never again would she whimper with pleasure when a man's mouth touched her breast. There was no pleasure in that kind of vulnerability, only pain.

Lara turned away from the mirror, frightened by the unexpected, dangerous female vanity that had wanted Carson to admire what he had once rejected so cruelly.

What she didn't understand was just how womanly she looked despite her casual clothes. She had worn jeans for so many years that she didn't realize how they emphasized the length of her legs, the tempting curves of her hips and the contrasting slenderness of her waist. The cotton blouse was soft, fitted and clung to her breasts like an ice-blue shadow. The windbreaker she had tossed over her shoulders was a vivid scarlet that brought out the natural color in her cheeks and made her hair shine like polished obsidian. Her lips, too, were red, and their wide bow hinted at both humor and passion. Despite her lack of fancy clothes, she was more than enough to make a man's hands itch to follow her curves.

Lara had discovered long ago that a backpack was more practical for her than a briefcase and purse. The navy-blue pack was propped against the doorway in the living room, already stuffed with everything she might need for her research that night. She shrugged the straps into place and went through the door, closing but not locking it behind her. Because she had never looked in the mirror while wearing the backpack, she didn't know that its straps snugged the blouse tight across her firm breasts, subtly revealing the sheer pink outlines of her bra and hinting at the deeper pink of her nipples. The button between her breasts strained at its fastening, allowing the puckered cloth above and below to reveal flashes of smooth flesh with each breath.

The slanting evening light turned the land to green and gold and ruddy bronze as Lara walked along the edge of the dirt road curving down into the big valley. She could have driven to the ranch house or ridden Shadow, but the mild evening fairly begged to be enjoyed on foot. One of her best memories of the time when her mother had been alive was of walking over the land with her in the evenings, when the earth itself lay hushed beneath the condensing weight of night.

It was from her mother that Lara had learned the savage beauty of mountain thunderstorms. Even after her mother had died while hiking alone in an unexpected hailstorm, Lara had continued to walk the land during times when the wild wind blew, seeing lightning even through her closed eyelids and feeling thunder in the very marrow of her bones.

As Lara approached the old ranch house, her steps slowed. She had been in the big house eighteen times, once for every Christmas before she went away to school. It was not a unique tribute to her status as a bastard Blackridge. Every other child whose parents worked or lived on the ranch had also been invited to the Rocking B's Christmas Day festivities. Santa— usually Cheyenne plus pillows, towels and the most unlikely white beard ever to grace lean cheeks—had handed out presents to squealing children in the shadow of a huge tree cut from a forest high in the mountains.

Lara didn't know when she had first looked at Lawrence Blackridge standing next to the tree and realized that he was her father. She did know that she had always instinctively avoided Sharon Blackridge, whose cold gray eyes were a fitting match for her tight-lipped smile.

That's over now. Mrs. Blackridge is dead. When I knock on that door, I won't have to pray that I'll be able to avoid her. So relax. I'm an adult now, a scholar invited here to do a history of the Rocking B, not just someone's bastard kid.

There was an assortment of ranch vehicles parked along the circular blacktop drive, including a flashy convertible that Lara didn't recognize. Somehow it didn't look like something Carson would have owned, which meant that the car probably belonged to one of the temporary hands the ranch hired every summer to help with branding, calving and rebuilding winter-ruined fences.

The ranch house was only a few decades old. Gossip said it had been built to amuse the Queen Bitch after she had discovered that she couldn't have children. The house was big, well insulated and finished in a combination of native stone and lumber, which blended beautifully with the spectacular setting. The door knocker was a polished brass horseshoe turned upside down to hold good luck within its deep curve.

The first time Lara used the knocker, she was so hesitant that the sound barely reached her own ears. The second time the clean metallic cry carried throughout the house. As the door began to open, Lara's heart wedged in her throat. She wanted to see history, not Carson Blackridge. When Yolanda's wrinkled face and wide smile appeared in the opening, Lara was almost dizzy with relief. The smile she gave the cook was so brilliant that the woman blinked.

"*Ai,* Lara, you are even more pretty than your mama. Come in. Let me look at you."

Lara walked inside and hugged the old woman who had been Cheyenne's favorite card partner as well as the ranch housekeeper and cook who had always had a treat on hand for any child brave enough to sneak through the backyard and tap on the kitchen window. Yolanda had been on the ranch for as long as Lara could remember.

"Hello, Yolanda. You haven't gotten a bit older. What's your secret?"

"You are too young to know," Yolanda said promptly, grinning and showing three gold teeth.

"Then I guess I'm just going to have to get old," Lara said, laughing.

Yolanda smiled. "You have eaten dinner?"

"Yes."

"Alone? At the homestead?"

She nodded.

Yolanda shook her head disapprovingly. "You must eat here from now on. It is not good to eat alone."

For a moment Lara couldn't believe what she had heard. More than any other single thing that had happened since she had come back, the invitation to dinner brought home to her the fact that Mrs. Blackridge was truly dead. Had she still been alive, Lara could have starved to death on the front porch before she would have received an invitation to eat inside with Sharon Blackridge.

Yolanda nodded as though she knew what Lara was thinking. "*Sí*," she said. "It has changed now that the Queen—Mrs. Blackridge is dead. It is a big house for just one man. Carson, he is lonely, I think."

Lara made a sound that could have meant anything or nothing. "Is he around now?"

"*Sí*. He told me if you come to bring you right to the library." Yolanda's face changed. "I think he will be glad to have some help with *la huera*. *Ai*, that one is as stubborn as a burro."

From the kitchen came the sound of a strident buzzer. Yolanda muttered a few Spanish words under her breath. "The cake," she explained. "It is ready."

"Go ahead. I'll wait."

Yolanda shook her gray head vigorously. "The library," she said, turning Lara and pointing her down the hall. "It is the room on the right. Go, go. He is waiting and so is my cake."

For a moment longer Lara hesitated, watching Yolanda's broad form vanish into the kitchen. Then she took a deep breath, squared her shoulders beneath the backpack and walked quickly through the living room. Everything looked strange to her, subtly out of place. She realized that it was the first time she had ever seen the room without a huge evergreen dominating the corner opposite the fireplace and holly wreaths burning greenly along the stone walls.

The library door was ajar. Lara knocked lightly on it, heard Carson's growled "Come in" and pushed the door fully open, taking a step into the room. That step was as far as she got before she froze.

Carson's shirt was open to his waist, revealing a thick mat of dark, curling hair. Light from the room washed over him like a caress, igniting small fires in his golden eyes and bringing the powerful muscles of his chest into high relief. His hand was rubbing the back of his neck as though to relieve muscles tightened by fatigue—or desire.

Too late Lara remembered that *la huera* meant "the blonde." And that was just what the woman was, a tall, lushly built strawberry blonde who was reaching for Carson with manicured hands and pouting mouth. Her silk blouse was all but undone, showing the swell and sway of breasts unconfined by any bra. Carson was looking down at the smooth flesh being offered to him, and there was a sardonic curl to his hard mouth.

"What is it, Yolanda?" asked Carson, closing his eyes and rubbing his neck. "Does one of the hands need me?"

Lara couldn't force an answer past her lips. The sight of Carson's unbuttoned shirt had brought back an explosion of sensual memories she had kept buried for years, except in her uncontrollable, hotly twisting dreams—Carson stripping her clothes away with those big, warm hands and then bending down to her, his mouth caressing her breast until she thought she would die of the sweet fire bursting through her body.

But she hadn't died. Not in fire. She had frozen to death when he had turned away from her nakedness as though it repelled him.

Would he turn away from the blonde at the last instant as he did with me?

Lara looked at the woman's exposed breasts and open, shining lips. The blonde didn't look like a woman who expected rejection. She looked like a woman who knew very well how to please the man smiling down at her. The thought made Lara shudder as sweat broke in a clammy wave over her skin. A soft, choked sound came from her throat.

Carson's eyes opened as he spun swiftly and saw Lara standing in the doorway, her eyes blank, her hand raised as though to push something away.

"I'm—I'm sorry," Lara stammered. "Yolanda told me to—she said you—"

"No problem," Carson said dryly. "Susanna just stopped by to see if I needed company. I don't so she's on her way home." He rubbed his neck and moved his head to ease the tight, aching muscles. "Coffee?" he asked Lara, ignoring Susanna and gesturing with his free hand toward a tray sitting on his desk.

"Let me, darling," Susanna said, standing on tiptoe to knead Carson's shoulders. "I know just where those old headaches tie you in itty-bitty knots."

Lara turned away before she saw Carson pull Susanna's hands from his body with a gesture that shouted of impatience.

"I'll—maybe tomorrow, or—" Lara gave up trying to talk coherently while her mind was reeling. She spun and all but ran toward the living room. She was halfway there when she heard Carson calling her name. She didn't even hesitate. Yolanda came rushing out of the kitchen as Lara reached the living room.

"You are leaving so soon?"

"Carson's—busy."

Lara's pale face told Yolanda that she should have been the one to open the library door. "*Ai*, that damned *huera!* She was after him again, no?"

"She was after him, yes. And she caught him."

Yolanda realized that, short of wrestling Lara for the door handle, she couldn't prevent her from leaving. "Go to the bunkhouse," Yolanda said quickly. "The hands, they are all hoping to talk with you. They tell me so just tonight. Go. You will see."

Lara bolted through the open door just as she heard Carson call her name again. She kept going without looking back.

"Damn!" snarled Carson as he stood in the hallway, frowning fiercely, his open shirt flapping in the breeze from the front door.

"*Ai*, no wonder the little one runs," Yolanda said, closing the door and throwing up her hands. "That is no way to win a wife, señor!"

Carson turned toward Yolanda. "What the hell—"

"I am old, señor, but not deaf or stupid. I hear the old man and his wife yelling at night. I know that he wanted what was only right and just for his blood child. I know that he wanted to see grandchildren from his own body inherit the Rocking B." Yolanda grunted. "And how can that happen but to have Lara Chandler become your wife, *verdad?* It is a thing much to be desired."

"Is that what you told Lara?" asked Carson, his voice low, deadly.

Yolanda lifted her hands to the ceiling and called upon God in torrents of Spanish.

"Answer me!" snarled Carson.

The old woman muttered and dropped her hands. "I am not a cow to be stupid about such things. I said nothing to the little one of what I know. The heart of a girl is not moved by what is necessary or right. It is moved only by love." Yolanda shrugged. "Or the appearance of love, *verdad? Ni modo*. It does not matter. Once *los niños* arrive, a girl loses her foolishness and takes her man for what he is—an animal made by God in one of his weaker moments." Yolanda glared at Carson. "But she is not yet big with your child, *hombre*. Walk soft, and whisper sweet things to her. And get rid of that *huera* cow!"

Carson's lips twitched, and then he threw back his head and laughed. Yolanda tried to continue glaring but couldn't. She laughed, too, shaking her head. She had raised Carson as much as his mother had. He could always get around Yolanda, and he knew it.

"All right, I'll whisper sweet nothings," Carson said, smiling. Then his smile faded, and his expression became as hard as the stone mountains. "But you be damn sure you don't say anything to Lara about Larry's last wishes, *comprendes?* I mean it, Yolanda. Stay the hell out of this."

The old woman looked at Carson and nodded slowly. She understood. If she interfered, nothing would save her from Carson's wrath. In that he was very much like the man who had adopted him.

"Carson?" called Susanna from the library door.

"Goodbye," Carson said carelessly, heading for the stairway that led to the second-floor bedrooms.

"I thought we were going to—"

"No." Carson's voice was firm. He didn't pause on the stairway. "I told you seven months ago that it was over. Go back to town and your banker boyfriend. Yolanda," he continued, raising his voice, "what kind of cake did you say Lara liked?"

"Chocolate," called the old woman to Carson's broad, retreating back.

"Bake one."

"Is your nose dead from *la huera*'s cheap perfume?" demanded the old woman. "Such a cake is right now cooling on the kitchen counter!"

"You're an angel from heaven," retorted Carson, pausing long enough to wink over his shoulder at Yolanda.

Susanna watched the long, powerful legs vanish up the stairway just beyond her reach, heard the bedroom door slam shut and said a few very inelegant words as she stalked to the front door. Under Yolanda's baleful eye, *la huera* climbed behind the wheel of the convertible and roared up the driveway with far more speed than skill.

Carson didn't notice Susanna's angry departure. He was standing by the bedroom window, watching Lara hurry toward the bunkhouse. As he remembered the stunned expression on her face when she had seen his shirt open to his waist, he smiled like a chess player whose opening gambit has been an unqualified success. Whistling softly, he tested the stubble on his cheeks, decided it was too harsh for Lara's luminous skin and went to shave.

He would give her an hour. Maybe two. Then he would go after her. The thought of catching her brought a slow smile to his mouth and a flood of heat through his body. He never should have let her get away four years ago. He had wanted her ever since.

Now he would have her, and the Rocking B as well.

Chapter Three

WILLIE'S NARROW FACE SPLIT INTO a grin when he spotted Lara standing on the bunkhouse steps.

"Come in, gal, come in! We was just talking about you and wondering if'n you was going to drop by soon."

Lara's smile was a bit grim and her face was flushed, but no one seemed to notice. She was grateful. She had been as shocked by the sudden flood of anger she had felt while she walked to the bunkhouse as she had been by her response to the sight of Carson's bare chest.

Who did he think he was to ask me over to look at the Blackridge photos and then to dangle a cheap blonde under my nose?

Even as the words echoed in Lara's head, she realized that she had no right to ask the question. In the first place, she hadn't told Carson that she was coming over that night; she had left him standing at the gate without a word as to when—or if—she would come to the ranch house. In the second place, if he wanted to chase cheap blondes—or even expensive ones—through his library, it was none of her business. In the third place—in the third place—Lara's thoughts fragmented on the memory of Carson standing and rubbing his neck wearily, his shirt open to the waist and light shifting over his powerful torso with each of his movements. It had been all she could do not to simply turn and run without saying a word. She had been very shy of men since Carson had rejected her. Even the thought of being naked and being touched by a man frightened her. She had once thought that making love would be beautiful, but Carson had taught her that it was hurtful and unspeakably tawdry. The shame of the moment when she had offered herself and he had refused still splintered through her at unexpected moments, freezing her.

"You remember Murchison, don't you?" asked Willie.

"Of course. Hello, Murchison." Lara repeated the greeting to Jim-Bob and Dusty. "Which one of you do I have to thank for repairing Shadow's tack and shoeing her?"

A chorus of disclaimers went up, capped by Willie's calm words. "Musta been Carson. When he heard you was coming, he had the old homestead cleaned. He caught Shadow and shook the kinks out of her, too. Guess he don't want you getting thrown. That's a right lively little mare, 'specially after running loose for durn near a year."

Lara's mouth opened, but no words came out. She could hardly believe that Carson had gone out of his way to help her. Carson, who had barely spoken to her at Cheyenne's funeral. Of course, if she was honest, she hadn't given Carson much of a chance to say or do anything. She had looked right through him when he had tried to offer her comfort. The only crying she had done had been in Yolanda's understanding arms while Larry Blackridge had sat nearby in his new wheelchair, looking exhausted by the strokes that had ultimately killed him. Sharon Blackridge hadn't been at the funeral; she had died weeks before.

With an involuntary shake of her head, Lara put away the memory of Cheyenne's funeral and her unacknowledged father's illness. Both men had lived full, productive, active lives, surrounded by the country and the ranch they loved. There was nothing for her to pity or regret in that, no cause for her sorrow or grief. If she could die after a life that was half as interesting and constructive as theirs had been, she would know that she had lived well.

Willie finished the introductions without noticing that Lara's attention was divided between the past and the present. She smiled and murmured the correct words as she memorized the faces young and old that were in the bunkhouse. Twelve men, more than she ever remembered having lived on the Rocking B. The ranch had flourished under Carson's leadership in the past few years, as illness forced Larry Blackridge to give over the reins to his adopted, well-educated and very shrewd son.

The men who lived in the Rocking B's large bunkhouse were a mixture of youth and age and everything in between. That was common to big ranches, where men came and went with the seasons. Most of the hands had been born on a farm or a ranch somewhere in the West, but some of them had come from the East's overcrowded cities and had found a home in the uncrowded lands where cattle and sheep grazed. Some of the men, like Willie, were determined bachelors who were painfully shy with any woman they hadn't known as a little girl. Others, like Murchison, were divorced. Still others, like the handsome young man known only as Spur, had an appreciation of women that was uncluttered by any shyness or notions of the necessity of rings and vows.

Lara smiled around the circle of attentive faces once again. Behind the men she saw overstuffed chairs and well-used card tables with worn playing cards placed facedown where men had been sitting. Materials to write a letter were scattered across a scarred desk, and magazines were heaped at one end of a long coffee table. A television crackled in the corner as a laugh track tried to coax watchers into believing that the flickering sitcom was amusing rather than merely simpleminded.

"I'm interrupting you," Lara said. "Please, go back to whatever you were doing. I just wanted to talk to Willie for a few minutes."

Another chorus of disclaimers went up as Spur walked over and snapped off the TV. "No way," he said, smiling as he turned to face Lara. "Willie's been telling us all about you, but somehow he didn't get around to saying how pretty you are."

Lara smiled slightly. Spur's charm was of the generic, automatic sort common to some men. It wasn't the specific kind of charm used by a man who was interested in a particular woman.

"I'll bet you have a lot of success with that line," Lara said dryly, smiling even as she let Spur know that she wasn't in the market for any lines, new or old.

Immediately the rest of the men relaxed and started ribbing Spur about his success with the ladies. Spur laughed, not at all put off by the teasing or by Lara's deft refusal of his invitation to join him in the oldest game of all.

"Is that what you're doing your research on—Western lines?" he asked.

She shook her head, smiling. "Nothing that spicy. I'm doing a history of the Rocking B from 1860 to 1960."

"Before my time," said Spur. "Before yours, too," he added, giving her an appreciative once-over with vivid blue eyes.

"That's what makes it interesting to me," Lara said, shrugging out of her backpack before Spur could offer to help. As she unzipped the biggest pocket, she glanced up. "You're sure I'm not interrupting?" she asked, looking particularly at the older hands.

"Hell, honey," said Jim-Bob, rubbing his grizzled head, "we been playing gin with each other so long we know the discards before we see them. No sport to it a'tall. We'd much rather talk to a sweet young thing."

"Well, if you find one, tell me and I'll let you go talk to her," Lara muttered as she rummaged in the backpack's huge pocket.

The men laughed and nudged each other appreciatively while Willie looked on like a proud papa. Knowing that Lara had not come to flirt with any of the hands allowed all of the men to relax and enjoy her company.

"The kind of history I'm doing," began Lara, laying out the tape recorder, "is informal. I don't care if you remember who was governor and who was president during the time your story takes place. What matters to me are the events and the people of the Rocking B ranch itself. I want the kind of stories your grandfathers told you, and the kind you would tell your friends or your children and grandchildren."

Lara looked up, glancing at each man's face, trying to make them understand why memories that might seem trivial to them were important to her.

"The Rocking B of the old days is gone," she said quietly. "It lives only in your memories, and in the stories you know about men and women who are now dead. Some of you have been here all of your lives, and when you were young, you worked with older hands who had also been here all of their lives. It was the same for those older men. They had been young once, and they had listened and learned from the Rocking B's old hands."

The older men nodded slowly, remembering their youth a half century before, when they had listened to stories told by men who had been young before the century had turned.

"In a way," Lara continued, "the men who have lived in the Rocking B's bunkhouse are like a family passing stories down through the years. At least, it used to be that way," she said, grimacing toward the now-silent TV. "Telling stories used to be a major form of entertainment for ranch hands. That time is past. I want to gather all the old stories before they're forgotten. I want anyone who reads my history to be able to close his eyes and hear voices from the past whispering of horses and cattle and storms and sweethearts. I want people to know, really *know*, what it was like to live on the Rocking B a long time ago."

Jim-Bob, who had once been quite a lady's man and who still cut a fancy figure among the local widows, rubbed his chin slowly. "You sure you want to know about the women, too? Not all of them were what you'd call respectable. Not that I'd know anything about it firsthand," he added hastily. "But I've heard some stories, sure enough."

Lara hid her smile. "If my tape recorder blushes or faints, I promise I'll throw it away and get a sturdier model."

Jim-Bob chuckled.

"The people who live on the Rocking B now aren't saints," Lara said matter-of-factly, "and neither am I. I'm sure it was the same in the past. I don't want a sanitized kind of history. I want it just the way you'd tell it if I weren't here listening. In fact, if my being here bothers you, I'll show Willie how to change the tape and bow out right now. Or, if you like, you can write down any story you'd be embarrassed to tell out loud. But whatever you do, please, please pass on the story. Don't let a wonderfully funny or sad or simply human piece of history die because you're embarrassed to share it with a woman."

Jim-Bob looked dubious. "Some of the stories are kinda raw, if you get my drift."

Lara smiled and said calmly, "If you're thinking of the story about Hustlin' Annie and the bunkhouse fire, or about Big Sally's Halloween surprise, or the night Cheyenne's daddy ran naked all the way back from town with a buttful of rock salt after getting caught in somebody else's saddle—"

The laughter of the old hands drowned out Lara's words. She smiled widely. "I grew up here, remember? And if it helps, the first informal history I ever participated in researching was the life of a ninety-year-old spinster living over on the Firehold River who had worked in every whorehouse in Montana. After that charming old bawd, I'm shockproof."

"Sounds like Tickling Liz," muttered Willie.

"She said to say hello if I saw you," Lara murmured without missing a beat, "and to ask you if you still were partial to dancing barefoot in the spring grass."

Willie flushed to the roots of his thinning hair while the men around him howled with glee. Then Willie began to laugh, too, and there was a remembering kind of gleam in his eyes as he thought of the easy-smiling older woman who had long ago taught him why God had made girls one way and boys another.

After that the stories began to flow. Unobtrusively Lara finished setting up the tape recorder, checked the sound level and settled back to be an attentive audience. Tonight she would make no attempt to direct the stream of reminiscence and memories. The time for that would be later, after the men were accustomed to seeing her in their midst. Then she could ask for their oldest memories; they would answer in ways that would surprise even themselves, for the human mind works in amazing ways, dredging up incidents that the men would have sworn they had forgotten.

"...had this old spotted mare that just wouldn't hit the trail unless he had a cup of Java like the rest of the hands. Well," Murchison said, stopping long enough to light up a cigarette, "the new man, Perkins, couldn't believe the mare liked coffee. He thought the hands were pulling his leg. So he ups and saddles the mare after breakfast, and she walks about ten feet and then she sits down in the middle of the trail," said Murchison. "Swear to God. She sat right down like a big ol' hound dog and just dared Perkins to do something about it. Well, he kicked and he cussed, and that old mare just sat tight and rolled her eyeballs at him."

"What'd he finally do?" asked Spur, grinning.

"Well, by the time he gave up, the chuck wagon was long gone over the hill," Murchison continued, blowing out a stream of smoke. "So Perkins spent half the morning chasing the wagon on foot and the other half hauling a bucket of coffee back to that walleyed ol' mare."

"Did it work?"

"Nope."

"Why not? Were they funning him all along?"

"Nope. Mare only liked coffee with cream. Last anyone saw of Perkins, that poor fool was running over the hills, trying to rope a mamma longhorn. To this day,

I've heard that you can see him when the moon is just right and the calves are just getting up to weaning size."

Lara's laughter blended with the deeper sounds of masculine amusement. She loved it when the men started talking about the horses they had known, for each man's life was intimately involved with the big, affectionate and sometimes epically willful animals.

"Did you ever hear about Wild Blue?" asked Dusty.

Lara shook her head, although the name sounded vaguely familiar to her.

"He was a big stud that roamed around here way, way back, about the time the first Blackridge rode into the valley through South Pass. The Indians had tried to catch that mustang, but it was like trying to catch the wind. So they took their best mares and turned them loose to get bred by the wild blue roan. He threw some of the prettiest Appaloosa colts ever to eat Montana grass," Dusty said.

The cowhand's voice was slow, the words almost hesitant. He was more than seventy years old and had been born on the Rocking B. He had a lot of memories to search through for the threads of the story he was telling. Lara listened to both the words and the silences, letting the story grow in her mind, seeing again a time when horses ran free and were pursued by men just slightly less wild than the mustangs themselves.

The stories blended one into the other like streams joining a river running back through time itself. When it was necessary, Lara changed the tape unobtrusively, not interrupting the flow of words as she labeled each tape and entered it into her interview log.

Eventually the talk turned to the raucous celebrations that used to follow a roundup, when everyone would let off steam after the brutal work of catching, branding, dehorning and castrating spring calves. The square dances would go on until dawn and beyond, with couples sneaking away to be alone and then returning later, flushed with secrets.

Spur, who had been pretty well left out of the storytelling up to that point, brightened at the mention of dancing. With little urging Willie hauled out his fiddle, cranked the strings into tune and began to play all the old hoedown songs with surprisingly agile fingers. Spur turned out to be a superb square dancer whose family had a long tradition of calling dances all over the West. He began to chant the dances that he had learned and to demonstrate the rhythmic, exuberant steps that accompanied the words.

"This step is known as Over the Moon and Around the Mountain," Spur said.

Lara blinked. She was no authority on square dances, but she had the feeling that her leg was being very gently pulled. On the other hand, that kind of droll teasing was very much a part of ranch life both today and in the past. She had no objection to providing the men with a little entertainment at her own expense.

"Over the Moon and Around the Mountain," she repeated gravely. "That sounds, er, strenuous."

"Oh, it's not bad a'tall," drawled Spur. "Here, I'll show you."

He held out his arms. Lara hesitated for several seconds before lifting her own arms and stepping forward.

As Spur pulled her into dancing position, she realized that Spur was every bit as tall as Carson and nearly as strong. The young cowboy's eyes were a very vivid blue, and his long, light mustache was worn in a drooping handlebar style that would have gone unremarked more than a century before.

"Ready?" he asked.

"I doubt it," Lara said, "but I'm game."

Spur winked. "That's my girl. Now start with your right foot."

Lara obediently put her right foot forward. Instantly she was swept off her feet, tossed into the air like a child, caught and swung around shoulder-high in a complete circle. She gave out a startled shriek and hung on to Spur as though he were a runaway horse. He laughed, set her on her feet carefully and grinned down at her.

"Over the Moon and Around the Mountain," he said. "Like it?"

"Er—"

"One more time."

"Spur—!"

Too late. Lara's feet left the floor before she could finish her sentence. This time Spur tossed her even higher, caught her even closer and swung her around twice. The men were all stamping and applauding and whooping their approval, and cutting a few fancy steps of their own while Willie made the old fiddle sing. Lara went Over the Moon and Around the Mountain so many times that she lost count. Before long she was laughing, breathless and too dizzy to do more than cling to Spur when he finally relented and set her on her feet to stay.

Suddenly the room fell silent. Lara pushed the hair back from her eyes and looked up. Carson was standing just inside the bunkhouse door. His expression was hard, and his eyes were the cold yellow of a winter sky after sunset. Although he was leaning casually against the door frame with his thumbs hooked into the waistband of his jeans, the angry tension of lhis body belied his relaxed stance.

"Any of you yahoos know what time it is?" Carson asked, his voice the temperature of a February wind.

"'Bout eleven," Spur said. "Why?"

"Going to be a long day tomorrow," Carson said flatly. He pinned Lara with a glare from his narrowed eyes. "Have you lived in the city so long that you've forgotten how early dawn comes? These men have work to do, and they can't do it if they're staggering around half blind for lack of sleep."

"I'm sorry. I lost track of time," Lara said. Hurriedly she shut the tape recorder off and stuffed it into her backpack. "It won't happen again."

"You're damn right it won't," Carson retorted, straightening and walking slowly toward Lara with his hand out. "I'll carry that pack for you."

"Now wait a minute," Spur said, catching Lara's hand as she jammed the rest of her stuff into the backpack. "None of us are riding nighthawk so what we do after dinner and before dawn is our own lookout. If we want to help you with your research, we'll damn well do it!"

If the room had been quiet before, it became absolutely dead still as the older hands held their breath in anticipation of Carson's explosion. He had a well-deserved reputation for his rough temper. The men who knew him expected him to fire Spur on the spot. Instead, Carson simply looked at the young cowhand. Spur realized he was in trouble, but he wasn't going to back down from what he had said. He had a full measure of the proud independence that had been the hallmark of cowboys since the first man saddled a horse and tried to keep track of his cattle in the West's endless open range.

"It's all right, Spur," Lara said quickly. "Carson's right. I shouldn't have—"

A curt motion of Carson's arm cut off the flow of Lara's words. She bit her lip and wished she knew why Carson was so angry. It was late, yes, but not that late, and as far as she knew, only routine ranch work was scheduled for tomorrow. It wasn't as though she had kept everyone up late carousing on the night before branding or haying.

"This is the damnedest so-called 'research' I've ever heard of," Carson said icily to Lara. "Unless you're doing a thesis on how to pick up men. Is that it?" he demanded, glaring at her right hand.

Suddenly Lara realized that Spur still had his hand on her right wrist to prevent her from packing up and leaving. She eased herself from Spur's grip.

"Now that would make sense," continued Carson, warming to his topic with a vengeance. "You go around to all the bunkhouses and get handled by all the young cowboys and they take up a collection to thank you for being so soft and warm and willing. Hell, I'll bet a girl could make quite a nice living that way, if she didn't mind being known as an easy kind of female—or worse."

The anger that Lara had felt earlier that evening returned in a rush as Carson's sarcasm cut into her.

"An easy kind of female," repeated Lara tightly, yanking her backpack into place and pulling her hair out from beneath the straps with abrupt motions. "Yeah, I guess you'd be an expert on loose women— or worse—if that blond number who was undressing you earlier tonight is any sample of your taste." Lara's disdain vibrated in every word as she walked toward Carson. "Well, Mr. Expert, if you wouldn't hang around with easy females like that, you wouldn't think that every woman was dying to go to bed with the first man who would have her!"

Carson's hand shot out and clamped around Lara's arm as she swept past. He leaned down and spoke so softly that only she could hear.

"Maybe you're forgetting who was doing the offering and who was doing the refusing a few years ago," Carson said in a low, deadly voice.

Lara looked up into his clear, cold eyes and felt herself freezing inside, shame splintering through her in shards of razor ice, cutting right through to her soul. It was as though the years had never intervened. She was vulnerable, naked, trusting, wanting—and he was none of those things. He was armored, ruthless, and all he desired was to see her shame.

A shame that she couldn't conceal. Naked.

Nothing had changed. She was as helpless now against Carson as she had been years ago. The realization was devastating.

"Damn you," she breathed, shaking with humiliation. "*Damn you!*"

Lara slipped past Carson and ran out into the night without stopping. She heard him call her name once and then again, urgently, as though something other than anger moved him. She didn't even hesitate in her flight.

Carson got to the doorway just in time to see the pale blur of Lara's blouse retreating along the road between the ranch house and the Chandler homestead. Behind him, in the explosive silence of the bunkhouse, he sensed movement. His hand shot out, and his long, work-hardened fingers clamped around Spur's arm in an unbreakable grip before the younger man could push past him and out into the night after Lara.

Unceremoniously Carson yanked Spur down the bunkhouse steps and around to the back, where no one could overhear.

"I'm going to tell you this once, cowboy, and only once. You listening?" snarled Carson.

Spur opened his mouth to say something, looked at the icy gleam of moonlight in Carson's narrowed eyes and decided that discretion was definitely the better part of valor.

"You're new to this valley," Carson continued, his words clipped. "You don't know about the Blackridges and the Chandlers, and I'm not going to waste my time educating you. All you have to know is this—Lara Chandler is mine. Got that?"

Spur hesitated, then nodded.

Carson looked at the younger man for a long moment, then nodded in turn, releasing him. "Good. Remember it."

"Or you'll fire me?" Spur asked, both curiosity and aggression in his voice.

Carson smiled thinly. "Hell, no, kid. I'll trash you. You want to work for me after you heal up, you're more than welcome. You're a good hand, Spur. One of the best I've got, despite the fact that you're barely old enough to drink hard liquor. But there are other good hands, and there's only one Lara Chandler."

Spur opened his mouth, shut it and smiled crookedly. "Well, you're living up to your reputation, Blackridge. Hard but fair. Know something? If Lara had given me the slightest come-on, I'd fight you and welcome to it. She'd be worth it. But she wasn't handing out any invitations to me or to anyone else that I could see." Spur shrugged. "So she's all yours and good luck to you. You're gonna need it. That filly is plumb skittish around men. She's real nice about it, but no is written all over her in letters a blind man could read."

Although Spur said nothing more, it was plain that he thought Lara's refusal extended to the tall, hard-looking boss of the Rocking B.

As Carson turned and went back to the ranch house, he was thinking the same thing. It had seemed so easy when Lara had flinched at the thought of him with another woman, and then she had found Susanna with him. Lara had taken one look at his open shirt and suddenly her eyes had blazed with memories. It was exactly the reaction he had hoped for.

What he hadn't expected was Lara's fleeing from him as though pursued by the hounds of hell. Before Susanna had dropped in, he had been set up in the library, hoping Lara would come over that night. He had expected to remind Lara of the sensual pleasures they had shared by the implied intimacy of the open shirt, then accept Lara's offer of a neck rub to ease his headache. She had the most marvelous hands. No one had ever been able to chase pain away as she could, with her sweet concern for his comfort and her knowing, gentle hands.

Carson cursed savagely under his breath. He hadn't meant to hurt Lara four years ago, and he certainly hadn't meant to hurt her tonight at the bunkhouse. Four years should have been plenty of time to get over being turned down by him. Until he had seen her flash of jealousy at the thought of him with another woman, he had been afraid that four years had been too damn much time to get over him, that she had forgotten entirely the months they had shared. He had assumed that during those years Lara had found more than one man willing to take what she had so sweetly offered Carson, a gift that he had been too caught up in the war between himself and his father to accept.

As always, the thought of some other man knowing Lara's warmth and lovely body made Carson's jaw tighten until it ached. He had been a pure, double-dyed fool to turn away from her, hurting her and complicating the hell out of his own life in the process; but nothing could be done about that now except to be sure not to repeat the mistake. He had missed his chance to be the first to teach Lara about the pleasures of sex. He would regret that the rest of his life. The thought of someone else sliding into that sweet young body had kept him awake more than once in the past few years. The memory of her bewilderment and pain and finally her overwhelming shame when he rejected her had kept him awake even more often than his enduring hunger for her.

Lara had looked the same tonight, surprised and hurt and then shamed all the way to her soul. The memory of her pale, absolutely bloodless face and haunted eyes turned in Carson like a knife, cutting him, making him grimace with the pain he had never meant to cause her. She was so fragile, so easily bruised, as sweet as a sun-warmed flower; he was a man not known for his gentle words and easy nature. The fact that Lara was still so vulnerable to him gave him both hope and fear—hope for his ultimate success in making her his wife, and fear that she had been too badly hurt ever to trust him again.

Damn you. Damn you!

Lara's words echoed in Carson's mind every step of the way to the dusty blue pickup. He got in, slammed the door and gunned the vehicle down the dirt road, wishing to hell that he had acted differently tonight. But he hadn't. He and his damn temper had taken one look at Lara all flushed and mussed from Spur's arms, and it had been all Carson could do not to take the young cowboy apart right there.

With an abrupt gesture Carson flicked the headlights on to high beam, hoping to pick out the pale color of Lara's blouse against the black of night. Nothing came back at him but the twin ghostly reflections of a cow's eyes as it grazed along the fence line.

Despite the urgency and impatience that was riding him, Carson kept his speed down well below the range of his headlights as he looked for Lara. He doubted that she had had time to get all the way back to the homestead, but there was no sign of her along the pale, moon-washed curves of the ranch road. Automatically he stopped, opened the homestead gate, drove through, then got out and closed the gate again. As he did, he heard the grating of wood over dirt and made a mental note to fix the gate. If it sagged any more, Lara wouldn't be able to handle the gate by the time the summer was over.

If she was still on the homestead.

The thought made Carson swear again beneath his breath. Lara had to stay. He simply would not accept any other possibility. It had seemed so easy after his mother had died. Even though Lara had refused to speak to him, he had been sure that if he could just lure her out to the Rocking B, time and proximity would take care of her coldness. For he knew that she wasn't a cold person at all. She was the exact opposite, at least as volatile and passionate as her own mother had been.

Carson frowned. He didn't like to think about Larry's mistress. He had grown up thinking of Becky Chandler and her bastard child as his enemies. Like his mother, Carson had blamed the Chandlers for the fact that Larry had never been much of a husband and even less of a father. Years later—far too late to prevent Carson from badly wounding Lara—he had realized that Larry's failings were his own and were not the responsibility of the passionate, blue-eyed woman Larry had loved when he could not love his own legal family.

It hadn't been an easy thing for Carson to admit to himself, but he had faced the reality of his adoptive father's lack of love and the reasons for it; then Carson had put it behind him and moved on to other things, things that were within his own ability to change or control.

It had always been that way with Carson. After he had learned whatever lesson was to be learned, he never looked back. For him, the past was a place of pain and mistakes, disillusionment and broken dreams. It held no fascination for him. He had never known his biological parents, and the people who had adopted him had done so for reasons that had nothing to do with wanting a child to love. He had no shared legacy of roots stretching back into time, securely placing him within a family history.

Carson had the future, though, and the future was his. He had earned it, and he was damned if he was going to let the mistakes people had made in the past take it away from him.

Chapter Four

USING THE BRILLIANT MOONLIGHT as her guide, Lara climbed quickly up the grassy ridge that rose between the ranch house and the homestead. The road snaked around the shoulder of the ridge, but instead of staying with the road, she had cut through the Rocking B's northeast pasture. It was a shortcut to the homestead, but she had no intention of going home just yet. She knew that would be the first place Carson would go looking for her, and somehow she had no doubt that he would pursue her. After all, she had run despite their agreement and his warning.

As Lara climbed, the memory of Carson's sarcasm on the subject of easy women flooded through her, goading her to greater speed. She couldn't blame him for thinking that she was easy. Once she had quite openly offered herself to him. He hadn't even had to ask. The aftershocks of that night and his refusal still shivered within her, shaking her, shaming her.

The top of the ridge was smooth, gently rounded and grassy. A breeze moved faintly, bringing with it sounds from the valley below. In the distance moonlight glittered along the length of the river that ran through the center of the Rocking B. The Big Green nourished the ranch's cattle and crops with water that had come down from the sawtooth mountain ranges that rimmed the broad valley. Much closer in, at the foot of the ridge, the ranch's lights glowed in shades of molten gold. The back door of the ranch house shut loudly, and a flashlight bobbed as someone walked across the yard. The air was so clear that it seemed as though the person were coming straight toward Lara.

She held her breath in the instant before she told herself that whoever was out walking couldn't be Carson. She had already heard his pickup go by on the ranch road and then turn up the fork that led to the homestead. When the flashlight vanished and the lights of a cottage came on, Lara let out her breath in a sigh, realizing that it had just been Yolanda going to her quarters for the night.

For a few minutes it was so quiet that Lara could hear her own heartbeat. Then two men came out of the bunkhouse and went toward the barn. She was too far away to distinguish words or identities, but the sound of easy male voices floated up to her in quiet counterpoint to the whispering of grass caressed by a summer breeze. A shiver coursed over Lara, a feeling that Cheyenne had once described as *the sensation of someone walking on my grave.*

Lara shrugged off the backpack and put on her wind-breaker, even though the night wasn't chilly. She drew her knees up to her chin, stared down at the Rocking B and listened to voices drifting up into the beautiful, fathomless silence of the Montana night.

Once she had dreamed of being a recognized part of the family at the big house, of having Larry Blackridge acknowledge her as his daughter. She had believed that, if only those things would happen, she would be one of the people living forever amid the golden lights.

Lara's mouth turned down in a sad smile at her own expense. She had been very young then. Certainly too young to protect herself from her own dreams. Far too young to realize that she was Mrs. Blackridge's natural enemy, a living symbol of her husband's adultery, not a motherless child that Sharon might want to call daughter. Even so, the dream of belonging had died slowly, stubbornly, not breathing its last until Lara was a shy, awkward teenager whose greatest pleasure was watching Carson Blackridge from afar.

He had always fascinated her. From the very first time she had met him, he had been different from other men. As soon as she had stood in front of him, she had felt a shock of recognition that had shaken her, as though unseen, unknowable emotions already joined her and the tall, roughlooking adopted son of Larry Blackridge. She had been thirteen years old when she had taken a Christmas present from Carson's hand. He had been twenty-two. It had been the first time that Carson had come to the Rocking B's celebration for the hands' children.

Even at thirteen, Lara had sensed the tension between Carson and his father. She had known without being told that Carson was giving out gifts under protest. Other people might not notice it, but to Lara, Carson's hostility was as tangible as the Christmas scent of evergreen that permeated the room. It had always been like that for Lara—she was as instinctively sensitive to Carson as a flower was to the sun.

Lara had neither sought nor discovered an explanation for her instant response to Carson Blackridge. It was simply a fact, like the color of the sky. Because she had no memory of a time when she hadn't been aware of Carson, she had never questioned that awareness. She had simply worshiped him with all of her young heart, and always at a distance. Her sensitivity to Carson's feelings had quickly told her that he wanted nothing to do with the thin, blue-eyed bastard whose mother had recently died in a storm. So she had watched him from afar, her eyes full of dreams and stirrings she was too young to name. He was aware of her, too; she was sure of it. It could not be an accident that he was never where she was on the Rocking B.

Years later, when Lara was eighteen and working at a restaurant in town during the summer before she began her classes at the university, Carson had allowed himself to admit that he noticed her. Not only did he acknowledge her, but he actually seemed to pursue her. He started coming several times a week to the café where she worked, and each time he was there, he flirted with her. When he had finally asked her for a date, it had seemed like a dream come true....

"WHOOPS!" SAID CARSON, withdrawing his feet and catching the tray before anything could spill.

"Sorry," Lara said, feeling the heat of embarrassment climb up her cheeks.

"My fault," he said, smiling at her. "I'm a little big for these booths. I sort of spill out into the aisle."

She couldn't help looking from his stirrup-scarred cowboy boots to the muscular length of his legs straining against the faded fabric of his jeans. As always when he was within view, her heart beat too fast and simultaneously a strange weakness flooded through her, making her clumsy. She had nearly dumped a dinner in his lap out of sheer shock when she had recognized him sitting in her section of the café. He looked so relaxed, so utterly male, like a big mountain cat resting in a meadow, eyes half closed against the summer sun. Carson's eyes were like a cougar's, too, clear amber with a flash of dark green in their depths.

"You're perfect—it's the booth that's too small," Lara said without thinking. As she heard her words, she flushed again, feeling like a complete fool. She had overheard enough of the local girls talking about Carson to know that he was much chased by women and rarely caught, and even then only for a short time. "Ketchup?" she asked quickly, setting a big hamburger and fries in front of Carson.

"Thanks, but I think the half bottle you brought earlier will hold me."

Lara looked away from Carson's thick, dark eyelashes long enough to realize that there was already a bottle of ketchup on the table, as well as steak sauce and mustard. She retreated without looking at him again.

It was the same the next three times he came in—her sudden heat and weakness, her clumsiness and unguarded tongue. She had dreamed of him for so long that his reality was overwhelming. She kept telling herself that she was being foolish, that he wasn't pursuing her, that he would never pursue her. His opinion of his father's former relationship with Becky Chandler was no secret. Besides, Carson had his pick of the sophisticated, experienced women who found their way to the Rocking B in hopes of catching and holding the interest of one of the most eligible bachelors in the state of Montana. What possible reason could Carson have to pursue a tongue-tied, blushing teenager?

The fifth time Lara glanced up and saw Carson watching her from what she had come to think of as "his" booth, she felt her heart turn over at the intensity of his look and the male heat in his slow, approving smile as she walked over to him.

"Hello, little fox," he said, gently brushing aside the menu she offered and running his fingertips over her right hand. "How's the burn?"

The teasing endearment sent a helpless flush over Lara's cheeks, as did the gentle touch. The last time he had been in the café, he had told her that she looked like a fox at twilight—dark, shy, mysterious and very, very soft.

Lara looked down at her fingers, barely remembering that she had burned her hand a few weeks before. "Fine, thanks," she said, her voice husky. Her right hand felt as though it were on fire again, but this time it was from Carson's quick, gentle touch. "Do you want the usual?"

"Yes and no."

Lara smiled and prepared to make some revisions in the menu. Carson was one of the few customers who regularly got away with special orders. The café's owner was Yolanda's brother. Whatever Carson wanted was given to him without question, for the Blackridges had been very good to Yolanda's family through the years, sending their children to college and helping them get started in various small businesses.

"I'll have the steak and fries and blue-cheese dressing on the salad," Carson said.

That was the "yes" part of his order. Lara looked up from the pad, waiting for the "no" part.

"And for dessert I'll have you for a partner at the cattleman's dance this Saturday," Carson continued calmly.

Lara had actually started to write Carson's words on the order pad when their meaning penetrated. Her head snapped up, and her blue eyes widened.

"What?" she asked, afraid to believe her own ears.

"I promise to hold your feet off the floor so you won't need to worry about getting trampled," he said, his eyes glinting with humor. The dances were notoriously crowded and sometimes rather rowdy.

Lara just barely prevented herself from blurting out that, if Carson was her partner, her feet would be so far off the floor anyway that they'd have to keep her on a leash like a carnival balloon.

"I—I'd love to—" Lara closed her eyes, hating the words that she had to say next.

"But?" he asked softly, watching her with eyes that missed nothing, seeing both her eagerness and her disappointment.

"I have to work," she said, her voice plainly unhappy.

"What time do you get off?"

"Ten o'clock."

"I'll pick you up at your apartment at 10:30."

Lara looked at Carson for a long moment before a smile transformed her face, making her glow like a delicate porcelain sculpture lighted from within. "Thank you, Carson. I'll look forward to it."

He hesitated, then smiled in return. "So will I."

Only later did she realize why his tone had struck her as strange. It was almost as if he had been surprised to find himself looking forward to their date. But that was absurd. If he hadn't wanted to take her out, there would have been no reason for him to ask her to the dance in the first place.

Lara left work early Saturday night and raced to her apartment, tearing the hated hairnet in her eagerness to be rid of it. She showered, washed and dried her hair and then brushed it until it shone like a raven's wing. The natural wave in the breast-length strands made her hair thick and luxuriant. Freed of the hairnet, her stylish, subtly layered haircut framed her face in soft, open curves that caressed her fine-grained skin like black flames. Against the darkness of her hair, her blue eyes had a jewel-like intensity and depth. She wore just enough makeup to emphasize rather than overwhelm her natural coloring, and a perfume that was as fragile as moonlight.

She hesitated in front of her closet, wishing that she had a dress as special as the occasion. Finally she settled for a white silk blouse that she had bought on sale a few weeks before and a swirling, floor-length skirt that was as black as her hair. A scarlet sash tied gaucho-style around her waist added a vivid splash of color that was repeated in her enamel earrings and matching bracelet.

With a frown Lara studied her reflection in the mirror, wishing she were older or had a spectacular figure or blond hair to her waist or a splashy designer dress or all four together. Then she wouldn't have to worry about Carson comparing her to the glittering, slinky women who always seemed to turn up at these affairs, making life miserable for their plainer or less wealthy sisters.

"Carson didn't ask one of those flashy types to the dance," Lara reminded herself out loud. "He asked me."

That continuing miracle still swept over her at odd moments, making her shiver with pleasure.

Another wave of pleasure went over Lara when she opened the door and saw Carson's surprise, quickly followed by his frank male admiration.

"Little fox," he murmured, looking at Lara from her gleaming hair to the black-nylon-clad toes peeking out of her high-heeled, patent-leather sandals. "You make me wish I weren't taking you out among the wolves tonight. I want to keep you all to myself."

Lara smiled and relaxed beneath Carson's genuine admiration. "Thank you," she said softly, no longer nervous about the coming date. Then, without stopping to think, she added, "Mountain lions don't need to worry about wolves."

Carson looked surprised again. His mouth curled into an odd smile. "Is that how you see me?" he asked. "A cougar?"

A quick sideways glance assured Lara that Carson was amused rather than put off by her frankness. "Yes," she said, picking up her little black purse. "Strong, rangy and graceful in a very masculine way. Not to mention your eyes." She smiled and looked away from him, saying, "But I suppose you're awfully tired of girls going on and on about your eyes."

Again Lara managed to surprise Carson, who had thought himself long past the age when a woman could show him anything new. He laughed suddenly and took Lara's hand, tugging her close to his side after she locked her apartment door.

"This may come as a shock," he said dryly, "but none of my dates have mentioned my eyes."

Lara looked startled. "Oh. Er, maybe it would be better if I went back to being tongue-tied."

"Only if my tongue gets to do the tying," Carson retorted, leaning past Lara to open his car door and glancing aside in time to watch the blush climbing up her face as the meaning of his words registered. He laughed again and ran the back of his fingers over her hot cheek. "Little fox, you're a real pleasure to tease. I didn't think girls still knew how to blush."

Lara groaned and tried to shield her face behind her hands. Gently Carson pried her fingers away.

"Don't hide," he said, kissing her flushed cheek and the corner of her mouth.

"You must think I'm a little fool," she whispered helplessly, shivering as she felt his mustache move over her sensitive lips like a silk brush.

"I think you're like a mountain creek on a hot summer day—clear, sparkling, sweet and tempting as all hell."

Lara would rather have been thought of as mysterious, sexy and complex, but she had just enough self-control not to say so out loud. She quit trying to hide her face and smiled at Carson rather uncertainly. He returned the smile with one of his own, a smile different from any she had seen from him before, as gently approving as a man watching a kitten chasing a teasing piece of yarn. When he bent and kissed her softly on the lips, she couldn't control her reaction or the small sound of her swiftly indrawn breath.

"Get in the car," Carson said, his voice deep, "before I decide to spend the night right here, kissing you."

Lara's red lips parted slightly as her breath came out in a rush. The thought of being kissed—really kissed—by Carson was both exciting and unnerving. His eyes narrowed as he read her instant response, but before he could move, she slid into the car. As he shut the door after her, he let out his breath in a soundless curse, surprised at the heat racing through his body.

The dance was held in the local Grange building. What the ballroom lacked in elegance it made up for in warmth and laughter. Everyone there knew everyone else, and the band knew all the favorite songs both old and new. By the time Carson and Lara arrived, most of the older couples had already gone home, leaving the floor to the violently energetic under-thirty set. The band had responded with the driving rhythms of rock music interspersed with slow, sexy ballads.

Carson found a small table, brought Lara a cola and himself a beer and pulled a chair around until he was sitting right next to her.

"To surprises," he said, smiling and clinking his glass lightly against hers.

She smiled almost shyly and took a sip. When she found that the drink hadn't been spiked, she let out a silent breath of relief. She hated the taste of alcohol, and she distrusted the dates who handed her a strong drink without asking her preference.

"Thank you," Lara said.

Carson's dark, thick eyebrows raised in silent question.

"For not giving me a drink that would bring down a bull," she explained.

Deep male laughter wrapped around Lara like a caress. After a moment she began to laugh, too.

"I outgrew that kind of maneuvering before I graduated from high school," Carson said, shaking his head.

"I wish more men had," said Lara.

"You have something against alcohol?" he asked innocently.

"Nope. It sure has something against me, though. First my forehead goes numb, then my head goes all twirly, and then I get sick as a hound dog that's been eating tall grass."

Lara's words stopped suddenly when she realized that she must sound about as sophisticated as a six-year-old. Carson shook his head and tried not to show his amusement, but in the end he gave up trying to control himself. He threw back his head and laughed with the kind of contagious humor that had other people turning and looking in his direction with a pleased smile. It got to Lara, as well. She forgot her embarrassment and laughed with Carson. She realized that she liked making him smile, hearing his deep laughter, watching the tight lines vanish from his face. It made her feel like a court magician bringing pleasure to a hard-working king.

Long, strong fingers closed over Lara's as Carson took her hand and squeezed gently. "You're not at all what I expected," he said.

The feel of Carson's warmth and strength radiated up Lara's arm in a wave of pleasure. When her breath came back, she asked, "What did you expect?"

As soon as the words were out of her mouth, Lara could have bitten her tongue. She knew precisely what Carson might have expected from an illegitimate child who was living alone in an apartment at a time when most girls of her age were still living with their families. Unfortunately, her grandfather couldn't afford a car for her to commute from the homestead to a job in town. Without a job there would have been no money for university tuition and books in the fall. Her apartment was very small; that and the fact that it was in a building partially owned by one of Cheyenne's old friends made the rental cost minimal. It was lonely living on her own but necessary if she wanted an education.

"Never mind," Lara said quickly, looking away from Carson. "I can imagine what you expected. Sorry about that, but I'm definitely not what the local gossips probably advertised. So don't feel like you have to stick it out here with me just to be polite. You can take me home anytime."

"How about tomorrow morning?"

The casual proposition shocked Lara. Her head snapped around toward Carson so quickly that her hair flew out and shimmered like black silk. She had called him a mountain lion—a predator—and that was exactly what he looked like then, his powerful body poised as though to pounce and his eyes almost yellow, narrowed in calculation.

A feeling of bitter disappointment washed through Lara, taking all the color from her, leaving behind only a pale shadow of her former animation. Carson hadn't wanted to be with her. Not really. He had just wanted to go to bed with her. She opened her mouth to tell him that she didn't sleep with men, even one that she had admired all her life. Her lips moved, but no words came out.

"You're totally innocent, aren't you?" asked Carson, watching Lara intently.

"Yes," she whispered finally, getting her voice back. She slipped her fingers from his and pushed back from the table. "I'm sorry. Thanks for being so honest about what you wanted from me. I should have guessed, but I'm not very...experienced." Lara's lips trembled, and her voice dried up. She swallowed, tried to speak and couldn't. "Goodbye, Carson," she managed, her voice so frayed it hardly carried beyond her lips.

Lara turned and quickly began to work her way through the fringes of the people crowding the dance floor. The band was playing a slow ballad that had a provocative, erotic rhythm. Couples clung to each other and swayed slowly from side to side, lost in a sensual world of warmth and closeness. Blindly Lara tried to slide through the dancers without causing a disturbance. She had just reached the edge of a small clearing in the crowd when Carson's hand closed around her wrist and tugged, using her own momentum to spin her around toward him.

"Carson, I won't—"

"Hush, little fox," he said softly, ending Lara's protest by pulling her into his arms.

"But I won't—"

"I know," Carson said, cutting across Lara's words and then kissing her lips gently. His hand slid beneath the black fall of her hair and stroked her spine soothingly. "Dance with me."

Lara hesitated, torn between her desire to be with Carson and her fear that he expected more from her than she wanted to give.

"Look at me," murmured Carson, taking both her hands and pulling them around his neck.

In the mirrored darkness of the dance floor, Lara's eyes were as enigmatic as twilight.

"I won't push you. I won't take anything you don't want to give me," Carson promised. "All right?"

"But you're used to—" Lara's voice broke as she tried to find a polite way to say that Carson was used to having women whenever the sexual urge struck him.

Carson's lips shifted into a smile that warmed Lara all the way to her toes. "That's my problem, not yours. You're different from my usual women. Let me enjoy that difference and don't worry about it. Okay?"

The breath sighed out from between Lara's unconsciously parted lips. "Okay," she said softly.

Carson's arms shifted subtly, moving Lara closer without making her feel trapped. His hand stroked the satin length of her hair, silently urging her to rest her head on his chest. As she did, her arms slid more tightly around his neck. With every breath she took, she smelled his unique male scent, a heady mixture of warmth and soap and a clean, faintly citrus aftershave. She matched his slow movements easily, unconsciously, fitting so perfectly into his arms that it was as though she had been born to be held by this one man.

Later, when Carson took Lara home, he did no more than brush his lips over her mouth and stroke her cheek with gentle fingertips. It was the same on the next date and the next. They talked and laughed and danced, and the weeks flew by. He never took her to the drive-in where couples groped and wrestled behind steamy windows. He never came into her apartment at the end of a date. Nor did he take her home to the Rocking B.

At first Lara was grateful that Carson was so careful not to push her sexually. It was a distinct difference from the way she had been treated before by boys her own age, most of whom seemed at the mercy of their newly rushing hormones. She had no doubt that Carson wanted her. She was inexperienced, but she wasn't ignorant. She knew exactly what caused the change that came over his body when he held her, kissed her gently, hugged her and kissed her and kissed her again before he slowly released her at the end of each date.

And at the end of each date, Lara wanted more.

It was almost three months before Carson slipped the leash on his control. They had been chased inside her apartment by a summer rainstorm that had washed out their mountain picnic. Lara had set up the picnic dinner all over again on the floor of her living room and had sworn not to use any furniture or electricity. They would sit on the floor, and when the sun set, they would just light a camp lantern and pretend they were back at Avalanche Creek's lush meadow.

As usual, Carson and Lara talked and laughed, and with each word, each moment, she fell more and more under his spell. She watched him with an intensity that she didn't understand. Every breath he took, every movement of his body, every small touch of his fingers against her, sent shivers of awareness coursing through her. And every instant brought her closer to the moment when he would leave. Then he would kiss her gently, hug her and let her go. She didn't want it to end that way today. She wanted more. She needed it in some mysterious, seething way that was so new to her that she had no defenses against it. She didn't even know that she needed any defenses.

Carson wanted more than chaste kisses, too. Lara could see it in the hot gold of his eyes reflecting the camp lantern and in the way his glance lingered on her mouth, her hands, her breasts. When it came time for him to go, he rose to his feet, pulling her after him. As usual he kissed her, held her, kissed her again; then he looked down at her parted lips silently begging for him. He made a husky sound that was almost a groan. His arms tightened around her like steel. In the flickering illumination of the camp lantern, his eyes were nearly pure gold, and like the light itself, they burned.

"Carson?"

"Little fox," he whispered, "would it shock you to feel my tongue touching yours?"

Lara hadn't liked it when other men had tried that particularly intimate kind of kiss on her, but the thought of being that close to Carson sent a shiver of excitement over her. She went up on tiptoe, circling Carson's neck with her arms, and then felt herself being lifted off her feet until her face was level with his. He fitted his mouth over hers with a single smooth motion. At the first hot touch of his tongue, she trembled and made a sound deep in her throat. Her arms tightened and her lips opened further as she tried to blend her mouth completely with his. When she moved her tongue over his, he tore his mouth away and let her slide down his hard body.

"Did I—did I do it wrong?" Lara asked. "Shouldn't I move my tongue, too?"

Half laughing, half groaning, Carson hugged Lara close and hard. "You did everything just right," he said hoarsely, fighting for control. "Oh, God, honey, you set me on fire all the way to the soles of my feet."

Her breath caught, and she looked up at him with blue eyes darkened by the beginnings of arousal.

"Is that good?" Lara whispered. "Do you like being—"

The words ended as Carson bent down and took Lara's mouth completely. Long fingers tangled in her hair, bending her head back and arching her body so that her breasts pressed against his hard chest. At the same instant his other hand slid down to her hips, lifting her into the cradle of his thighs, rocking her slowly over the hot, erect male flesh that strained against his slacks. His tongue moved in the same sensuous rhythms as his powerful body, the same rhythms that she instinctively gave back to him with her own tongue, her own body.

By the time Carson released Lara, she was dazed, trembling, half wild with feelings she had never known before. When his hands caressed the length of her body and then eased up over her breasts to seek and find the sensitive tips, her breath came in with a sound that was almost a moan. Her back arched again in a reflex as old as passion. He didn't have to ask if his hands on her breasts pleased her; her eyes were half closed, her lips were parted and her nipples had hardened into points that showed hungrily against the thin cotton of her blouse.

Gently, skillfully, Carson caressed the hard buds that had risen to his touch. Lara's whole body quivered in response. She didn't even know that he had unfastened her blouse and bra until she felt air bathing her flushed skin. The first touch of his fingers on her bare breasts was so exquisite that she moaned. When he plucked delicately at the eager nipples, she felt it all the way to her knees.

"Carson?"

The huskiness of Lara's voice was like an intimate caress. It fed the fires eating through Carson's control, burning him, consuming him. With one hand he flicked open the buttons of his shirt. Her eyes widened as she saw the dark thatch of hair curling across muscles and arrowing down to his belt buckle.

"I want to feel your breasts against me," he said quietly. "I want to watch those beautiful pink nipples nuzzle against my skin. Does that shock you?"

Slowly Lara shook her head, sending tendrils of hair whispering across her breasts. His hands tightened on her back, bringing her gently against his chest. He turned slightly from side to side, caressing her sensitized flesh with each small motion. She made a tiny sound and threaded her fingers through the male hair, kneading his muscular chest like a cat. Her eyes closed slowly, and her head tilted back as she gave herself to the subtle, ravishing sensations of her breasts caressing him and being caressed in turn. Pleasure expanded through her in wave after wave, shortening her breath until she was dizzy. She called Carson's name brokenly, barely able to stand.

"Yes?" he asked, his tone deep, gritty.

"I feel so strange." Lara's voice broke as Carson plucked at the tight pink crowns of her breasts, sending both fire and weakness radiating through her. As her knees sagged, she swayed against him. "Carson—"

He steadied her even as he eased her down to the floor. "It's all right, little fox," he murmured, nuzzling her ear and then biting it delicately, making her shiver.

"Everything's all right," he said soothingly, smoothly removing her blouse and bra as he spoke, fully revealing the rose-tipped beauty of her breasts.

Lara heard the hiss of Carson's breath coming in swiftly, suddenly, and opened her eyes. He was looking at her bare breasts with a sensual approval that made her feel weak. If she hadn't already been lying down, her knees would have given way.

"Tell me if I shock you," he said huskily, bending down to her. "I'll stop. I promise you."

Before Lara could ask what Carson meant, his mouth had replaced his hand on her breast. The kiss was so sweet, so hot, that she cried out, arching helplessly as her nipple became even more erect beneath the moist, searching caresses of his tongue. Her breath came quickly, raggedly, reflecting the wild pleasure he was giving her. Without knowing it, she rubbed her fingers through his thick hair and held his head hard against her breast. He responded with a taut, urgent suckling that made her breath come out in a fragmented moan.

The wild race of fire through Lara's body left her defenseless, violently sensitized, seething with hungers she had never known. When Carson lifted his head to look down at the wet, erect nipple, she reached for him with a cry, aching for the feel of his mouth loving her again.

"Carson," she said throatily.

"More?" he murmured.

But even as Carson spoke, he was lowering his mouth over Lara, pulling her deep inside, suckling hard on her until she made a ragged sound and her hips moved in the rhythms of his mouth tugging at her. His left hand kneaded her other breast, rolling the taut tip between his fingers, sending wave after wave of pleasure through her. Her eyes closed and her back became a bow that gave him her breasts with a sensual abandon that made him groan.

The hoarse sound was another kind of caress shivering through Lara, another flame licking over her hot skin. Pleasure swept away all her thoughts, all her inhibitions. She didn't even know the exact moment when he removed the rest of her clothes; she only knew that his hard, wonderful hand was stroking her bare stomach, her thighs, the midnight mound of hair at the apex of her legs. When he pressed lightly at her closed thighs, she shifted automatically, easing his way, too aroused to be hesitant or shy.

And then his fingers found the hot, aching nub hidden in her softness. She gave a broken sound as her hips rose against his caressing hand. When she felt fingers searching the rim of her softness and then sliding inside her, her eyes flew open in a wave of surprise and unexpected pleasure. She saw his face—taut, expressionless but for his mouth drawn with restraint. He was looking at her as he touched her, and his eyes blazed with hunger.

Suddenly his face changed as though pain were replacing passion. Slowly he began to ease his fingers from her body.

"Carson," Lara cried softly, lifting her hand to touch the hard line of his mouth. "It's all right. I'm not frightened. You don't have to stop. I love you. I've always loved you."

Carson closed his eyes and shuddered violently. He came to his feet in a single savage motion. For a moment he stood looking down at Lara, and then he said grimly, "You are your mother's daughter, all right, but I'm not my father's son. Using little girls just isn't my style. I'll find another way to get even with him."

NAUSEA ROSE IN LARA'S THROAT as her memories churned queasily. She had never remembered that night so vividly, her naked vulnerability and Carson's contempt like an impenetrable armor around him, her sickening eagerness for sex and his easy self-control, her trembling words of love and his cruel reminder of the circumstances of her birth.

She had borne much sly whispering for being the illegitimate, unacknowledged daughter of one of the biggest ranchers in the state, but it had been Carson's rejection that had nearly destroyed her. She had survived it but only at the cost of her ability to respond to men. Even the thought of being touched like that again literally made her go cold.

Only in her dreams was she a woman again, held once more in the arms of the man she loved.

Chapter Five

LARA SAT ON THE DARK RIDGETOP, her knees drawn up to her chest and her eyes staring blindly at the lights below while the past burned through her like black lightning. There were no tears in her eyes to reflect her memories of the night that Carson had rejected her so cruelly, so completely. She had called his name and had heard her answer in the door closing behind him. She had cried then, once, but never again. Humiliation had ultimately burned away her tears. After that there had been only shame. That had not burned away. She wondered if it ever would.

"I didn't mean to hurt you like that."

For a moment Lara thought that the voice was an echo from her former dreams, when she had longed to hear Carson explain what had happened, why it had happened, what had gone wrong that she had loved him and he had had no love at all for her.

But the voice wasn't a dream from the past. The voice was here, now, beside her; so was Carson Blackridge. With a muffled sound Lara looked away from him into the limitless Montana night.

"Don't turn away from me, little fox," Carson said softly. "Please. I'm sorry if I hurt you tonight. Seeing you with Spur made me jealous, and I lost my temper."

Lara's head snapped around so quickly that her hair flew out, brushing over Carson's hand as he reached for her. She had never heard Carson apologizing for anything. Not once.

"Jealous? I doubt it," she said finally. "A man who's interested in one woman doesn't spend the evening undressing another one. Or were you having some kind of complicated revenge on Susanna, too?"

There was more than enough moonlight for Lara to see the sudden narrowing of Carson's eyes and the flattening of his mouth.

"I didn't invite Susanna to the ranch, and I sent her on her way as soon as you ran out. She hadn't undone any buttons but her own. As for me—" Carson shrugged "—I'm used to being alone in the ranch house. Half the time I go around without a shirt. I didn't think that would shock you. Interest you, maybe," he added, smiling slightly, "but not shock you."

Lara looked at Carson's sensual, off-center smile and felt something in herself stirring as though awakening from a long, long sleep. The feeling frightened her.

"Interest me?" she asked, her voice tight as she forced herself not to remember the one time she had curled her fingers into the warm mat of hair that covered Carson's chest.

"It worked, too," he said bluntly. "If your eyes had been hands, I'd have been touched all over."

"No, thanks. I'll leave that to Susanna," Lara retorted.

"I doubt it," Carson said. "You don't like the idea of me with another woman, and it shows."

Carson's voice was calm rather than baiting. It was his very lack of inflection that was shocking, as though he had stated that Lara preferred her coffee black instead of with cream.

"I don't like the idea of sex, period," Lara said, but her tone wasn't as calm as Carson's had been. Emotions seethed through her words, through her hunger, confusion, fear and a sexual denial so deep, so ingrained, that she didn't even realize that it was underlying her other emotions, driving them, driving her. "I was—" Her voice shifted, splintered. She swallowed. "I was revolted by what I saw."

Carson's mouth flattened into an angry line. "I don't believe you."

She shrugged. "It's true. I don't like sex. Period."

"You liked it real well four years ago."

"People change."

"Not without reason," he retorted.

Lara shrugged again, but her body was so tight it ached. She hated talking about sex, thinking about it, because every word, every thought, led straight back to the freezing humiliation of four years ago.

Carson looked at Lara and saw again the shame that had come over her in the bunkhouse when he had mentioned the past. He also remembered the look in her eyes tonight when he had stood before her with his shirt open. He remembered her reaction when he had mentioned that other women didn't run away from him. But most of all he remembered the shiver of response when he had gently bitten her palm. No matter how violently she protested, she was still vulnerable to him. He knew it. He could prove it.

And he was going to.

"When I touched you this morning, you trembled. That isn't the response of a woman repulsed by sex," Carson said flatly.

"I was afraid."

"Then it must have been because you were responding to me," he retorted.

Lara looked at her hand as though she could still see the marks of Carson's teasing, sensual caress. Her throat closed and her breath caught. She swallowed hard.

"You're known for your temper," she whispered. "You were angry with me this morning. You're much stronger than I am. You even admitted that what you were doing to me was punishment for running away from you. It...frightened me. If you had decided to punish me more, there wouldn't have been anything I could have done about it."

"Hell of an idea," Carson muttered.

With no more warning than that, his hard hands fastened onto Lara's arms. Carson's shoulders blocked out the moon as he bent over her. Before she could protest, she was lying on her back looking up into his face. Moonlight and night made a mystery of his expression. She saw his lips part, saw the white flash of his teeth and knew that he was going to kiss her with a lover's intimacy. The moment was like her dreams—and her nightmares. He would kiss her and she would respond, and when he had her helpless again, he would turn on her, tearing out her soul, leaving her empty of everything but pain. She couldn't go through that again. She simply *could not*.

Carson sensed the sudden stiffening of Lara's body as he brushed his mouth over hers. He felt the trembling warmth of her lips, tasted the freshness of her breath, and memories exploded through his body. He had never known anything half so sweet as the taste of her innocence when she had responded to his kisses long ago. He didn't believe that she was still innocent. Anyone as naturally sensual as she was would have experimented thoroughly before she gave up on sex, if she had really given up on it. Remembering her abandonment when he had made love to her four years ago, he doubted that she had given up anything that had obviously brought her so much pleasure.

God, he had been a fool to walk away from Lara, no matter how much he had hated his father at the time.

"Little fox," Carson whispered against her mouth, "I—"

Whatever he had meant to say was lost in Lara's choked cry as she tried to throw herself aside, twisting and turning, struggling to evade the kiss. Reflexively Carson held her still, controlling her with an ease that only increased her fear. She fought wildly, futilely, for he was far stronger.

After the first few instants Carson no longer tried to kiss Lara. He simply tried to protect both of them from her frantic struggles. Quickly the weight of his body pinned her against the ground as his legs and arms captured hers, stilling her, making it impossible for her to fight.

"Lara," Carson said urgently, "it's all right, honey. I'm not going to hurt you. Lara! Listen to me! You're safe!"

For a terrible moment Carson thought that she was too frightened to hear him. Then he felt her shudder and go absolutely limp beneath him. Instantly he rolled aside. He wanted to gather her against him, to rock her in his arms, to touch her reassuringly; but most of all he wanted to erase even the memory of the fear he had seen on her face when he had bent over her.

"Lara," he breathed, touching her pale cheek with aching tenderness. "Honey, I didn't mean to frighten you."

She looked up at him with wide eyes that were black in the moonlight, haunted. Then she turned her head aside. Carson took a deep breath and fought to keep his voice gentle when he would rather have screamed his raw rage at the man who had done this to her. After a few more breaths he felt calm enough to speak.

"Who was he?" Carson asked, his voice shaking with the effort of keeping it under control.

Lara drew a broken breath, too upset by her own wild, unexpected panic at Carson's touch to think coherently. She had had no warning, no chance to control her fear in the searing moment when she fought against herself and him without a thought to anything but getting away, fleeing, running and never stopping.

Suddenly Lara realized that that was what she had been doing for the past four years. Running from Carson. Running from herself. Running in a panic that knew no end. She thought she had gotten over him, but all she had done was flee from that awful moment when she had whispered her love and his expression had changed from passion to disgust.

"Who was he?" repeated Carson.

"What?" Lara asked, still dazed by her discovery that she hadn't solved her problem, she had merely run from it.

"Who was the man who raped you?"

Her head turned quickly toward Carson. "What are you talking about?"

"Don't be afraid to tell me," Carson said gently. "Who was he?"

Lara's mouth opened in disbelief, hardly able to accept that she had heard correctly. "No one," she said distinctly, "has ever raped me."

Carson's lips turned down in a sad smile. "It's all right, little fox. You can tell me."

"There's nothing to tell."

Slowly he shook his head. "It won't wash, honey," he said softly. "No woman as sensual as you were just turns off sex for no reason at all. What happened?"

Anger leaped suddenly in Lara, a bright, white-hot flame that burned through all her hesitations and fears. To hear Carson ask the same question that had pursued her through the years made her furious. He didn't know why she had run, why she was still running. He didn't even have the least idea of what he had done to her.

"How would you feel if you had been inexperienced and fascinated by a woman, but she wouldn't have anything to do with you for years, no matter how much you wanted her? Until one day she turned around and smiled at you and held out her arms and you ran into them."

Lara drew a shuddering breath and continued talking quickly, as though her life depended on crowding as many words as she could into as few seconds as possible. And in some ways it did. She couldn't run anymore. She was appalled that she had run so long and still had stayed in the same place—disarmed, vulnerable, frightened.

"And then she hugged you and kissed you and undressed you despite your hesitations," Lara continued almost wildly, "and when she had you naked and begging and crying for your love, she looked at you as though you were dirt and walked away saying you weren't good enough for her because you were a bastard. How the hell would you feel about that, Carson? Would you run right out and jump on the next woman who smiled at you, or would the mere thought of sex make your stomach turn over?"

Carson flinched as though Lara had struck him. "Lara," he said hoarsely, "little fox, listen to me. That isn't why I walked away from you that night. I never meant to—"

But Lara was still talking, four years of anger and betrayal pouring out in a headlong rush that nothing could silence.

"That's exactly what happened!" she countered, her voice raw. "Denying it won't change it, and it certainly won't change the way I respond to men because of it. I'll never be that vulnerable again. I'd die first!" She shuddered and turned her face away from Carson. "In a way, I suppose I should thank you for curing me of an affliction that seems to run the rest of the population ragged." She smiled bitterly. "But I'm sure you'll understand if I just tell you to go to hell instead."

Carson studied Lara's profile, her long lashes throwing lacy shadows on her moon-washed cheeks, her lips trembling slightly. He let out a long, ragged breath and examined his clenched fists as though they might hold answers to questions he had never thought to ask until that moment.

"I've made it a rule never to look back," he said finally, bleakly. "The past is for people with roots, people who know where they came from. I don't. All I know is where I'm going." He looked at Lara. She was still turned away from him, still living in the moment when he had hurt her so badly and had never even realized it. "I said I made a mistake four years ago and I meant it. Just like you're making a mistake now."

Carson heard the whispering of Lara's hair as she turned back toward him. "What do you mean?"

"You think I walked away from you because you're Larry's illegitimate daughter."

Lara went very still. It was the first time anyone in the Blackridge family had openly acknowledged who her father was. "Yes," she said, her voice as thin as moonlight.

"No," Carson said flatly. "All my life I had two things shoved down my throat by my dear 'father.' The first was that I wasn't of his blood. The second was that you were. No matter how hard I tried, how much I accomplished, how good I was at what I did, it wasn't good enough. A *real* Blackridge would have done better. And you were the living proof. Dear old Larry never tired of telling me that you were the brightest, quickest, most beautiful, polite, respectful, graceful kid in Montana. You were better than any other kid at anything and everything you did. In short, you were a *real* Blackridge, although he never said it in so many words."

Lara's mouth opened in silent shock. Never had Larry Blackridge said or done anything in her presence that made her think she had even been noticed by him in any special way. "But—" she began.

"No," Carson said, cutting across Lara's attempt to speak. "I'm going to tell you why I walked out four years ago, and I'm only going to tell you once. Then the past will be buried in the same grave our parents are, and I'll be damned if I'll go digging it up again. Ever!"

The hostility Carson felt toward the past crackled in every word he said. Lara could imagine what it had done to a man of Carson's pride to be belittled for something over which he had no control—the fact that he hadn't been born from Blackridge loins. Nothing he could say, nothing he could do, could ever change that simple fact.

It had been the same for Lara when she had been belittled by schoolchildren for being a bastard. Nothing she did, nothing she said, could change the fact of her

illegitimate birth. She understood how that kind of unfair rejection could eat into a person's soul. She wanted
to tell Carson that, but she didn't. She was afraid that
if she interrupted again, he would simply stop talking.
Then she would never know the answer to the question
of why he had walked away from her love, if not because she was his father's bastard child.

"The older you got," continued Carson, "the more
Larry shoved you down my throat. Partly he did it just
to needle me because he was old and sick and I was
young and strong and there wasn't a damn thing he
could do about either one. But mostly he baited me as
a way of getting even with me for not being his real
son." Carson swore tiredly and rubbed the back of his
neck, trying to ease muscles knotted by tension. "Anyway, I decided that I'd get even, too. I'd go find this
paragon of perfection, this *real* Blackridge, and I'd
screw her and then I'd shove that fact down Larry's
throat until he gagged on it."

Lara made an odd sound as she realized where Carson's words were going, why he had sought her out four
years before, flirted with her, dated her, seduced her, rejected her. She put her fist against her mouth and tried
not to cry out in protest. He had never wanted her, not
ever, not even in the beginning.

"So I went to the café where you worked," Carson
said. "I stood outside in the dark watching you for
about an hour before I went in. You reminded me of a
fox at twilight—graceful, wary, elusive. I expected you
to flirt with all the men. You didn't. You had the same
polite smile for everyone. You worked hard."

Carson rolled his head and sighed. He hated talking about the past. He hated even thinking about it. Talking and thinking only brought it all back, all the pain and the rage and the hurt. And to what purpose? None of it could be changed. Not one damned second of it. But if it helped Lara to know why he had walked away from her, he'd talk until his jaw locked. He owed her at least that much.

And he needed her. Having her was the only possible way to defeat the past.

"So I went into the café and the first thing that happened was that my big feet got in your way." Carson smiled wryly, remembering despite himself, and not all of the memories were bad. Some of them were like rainbows shining in the midst of the stormy past. "You were so sweet about it. You acted as though my clumsiness were your fault. That surprised me. It wasn't what I'd expected. I'd thought that any girl with looks as stunning as yours would have been spoiled to death by the men around her."

Lara's eyes widened as she stared at Carson. She had never thought of herself as unusually attractive. The realization that he had thought of her that way warmed her subtly.

"After the first few times I ate at the café, I found myself looking forward to going back. I enjoyed watching you, and you enjoyed watching me. I could tell by the blush when I turned and caught you at it." Carson's voice softened. "When you said you'd go to the dance with me, I could hardly wait for the weekend. I had heard all the gossip. I thought that your sweet innocence was just an intriguing kind of act, a way of making the moment even hotter when you finally gave in. Then you opened the door and stood there in that sheer silk blouse and sexy, floaty skirt, and your hair was all soft and loose and begging for a man's fingers, and I was sure that I'd have you before the night was over."

A tiny shiver coursed through Lara as she listened to Carson's deep, gritty voice painting a picture of the past that was unlike any she had in her own mind. *Is that how he saw me? A sexy little tease who pretended innocence only to make the chase more interesting?*

The realization that Carson's image of Lara had been so different from her own image of herself expanded through Lara's mind like a shock wave, rearranging every memory it touched. It was as though reality were a book in which each chapter contained a different version of the same story, and everyone who looked at it saw a different chapter, a different slice of history, a different view of life; now she was reading the chapter Carson had read, with the result that her own view of the reality of the past was changing with every word, every new insight. It was disorienting, dizzying, and at the same time it was exciting, almost miraculous, another page from the past revealed.

Lara had felt a similar excitement before, when her research had turned up a fact that changed everything, rearranging the past before her very eyes. That had been the fascination of history for her. History wasn't dead—it was alive, immensely vital, capable of infinite change. The realization that her own personal history was also fluid, vital, changing, gave Lara hope for the first time in years. Nothing was fixed. Nothing was final. Everything was possible.

Carson's words sank into Lara, sliding past old barriers and fears, touching the vulnerable core that had never died.

"And then you looked so shocked when I called your bluff," Carson said. "I couldn't believe you were that innocent, until I saw your face. You had gone pale. No actress is that good. When you apologized for being a virgin and told me you understood that I wouldn't want to waste any more of my time on you, I felt as though I'd been sandbagged. By the time I realized that you were every bit as sweet and innocent as you seemed, you were lost in all the dancers."

Lara bit her lip, remembering again how she had fled across the dance floor. It had been like a nightmare. No matter how she had twisted and turned, there had been no clear exit, no way out of the room. Trapped. Even the thought of it made her heart beat faster.

"I sat there and told myself there was no point in chasing you, I wasn't going to get my revenge by screwing you. And then I remembered how you had smiled when you saw me walk into the café. You didn't smile at other men like that. Whether you knew it or not, you wanted me." Carson hesitated, then added, "I wanted you, too. You could make me hot with a look. And you kept surprising me. I enjoyed that. It had been a long time since I'd found anyone half so intriguing." He smiled a swift, off-center smile and ran the back of his index finger along Lara's cheek. "Hell, little fox, I still haven't found anyone like you."

Startled, she flinched at the touch. Carson's mouth flattened into a grim line. He wished that he had never started talking, wished that all of it had never happened, wished that he had a clean slate with the woman lying so close to him, wrapped in the black shroud of the past, a past that was strangling the only future he had ever wanted. He had to find a way to unwrap the clinging shroud or there would be no future, nothing but the past repeated, hopes and dreams dying.

"Then you curled up so trustingly in my arms on the dance floor," he said, the words clipped. "You fit perfectly against me and you smelled like a sweet, wild spring wind. I wanted you until it felt like I was being pulled apart."

Again Carson had surprised Lara, making the huge pages of history turn again, shifting reality, revealing yet another new truth. He had wanted her. No matter the ultimate outcome, he had truly wanted her once. She heard it in his deep voice, saw it in his hands clenched against the memories of hunger.

"I kept on wanting you," Carson said. "I told myself it was revenge I really wanted. That was why I kept on seeing you, talking with you, laughing, enjoying myself. Revenge. Every day brought me closer to the time you'd give in and I'd go back to Larry and tell him 'like mother, like daughter.'" Carson's breath hissed out in a savage curse. "Most of the time I even believed that it was revenge I was after. I had to believe it. There couldn't be any other reason for seeing you. Larry couldn't be right—you could *not* be the perfect woman for me. You were my mother's enemy and my enemy. You always had been. You always would be."

Lara lay very still, trying not to even breathe. The complex emotions in Carson's voice flicked over her like burning threads, scoring her.

"I didn't ask myself why I avoided any chance of actually getting my revenge by seducing you," continued Carson. His tone was oddly distorted, as though he had flattened all emotion from it. "I could have teased and nudged you into bed a lot sooner, but I avoided even being alone with you. Damned funny way for me to go after my revenge, wouldn't you say?"

Carson resumed rubbing his neck, speaking matter-of-factly, not expecting an answer from Lara. "Then the storm came that day and chased us inside. We were alone, and you were watching me with eyes that made me ache. So beautiful. So curious. So hungry. I tried to leave before I touched you. I swear to God I tried not to—"

Carson made an abrupt sound, a harsh word that was bitten off before it could offend Lara.

"Then I told myself one kiss, just one," he said, turning toward Lara, looking at her. "I should have been able to stop, but I couldn't. I'd wanted you so long, and you trembled when I kissed you. Passion, not fear. You were burning and so was I. When I kissed your breasts and you moaned, I nearly went crazy. You were more beautiful than I had imagined, and I'd spent more than one night undressing and loving you in my mind."

A visible shiver went through Lara. Once Carson would have assumed that it was desire. Now he was afraid it was revulsion. He continued speaking quickly, not wanting her to get up and flee his words as he described things she no longer could bear even to think about.

"And then you were naked," he said. "All that softness, all that fire. Mine. When I touched you, really touched you, I felt the proof of your innocence. So did you. You looked at me and said that it was all right, that you weren't frightened, that you loved me."

Carson's voice changed as emotion seethed beyond his control once again. "At that instant I knew I couldn't do it. I couldn't take your virginity for revenge. Suddenly I despised my father and your mother for their years of adultery, for all the pain they had caused other people in the name of the lie called love." Carson grimaced, his face expressing exactly what he thought of love. "I knew all about love. At best, love is a trick you play on yourself. At worst, it's a trick you play on the unwary, the innocent—like you that night. Innocent. Trusting."

Carson's fingers dug into the muscles knotted at the base of his neck, physical symbol of the tension knotting his mind. He hated digging through the pain and failures of the past.

"I wanted to yell at you to wake up, to look at reality, to understand that I was your enemy," Carson said harshly, his voice resonant with anger. "Your innocence enraged me. But most of all I was furious and completely disgusted with myself for being so caught up in the past that I would use another person as I had almost used you. I had hated Larry for years for not being able to control his sexuality even to the point of preventing his mistress's pregnancy. Yet there I was, about to do the same thing with you. I had no way of protecting you that night, and you were too naive to have protected yourself."

Carson shuddered suddenly. "And you know what?" he asked roughly. "That thought was the most exciting of all. Something of me growing in you. Something new. Something untouched by the past. A child. Our child."

The sound Carson made then was too harsh to be called a laugh. It was more like a hoarse echo of pain. It cut deeply into Lara, telling her how little she had known about Carson four years ago—and how much she still cared that he had been hurt by the past, too. He was still hurting. Like her. Hurting and not knowing how to make it stop.

Without realizing it, Lara's hand went out to Carson in an instinctive gesture of comfort that stopped short of actually touching him.

"Nothing escapes the poison of the past," Carson said flatly. "I spent most of my life fighting that particular truth. I lost. But I finally learned that you can limit the damage by not looking back. So I don't look back. I go after what I want for the future and *to hell with the past*." He turned and searched Lara's face, trying to read her emotions beneath the mysterious veils of moonlight and darkness. "Do you understand now?" he asked softly. "It wasn't you I walked away from that night. It was the past."

Lara didn't realize that she was crying until she felt the heat of her tears against her cool skin. Carson brushed away the tears with a gentle fingertip, then brought his hand to his lips, tasting her tears.

"Don't cry, little fox," he said hoarsely. "The past isn't worth the salt in your tears. The past is dead. Buried. Don't let it hurt you anymore. Don't let it hurt us. Don't let it ruin our future."

Lara closed her eyes, releasing the last of her tears. "Carson," she whispered shakily, "what do you want from me?"

He started to speak, then remembered her raw fear when he had tried to kiss her a few moments ago. The sexual implications of marriage would send her fleeing down the hillside like the wind.

"Another chance," he said, which was as much of the truth as he felt Lara could handle, as much of the past as he would allow to intrude into the present.

"Why?"

"I enjoyed being with you four years ago," he said simply. "I want that again. We had something that I've never found with any other woman. I've wanted you for years, but I let the past get in the way."

Slowly Lara shook her head. "I don't have anything to give you anymore," she said, her voice breaking.

"That's not true."

She looked at Carson's narrowed, intent eyes and didn't know whether to laugh or cry. "Haven't you listened to me?" she asked hoarsely. "Even when I was a child, I had already learned to fear the passion that drew my mother and your father together, causing so much pain for her. Then you—we—" For a moment there was only silence while Lara fought to control herself. "I didn't know how very powerful desire could be, until you touched me. I didn't know how much I could love, until I loved you. And I didn't know how much I could be hurt, until you walked away from me." She let out a shaky breath. "I can't be that vulnerable again, Carson. I simply can't. If you walked away again it would destroy me."

"I'll never walk away," he said flatly. "I can't."

Lara bit her lip and shook her head slowly.

"So to avoid the possibility of being hurt in the future, you're killing yourself by inches now," he said. "Is that it?"

"I was fine until I came back here."

"Were you?" asked Carson softly. "Or were you just so badly poisoned by the past that you were afraid to let yourself feel? Like me." He ran his fingertip down the silver trail of a tear until he reached the corner of Lara's mouth. "When you trembled today, it wasn't all fear, was it?"

"Carson, I—"

"Was it?"

Lara shivered as the ball of Carson's thumb stroked her lower lip very lightly, tracing the full curve.

"Give us a chance," he said, his voice low, coaxing. "Stop running long enough to get to know me again. I won't drag you into bed. I promise." He smiled crookedly. "As Cheyenne would say, my intentions toward you are strictly honorable, more than you know." Carson hesitated, then made a movement with his hand that was impatient, almost angry. He wanted to talk of marriage but knew it was too soon. "I won't do to you what my father did to your mother," Carson said finally. "I won't dishonor you."

"But if you don't believe in love—" Lara's voice stretched and broke into silence as she remembered his words. *Love is a lie, a trick played on the unwary.*

"Do you?" Carson asked, his tone curious, his expression surprised.

"Despite all the pain, my mother loved your father," whispered Lara. "My grandfather loved the grandmother I never knew. He talked about her until the day he died. And he and my mother loved me. I loved them. Yes, I believe in love."

Carson's smile was bittersweet, almost yearning. "Then you're stronger than I am, little fox, or much more naive." He lifted Lara's hand to his mouth and kissed her palm with such exquisite restraint that she barely felt the warmth of his lips before he lifted his head and looked straight into her eyes.

"If you eventually decide that you want me, remember this: I would never turn you into a kept woman for others to sneer at and condemn. I would never get you pregnant and then not marry you. I would never allow a child of mine to be sold like I was or to be raised as a bastard like you were. If you trust yourself to me, I will take care of you and our children. Always. The future, Lara. Not the past."

Lara closed her eyes and felt her palm tingling where Carson's lips had brushed over her. He was sometimes a hard man, even a fierce one, yet even his worst enemy had to admit that Carson's promises were as solid and unchanging as the mountains themselves. As she listened to his words again in her mind, she felt them sinking into her like an intangible balm, healing places she hadn't even known were raw. Carson would not seduce her and then abandon her to a lonely pregnancy and an even more lonely life as a single parent. Nor would he condemn his own child to a life of illegitimacy in a time and a place where such things still mattered. He might not believe in love, but he did believe in personal responsibility.

That was why he had walked away from her four years ago. It hadn't been disgust with her. It was simply that he had been too decent to use her for revenge like that.

Slowly Lara's eyes opened. She looked at the long, powerful body of the man stretched out on the grass so close to her. Moonlight and shadows outlined his strength, heightening every line of his body; his need was a long ridge of moonlight and darkness rising against his jeans. Oddly, the blunt evidence of Carson's desire reassured her. Despite his obvious physical hunger, once he had understood her fear, he had made no move to touch her in any way but gently.

She drew a slow breath.

"All right," Lara whispered. "Another chance."

"No more looking back?" Carson asked, his voice urgent, as though he needed reassurance as much as she did.

"Carson," Lara said very softly, her voice breaking. "Oh, Carson, the past isn't dead. The more you learn about it, the more it changes. That's not something to fear or avoid. It's a miracle. It allows you to grow past pain, to heal."

"You're wrong," Carson said flatly, his voice as bleak as his eyes. "For us, the past is dead. It has to be, or the future is dead, too. Believe me, Lara. Please. The past can't heal us, but it can destroy us. Let it be. Let the dead bury the dead."

Lara opened her mouth. No words came out. There was an emotion close to desperation in Carson's flat words. He believed what he was saying and wanted her to believe, too. He wanted the past dead, buried, gone, untouchable, unspeakable.

Carson came to his feet in a swift, lithe movement and held out his hand to Lara. After an instant's hesitation she took it, allowing herself to be pulled toward him. She walked with him back down through the moonlight and darkness over Blackridge land, going toward the Chandler homestead—going toward the past, feeling the future tugging at her hand, letting the warmth of Carson's skin drive away her doubts.

Chapter Six

LARA TURNED OFF HER TAPE RECORDER and stretched, flexing fingers that were numbed from working the old manual typewriter that was all she could afford. Despite her aching back and sore fingers, she smiled at the neatly stacked sheets of paper. Willie had finally broken down and told her a carefully edited version of the day he had danced barefoot in the spring grass with the woman who later became known as Tickling Liz. Willie's halting, hesitant words had sketched in the lines of a society and a time when *lust* was the only word used to describe all sexual feelings outside marriage. Yet it had been more than lust for Willie, and perhaps even for Liz. Surely no woman who was merely a whore would have taken so much gentle care in seducing a terribly shy boy.

Slowly Lara leafed through the papers again, but she didn't need to see the words. She could still hear Willie's thin voice and see the memories glowing in his eyes.

...and I took off my boots so I wouldn't hurt her if I missed a step. She smiled up at me and laughed soft and low, and for a time life was warm and sweet as summer honey.

Lara knew she would never again look at Willie and see simply a gnarled old cowhand. She would also see the boy he had once been, dark-haired and strong for his years, holding a woman in his arms while she taught him all the different ways there were to dance.

That was the kind of knowledge that Lara wanted in her history of the Rocking B. It was a ranch and a state and a country built by men and women like Willie and Liz—neither saints nor devils, simply people who had been born into and had grown up in a world they hadn't made, a world inherited from their parents. And, like their parents, like themselves, the world was imperfect. Often it seemed that there was more hate than love, more hurting than healing, more death than life. Yet even in the very worst of times, some people still loved, still healed, still created life in the midst of death. It was those people who left the world a better place than they had found it, not the conquerors and kings who marched hard-shouldered through history.

Smiling, Lara let the pages of Willie's memories drift from her fingers back onto the scarred oak table. She knew her gentle views of history would never be as popular as the fierce cycles of ambition and bigotry, war and betrayal that most people thought of when they heard the word *history*. Those things existed, of course, and they had changed the outward appearance of countries and the distribution of various peoples since the beginning of time. But beneath those outward changes lay the unchanging reality of human emotions, human needs. That, too, was history, and it was a history far more enduring than any royal dynasty or national boundary.

"Lara?"

The sound of Carson's voice whisked Lara out of her history project and into the present. Her breath caught for an instant and her heartbeat speeded up. It had been two weeks since she and Carson had made their truce on the ridge between the ranch house and the homestead. She had seen him every day and most evenings, but it hadn't been to research the Rocking B by going through the boxes of old papers and cabinets of photographs. Instead, they had simply talked after dinner about what Carson had done that day on the ranch or what interviews Lara had done for her history project. After they had discovered a mutual passion for cribbage, they spent many hours pegging up and down the ivory cribbage board that Larry Blackridge's great-uncle had carved from the horns of a massive elk he had shot for winter meat nearly a century before.

"Door's open," Lara called, frowning and wishing that time hadn't gotten away from her. Now it was too late to shower and change clothes before she went riding.

Even as Lara realized that she wanted to look pretty for Carson, uneasiness prickled through her. She shouldn't care whether he found her attractive. But she did. It was there in the quickened beat of her heart and in the breath wedging in her throat as he walked into the small living room. He filled the doorway. Even with his hat off, he had to duck beneath the lintel. In his cowboy boots he was six feet six inches tall.

Carson saw Lara's sudden, intent stare and stopped moving toward her. "What's wrong, honey? Did I startle you?"

"No. It's just—you're so much bigger than the men who built this house."

Carson's green-flecked, golden-brown eyes traveled down the curving length of Lara's body with a possessiveness that he didn't bother to conceal. "Don't let it bother you. You're bigger than the women were then, too. We'll fit together perfectly, just like we did when we danced."

For a moment Lara was speechless, totally surprised by the sensual implications of Carson's words. He hadn't touched her even in the most casual way since the night he had led her down off the ridge and squeezed her hand in farewell at the homestead's door. Yet the look in his eyes right now was enough to light fires in a snowbank. Even as Lara's own eyes widened, she felt a soft bloom of heat deep within her body.

"Carson, you promised," she said, her voice sounding husky, almost breathless.

"I'm not touching you," he pointed out, smiling slowly as he looked at the escaped tendrils of her hair curling around her face, teasing her red lips.

Carson may not have been touching Lara physically, but his smile sent another pulse of heat expanding through her. She realized that at some level she wanted to be touched by him, just as she wanted to be pretty for him. For a moment fear and excitement warred within her.

Carson saw the fear. Even as he told himself not to worry, it had only been two weeks, his smile faded. Two weeks, and nothing had changed. She was still afraid. Would it be the same after two months? Six? Sixteen? Would he lose the only future he wanted because of the mistakes of the past?

He closed his eyes, fighting the rush of fear that came when he thought that Lara might not change in time, might not turn to him with trust instead of fear in her eyes before it was too late. He could not let that happen. He could not let the past win again, taking everything he wanted, everything he needed.

Suddenly Carson felt each separate ache in his body, legacy of the tiredness that had come to him because he had cut short his sleep in order to spend more time with Lara and still get all the ranch work done. Unconsciously he rubbed his neck, trying to loosen muscles knotted by too much work, too much tension, too little peace of mind.

"Carson?" asked Lara softly, hating to see the light and laughter go out of his eyes.

He looked at her, forcing a smile. "Ready to look at those old boundary markers?"

"I—I packed a picnic lunch if you...that is, I know how busy you are and—" Lara stopped speaking and made an uncertain gesture with her hands.

Carson's mouth softened into a true smile. "Clever little fox. How did you know that I needed to get away from accounts and breeding books for a while?"

"Because it's so beautiful outside," she said promptly, smiling because she had chased the darkness from his eyes. "Everyone knows it's bad for your health to be inside on a day like this."

"You have a swimsuit?" he asked.

She nodded.

"Bring it. We'll go up to Long Pool."

"Is it warm enough?" she asked, thinking of the clear green water of the Rocking B's favorite swimming and fishing hole.

"We'll swim fast," he suggested wryly. "Or if you're too chicken—"

"Never," she interrupted quickly, rising to the bait. "I joined the Polar Bear Club as soon as I was old enough to swim. I was so little they had to put me on a fishing line and dunk me like a worm."

Carson laughed, and the lines of strain bracketing his mouth dissolved, making him look much less intimidating. For an instant his hand stroked Lara's shining black hair in a gesture of appreciation for her company. Even though he withdrew his hand almost as quickly as he had extended it, she felt the brief touch all the way to the soles of her feet.

"I've got to get a few things," Lara said huskily. "Why don't you sit down?"

"I'm afraid I'd fall asleep," he admitted, muffling a yawn.

"There's coffee on the back of the stove."

Carson's eyes flew open, revealing flecks of green as well as the familiar golden brown. "You have no idea of the things I'd do for a cup of coffee right now."

"Then I'd better get you one before I find out," she said quickly, a smile tugging at her lips.

"Chicken," he said as she retreated.

"I'm a fox, remember?" she shot back, refusing to rise to the bait again. "They aren't chickens—they eat 'em."

Carson's low chuckle warmed Lara. She loved being with him like this, teasing and laughing and enjoying each other. And if his eyes flared with desire from time to time, that, too, was warming.

By the time Lara had combed her hair and added a swimsuit and towel to her picnic collection, Carson was finishing his second cup of coffee. He looked more alert, but Lara couldn't tell whether that was the result of the coffee or the sight of her teal-blue two-piece bathing suit dangling from one end of the rolled towel. Although he said nothing, his dark brown eyebrows rose in a silent show of anticipation.

They decided to swim and eat lunch before tackling the photographing of the Rocking B's various boundary markers. The ride to Long Pool was only a few miles, but there were six gates. Lara got in and out of the pickup each time like the well-brought-up ranch child she was, grumbling for the last three fences that the only reason Carson had brought her along to the swimming hole was so that he wouldn't have to open all the gates himself. He agreed with a solemn voice and a wicked smile that lighted up warning signals and nerve endings all through Lara's body.

The first rush of the spring melt had already passed, restoring the Big Green to its normal summer size and clarity. Despite the river's name, it wasn't very large. In most places the Big Green wasn't a lot more than a hundred feet wide. Nor was the river particularly deep, except in the pools, which were often twenty-five feet deep or more, having been gouged out during spring floods. At the pools the water poured in swiftly on the upstream end, churned in shades of white and green and blue, and then flowed sedately toward the shallow, downstream end of the pool where eddies swirled slowly and smaller trout fed.

Thickets of willow and an occasional granite boulder taller than Carson studded the riverbanks. He spread their picnic quilt in a nest of grass shielded from the wind by one of the huge boulders. In addition to being a windbreak, the pale granite made a very good heat reflector, adding several degrees to the already warm picnic site.

With a sigh of pleasure, Carson sat down on the quilt, pulled off his boots and socks, tossed his hat aside, unbuttoned his shirt halfway to his belt and rolled up his sleeves. Lara watched the quick, efficient motions of his hands with something close to fascination. It had always been like that for her—watching Carson's combination of size, strength and coordination had never failed to please her.

When Carson had finished making himself comfortable, he closed his eyes and turned his face up to the sun with an appreciation that made Lara's heartbeat quicken. More than anyone she had ever met, Carson was alive to his senses and to the physical world around him.

"You can change here or in the thicket," Carson said without opening his eyes. "I won't peek."

Lara's cheeks flushed suddenly with a warmth that had nothing to do with the sun. The thought of being naked in front of Carson frankly terrified her. It was too close to her memories, to her nightmares. Even the idea of wearing a swimming suit around him made her very uneasy.

"I don't—it's not hot enough to swim," she said quickly, looking away from him.

Carson's eyes opened. He looked at Lara for a long moment, seeing her fear, sensing the darkness of the past reaching forward into the sunny day. He could have pointed out that it was at least eighty degrees in the sheltered spot, more than warm enough to be comfortable in a swimsuit, but he knew that it wasn't the temperature that was preventing Lara from swimming. She had been naked when he had walked away from her four years before. He had been fully dressed. She remembered that as well as he did, probably better, and she had no desire to duplicate the humiliating moment.

With a silent curse Carson yanked off his shirt. He had hoped that swimming together would help diminish Lara's nervousness about being less than fully dressed around him. He had even hoped to see a flash of sensual interest in her eyes when he eventually stripped to his swim trunks. Instead, he was afraid that he had done nothing but increase her fear, reinforcing the past's dark grip on his future.

Wide-eyed, Lara watched Carson's lithe, muscular body emerge from the concealment of his clothes. She was so caught up in the moment that she wasn't even aware of staring at him. She hadn't fully realized just how powerful he was until she saw the bunch and flow of his strength unblurred by concealing cloth.

Carson's legs were long, muscular, and gleaming with hair that was so intense a brown it was almost black. Vaguely Lara noticed that he had worn swim trunks beneath his jeans and that he must have spent a lot of time at Long Pool through the years because his legs had the same tan that his chest did. His shoulders were half again as wide as her own, and his chest tapered to a lean waist and hips that were the result of both a lifetime of hard physical work and a genetic heritage that was unknown but must have been excellent.

"What are you thinking?" asked Carson, his voice low.

The words were as soft and unthreatening as the breeze sliding through the grass. Lara answered automatically while she admired sunlight pouring like honey over Carson's body, making everything it touched gleam with golden light.

"Your parents must have been physically perfect," Lara said simply.

For an instant Carson didn't understand that Lara wasn't referring to Sharon and Larry Blackridge but to the unknown man and woman who had conceived him. When Carson did understand, he looked down at his own body as though he hadn't ever seen it before. It was the first time he had looked at himself through a woman's eyes, seeing the raw strength of his own flesh compared to Lara's smaller, softer body. It occurred to him that it was a miracle she trusted him enough even to be alone with him. The difference in their physical strength was so great that it had to be frightening.

And then Carson realized that not only did Lara trust him, but also she approved of the very differences between their bodies.

"You're amazing," he said, shaking his head.

Lara looked up into his eyes, surprised. "What?"

"I'm twice your strength, half again your size and must look about as hairy and generally cuddly as a hungry grizzly. Logically, you should be running away from me and screaming. Yet you stand there and tell me that my parents must have been physically perfect. You're amazing." He laughed and held out his hand to her. "Come on, my brave, crazy fox. Walk with your tame grizzly down to the river."

Smiling almost shyly, Lara took Carson's hand, enjoying the warmth and strength of his touch. He interlaced their fingers until their palms met and rubbed with a sweet friction that sent tiny quivers of awareness through her. She giggled when Carson winced as his unprotected feet found the stones lying in ambush along the way to the river.

"Tenderfoot," she teased.

"Literally," he agreed, smiling crookedly as he boosted Lara onto the top of a huge, water-smoothed rock ledge that overlooked the deepest part of the pool. "Even though I go barefoot around the house a lot, I still have to toughen up my feet every summer." He braced his hands on the chest-high granite outcropping that made up the ledge and levered himself up next to Lara in a single, easy motion. "It's worth a few stone bruises, though," Carson continued, sitting next to her, close but not crowding. "The men have learned not to bother me when I head for Long Pool. They know I come here when I need some time to myself."

Glancing sideways at Carson, Lara saw both the lines of strain on his face and the subtle signs that he was relaxing in the presence of the rushing water and radiant sun. She could understand the soothing lure of the pool. The patterns the water made were almost hypnotic, as was the sound of the river itself, and the sun was a continuous caress over her whole body. Deep inside herself, she sensed knots loosening, releasing her from a tension that had been part of her for so many years that she had come to accept it as normal. But it wasn't. She was learning it with every breath she took, relaxation overtaking her like a benediction.

Lara wished she were in her swimsuit so that her body would be free to absorb the warmth and peace unhindered by clothes. Being naked would be even better, feeling the sun over every inch of her skin, all knots loosening until her body softened and turned to honey.

The thought would have startled Lara if she hadn't already been so undone by the sun and the murmuring green water. She hadn't enjoyed being naked for years, not since she had curled around herself after the door had closed behind Carson and she had felt cold to her soul.

That was the past. This is now. Go away, memories. Let me dream in the sun. It feels so good, both the sun and the dreaming.

Closing her eyes, Lara leaned back to brace her weight on her hands and turned her face to the sun.

Carson watched hungrily, wishing that it had been his touch that had brought the sensual softening to her mouth. He wished that he could settle her gently between his legs, letting her rest her weight on his chest while he kissed the sensitive center of her palm and the tempting line of her neck. Then she would use his bare thighs as an armrest, stroking him with her soft fingers while he unfastened her blouse and her bra and held her breasts in his hands.

The direction of Carson's thoughts had an immediate and unmistakable effect on his body. Abruptly he decided that it was time to go swimming in the river's bracing green water. If Lara saw him before he had his unruly sex under control, he doubted that she would feel quite so relaxed around him. In fact, she would probably run like hell.

The small sounds that Carson made as he stood up were lost in the soothing rush of the water. He went into the pool in a shallow dive. Lara blinked, looked around and saw Carson swimming cleanly downstream. When the water became too shallow for swimming, he turned and swam upstream, his body slicing through the water with the speed and grace of an otter. She remembered hearing that he had been on the swimming team at the university during one of the best seasons the team had ever had. As she watched, she had no doubt that Carson's presence had contributed to the team's success.

It was also clear that he was at home in the water in a way few Montana ranchers were. He swam easily, swiftly, powerfully, as though the pool were only fifty feet long instead of more than fifty yards. She wondered if Carson's father had been a swimmer, too, and if his sheer physical beauty had caused some girl to succumb to an ill-advised passion.

But that was something Lara suspected she would never know. If Carson had any curiosity about his biological parents, he had never expressed it aloud. As he had told her two weeks before, he never looked back. In all their hours of talking, if the past had been discussed, it was because Lara brought it up. That included any of the past, not merely what had happened between them four years before. Carson would talk freely enough about the ranch's history and the old stories the cowhands told around the bunkhouse at night, but when it came to talking about the Blackridges and the Chandlers, Carson usually found a way to change the subject; and the closer the questions came to the past four years, the more quickly the subject was changed.

The soothing, sibilant, rushing sounds of the river beckoned to Lara, unraveling her thoughts. It was warm on the big rock where she sat, almost hot, and the breeze had died to nothing. A sheen of sweat slicked her skin, making her itch to go swimming. Carson was heading upstream on either his fifteenth or sixteen complete circuit of Long Pool. She had lost count, and he showed no signs of slowing.

Lara slid off the ledge, went back to the picnic blanket and shook out her swimsuit. She undressed almost slowly, savoring the feeling of freedom that came as her confining clothes dropped onto the quilt. She hurried only when she replaced her bra with the swimsuit top, and her panties with the bottom. The suit was the most modest one she had been able to find short of buying from the granny racks in the local department store.

The one-piece suits that were cut up to the hipbone and down to the navel weren't to Lara's taste. Nor did she like the handfuls of strings and tiny patches that were called bikinis. The blue two-piece she had finally selected was more than most women wore and less than Lara had hoped to find. Yet she had to admit that the sun felt like silk on her exposed skin. It made her want to close her eyes and stretch completely, holding out her arms to the pouring warmth.

The river, however, was a good deal less warm. Lara stood undecided on the edge of the rock ledge that rimmed the deep pool, letting water drip from the foot that she had dangled briefly in the pool. A long, dark shape glided closer to the ledge. The shape evolved into Carson shooting up out of the depths, shaking hair and water from his eyes. He hung suspended in the clear water, making lazy motions with his hands to stay in place against the current.

"Come on in," he offered, watching Lara through half-closed eyes. He was grateful for the hard swimming and the cold water because she looked delicious standing there, her body poised between advance and retreat. He wanted to pull her into the water and feast on every lovely inch of her.

"Aren't you going to tell me the water's fine?" Lara asked hopefully.

"Actually, it's pretty warm for early summer."

"Damned by faint praise, as Shakespeare would say," she muttered.

Carson laughed. "It's not that bad, honey."

Lara gave him a look that clearly said she didn't believe him. Then she dove in and came up gasping.

"You beast!" she said, trying to get her breath. "Why haven't you turned blue!"

"You just got all hot lazing around on that rock," Carson said, grinning. "Come on. We'll swim you warm again."

After Lara had done a few quick circuits of the river pool, she was warmer. After six more she was getting a little breathless. When Carson turned and began the thirteenth full circuit, she groaned and rolled over on her back, letting the current take her downstream the easy way. Carson noticed that she was missing, turned, swam back and drifted alongside her.

"I've found—the secret of—your great body," Lara panted, fighting for breath.

"Swimming?" asked Carson lazily, smiling at her, pleased by her words.

"Sort of. Your father was—a deep-sea diver. Your mother—was a mermaid."

"That explains everything but the fins," Carson said gravely.

"Fins?" Lara asked, looking at the clean, powerful lines of his body as he drifted next to her. "You aren't wearing any swim fins."

"Right. No fins a'tall," he drawled. "Just fur."

"That explains it," she said, smiling slightly.

"What?"

"Why I'm cold. No fur," she said succinctly.

Carson remembered the sight of Lara standing in the sun, her smooth skin gleaming with warmth between the blue bands of her suit. She was right. There hadn't been a bit of fur showing on her. With an effort he dragged his thoughts away from the memory that there was one place where she was softly, beautifully furred.

"Ready to get out?" he asked.

"What was your first clue?"

"Shriveled blue lips."

Lara buried Carson in a wave of water plowed up in front of her cupped hand before she turned and raced for the ledge. She thought she had made it when she felt his hands clamp over her thigh. Then his fingers slid slowly down her leg and off her foot, freeing her. She felt suddenly weak, but she pulled herself out onto the ledge in time to watch Carson come out of the water in a smooth rush. He shook his head, spraying water every which way. She would have done the same if she hadn't been afraid of beating herself half to death with her heavy single braid.

The first thing Lara did on the way back to the quilt was step on one of the rocks lying in ambush. Her breath caught at the unexpected pain, and she stumbled. With no warning Carson scooped her up into his arms and calmly continued walking toward the quilt.

"And you call me a tenderfoot," he said teasingly.

Carson looked down at Lara for only an instant before he concentrated on the vague trail to the quilt. The ground didn't need that much of his attention; he was simply afraid that she would see the desire in his eyes.

Her breasts swelled temptingly from the top of her suit, water beaded like diamonds in the shadow cleavage between and her cold-hardened nipples were clearly defined by the blue cloth. He remembered all too well a time when it had been the heat and moisture of his mouth rather than a cool river that had made her nipples hard. He wanted that time to come again with a force that shook him.

"There you go," Carson said lightly, depositing Lara on her feet on the soft quilt. With swift motions he shook out her towel and wrapped it around her shoulders. "Warm enough?"

Lara nodded. "Thanks," she said, knowing that she sounded a bit breathless but unable to control it. "You're so strong." Instantly she winced, wishing that she had said anything else or at least hadn't sounded quite so awed. "I'm not used to being carried," she added quickly, as though that explained her words. "In fact, no one but you has called me little since sixth grade."

"Strength comes in handy with a mean steer," Carson said matter-of-factly as he dried his face on his towel.

He concentrated on briskly rubbing his hair dry and biting his tongue so that he wouldn't say how soft Lara had felt in his arms and how sweet it had been to know that she trusted him at least that much. She had allowed him to carry her. That simple fact went through him like lightning, warming him more than the sun.

Lara sat down and buried her face in her own towel, grateful that Carson had accepted her words as though people told him every day that he was surprisingly strong. Perhaps they did. Especially women. After all, it was only the truth. With unnecessary force Lara jerked out the rubber band that was holding her braid and yanked her fingers through her dripping hair, wincing and wishing that she had never thought of Carson's powerful arms wrapped around other women.

"Hey, easy there," Carson said, kneeling and gently pulling Lara's hands away from her hair. "Let me do it."

Without waiting for her agreement, he began carefully separating her braid until black strands fell slick and gleaming halfway down her back. He took his towel and wrapped her hair in it, squeezing gently until the excess water was absorbed. Then he shifted to a dry part of the towel and rubbed her head slowly.

A small sound of pleasure escaped Lara as Carson massaged her scalp. The flash of uneasiness she had felt when he had picked her up was completely gone. He had made no attempt to increase the intimacy of the moment, although she knew he wanted her. It was as clear as the blunt ridge of flesh rising against his swim trunks.

The fact that Carson was aroused didn't frighten Lara. She knew that he couldn't prevent his desire from showing—but he could prevent himself from pushing her, demanding something that she wasn't prepared to give.

"Where's your comb?" Carson asked, rubbing Lara's scalp slowly, feeling its warmth seep up through the towel to his fingertips. His hands paused. "Unless you mind?"

Lara opened her eyes slowly, mesmerized by the gentle massage. "Mind?" She blinked against the bright sunlight and closed her eyes again. The twin black arcs of her eyelashes cast delicate shadows over her cheeks. "Mind what?" she murmured, sighing with pleasure.

Carson smiled as he bent and kissed Lara's hair so lightly that she felt nothing. He glanced around the quilt until he spotted a bright red comb peeking out from beneath Lara's discarded jeans. Carefully he combed out her long hair until it lay over her back like a polished ebony fan. Then he picked up the brush that had also been underneath Lara's clothes. With slow, firm movements he brushed her hair until it was dry and silky and clung to his fingers like a lover with each stroke of his hand.

After the first few minutes Lara stopped trying to stifle her appreciative murmurs. Having her hair brushed was a luxury as unexpected as relaxing beneath the sun's heat had been. Carson absorbed her small sounds of pleasure hungrily, for each one was a separate caress, a separate sign of hope. The brush dropped unnoticed to the quilt as he substituted his palm smoothing over the glistening black strands, stroking her slowly, taking an intense pleasure in the softness of her hair against his skin.

Long, strong fingers eased into Lara's hair, searching beneath the silk, finding the warmth of her. Carson massaged her scalp with slow, sure motions until she came unraveled in his hands and leaned against him, letting him support her relaxed body.

"You're very good at this," Lara said. Her words were as languid as the motions of her head rubbing against Carson's hands in return, increasing the pressure of his fingers. She was too relaxed to guard her thoughts and questions. She sighed and asked, "Who taught you?" And then she bit her lip at the question. It was none of her business who Carson had been with, who he had caressed, who he had seduced. "Never mind, I—"

"You taught me," Carson interrupted, leaning down to inhale the sweet fragrance of Lara's hair. "I've never forgotten how good it felt at the end of a long day to have your hands rubbing through my hair, unraveling all the knots of tension and disappointment, leaving me at peace."

Carson's words were another kind of caress touching Lara, sliding past her defenses, making her eyes brim with unexpected tears.

"Was it really like that for you?" she whispered, turning to look at him over her shoulder.

"Such beautiful eyes," Carson said. "They've haunted me." He bent and brushed his lips over Lara's. "Yes," he whispered. "It was really like that. And that, too, has haunted me."

For a long moment Carson looked at the memories and shadows darkening Lara's eyes. He knew she was remembering how it had ended between them—pain rather than peace. Silently he cursed himself for bringing up the past when the present had been so unexpectedly sweet.

"If you must remember the pain," Carson asked in a low voice, "why can't you at least remember the pleasure, too? I remember, and I wake up hot and shaking. Pleasure, Lara, not pain. I want a chance to make more of those memories so that when we look back years from now, the past won't be a cold chain wrapped tight around our lives, strangling our future."

Lara closed her eyes and shivered, and even she didn't know whether it was from fear or the sudden memory of Carson's face taut with need and pleasure as his tongue laved the sensitive pink peak of her breast. As though he were caressing her like that again, her nipple tightened, sending currents of pleasure radiating down through the pit of her stomach, making her want to moan. She wanted to see his mouth on her again, to feel his heat and need—and she was afraid to give herself to him again, to share his heat and need.

"What is it that frightens you so?" asked Carson. His voice ached with the effort of being gentle when he wanted to tear the answers from Lara, ending her pain and his own, putting the past behind them once and for all. "Did I ever hurt you physically?"

Silently Lara shook her bowed head, sending a soft black cloud of hair sliding over her shoulders, concealing her breasts.

"Are you afraid that I will?"

Again she shook her head. Despite Carson's physical strength, she didn't fear him in that way. Even when he had wanted to use her only for revenge, he had been unfailingly gentle with her.

"Did you like being touched by me?" he asked, his voice both soft and persistent.

This time Lara nodded her head, but she still didn't look up at him. She didn't want to meet his eyes, for she knew that too much of her hopes and fears could be read on her face.

"Then what is it, little fox?" Carson asked, tilting Lara's head up with his hand beneath her chin.

Lara didn't fight his touch, but she refused to open her eyes. She tried to speak, swallowed and forced out the words. "I'm just afraid to give myself to you again."

There was a long, taut pause while Carson looked at Lara's beautiful, troubled face. He smiled suddenly, crookedly, and his thumb touched her lips like a kiss. "Then I'll just have to give myself to you instead."

Lara's eyes flew open. "What?"

"Yeah, I know. It's a terrible sacrifice," Carson said gravely, his eyes brilliant with laughter and other emotions that were far stronger, far more complex. He held out his hands to her. "Take me, honey. I'm all yours. You can comb my hair and rub my scalp until I turn to butter and melt in your hands. You can talk to me, ride with me, stand quietly and watch the sun go down with me, dress or undress me, touch me, explore me, do as much or as little as you like. Anything. Everything." The laughter faded from Carson's eyes but not the emotions that turned his eyes to molten gold. "Except run from me," he said. "No more of that, Lara. That belongs to the past, and the past is dead."

Carson's eyes were intent, golden, and the hands he held out to Lara didn't waver. Slowly she put her hands in his. She expected her fingers to be enveloped in his warmth and strength, but he made no move to hold her

more tightly. She realized that he was silently reinforcing his words. He had given himself to her.

What she did with that gift was for her to decide.

Chapter Seven

THE FADED DAGUERREOTYPE showed a ragged pile of rocks on a windswept ridge. Below the ridge was a wide, fertile valley with a river winding through it. There were no fences, no man-made landmarks, nothing but grass, the river and thickets of willow and alder. Tiny dots scattered across the grass in the picture could have been deer or perhaps even elk.

Lara knew that the dots weren't cattle, for the first of the Blackridge herd was being driven up from Texas when the photo had been taken more than a century ago. She had found the daguerreotype tucked in among her grandfather's mementos. It had been Cheyenne's old-fashioned, formal hand that had written the note glued to the back: *The first marker on the Rocking B. Photo probably taken by Carson Blackridge after Civil War and before first herd arrived in 1867.*

The curved lens of Lara's magnifying glass glittered in the sunlight as she slowly moved the lens over the length of the photograph. After a moment she looked up, studying the valley below her, searching for landmarks that hadn't changed in the past century. Over the past few weeks she had learned to ignore the modern reality of fences and missing trees, the houses that had been built and the bend in the Big Green that had moved subtly south.

Shadow shifted her weight, stamped to discourage a fly and went back to her three-legged doze. The horse's motions didn't distract Lara. She had become accustomed to Shadow's habits in the four weeks that she had been living on the old homestead. A lot of Lara's time during those weeks had been spent on horseback, talking to the older hands as they rode the land and remembered other rides, other times. Between interviews she had searched for and ultimately found all but one of the Rocking B's original boundary markers.

Even Carson had been drawn into the search for the missing marker after the picnic at Long Pool. Together Lara and Carson had gone through the old deeds and surveys that he had brought out of safety-deposit boxes in town. With his help Lara had compiled a list of boundary markers and their probable locations. She had spent days tracking down the markers and photographing all of them. Except one. The one whose daguerreotype was in her hands right now.

"Dammit," she muttered. "This has to be the ridge and the right place on that ridge. And it was about this time of year, too. The flowers in the foreground are blooming, and the snow has melted back to the higher peaks. It was about this time of day, as well. The shadows match, and the angle of the sun on the Big Green and even the wind bending the grass so that—"

Abruptly Lara straightened in the saddle. "Of course! The grass!"

She slid off Shadow and began quartering the ridgetop for several hundred feet in all directions. It was hard work. This part of the Rocking B had been withdrawn from grazing for the past three years, allowing the land and the plants to rest. As a result the grass was waist-high in places. Lara waded through it as though it were a living green river. Several times she spotted the pale gleam of stones jutting up through the grass, but each time she was disappointed. The stones were naturally scattered rather than gathered by man and piled to mark the first eastern boundary of the Rocking B.

After a few minutes sweat began to shine on Lara's cheeks. Though it was barely a week into June, the land was hot and sweet with summer's bounty. At the moment Lara wished the sun were a wee bit less generous with its presence. A cooler day would have made plowing through the grass more pleasant.

"Lose your watch?"

Lara's head snapped up at the sound of Carson's voice. She had been so intent upon her search for the markers that she hadn't even heard him ride up.

"Carson! Where did you come from?" she asked, her eyes lighting up with pleasure at seeing him so unexpectedly.

The look on her face went through Carson in a shock wave of warmth. Lara had smiled at him like that in the past, when he had appeared without warning in the café where she had worked. He hadn't seen that particular smile in years. He hadn't known just how much he had missed seeing it.

"One of the cows was down along Hat Creek," Carson said, gesturing over his shoulder with his thumb. "I saw you pacing back and forth up here and came to see what was going on."

"Looking for that darn boundary marker. How's the cow?"

"Dead," he grunted, rubbing his neck. "Third one this week. Probably just a coincidence—they were all old cows—but I called the vet, anyway." Carson sighed, and his hand dropped to the saddle horn. "So you're still looking for that pile of rocks. Why? Do you need it that bad for your paper?"

Lara paused, wondering how she could make Carson understand. It wasn't that she needed the marker for her personal history, it was just that the marker was a lost piece of the past waiting to be discovered. "I guess I just love finding missing pieces," she said.

"Never give up grubbing around in the past, do you?"

"Nope," Lara said cheerfully. "It's too much fun."

She wiped her forehead on her sleeve and pulled her hat back into place, missing the sudden tightening of Carson's face as he realized that the longer a piece of the past's puzzle eluded Lara, the harder she would look to find it.

And there was one piece of the past that simply had to be left unfound.

All Carson could do was thank God that what had to remain hidden wasn't part of the time covered by Lara's history. That part of the past would be exempt from her too-intelligent, too-careful scrutiny.

Lara looked up and saw Carson's changed expression. "I know, I know," she said, smiling uncertainly, "you'd just as soon never have to look at any part of the past. Well, I'm a historian, and I love grubbing around in the past."

After a moment Carson smiled almost unwillingly. Despite his fear he enjoyed seeing the light in Lara's eyes when she was in close pursuit of something she enjoyed.

"Hell, I don't suppose much harm could come from finding an old pile of rocks." Carson dismounted and walked over to Lara. "Let's grub together until suppertime."

"You're sure?" she asked hesitantly. "I know you're not interested in the Rocking B's history."

That was putting it tactfully. Lara knew that Carson had a hostility toward the Rocking B's past that was both deep and, to her, inexplicable. Sometimes she wondered if the hostility might have come from the fact that he had been raised knowing that he didn't "belong" to the ranch's history. Would that be enough to make Carson hate the past?

Although Lara very much wanted an answer to that question, she knew that she wouldn't bring up the subject directly. She hated to see Carson's face tighten into harsh lines, and it always did when they talked about the recent past and the Rocking B ranch.

"I'm sure I don't mind," Carson said, rubbing his neck again. "Beats hell out of looking at dead cows."

"No argument there," Lara said, making a face.

"So how do we go about this low-budget historical survey?" Carson asked dryly, kneading his neck one more time before giving up. The headache had started the day he had held Larry Blackridge's will in his hands; there were nights when Carson wondered if the pain would ever end.

"First you hold my hand," Lara said.

"Yeah?" Carson's face softened into a smile as he peeled off his work gloves and stuffed them into his back pocket before offering his hand to her. "Holding hands, huh? Maybe I've been wrong about this history stuff all along."

Lara looked at Carson's gentle smile and tired eyes. Impulsively she took his hand between both of hers and brought it to her lips. She kissed his palm softly, brushing her lips over the sensitive skin before pressing it to her cheek. She felt his fingers tightening slightly, returning the caress. The restraint of the gesture made her want to cry. He had been so careful to keep his word, not to press her in any way. He had given her so much companionship and laughter—and she had given him nothing in return.

"You're working too hard, Carson," Lara whispered. "You look so tired. I don't want you to wear yourself out over an outdated boundary marker that means nothing to you."

Carson closed his eyes for an instant, feeling the softness of Lara's cheek pressed into his hand, savoring it with an intensity that was just short of pain. Since the picnic by Long Pool, Lara had touched him more frequently, been more at ease with him physically, but not nearly as much as he had hoped; and at no time had she suggested that the touching go beyond her hand in his as they walked out across the ranch and watched sunset transform the land into a place of fire. Yet he looked forward to those times with an intensity that made him ache.

And now she was looking at him with concern in her beautiful eyes.

"I don't mind, little fox," Carson said, his voice deep. "The best part of my day is the time I spend with you."

Lara didn't know whether she stepped into Carson's arms or he stepped into hers. She only knew that she felt as though she had truly come home.

At first they held each other tightly, as though they were afraid that something would happen to separate them. Gradually their arms loosened while Carson rocked Lara slowly against his chest, stroking her hair and back with his big hands, wordlessly telling her how much it pleased him to hold her. It was the same for Lara. Her arms were around his lean waist and her head was resting against his chest as her hands kneaded gently down the muscles of his back, trying to relax the tension that was rooted so deeply in Carson that he had forgotten a time when it hadn't been there.

When Lara finally tilted back her head to look at Carson's face, his eyes were closed and an expression of peace had replaced the lines of strain on his face. The knowledge that she could bring him such ease with something as simple as a hug made her ache with emotion. She should have done this weeks ago. She had wanted to. Every time she saw him at the end of the day, his face weary, his right hand automatically rubbing his neck, she had wanted to hold him and soothe him until he relaxed and smiled down at her as he had done years ago.

"I have a better idea than tramping around up here until it's too dark to see," Lara said softly.

Carson rumbled deep in his throat, a sound that was more a bass purr than a word. Lara smiled. Without thinking, she brushed her lips lightly over his shirt. He felt it. She could tell by the subtle tightening of his arms around her. Yet his hand never hesitated in its slow, gentle stroking of her hair.

"It's Yolanda's night off, isn't it?" continued Lara.

Carson rumbled again, somehow managing to make the sound both contented and questioning at once. She laughed softly and hugged him close for just an instant.

"Why don't I cook dinner for you at the homestead?" Then, quickly, Lara added, "Bring the ranch accounts with you, if you like. I know you're behind in them. After dinner you can work on them while I go through some of Cheyenne's mementos. Then I'll feed you dessert and give you a back rub because you hate doing the accounts so much that it always ties you in knots. How does that sound?"

Carson's smile radiated through Lara. "Like heaven. We'll do it right after you show me a little more of your hand-holding history research. I figure you should get something out of this deal, too."

"You don't have to plow through all the grass with me."

"But I want to," Carson murmured, shifting his weight, subtly easing Lara closer to his warmth. "I like holding hands with you. And I like this so much that—" A tremor went through him. "Oh, God, Lara, I love holding you."

The whispered, barely audible words sent an answering tremor through Lara. Her arms tightened, and she held Carson very hard for a few moments. Then she looked up at him. The intensity of his amber eyes made her breath shorten. She wanted him to kiss her but knew that he wouldn't, even though it was obvious he wanted to very much. He had been careful to keep the promise he had given to her a few weeks before. He had done nothing to make her afraid. Nor would he do anything now. If she wanted to be kissed, it was up to her to take the initiative.

"Can I...kiss you?" Lara asked. Her voice was hesitant, and her eyes mirrored her own inner conflict. She wanted the kiss, yet even as she leaned toward him, her memories warned her of danger.

"I'd like that," Carson said, looking at her mouth, his voice gritty.

Again Lara felt the small shiver of response take Carson's strong body. And again he did no more than tighten his hold on her for an instant. That reassured her. As much as she wanted to be in his arms, to know again the pleasure of his touch, the memory of what had happened four years before still had the power to make her want to turn and flee.

Carson could sense Lara's uncertainty. Despite the hunger that sent tiny, uncontrollable tremors through him, he didn't bend down and take the lips that trembled very slightly as Lara looked up into his eyes. She knew that he wanted her. Standing as close as they were, she could feel the proof of his desire. So he waited for her to come to him, knowing that she would feel more secure that way, knowing that she had to want him enough to overcome her fear.

Lara stood on tiptoe and kissed the corner of Carson's cleanly shaped mouth, then pressed her lips against his. She had meant to feel only briefly the firmness and warmth of his lips and then to retreat as gently as she had advanced. But the silky texture of his mustache and the smoothness of his mouth sent sweet memories rippling through her. Some small corner of her mind recognized that Carson was right; she should try to remember the good as well as the bad.

And it had been very good to open her lips beneath his, to taste and feel his mouth consuming her softly.

Hesitantly Lara's hands crept up the front of Carson's shirt. Her lips brushed over his once, twice, and then her arms came around his neck, allowing her to lean against him. Instantly his arms shifted, supporting her as he gathered her even closer to his body. She opened her mouth slightly and kissed him again, expecting him to take her mouth with a single hot stroke of his tongue.

When that didn't happen, Lara pulled back and looked up at Carson. His eyes were closed. The taut, intense look of concentration on his face left no doubt that he was enjoying the soft kisses. Reassured, Lara kissed him again, nuzzling against his firm lips, hoping that they would open in response to her caress. But they didn't.

Puzzled, frustrated, Lara wondered how to get Carson to open his mouth for her. She had had no experience in being the leader in this kind of sensual play. It had taken her a long time even to accept a date after Carson had rejected her, and the men she had dated had been more than willing to be the aggressors. In the end that was what had made Lara retreat; the men were demanding the very thing that she had once offered Carson. She simply hadn't wanted any of the men enough to take the emotional and physical risk of offering herself again. As a result she was no more experienced in lovemaking now than she had been four years ago. She wanted to increase the intimacy of the kiss she was sharing with Carson, but she didn't know quite how to go about it.

Lara kissed Carson again, pressing harder against his mouth. That was more satisfying because she could almost taste him, but it was still much less than she wanted. Again she pulled back, looking at his mouth as though it were a puzzle she was trying to solve. When she finally glanced up, he was studying her own mouth with equal intensity.

"Carson?"

A questioning kind of purr was her answer.

"Why won't you—" Abruptly Lara's courage deserted her. Putting what she wanted into words suddenly seemed more intimate than any kiss she could imagine. She was about to abandon the whole idea when she shifted her weight and felt the blunt, hard ridge of Carson's sex pressing against her torso. The certainty that he wanted her gave her the nerve to try again. After all, he had already taken the risk for her; he had made her the gift of himself two weeks ago when they had been at Long Pool. Now it was up to her to find out how to unwrap that gift. "Why won't you open your mouth for me?" she asked in a rush.

"Do you want me to?" Carson asked, smiling a slow kind of smile.

"Yes," she said huskily, "but I don't know how to make you." She heard the last words and winced. "I don't mean 'make you,' exactly," she muttered. "That sounds awful. I mean I want you to want to—" She stopped again, realizing that she already had hard physical proof of his wanting her. "I mean, I don't know how to tell you I want you to open your mouth without just coming right out and saying it," she admitted in a rush, flushing. She buried her hot face against his shirt. "Oh, Carson, I don't know what to do," she said miserably. "All I really know about kissing is what I learned from you four years ago."

Carson's expression changed, surprise replacing passion for an instant. Somehow he had assumed that, even if Lara hadn't given herself completely to a man during the past four years, she had at least gone in for the kind of heavy petting that made the question of virginity a technicality rather than a real issue of inexperience.

The realization that he had hurt Lara so badly that he had all but crushed the expression of her sensual nature shocked him. She had meant what she said when she had cried *I love you*. He hadn't believed in love then. He still didn't—not in the same way she did. But he was learning just how deep Lara's feelings ran, and just how badly she could be wounded. It made him want to give her a pleasure as deep as her capacity to feel emotion.

Carson gathered Lara closer, kissing the top of her head. "There's nothing wrong with telling me what you want," he said, the words soft and gentle. "In fact," he murmured, moving just a little against Lara, teasing and easing his hungry body with the same motion of his hips, "it's sexy as hell to hear you say that you want my mouth. But if talking makes you feel shy, just run your tongue over my lips." He laughed softly, deep in his chest. "I can guarantee that I'll get the message. I'll even make you a deal. Whatever way you touch me, that particular kind of touching will belong to both of us. But until you do it first, I won't do it at all. Okay?"

Lara looked up, saw gentle amusement, anticipation and hunger in Carson's eyes. She smiled. "Okay."

She went up on tiptoe again, nuzzling against his lips, enjoying the firm feel of his mouth. Slowly her lips parted and her tongue hesitantly brushed the full curve of his lower lip before circling to trace the deeply indented peaks of his upper lip. She felt the shiver of Carson's response and heard the thick, stifled sound of his groan. His mouth opened, and his tongue repeated her caress exactly, leaving an exciting trail of warmth and moisture around her lips.

Breath rushed out of Lara's mouth in a sigh that sounded like Carson's name. The tips of their tongues met, retreated and touched again. It wasn't enough. She wanted her lips to be pressed hard against his and her mouth to be fully joined with him while his tongue stroked hers. It had been that way once. She remembered it vividly. He would kiss her like that again if she could just show him what she wanted.

Lara's fingers slid up into Carson's thick hair, sending his hat tumbling to the ground not far from where hers already lay. The pressure of her fingers brought his head down to hers. She tilted her head a little, then a little more, trying to find the angle that would allow the greatest contact with his lips. Even after their mouths were fully joined, she continued moving her head slowly, rocking back and forth, remembering that he had once kissed her that way and she had felt a wave of sensation clear to the soles of her feet.

Carson made a thick, inarticulate sound of pleasure as he felt Lara's warm breath sigh into his mouth. In an agony of suspense, he waited until Lara's tongue rubbed over his, silently telling him what she wanted him to do to her. His arms flexed as he straightened, lifting her off the ground until her face was level with his. He teased her tongue slowly, luring her deeper and deeper into his mouth until the sensual trap was sprung and he could fill her mouth in return.

The shiver of Lara's response set fire to Carson. It was all he could do not to carry her down into the tall grass and join their bodies even more deeply than their mouths. He wanted it with a violence that shocked him. In that instant he learned that, although he had taken other women since he had turned away from Lara, he hadn't really wanted them. Not like this, with his blood rushing and gathering heavily between his thighs until his head spun and his knees wanted to give way, tumbling him into the soft grass with Lara still in his arms.

With an almost harsh sound Carson slowly lowered Lara until her feet were touching the ground again. He didn't know how or where he found the control not to keep on going, to pull her down with him and cover her sweet, forgiving softness with his own hungry need.

When Carson's arms loosened, Lara swayed slightly as her legs gave way. She realized that if he let go of her completely, she would slide down his body and end up in a boneless heap at his feet. The certain knowledge that she would fall unless he supported her was all that gave her the strength to pull her mouth away from his, ending the deep kiss.

"Hold me," Lara said, her voice so husky that it didn't sound like her own. "My legs—" She tried to take a breath, only to have it break into pieces with a ragged sound. She laughed helplessly. "What have you done to me, Carson? I don't have any more bones than a spoonful of honey."

"Funny you should mention that," he said, his voice deep, almost rough. "I was going to say the same thing." Automatically he bent down to capture her mouth again, then realized what he was doing, the pursuer rather than the pursued. He straightened and took a deep breath. "You go to my head worse than Willie's 180-proof white lightning."

Lara blinked and then smiled, pleased that she wasn't the only one who felt a little weak in the knees. "Do I?" Her breath caught with a husky, intriguing vibration. "I like that idea," she admitted.

Carson made a sound that was a cross between a growl and a purr. Lara felt as much as heard it. Her eyes went again to his mouth. It was reddened from the force of their kiss and from the blood beating heavily through his body. Slowly Lara went up on tiptoe, supporting herself by leaning against Carson's chest, feeling his heat and strength radiate through her blouse until her heart beat as rapidly as his. She closed her eyes and strained upward until her lips barely touched his. The tip of her tongue went out and whispered over his lips as lightly as her breath.

"Are you doing it deliberately?" he asked, his voice both sensuous and rough.

"What?"

"Torturing me."

The tip of her tongue nuzzled the corner of his smile. "Am I torturing you?"

"Yes," he said, but there was no anger in the word, simply an underlying masculine purr of pleasure and laughter and hunger.

Suddenly Lara remembered one of the ways Carson had "tortured" her years ago. She caught his lower lip between her teeth and tugged delicately, running the tip of her tongue along his resilient, captive flesh. Carson's laughter was replaced by a deep sound of desire. His tongue slid beneath her upper lip, making her gasp. As her teeth parted, he tilted his head and fitted their mouths together smoothly, hotly, no longer worried about who was pursuer and who was pursued. She was asking for his mouth, aching for it, and they both knew it.

Lara felt the kiss throughout her whole body, lighting up nerves that had slept too long. The sweet friction of his tongue on hers, the taste of him, the heat and pleasure of his mouth, every aspect of the kiss swept through her. She didn't know that she whimpered deep in her throat as her knees gave way. Nor did she know that her breasts were pressed against his chest and her mouth was straining against his every bit as fiercely as his was straining against hers, as though they both wanted a single kiss to bridge the dark chasm of misunderstanding and years that lay between them.

It cost Carson all his strength to slowly, slowly end the kiss, although even then he held Lara as though she were his last hope of peace after a lifetime of conflict. They both were breathing quickly, unsteadily, soft bursts of sound and heat. He had never wanted a woman so much, not even the night he had turned and walked out on Lara.

"I never knew how hot a kiss could be," Carson said huskily, watching Lara with eyes that were dilated by passion until there was only a narrow ring of green-flecked gold around the pupils. "You'll have to let me take time out, or I'm going to forget all my fine promises and drag you down into the grass."

The thought both intrigued and made Lara wary. Carson could sense passion in the rosy softness of her mouth and uneasiness in the sudden stiffening of her body against him. He nodded slowly.

"I know," Carson said heavily. "It's too soon for you, isn't it?"

Lara closed her eyes. "I'm sorry," she whispered.

His thumb stroked lightly over her sensitive lips, silencing her. "Hush, little fox. There's nothing to be sorry for. You gave me more with that kiss than I deserve."

"But you...that is, you're—"

Helplessly Lara's glance went down to the thrusting evidence of Carson's desire. His own eyes followed hers, and he smiled crookedly.

"Yeah, I sure am. Sorry if it bothers you, but there's not a hell of a lot I can do about it when I'm around you."

"Bothers *me*? What about you?"

Carson laughed softly as he brushed his lips over Lara's forehead. "Honey, after a kiss like that, I'd be a lot more bothered if all I had in my jeans was a pocketknife."

Biting her lip, Lara tried not to laugh as she looked up at Carson from beneath a black fringe of eyelashes. Then she gave up and let laughter bubble out.

"Just for that," Lara said finally, fighting for breath as she held out her hand to Carson, "I'm going to lead you down the primrose path of history."

"Is that where the primrose path leads?" Carson asked dubiously, lacing his fingers through hers. "I always thought it went to something more, um, exciting."

"Depends on how you define excitement."

"Guess," he said succinctly.

Lara flushed, but the color had more to do with pleasure than embarrassment. "Did you really like it?" she whispered, hardly able to believe that the kiss had been real.

"Oh, yes," Carson said, slanting her a sideways grin. "I really liked it. But I know scholars are trained to go to the original source for their information. So feel free to do some truly original research. Rummage around in my pockets and see what comes to hand."

Carson's expression was such an outrageous combination of sober encouragement and frank sensuality that Lara forgot to be embarrassed. With a small shock she realized that the thought of sliding her hands into his pockets right now made nerves quiver deep inside her body.

She was quite certain that she would find more than a pocketknife.

"I think, for now, I'll settle for researching the Rocking B's first boundary marker," Lara said, unable to meet Carson's eyes or to entirely suppress the small, very female smile that tugged at her mouth.

When Carson saw the smile, a raw stroke of desire ripped through him. His hand flexed slowly, making his palm rub over hers as hotly and completely as his tongue had. "Where do we start?"

It took a moment for Carson's question to register in Lara's mind. The sensuous promise of his skin moving over hers had scattered any thoughts of history and the Rocking B's original boundary markers. At the moment the present was far too sweet for her to care about the past.

"Where do we start to...?" she asked, her voice trailing off as she met Carson's eyes.

Lara looked at Carson. The angle of the sunlight had caught his eyes and turned them into brilliant topaz jewels. Light tangled in the thick hair she had so recently run her fingers through. The slanting radiance brought out high-lights of deep chocolate and darkest bronze. The play of colors and sliding light shifted with each of his breaths, changing before her eyes, fascinating her.

"Lara?"

She blinked, but he didn't vanish. He still stood before her, radiant with the late afternoon light, as strong and as perfect as though he had condensed from the land itself.

"Lara?" asked Carson softly, wondering why she had gone so still.

"You are so...perfect," she said helplessly.

The emotion that closed Carson's throat for a moment had nothing to do with desire. She was coming to him so trustingly, so...perfectly. And he knew that he could not match her perfection.

"Oh, God," he said raggedly, closing his eyes against the light's burning clarity. "I wish I were, Lara. For you. Just for you. But I'm not perfect. Remember that when I fail you," he whispered. "Remember, and try to forgive me."

Lara felt herself being lifted even as she reached for Carson. She held him tightly, trying not to cry, wanting desperately to ease the wild pain she had seen in his eyes before they closed.

"It's all right, Carson," she said huskily, holding him. "Whatever it is, it's all right."

He held her until he ached, knowing that it wasn't all right, knowing and praying that she would be able to forgive him when she discovered what he had done.

Chapter Eight

"YOU'RE SURE YOU'LL BE ALL RIGHT?" asked Lara anxiously.

"The doctor, he told me there was nothing wrong that a few weeks off this ankle will not cure," Yolanda said, gesturing to her left ankle, which was thoroughly swathed in elastic bandages. Sighing comfortably, she propped her foot on a hassock and settled back in the worn, overstuffed chair that dominated her cabin's small living room. "Now do not worry about me. The bunkhouse cook, he said he would bring me my meals until my sister's daughter gets here tomorrow. And the hands—they have spent more time walking through my house than watching cows."

Lara smiled, knowing that it was true. Ever since Yolanda had sprained her ankle slipping on a throw rug, two things had happened: all throw rugs on the Rocking B had vanished or had been fixed in place, and the men had taken turns watching over Yolanda until her niece arrived from Billings.

"There is one thing you could do," Yolanda said slowly, "if you would not mind."

"I don't mind," Lara said, without waiting to hear what Yolanda needed. "What is it?"

"Carson he hates old Mose's cooking. If you could fix dinner for him, I would not feel so bad."

"Of course."

Yolanda smiled like a cat curled around a bowl of cream. "Thank you, *niña*. That is very good. You better hurry. Carson, he is a very big man, very hungry, and the hour, it is getting late."

Lara glanced at her watch. "Do I need to run to town for supplies?"

"No. Everything that a woman needs is already there." Yolanda closed her eyes and smiled to herself, nodding slowly. "*Sí*, everything."

Shutting the door softly behind her, Lara crossed the ranch road and hurried toward the big house. It was no trouble for her to cook for Carson. Lately he had eaten more meals at the homestead than he had at the ranch house. In fact, Lara hoped that this evening would provide the perfect opening to ask if she could finally see the documents, photos and other memorabilia that composed the Blackridge archives.

She had hinted around the subject several times before. Each time Carson's expression had subtly changed, telling her that he would just as soon not confront the question of the past and the Rocking B, the Blackridges and the Chandlers. Sometimes Lara thought that it was almost as though having found a way to bring her close without using the Blackridge collection as a lure, Carson regretted having promised her access to it at all.

After Lara did a quick survey of the kitchen garden and refrigerator, she decided that Yolanda had enough food to feed the Rocking B and the neighboring ranches as well. It was too late to cook a roast, but there were some thick steaks that would be more than enough for dinner. A few minutes in the garden yielded tiny new potatoes, baby carrots and baby peas. Lara remembered that Carson loved raw spinach but wouldn't touch it cooked so she gathered two handfuls of greens for a salad. Humming quietly, she carried her vegetable loot into the kitchen.

By the time Lara heard Carson walk into the laundry room just off the kitchen, the whole house was filled with the smells of dinner. She heard the water run as he sluiced off the worst of the sweat and dust, but she didn't hear him come into the kitchen behind her. As always, he had left his boots in the laundry room. He came in barefoot. There were moccasins set out for him to wear, but he ignored them unless the house was really cold.

"And here I thought all those good smells meant that I was going to have to apologize to Mose for slandering his cooking all these years," Carson said, coming up to stand behind Lara as she washed spinach leaves in the sink. His arms slid around her waist as he bent to nuzzle the line of her neck. "You look good enough to eat." His tongue flicked out over her warm skin. "You taste good enough, too. You're in trouble, woman. I'm a very hungry man."

A spinach leaf appeared beneath Carson's nose. Growling rather fiercely, he ate the green leaf all the way down to Lara's fingertips and then began nibbling on them, too. She laughed and turned in Carson's arms to give him a welcoming kiss. Since they had searched hand in hand for the boundary marker nearly a week before, she had become much less wary of him physically. Despite the hunger that Carson couldn't conceal, he had kept his word; he kissed Lara often, and passionately, but he didn't push for any greater intimacy than she had already offered in her previous caresses.

At the times when Lara felt herself aching for more than kisses, she knew that she would have to be the one to take the lead. Without a word being said, Carson's actions had assured her that there was no way she would ever be undressed and then rejected again; it was for her to do the undressing and, if she wanted, the rejecting. That reassured her, just as Carson's passion and restraint reassured her. He was doing everything he could to make their growing relationship risk free for her. The realization that he was perceptive as well as passionate made her feel cherished. These days when Carson touched her, she responded without fear.

Slowly Carson pulled Lara close, fitting her along the length of his body with a sensuous precision that sent fire racing through both of them. There was no question of giving or taking, pursued or pursuer. The kiss claimed both of them equally, making a shivering heat blossom deep within Lara. She loved the feeling of being pressed along Carson's powerful body, and she trembled with pleasure to feel the hard rise of his desire and know that she was causing it.

Only after the long kiss was over and Lara looked up into Carson's face did she see the lines of fatigue and the darkness beneath his eyes.

"Carson," she whispered, kissing him very gently, "you look so tired. Aren't you sleeping well? Is something worrying you?"

His whole body tightened at the question. "I sleep," he said, nuzzling the corner of Lara's mouth.

What he didn't say was that he lay awake for a long time each night, trying to decide whether it was better to tell Lara the whole truth now and almost certainly lose everything he had ever wanted, or to wait and pray that he would never have to tell her at all. There was no guarantee that she would ever find out. And even if she did, it might be years and years in the future. By then she might understand. By then she might care enough about the life they had built together to be able to forgive him.

"Is something wrong with the ranch?" Lara asked hesitantly. "Are the inheritance taxes—"

"No," Carson interrupted, his voice almost harsh. "Larry planned for everything. Too damned well!"

Carson's arms tightened as he bent down, asking for and taking Lara's mouth in the same motion. She wondered what Carson had meant by his comment, but as always the heat of his kiss scattered her thoughts. Even as part of her realized that this always happened when the subject of the Rocking B or Carson's father came up, the rest of Lara responded to the need that lay beneath Carson's searching kiss, a need that transcended the hard insistence of his sex pressing against her softness. She didn't know where that greater need came from; she only knew that she ached to answer it, to ease Carson's mind as well as his body.

Slowly Carson and Lara separated, sharing many tiny, swift kisses that spoke eloquently of their reluctance to be parted.

"I'll shower," Carson said, his voice husky. "I must smell like a polecat."

Lara smiled. "You smell like a man who has worked hard and ridden hard. You smell hot and—wonderful."

With a thick sound Carson stepped back quickly. "You keep that up and I'm going to find myself suggesting that you take a shower with me," he said, smiling and very serious at the same time.

Carson turned away before he could see the widening of Lara's pupils or the sudden intake of her breath as she thought of sharing a shower with him. She waited for fear to come at the thought of being naked with him. All she felt was a flash of uneasiness that was quickly overwhelmed by a rush of desire.

"How long before dinner is ready?" he asked, not looking back.

"How long do you want?"

"Give me fifteen minutes."

"Fifteen minutes," she agreed.

It seemed like a very long quarter hour to Lara before Carson returned, filling the kitchen with his male presence and deep voice.

"I'd kiss you again," he said, "but I don't trust myself to stop before dinner is as cold as well water."

Lara looked at Carson's damp, freshly combed hair, dark mustache and smiling lips and decided she didn't trust herself, either. She served the dinner with easy, efficient motions, then sat at his right hand and began to eat. Between bites she asked questions about the water and the grass, the calves and the cows, the price of beef and feed. The ebb and flow of the Rocking B's seasonal work had always fascinated Lara, for it gave her a deep sense of being involved in processes and cycles that went far back in time and would continue far into the future.

"...vet said that it was nothing but coincidence that I lost those three cows so close together," finished Carson.

Lara let out an audible breath of relief. "I was worried that the cattle you bought at the beginning of summer might have been carrying some disease."

"That thought occurred to me about once an hour after the third cow died," Carson agreed wryly. "Just old age, though. It was a hard winter, and raising a calf takes it out of old cows. They dropped strong calves, though. They're going to make it."

"Doesn't surprise me," Lara said tartly. "They darned near pulled my arms out of the sockets tugging on the bottle."

Carson's eyes kindled with laughter and pleasure as he remembered the picture she had made with her legs braced and a healthy bull calf nursing hard on the oversize bottle she was holding. Carson had finally moved to stand behind her, wrapped his arms around her waist and anchored her so that the calf didn't pull her right off her feet. As they struggled to keep the bottle from being yanked free by the eager calf, they had begun laughing so hard that they had ended up falling down in the hay while the calf trailed milk all over both of them.

And then they had forgotten the calf and the barn and the men working nearby in the other stalls. Carson had pulled Lara into his arms for a kiss that had left him hard, aching, shaking with hunger at the feel of her body so soft and unafraid beneath his.

"You can hand raise my babies anytime," Carson said, leaning back in his chair, his voice gritty and his eyes tawny beneath the dining room's warm lights.

Something in his clear, intent eyes made Lara breathless, as did the thought of feeding his babies—and not the four-legged variety, either. She realized then how much she would like to feel Carson's child growing inside her, forever joining their destinies beyond any human ability to sever. The thought exploded softly through her, making her melt in waves of emotion that left her trembling.

"I'd like that," Lara whispered, her voice as soft as the sensations shivering through her.

Carson heard her words, and he knew that Lara wasn't talking about raising calves.

"Lara—" he began, looking at the woman sitting next to him at the table.

Then his words stopped as he saw Lara's tongue flick out to pick up a stray crumb from her lip. With a throttled groan he bent and caught her mouth beneath his, turning his head until her lips opened. He kissed her with slow, aching rhythms of his tongue. When he finally lifted his head, he was breathing too fast, and so was she.

"White lightning," Carson said hoarsely.

Once Lara would have blushed or felt uneasy at seeing the raw desire on Carson's face. Now, seeing his need simply made it more difficult for her to drag air down into her lungs.

"You make the coffee," he said, standing abruptly. "I'll take care of the dishes."

"I'll help."

"Honey," Carson said, his voice almost rough, "if I brush up against you in the kitchen right now, I'll trip you and beat you to the floor." He saw the sudden parting of Lara's love-bruised lips, heard the swift intake of her breath and wanted nothing more than to feel her naked and willing and hot beneath him. "Don't look at me like that," he warned, but his voice was caressing rather than harsh.

"Like what?"

"Like you want to eat me for dessert."

Carson's eyes narrowed into hot gold slits as he realized that Lara had never thought of touching him that way before—and thinking of it now had made the pulse in her throat beat faster. When a shiver of response coursed over her skin, it was all he could do not to grab her.

With a small sound Lara tore her eyes away from Carson's hard, hungry body. "Coffee," she said faintly.

Carson didn't trust himself to say anything at all. He grabbed two handfuls of dishes and went into the kitchen. After a few minutes he heard Lara walk into the kitchen and turn on the fire underneath the old-fashioned drip coffeepot he always used.

"Carson?" Lara's voice was hesitant, as though she were unwilling to disturb the increasingly fragile control that both of them had over their emotions.

"Hmmm?"

Carson's vague rumble of encouragement was all Lara needed. "Would it be possible for me to look at some of the Blackridge historical papers and photos tonight?" she asked in a rush, as though afraid Carson would somehow manage to change the subject in midquestion as he had so many times in the past.

It was the request that Carson had been heading off successfully since the day he had held out the family archives as a lure to draw a shy scholarly fox closer to him. He wanted to change the subject, to deflect her, to do anything but agree to let her rummage through the Blackridge papers, raking up a past that belonged to her in a way that it would never belong to him—a past whose cold shadow could extend even into the present and future, destroying the delicate growth of friendship and desire that was bringing Lara closer and closer to him with every breath.

Yet Carson knew that if he kept refusing to allow Lara into the Blackridge archives she would begin to suspect that his reluctance went much deeper than a simple dislike of the past. She would begin to ask questions. Once that happened, she wouldn't rest until she found the answers. There would be no hope of deflecting her. He had seen that already, her joy and persistence in uncovering historical facts that was as much a part of Lara as her stunning blue eyes. Once she had found out about the old boundary markers, she had pursued them like a prospector after the mother lode, even though the markers had no immediate relevance to her informal history of the Rocking B. They were simply there, a tangible part of history, and she wanted them.

It was the same for the Blackridge archives.

Although Carson had carefully removed any documents dating later than 1960 from the boxes, he still hated turning those records over to Lara. They contained too many hints of what had finally driven Larry Blackridge to draw up his morally crazy but legally unimpeachable will.

Carson didn't want Lara's curious, intelligent mind anywhere near the Rocking B's recent history. Yet he knew that he had stalled as long as he could without raising Lara's curiosity. As of tonight, giving the records to her had just become the lesser of two evils.

And Carson hated that, too—being forced by the past to choose among evils. But it was not the first time. Nor would it be the last.

"Take the coffee into the library," Carson said quietly, "but don't touch any of the stuff lying around until I get there. Bring some cognac, too. I could use it."

Surprised by Carson's tone and by the implication that she somehow wasn't to be trusted alone with whatever was in the library, Lara said nothing. She poured coffee into an insulated carafe, found two big mugs, put them on a tray and carried it over to the liquor cabinet. When she opened the polished walnut doors, she spotted an array of glasses as well as liquor. She pulled out a snifter for Carson. After a moment's hesitation she added another snifter to the tray, deciding that she wouldn't mind a taste of cognac herself. As always, the subject of Blackridge history had created tension between Carson and her. She wished that he would talk about the problem instead of ignoring it, but so far he had resisted every effort she had made to follow that particular line of conversation.

"It's the decanter to the left," Carson said without looking up from the dishes he was stacking casually in the dishwasher. "The square one."

Lara looked at the row of cut crystal decanters that had been Sharon Blackridge's pride. They were all filled with liquids of varying colors and potency. Only one of the decanters was perfectly square. It was filled with a liquor the exact shade of Carson's eyes when he stood at sunset looking over the land he loved.

The door to the library was ajar. Lara nudged it with her shoulder until she could carry the wide tray through. Cartons were stacked everywhere, floor and coffee table and couch alike, as though every closet in the ranch house had been cleaned out and the contents packed for storage elsewhere. The only place free of boxes was Carson's desk, which was covered with various papers, breeding books and ranch ledgers. Fortunately, there was enough room for the tray, as well. Lara would not have moved a single box even one inch after what Carson had said to her in the kitchen.

She set the tray down on the desk and poured coffee and cognac. Scrupulously not looking into the few cartons that were open, she eased down onto the couch in a narrow space between boxes. Cautiously, she drank her coffee and occasionally sipped the cognac, inhaling the fragrant, potent fumes. She moved as little as possible so as not to disturb the precariously balanced boxes.

From what Lara could see, nearly all the cartons were new. Each had been labeled in a general way. The words she could see—daguerreotypes, ranch accounts, personal mementos, old photographs—were all written in the same strong, blunt hand. Carson's, she assumed. From what she had heard, Larry Blackridge had been too ill before he died to do anything as strenuous as sorting through generations of accumulated family records.

Lara didn't notice Carson standing in the doorway watching her while she looked at all the cartons. He could read the intense curiosity and eagerness on her face as easily as he could read his own handwriting on the boxes. For a moment he wished futilely that Lara had been interested in knights and dragons or shoguns and warring city-states—anything except the history of ranching in general and the Rocking B in particular.

But that had always been her passion, just as becoming a "real" Blackridge had always been his.

Without a word Carson walked into the room, shifted boxes off the couch, grabbed his coffee and cognac and sat next to Lara. He sensed her watching him with a curiosity that grew greater with every second he didn't speak. From her reaction he knew that his expression must have accurately reflected how he felt inside—cold, closed, hard. Trapped. He put his foot against a box of papers and abruptly shoved it onto the floor, making room on the coffee table for something other than the dusty residue of Blackridge history.

Lara set her empty coffee mug and nearly untouched cognac beside his in the cleared space on the coffee table. Biting her lip unhappily, she turned toward Carson.

"I just realized how unfair this is to you," Lara said quietly. "There are six cartons of Cheyenne's journals and mementos back at the homestead, and I haven't had the courage to open even one of them. Even the thought of going through all the pictures and personal treasures was just too painful." Lara closed her eyes against the sudden sting of tears. "So instead of coping with my feelings and reading Cheyenne's journals, I come here and ask you to rummage through your own family mementos, your own pain. I'm sorry, Carson. That was terribly selfish of me."

Strong arms closed around Lara as Carson lifted her onto his lap. He tucked her head against his shoulder and kissed her gently, repeatedly.

"Sweet little fox," Carson said huskily, kissing Lara's eyelids, "you wouldn't know how to be selfish if someone gave you step-by-step instructions."

Lara's lips trembled as she tried to smile. "Oh, Carson," she whispered suddenly, burying her face again his neck, "sometimes I miss Cheyenne so much that—" Her voice broke.

Carson's arms tightened around Lara as he rocked her slowly against his chest. "Go ahead and cry," he murmured, stroking her gleaming black hair and kissing her forehead.

"It isn't the kind of pain that crying makes better. This makes it better, though," she said, closing her eyes, letting Carson's presence seep into her, filling her with warmth. "Having you hold me is...healing."

"Yes," whispered Carson. "For me, too."

For a long time there was no sound but that of Carson's hand gently stroking the raven silk of Lara's hair. Finally he began talking quietly, his voice so deep that she could feel the words resonating through the hard bone and muscle beneath her cheek.

"Larry was like you," Carson said, "obsessed with the Blackridge family history, the Blackridge bloodlines. He had genealogical charts drawn up that began with the Battle of Hastings and stopped with Larry Blackridge." Carson made a sound that was partly amusement, partly disgust. "I doubt if there's any truth in the damn charts beyond Great-Grandfather Blackridge—or was it great-great?" Carson shrugged, dismissing the distinction because it no longer mattered to him. "Whichever. The Blackridge who piled up those boundary stones you can't find on Windy Ridge. Beyond him, I think those fancy charts are a load of raw crap."

Carson leaned forward, holding Lara in place with one arm while he reached past her with the other and snagged a snifter of cognac between his fingers. He offered her some, watching hungrily while she took a delicate sip and licked her lips. He wanted very much to lick her lips for her, to bend his head and taste the sweet warmth of her mouth. But he knew that he had to talk first, to try to make her understand why he was so hostile to the recent past. He had to tell her enough to dull her curiosity about him personally...and not so much that her curiosity found a new, much more dangerous direction.

Frowning, Carson took a sip of the brandy, sighed and wondered how to begin talking about his least favorite subject. He leaned back against the couch once more, taking Lara and the snifter with him. The subtle movements of her body as she found a new balance in his lap were an exquisite torture. He hadn't known a man could want a woman so much, in so many ways. Not for the first time he cursed his parents for the power struggle whose ramifications were still shuddering through his own life, threatening to tear it apart. He should have married Lara four years ago, when she had wanted him.

But it had been impossible then.

"For a while," Carson said almost roughly, "I was just as wild about the Blackridge family tree and history as you or Larry. I was still young then. I still believed that one day my dear adoptive 'father' would look at me and see his son instead of a changeling who had been foisted off on him."

Lara's eyes widened and darkened. She wanted to ask what Carson meant. Hadn't Larry wanted to adopt a child? And if he hadn't, why had he gone through with it? But the sight of old pain and anger drawing Carson's face into dark, tight lines made Lara ache. She didn't want to hurt him by asking unnecessary questions, questions he might answer if she were just patient and listened quietly.

Carson swirled the rich amber cognac around and around in the crystal glass for the space of several breaths before speaking again.

"But no matter how much I tried, how hard I worked, how much I wanted it, Larry never looked at me as his son," Carson said finally. "It never seemed to occur to him that a baby might grow up feeling that the man and woman who raised him were actually his parents in the only sense of the word that mattered, and that the child might want to love and be loved by those parents."

Carson shrugged impatiently, as though throwing off the grasp of the unhappy past. "The only part of being a parent that mattered to Larry had to do with extending his bloodline. The rest was sentiment, and God knows Larry never had much use for that." Carson swirled the liquid again and added softly, "Except with your mother. I have a feeling that was as close as Larry ever came to loving. And you, probably. For your blood. His blood."

And may he spend eternity regretting his obsession with blood, Carson added silently, bitterly. *He sure as hell made everyone else regret it while he was alive.*

Lara's fingers moved to cover the strong hand that had tightened on her hip. She didn't know what to say. She did know that Carson's thoughts must have been even more painful than his words.

"None of it is your fault," she whispered, lifting Carson's hand and rubbing her cheek slowly over it. "You were everything a reasonable man could want in a son."

Carson's curt laugh made Lara wince. "Too bad Larry wasn't a reasonable man," Carson said savagely. "But it's over now, over and done and buried with him. He fouled up enough lives in the past. I'll be damned if I'll let him foul up any more in the future."

As Carson's words echoed in the silent room he knew that he had the answer to the question that had been keeping him awake nights: No. He would tell Lara nothing. The bitter result of the power struggle between Sharon and Larry Blackridge would be buried with them, never to see the light of day again.

"To the future," Carson said, lifting the brandy snifter, "and to hell with the past."

He drank swiftly, draining the potent liquid. He leaned forward, traded the empty glass for the other one and settled back again without loosening his hold on Lara.

"Where were we?" he asked. "Oh, yes. The precious Blackridge family archives."

Lara winced again and said nothing. She had a better understanding of Carson's bitterness now. Everything in the room was a reminder of a family that he had tried desperately to belong to. In the end Larry Blackridge had never allowed Carson to be more than a stranger who happened to share the same living quarters.

The thought of growing up like that made Lara ache in silent sympathy. Being a bastard had been difficult for her at times, but she had always known that she was loved. She hoped that Sharon Blackridge had somehow made up for Larry's inability to love his adopted son. Yet even as the thought came, Lara doubted that it had worked out that way. Sharon Blackridge had been a proud woman rather than a loving one.

"There they are," Carson continued, waving the snifter of brandy in a wide arc that included the chaos of cartons and boxes. "At one time I spent a lot of time pouring over this junk, looking for the key to Larry's respect. I guess I figured that if I knew as much as he did about the Blackridges, I'd somehow magically become one."

Carson's laugh was harsh, but the arm holding Lara was not. With a sigh he bent and brushed his lips over her silky black hair.

"I spent damn near as much time learning the family history as I spent on getting a bachelor's degree," he said. "It didn't make me a Blackridge, though. Nothing did. Nothing would. Larry told me that so often that I finally believed him. I'm not a Blackridge and I never will be. So after he died, I was tempted to burn all this junk to ash and throw it to the wind."

Lara's breath came in with an audible rush at the idea of so much history being destroyed. Eyes wide and dark, she studied Carson's face. Once she would have thought that the smile curling the corner of his mouth was cold, unfeeling, almost cruel. She knew better now. She could see the hurt beneath the hard exterior, the lingering remnants of the child who had never belonged, no matter how hard he had tried.

Sadly she realized that in some ways it must have been a relief for Carson when Larry died. The Rocking B was Carson's home now. He finally had a place where he belonged, a place where he would no longer have to feel like a stranger every time the man who refused to be his father looked at the son he had adopted but never accepted into his heart.

Very gently Lara brushed her lips against the warm, slightly rough skin along Carson's clenched jaw. He turned to look at her, and for an instant his eyes burned into hers like those of a cougar brought to bay. Then he bent and gave her a kiss that tasted like cognac and fire. When the kiss ended, he looked at her again, his tawny cat eyes clear and hot.

"Then I decided that what the hell, maybe some good could come of all this Blackridge stuff in the right hands. So it's all yours, Lara. May you get more joy out of it than we did."

Chapter Nine

CARSON WATCHED LARA'S DARK HEAD as she bent over the coffee table, sorting through yet another box. The floor was checkered with documents, photos and mementos divided into decades. When the pile of material Lara was building threatened to slither off onto the floor, Carson gathered everything up in his big hands.

"Are these for the 1910 pile?" he asked, stifling a yawn.

Lara made a noise that he thought sounded positive, but he wasn't sure.

"Lara?"

She looked up from the photograph in her hand. Tears magnified the blue depths of her eyes. Carson's hands opened. A cascade of photos and papers poured unnoticed to the floor.

"What is it, honey?" he asked, reaching out to her.

Wordlessly Lara held out a handful of faded color snapshots. "These were buried in with all the early 1900s photos. I don't know why."

Carson looked at the picture on top. He recognized Long Pool, the water-smoothed granite ledge and the swirling, tumbling wealth of the Big Green. There was a young woman stretched out on the pale granite, sunning herself as unself-consciously as a butterfly. She was slender, elegantly shaped, and her hair was the color of the sun. Although her face was turned away from the camera, Carson had a visceral certainty that the woman's eyes were the brilliant blue of a high-country lake.

"Your mother," he said, no question in his tone.

Lara nodded.

For a moment Carson's hand tightened on the snapshots as though he would fling them across the room. He stared down without seeing anything, wishing that he had looked for more than incriminating documents when he had gone through the archives. He could have spared Lara the pain of meeting her mother's ghost so unexpectedly. Slowly, almost against his will, he slipped the first photo from the group and put it underneath the others.

The sound of the camera must have alerted Becky. She had propped herself up on her elbows, turned and smiled. Carson's breath hissed out of him as though he had taken a blow. He had seen that smile before, when he came upon Lara unexpectedly and she turned toward him, her face glowing with pleasure. If he had had any doubt about who was taking the pictures, he no longer did. Only one man would have been able to light up Becky Chandler like that, the man whose mistress she had been for thirteen years, the man whose bastard child she had given birth to.

The next snapshot was a stunning close-up of Becky looking into the camera, approving of the man she saw. The angle of the light told Carson that this picture had been taken later in the day. Becky's lips were slightly swollen, her cheeks were flushed and her hair was a wild radiance around her face. She had the languid, sensual look of a woman who had been loved recently and well.

Carson's body tightened as he wondered if Lara would look at him half so approvingly after they finally made love.

The last snapshot made Carson go as still as Lara had. It was a close-up of Larry Blackridge, but it was a Larry whom Carson had never before seen. His father was smiling with affectionate indulgence while Becky took his picture. Despite the gentle curve of Larry's lips, his pale blue eyes blazed with emotion as he looked at the woman who held the camera.

And there was no doubt that it was Becky Chandler who had taken that picture. Larry had never smiled gently at anyone else. In fact if it weren't for the picture in Carson's hand, he would have sworn that Larry had been incapable of that much tenderness, that much intensity, that much passion.

Or was it love that Larry had felt, as well as passion? Had he loved Becky, but not enough? Had he loved the Rocking B more, and chosen it over Becky?

Because Larry couldn't have had both of them legally, the woman and the land. He had had to choose. Sharon had seen to that. Then Larry had tried to have the last word in the long, bitter struggle over love and the land; in doing so, he had inadvertently ensured that Carson would have neither love nor land if Lara found out what Larry had done.

"I—I didn't realize mother was so beautiful," Lara said, her voice aching. "The photos I have of her are either as a child or after I was born."

Carson looked down at the haunting, bittersweet pieces of the past held in his hand. He had hated Larry because he was cold, stubborn and occasionally cruel in his determination to have his way. Yet Larry had also been a man caught between two overwhelming loves. He had kept both the land and the woman, for a time. When a storm had taken the woman and left him with only the land, Larry's cruelty had become more than occasional.

Carson hadn't thought about any of that, even though he had been old enough to see Larry as more than the man who refused to be a father. Carson had been twenty-one when Becky Chandler died, yet he had not seen his father's grief. Carson had seen only his mother's hurt and humiliation, and his own. He had not asked if Larry might have found something in his mistress that his wife could not provide, or if a cruel necessity had doomed him to marry the wrong woman. Carson had simply hated Larry without trying to understand him at all.

And then Carson had gone out and poured that hatred like acid over a girl whose only crime had been to laugh with him, to ease his fatigue at the end of a long day, to bring him passion, to trust him and to make him feel alive in a way that he had been trying to recapture for the past four years.

"I've heard that women in the first flush of love often are beautiful," Carson said quietly, looking up at Lara. "I know that I've never seen a woman half so perfect as you were the night we ate a picnic in your apartment."

Carson saw memories darken Lara's clear eyes and draw her face into lines of pain. His mouth turned down in a bitter curve.

"That's all you remember of that night," he said. "Pain. Humiliation. I gave you no pleasure at all, nothing to repay your warmth, your trust, your—love." His fingers opened and the colored fragments of the past fluttered down like autumn leaves. "Oh, God, little fox," he whispered, his voice shaking. "There are times when I wish I could crawl out of my skin and die."

Carson came to his feet in a wild surge, but before he could turn away, Lara had thrown her arms tightly around his hips, holding him close.

"It wasn't like that!" Lara said fiercely, scratching her temple against his silver belt buckle and not even noticing. "You made me feel like the most beautiful woman ever born. And when you kissed me, touched me—" Her voice broke. She moved her cheek caressingly against Carson, feeling the hard warmth of his body beneath the faded jeans. "You turned me into fire and I— I burned. For you. With you. Nothing was ever that beautiful for me. Nothing. That's why it hurt so much when you—when you—"

Carson's fingers tangled in Lara's thick, silky hair as he held her tightly. "I'm sorry," he said hoarsely. "If I had known I was going to hurt you so much, I never would have walked into that café."

He felt the shudder that went through Lara as though it were his own.

"Then I'm glad you hurt me," she said, her breath ragged. "If that was the only way we could be here, now, together, then I wouldn't take back a second of the past. Do you hear me?" she asked urgently, tilting her head back from his waist and looking up at him. "Not one second. It was worth it, all of it, for this."

Carson looked at the deep, brilliant clarity of Lara's eyes and felt his throat close around emotions he had never felt before. "You are so beautiful to me," he whispered hoarsely, stroking her cheek with fingers that trembled. "I'd give everything I have to take back what I did to you."

"You can't take back the past," Lara said, turning to kiss the hand that was touching her cheek. "You can only understand it, forgive it and go on to build a different future." Her head pressed tightly against Carson as her arms held his hips in a hard hug. "But until you understand and forgive," she said, caressing his body with her cheek, her hands, her mouth, as though touches could make him understand what words could not, "until then you're like a fly in amber, imprisoned forever in the past. Don't do that to yourself, Carson. Please."

After a few moments he let out a long, ragged breath. He eased his fingers back into the silky warmth of

Lara's unbound hair and rocked her head slowly, gently, against his body.

"How did you get to be so wise in so few years?" he asked softly.

"I learned from you."

Carson laughed sadly. "Pain, yes," he said. "But not understanding or forgiveness."

Silently Lara shook her head, disagreeing. "I didn't understand what happened four years ago. It...froze me. Now I understand. I can grow again."

And forgive?

Carson thought the question had existed only in his mind. He didn't know that he had whispered the words aloud until Lara answered him.

"Yes," she said, her arms tightening around his hips. "Oh, yes."

"No," Carson said quickly, hating himself because he could not tell her about the rest of the past, the part of it that could be understood but not forgiven and overcome. "I have no right to ask you for anything, least of all forgiveness."

"And I have no choice but to forgive," Lara said, turning her face into Carson's warm body, kissing him blindly. "I love you." As she felt his hands clench almost painfully in her hair, she smiled sadly against the worn fabric of his jeans. "It's all right, Carson," she said softly. "I'm not asking you to love me in re-turn. I know you don't believe in love. But I do, and I love you."

Carson was still for so long that Lara finally loosened her arms enough to look up at him. His eyes were tightly closed, his expression almost agonized. A tear glittered against the thick darkness of his lashes.

"Carson?" she said, her voice breaking.

He opened his eyes and looked down at her. "You're right. I don't believe in love. Not the way you do. And I don't deserve your love," he said hoarsely, "because I can't return it. But I want it. Oh, God, how I want it!"

"It's yours," she said simply. "It always has been."

Carson pulled Lara to her feet and into his arms, kissing her eyes and her cheeks and the cool smoothness of her hair. His caresses were like warm rain falling over her, bathing away the bitter residue of the past. She gave back the kisses as tenderly as she had received them, holding his face between her hands, trembling as she tasted the single tear that had escaped his control.

The world shifted around Lara as Carson sank back down onto the couch and lifted her into his lap, holding her in his arms as he whispered her name over and over again. She closed her eyes and held him in return, drinking the soft sounds of her name repeated by the man she loved. Gradually she became aware of the hard warmth of Carson's body, the power of his arms and the trembling sweetness of his lips brushing over her hair, her eyelashes, her mouth. She shivered and knew that she wanted more than those tender, fleeting caresses. But did he?

Lara turned her head and caught Carson's mouth with a sensual skill that he had taught her. When her tongue touched the corner of his lips, she felt the instant shudder of his response. He opened his lips and waited for her to accept the invitation. Though he ached to, he was afraid to take control of the kiss. He needed her too much. If he slipped the leash on his control just one fraction, he didn't trust himself to stop until he was finally sheathed inside her softness, drinking her passionate cries while he poured himself into her as he should have done long ago.

When Lara's tongue teased his, Carson groaned and returned the caress with slow, deep, primitive rhythms of his tongue that were unlike any kiss he had ever allowed himself with her before. As she trembled, he realized what he was doing, seducing Lara rather than following her lead, breaking the spirit if not the letter of his promise to her. With an effort he forced himself to stop pleading for her body with every movement of his tongue.

"Again, please," whispered Lara, pressing against Carson as she slid her hands deeply into his hair. "Oh, yes, again. I like that kind of kiss."

"Do you?" he asked, opening his eyes, looking at the velvet warmth of Lara's mouth, wanting it.

"I felt it all the way down inside me," Lara whispered.

"Oh, God," groaned Carson, consumed by a wild lightning stroke of desire that was like nothing he had ever felt before. His fingers speared into Lara's rich, thick hair, holding her still for the claiming of his mouth. "I know where you felt it," he said huskily as he slowly lowered his lips to hers. "In a place that's soft and hot and made for me. Someday you'll let me touch you there, taste you, be part of you. But until then kiss me the way I just kissed you, kiss me and imagine what it would be like if our bodies were as deeply joined as our mouths."

The words sank into Lara and exploded softly, sending heat coursing through her, heat and a heavy sweetness that made her breath wedge in her throat. Carson's mouth fitted hers with hot perfection, and his tongue thrust slowly, completely, into her. As he resumed the primal mating rhythm of tongue against tongue, Lara made a sound deep in her throat and clung to him, giving her mouth wholly to him, imagining....

When the kiss finally ended, they were both trembling and breathing too fast, too hard. Lara's hand moved restlessly from Carson's hair to his shoulders and then to his neck. She loved feeling the masculine textures of his skin and touching the dark hair that curled up in the opening of his shirt. She dipped her fingers beneath his collar, seeking more of his heat, more of his textures. The feel of his skin against the palm of her hand made air hiss sharply into her lungs. She leaned forward, wanting to kiss him, to taste him, to rub her cheek against the thick, springy hair that lay like a shadow beneath his shirt; but everywhere she turned, every way she touched, cloth was between her and her desire.

"Carson, could I—"

"Yes," he said instantly, interrupting her.

Lara smiled and traced his lips with her fingertip. "You don't even know what I was going to ask."

"I don't care," Carson said simply, looking at Lara with eyes that were molten gold. "There's nothing you could ask me that I would refuse."

Lara looked at Carson's lips and felt weakness course through her. She wanted his mouth but not merely for another kiss. She wanted to feel his mustache brushing against her naked breast, his tongue stroking her nipple, the moist heat of his mouth caressing her. That was how it had been years ago. Surely it could be that way again. She wanted it until she ached, but she was too shy to put her need into words.

"Can I have the shirt off your back?" she asked wistfully.

Humor and passion flared in Carson's eyes, making the centers widen and darken even more. "Yes."

She waited expectantly, but he made no move to undress himself. "Carson?"

"It's yours, little fox," he said, smiling slowly. "All you have to do is take it."

Hesitantly Lara lifted her hand. Carson's shirt had snaps rather than buttons, and the snaps were stubborn. Sitting as she was with one of her arms around him, her body half leaning against his chest and wrapped in his arms, she could use only one hand to open his shirt. She tugged again at the first snap. The cloth pulled toward her, and the snap stayed shut.

Smiling despite the sensual anticipation that had made his whole body tighten until he ached, Carson lifted Lara, shifting her position until she was sitting astride his lap. The thought of sitting the same way without having clothes between them made him shudder. The hard length of his sex ached in response to the blood pouring through his body and pooling hotly between his legs. He pulled Lara's head down, drank deeply from her mouth and slowly released her.

"Now," Carson said huskily, "try again."

Lara's hands were trembling. She pulled on the snap and heard it give way, revealing the darkly sensuous gleam of his hair. She stroked him lightly, then more firmly until her fingertips were combing through the warm, springy hair. The second snap gave way more easily than the first, and the third more easily still. Her hands slid inside the shirt and then slowly pushed it open until she could rub her face across Carson's chest, turning from side to side, stroking him with her cheek as well as her hands.

Lara's curious, exploring fingertips brushed over and then returned to the small, erect nub at the center of Carson's nipple. She rubbed gently, savoring the unexpected, different texture. His groan caught her by surprise. She glanced up, startled.

"Shouldn't I—" she began.

"God, yes," Carson gritted, cutting across her hesitation. "Touch me any way you want, every way you can think of, whatever you dreamed. Do it all, honey, every bit of it." He stretched his arms out along the back of the couch. "I won't give you back the pleasure. Not yet. Not until I know without a doubt that you want me." He smiled with sensual promise. "Go ahead, my shy, curious little fox. No matter how you touch me, you won't shock me. I promise you."

Hesitantly, then with growing confidence, Lara found and caressed the tiny, erect points of his nipples, watching Carson as she did. She saw his eyes become heavy lidded and his mouth become frankly sensual. Seeing his pleasure so clearly was like being licked by a loving fire. She leaned forward until her hips were just brushing his, and then she stroked him with her tongue in the same rhythm as her fingers teasing his nipples. She felt him strain toward her, pulling against the boundaries of his self-imposed limits.

Knowing that Carson would keep his word was as exciting for Lara as the feel of his warm, naked skin. Slowly her mouth quit teasing his lips. She kissed his cheek, the line of his jaw, his neck, and then sighed as her tongue probed a darkly curling thatch of hair on his chest until she found the erect, eager nipple beneath. The thready groan that answered her caress made her shiver as though she were the one being touched. She had never guessed how exciting it would be to arouse Carson. She bent down and caressed him as she ached to be caressed, with teeth and tongue and mouth. His breath went in raggedly even as she felt his thighs tighten between her knees. That, too, was exciting.

Lara turned to find and tease Carson's other nipple, only to discover that his shirt kept on getting in the way of her exploring hands and mouth. With an exasperated sound she tried to open the rest of the snaps, only to be defeated because the shirt was tucked in at Carson's lean waist. This time she didn't wait to ask for permission. He had already told her she could do anything she wanted, and she was impatient to take him at his word.

Smiling, Carson watched as Lara tugged out the long shirttails. He leaned forward obligingly, making it easier for her to slide the shirt off his shoulders. When she got sidetracked tracing the lines of muscle on his left arm with her tongue and then her teeth, Carson moved slowly with each caress, increasing the pressure, silently telling her that he approved of her sensual exploration.

Lara straightened to look at the powerful shoulders she had just revealed beneath the dark cloth of his shirt. Carson was even more magnificent than she had remembered. She breathed his name and returned for another taste of his hot skin, hungry for him in a way that she could neither name nor satisfy.

"If I'm going to get this shirt off you, you'll have to take your arms off the back of the couch," Lara pointed out.

The husky sound of Lara's voice made desire twist through Carson. The low, intimate timbre told him that she was enjoying the sensual play every bit as much as he was. Slowly he lowered his arms. Rising slightly up on her knees, she pushed the dark fabric down his back. She had peeled the shirt all the way down to his wrists when she realized that the cuffs were still fastened. Not only that, but the shirt was now so tangled that she couldn't even find the snaps.

Suddenly Lara felt foolish. She had no practice at seducing a man, and everything she did proved it. Yet when she looked up into Carson's face, all she saw was approval and desire.

"You're very patient," Lara said quietly as she went back to work on Carson's cuffs. "I'm no good at this."

"You're sexy as hell," Carson said deeply, watching the fine trembling of Lara's fingers. "Knowing that you've never undressed another man, watching your face as you discover just a few of the things you can do to me, seeing you shiver every time your tongue touches my nipple—God, little fox, it's so sweet and hot it's a miracle I haven't lost control." Carson saw her startled look and smiled. "No, I didn't mean lose control as in pouncing on you. I meant lose control as in coming right here. Does that shock you?"

Lara started to say yes, then realized that it wasn't quite the truth. Surprise her—yes. He was so open with her, as though he wanted her to know at all times that he was vulnerable to her. And then she realized that that was exactly what Carson was saying. He had given himself to her. That meant being naked in more ways than simply not wearing clothes.

"No," Lara said softly, smiling as she bent over his cuff once more, "I'm not shocked. I'm...pleased."

Her smile almost undid every one of Carson's good intentions, as did the innocent pressure of her thighs on either side of his. So close, so very close, and so very far away from the blazing act of intimacy he wanted.

The last snaps gave way. Lara pulled off one sleeve and then the other, dragging the shirt across Carson's lap in her eagerness to get rid of it. She felt his hips jerk softly when her hand brushed across his jeans. As she looked down, she saw that he was fully aroused and that she had inadvertently touched him.

"I'm sorry," she said quickly. "I didn't mean—"

"Oh, God, little fox," he interrupted raggedly. "Just do it again and I'll forgive you."

Lara looked at Carson's face, wondering if he was joking. He stretched his arms across the back of the couch again, underlining his vulnerability.

"Whatever you want," he said, his voice a gentle rasp.

Lara stared into Carson's amber eyes for a long moment. The only sound in the room was his quickened breathing as he watched her in return. Almost imperceptibly her hand moved forward, hovering above his jeans. He held her eyes and smiled a slow, inviting smile that made her heart turn over. She let her hand settle over him. She felt the barely controlled surge of his hips, heard the sudden, fierce hiss of his breath and almost lost her courage. Then the heavy-lidded pleasure revealed by his golden eyes made heat and weakness shiver through her. Gently she increased the pressure of her hand on his hot, hard flesh.

"I can feel your heartbeat," Lara said, her eyes wide, her tone husky with surprise.

Carson felt an odd combination of tenderness and violent desire. Tenderness won. He let out a long breath and forced himself to relax against the couch, opening himself to whatever caress she might want to give him. As softly as a breath her fingertips traced his length. Against the sun-faded roughness of his jeans, her hand was slender, graceful and so utterly feminine that he had to look away or risk losing control.

"What should I do?" she asked softly.

"Pet me, honey."

His voice was too gritty, too thick, but he couldn't control that any more than he could prevent the blood from beating heavily in the erect flesh beneath Lara's caressing fingers.

"Oh, God," he said, moving subtly against her hand. "I wish I could make you feel as good as you're making me feel. I wish—"

The word ended in a hiss as Carson thrust almost helplessly against Lara's hand, increasing the pressure of her palm against his hungry body. Suddenly she wanted to be able to hold him, to run her hands over him without the barrier of clothes, to know him with an intimacy that she had never shared with any man. She wanted it so badly that her hands were shaking.

"Carson?" asked Lara raggedly.

The sound of his name was another caress, almost as hot and every bit as sweet as her hand stroking him, and her eyes watching him were like blue fire. Without a word Carson shifted his hands from the back of the couch to the waistband of his jeans. The steel buttons gave way in a fast, soft ripple of sound. Wordlessly Lara moved aside. He peeled off his clothes and kicked them under the coffee table. Watching her, he leaned against the cushions and forced himself to put his arms along the back of the couch again, leaving himself utterly open to her eyes and her touch.

It was the hardest thing Carson had ever done, to be naked when Lara was clothed, vulnerable when she was not, aching for her until he thought it would be easier to die than to go on without having her; and suddenly he wondered what it would be like if she told him that he didn't measure up and then walked out without a backward look. The realization of what it must have been like for her made ice twist through his guts.

"Lara—" he said hoarsely.

But Carson could say no more for Lara's hands were smoothing over his chest, his waist, the long, taut muscles of his abdomen and the rigid muscles of his thighs.

She traced the shadow of dark, curling hair as it tapered to his navel and then flared out again into a thick thatch. There her hands hesitated until Carson felt as though he were being stretched on a rack.

"I can see your heartbeat now," Lara whispered. "It's so fast, so hard. Oh, Carson, do you really want me so much?"

Before Carson could answer, Lara cradled him between her palms. To feel her warm hands holding him was like being connected to a soft current of electricity. To see her delicate fingers caressing him was like sliding into fire. Carson felt control slipping away beneath the sweet, wild friction of her skin over his naked desire.

"Oh, baby, stop," Carson groaned.

Stricken, Lara looked up into his eyes. "Am I hurting you?" she asked. Her voice, like her hands, trembled.

Carson's answer was a thick sound that could have been a laugh. Deliberately he moved his hips, sending his hot flesh sliding between her hands again and again, slowly, deeply.

"Harder," he rasped and then shuddered uncontrollably when she responded by giving him what he had asked for and more, her hair tumbling freely down his naked torso and her mouth learning the hot, changing textures of hair and skin. "No, that doesn't hurt," he said, groaning again. "It just feels too damn good to bear. A little more and I'm going to shock you."

"You won't shock me," Lara said. The words were as soft and hot as her breath trembling against his aroused skin.

Carson laughed roughly. "The hell I won't. I've wanted you for years, dreamed of you until I woke up sweating and tied in knots. But I never dreamed anything this hot, this wild. God, you're killing me so sweetly that I—" He groaned and moved even as Lara's hands did. "No more," he said, wrapping his fingers over her wrists, forcing her to be still.

"But I want to know," she whispered, smoothing her cheek and her hair over the hard muscles of his abdomen. "I want to know how it is for you when I please you."

The thought that Lara wanted to know his body that intimately almost cost Carson what control he had left. With a thick sound he covered her hands with his own. He moved once, very slowly, and then forced himself to stop.

Lara looked at Carson completely, from the thickly curling hair of his head to the powerful lines of his torso and down to the different, ultimately masculine flesh that responded so hotly to her touch.

"Oh, Carson, don't you know how perfect you are?" she whispered, caressing him with her hands, her cheek, her lips. "Nothing you do could shock me."

Lara felt the current of response going through him, felt the instant when his whole body tightened, felt the pulsing groan that came all the way from his soul, felt the sweet heat of him filling her hands to overflowing. Watching him with her eyes half closed, smiling, she pleasured him slowly, loving him.

"Come here," Carson whispered finally, pulling Lara up his body with hands that shook. "I have to kiss you, feel you against me, all of you, or I'll go crazy. I want to touch you the way you touched me, tease you until you shiver and cry and melt all over me like honey. Then you'll know what you've done to me. You'll know how it feels to want it until you could scream and then to have it, all of it, given to you with a loving smile. You'll know—"

The words ended in a husky sound as Carson's mouth fitted over Lara's and his tongue seduced her in the primal rhythms she had just learned. His big hands smoothed over her, shifting her until she fitted against him in a long caress. She felt him move beneath her, stroking her with his body and his hands as his tongue thrust into her soft, hungry mouth. By the time the kiss ended, she was twisting slowly against him, trying to ease the tension that had tightened her body until she shuddered repeatedly. She wanted his hands to soothe her and to set her on fire, she needed his touch, yet no matter how she twisted, his hands slid away from intimacy.

"Please," Lara whispered.

"Anything," Carson said, clenching his hands into fists to avoid breaking his word, taking her before she asked for him. "Just tell me."

"I want—" Her voice broke as she looked into the hot gold of his eyes. "Everything. I want things I don't know how to ask for. Undress me," she whispered, trembling. "Touch me. Help me, Carson. I—hurt."

His hands swept up her body until her breasts were cupped in his palms. The sweet pressure felt so good that Lara couldn't control a whimper. When he brushed her nipples with his thumbs, she had to bite her lip against a wild cry of pleasure. He teased her gently, hotly, tugging at her breasts until her nipples were hard and radiating bursts of fire that consumed her. When his hands moved away, she twisted helplessly, seeking his touch again, needing it with an intensity that made her groan.

"Easy, love, easy," Carson said thickly, gently laying Lara on the couch as he slid off and knelt beside her. "Let me undress you. It will feel even better without any clothes."

He wanted to unbutton her blouse slowly, kissing each new bit of skin until he found the dark pink buds that were hidden beneath cloth and lace. But her wild little whimpers and the thought of all her hot, sweet secrets waiting for him made it impossible to draw out the moment.

"Next time," Carson promised Lara hoarsely as he stripped away her clothes, tossing them onto the coffee table heaped with photos, scattering bits of the past on the floor. "Next time I'll go so slow you'll think you're dying, but now—ah, God, you're beautiful!" he groaned as the last bit of cloth fell away, revealing all of her.

Lara felt a flash of unease when the room's cool air touched her and she realized she was naked. Then she saw Carson's approval in the blazing gold of his eyes, heard it in his deep voice, felt it in the big hands smoothing reverently down her body. When his tongue touched the tight peak of her breast, she arched in helpless reflex, thrusting her aching nipple more deeply into his mouth. Carson's long fingers spread beneath her back, pulling her even closer, holding her for the loving, tugging pressure of his mouth.

Pleasure shimmered through Lara's body. She cried out, and her hips moved in languid, sinuous rhythms. Carson's teeth raked tenderly, and she cried out again. This time when she moved her hips, there was an answering warmth and pressure as his hand eased between her thighs, tenderly cupping her softness. Unerringly his thumb found the tiny bud that ached to be caressed. He stroked her slowly, gently, drinking in her small cries, and she opened to his touch, withholding none of herself. His deep voice told her of her beauty and of the pleasure she brought to him when she gave herself so sweetly to his caresses. He cherished the soft, feminine secrets that she had given to him, stroking her with his fingertips and tasting her between each husky, loving word.

Inside Lara an expanding wave of pleasure burst, showering her with tingling warmth. She felt another wave gathering and then another and another, each one more intense, each one both releasing and paradoxically increasing the tension that grew deep within her. She trembled suddenly, almost frightened by the unfamiliar sensations claiming her.

Her eyes opened and she saw Carson watching her as he loved her with his hands and his words. She felt the velvet brush of his tongue in her navel and then the unexpected, exciting touch of his teeth on her soft inner thigh. As she saw the vivid darkness of his hair against her pale skin, she knew that she should feel shy or fearful, but the passion that had flushed her body had burned away everything except her need for the hot, intimate caresses he was giving her.

When his hand moved between her legs again, testing her softness, the tension that had been gathering in her tightened with sudden violence. She moaned brokenly, balanced on the brink of a pleasure so great it was nearly pain.

"Carson!"

"Let it happen," he said huskily. "Give yourself to it, to me. It's all right. I'll keep you safe."

Carson's head bent down and he caressed Lara so tenderly, so intimately, that her fear splintered and fell away, leaving nothing to inhibit her pleasure. She abandoned herself to him as wave after wave of sensation swept through her, shaking her, melting her, setting her afire. Sensual triumph glittered darkly in Carson's voice as he encouraged her, in his eyes as he watched her and in the hot, knowing movements of his hands and his mouth over her softness. He felt the wildness gathering deep inside her, a wildness that he had called from her innocence, a wildness that he had focused within her and would finally release.

With a smooth, powerful movement Carson settled between Lara's legs, teasing her with his own violently aroused body. Her eyes opened, heavy lidded and black with desire.

"Carson?" Like her eyes, Lara's voice was dark, heavy.

"Yes, little fox," he said deeply. "You're finally going to be mine. Is that what you want?"

Lara's answer was a broken sound of pleasure coupled with a motion of her hips that brought Carson closer. She felt him gently pushing against her, easing into her, becoming a part of her. She had expected pain or discomfort or shyness, anything but the exquisite pleasure that radiated through her with each slow, rocking motion of his hips. Her skin was hot, slick with passion, and so was his, making every movement of his body over hers a shivering, sliding caress.

"Does it hurt?" Carson asked, the words rough with the effort of controlling himself.

Lara tried to answer, but the sight of him rising over her, shaking with passion and restraint, swept away her ability to speak. She breathed in suddenly—and that simple movement tightened her around him, sending the first currents of ecstasy racing through her. Her back arched, and she drew up her legs in an instinctive effort to hold him more deeply, to make the ecstatic instant last and last.

If there was any pain when Carson took Lara completely, it was lost in the pleasure bursting within her, melting her around him. When he felt her hot and sweet, tightly sheathing him, he pressed even deeper, rocking slowly against the bud hidden within her softness. He heard his name become a broken cry on her lips as she abandoned herself utterly to him, moving with him until they both were overtaken by the unleashed ecstasy they had called from one another.

And then they clung to each other, shaking with the wild pleasure that was sleeting through them, so deeply joined that neither knew whose skin was caressed, whose name was called, whose body had shattered and been reborn in the endless moment when they had been not two but one.

Chapter Ten

THE FIRST LAMBENT RADIANCE of dawn slid silently from windowsill to floor, then crept softly across the pillows, waking Carson. Slowly he eased from the warm, scented tangle of limbs and sheets, kissing Lara gently again and again. Then he stretched fully, smiling to himself. He could barely believe the changes that the past six weeks had brought. Before it had been as though he was stranded in the past, caught as Lara had been caught, an insect paralyzed within the unforgiving amber of time, helpless to go either forward or back. Then Lara had allowed him to make love to her, healing both of them and filling him with a radiance that even the sun could not equal.

The gold band on Lara's left hand gleamed in the same warm color as Carson's eyes. He bent and took her hand reverently, kissing the wedding ring before he turned over her hand and smoothed another kiss into her soft palm. She was so beautiful lying there asleep, smiling just a little as though she were feeling his loving caresses even within her dreams.

"Good morning, Mrs. Carson Blackridge, my beautiful little fox," he murmured, rubbing his cheek against her palm. His eyes closed and his fingers tightened almost imperceptibly, as though something were trying to take her away. Emotions burst through him powerfully, more emotions than he could name or understand. It was all he could do to breathe. He lay quietly, watching her, sorting out the explosion of feelings, separating the familiar from the unfamiliar.

One familiar feeling was desire. There was no doubt of it. Making love with Lara was an incandescent pleasure that grew hotter and better with each sweet repetition. It was the same for her. She came to him without inhibitions, eagerly, making him feel so much a man and then celebrating his manhood with him in the most elemental way. With her he drank the wild, consuming wine of sensuality and found ecstasy glittering in the bottom of the shared cup.

There was also the familiar, cold presence of fear. Carson had no doubt of that, either. He would never feel secure in his shared life with Lara nor even in her love, for it could be torn away from him at any instant by a past that might refuse to stay buried. Knowing he could lose her was an agony that sometimes brought him upright in bed in the middle of the night, his body clammy with the residue of a dream too black to remember.

That, too, was familiar to Carson. He had spent a lifetime knowing what it was to want and to want and

never to have. He had learned that wishing and wanting and hard work didn't necessarily make dreams
come true.

What was unfamiliar to Carson as he lay and
watched Lara was the aching tenderness he felt toward
her; he wanted to give her the sun and the moon, the
earth beneath her feet and the very air she breathed. He
wanted to infuse her with the sweet warmth she gave
to him simply by being alive. He wanted to make her
smile, to drink her laughter, to see her eyes light when
he called her name. He wanted things for which he had
no words, simply unfamiliar yearnings sweeping
through him until he could only murmur her name as
he bent down to her, breathing air that was still warm
from her body.

Lara stirred sleepily beneath the covers, reaching for
Carson before she was even half-awake. The gesture
sent a lightning stroke of tenderness and desire through
the man who watched her with eyes that were as gentle as the dawn itself. Lara's sensuality was a continuous revelation to Carson, but it was her generosity of
spirit that was unspeakably beautiful to him. She never
measured or withheld her caresses, waiting for him to
say or do something that might pleasure or repay her.
She simply smiled and touched him, pleasing him, because his pleasure was also hers. It was the same for him.
Seeing her face light up when he appeared, hearing her
breath catch when his kiss changed from welcoming to
consuming, feeling the boneless melting of her body
against him—those things transformed his lonely inner
silences as surely as sunlight transformed night.

Although Carson knew that Lara ached to hear *I love you* from his lips, she never pleaded or pouted until he gave in. She didn't even apply the unsubtle pressure of saying *I love you* and then waiting for him to speak in return. She rarely said the words herself except when the ecstasy he brought to her consumed all barriers and the words poured out, setting fire to him in turn. Her breathless, broken declarations of love satisfied him in a way that he could neither explain nor understand; he only knew that he lived for the words and the shared smiles as well as for the blazing, shattering pleasure he found deep within her body.

Carson lowered his head and nuzzled Lara's lips gently. He felt them shift into a smile as her arms snaked around his neck and a warm, impudent tongue teased the corners of his mouth. Desire arced through him. He pulled her into his arms and gave her a long, deep kiss. Before it ended, she was clinging to him hungrily.

"Last chance," he said, ending the kiss with a reluctance that told of the blood beating heavily through his veins.

"For what?" Lara asked. Her fingers slid down the long, powerful muscles of his back to his hips, caressing the resilient flesh, savoring his hard strength.

"Don't ask me, honey," Carson said, laughter curling beneath the words. "You're the one who told me to get you up at dawn."

"I did?" Lara blinked and frowned sleepily. "Oh, yes. Now I remember. I wanted to make the final selection on those pictures so I could take them into town to be duplicated before Mr. Donovan goes to court."

"*Donovan?*" Carson felt all the warmth of dawn change to icy midnight. He pushed up on his elbow and looked down at Lara. "What do you need him for?" Carson demanded. "Why do you keep wanting to see him? Is something wrong that you're not telling me about?"

Lara yawned and shook her head at the same time. "I've been trying to set up an interview with Donovan for weeks, but either you needed me for something on the ranch or he had to be in court, or—" Lara yawned again and turned to rub her cheek against Carson's warm, furry chest. "Anyway, I figured since half of the Donovan family has owned the neighboring ranch for the last century and the other half of the family has been the Rocking B's lawyers for the last hundred and twenty years, Donovan would have some good stories for my history. I hear he has an incredible memory. He's got to be almost eighty, and he's still practicing law."

Even as Carson opened his mouth to tell Lara that she couldn't see Donovan, he realized that he would have no reason to give her when she inevitably asked why. There were other ways, better ways, to put off the potentially dangerous interview. Much more pleasant ways. His hand slipped beneath the sheets. Slowly he smoothed up the taut flesh of Lara's thigh, traced the crease where leg joined torso, dipped into the dimple of her navel and continued upward to the soft weight of her breasts.

"I've got an incredible memory, too," Carson said, his tone deepening. "Want to reward me with an interview?" His fingertips teased Lara's nipple into a taut peak of desire. "I remember how hard and yet velvety you get," he said, rubbing a tight pink crown with his thumb. "Then I remember how sweet you taste and how warm your mouth is."

His tongue slid between Lara's teeth with a lover's ease, drinking the small catch of her breath as she turned toward him. He kissed her until their heartbeats were hard, rapid, and she was clinging to him.

"Then I remember how incredibly soft you are," he whispered, easing his hand down to the apex of her thighs. Delicately he sought and found her most tender flesh. He groaned as he felt her changing even while he touched her, becoming softer, hotter, preparing herself to accept the gift of his body. "God, Lara, you don't know what it does when I feel your willingness to take me. You're so damned sexy it's a wonder I ever get out of bed."

Lara laughed softly and tangled her fingers in the thick, rumpled thatch of hair curling down Carson's body. "It's you, not me," she whispered as she nuzzled his neck. "You touch me so perfectly." She shivered suddenly, and her hips began to move against his caressing hand. "Just thinking about how it's going to be makes me want to—"

Carson savored the moan that took away Lara's words, felt the hot melting of her at his touch. Then her warm, appreciative hands slid down his body, and he forgot to breathe.

"Come inside me, love," she whispered, caressing his hard length, pleasuring him, promising him even greater pleasures with her smile.

Carson swept aside the covers with one motion of his arm. For the space of several ragged breaths, he simply looked at the woman who could turn his body to fire with a look, a touch, a smile. Lara's skin was gilded by dawn and flushed by passion. She lay nude before him without fear or shyness, her body open, inviting him to become part of her once more. When he looked at her breasts, the nipples tightened as though he had touched them with his tongue. It was the same for her navel, a visible ripple of sensation chasing across her taut skin. When his gaze lingered over the glossy black mound below, her knees flexed and her body moved in helpless need.

"Carson," Lara said huskily, reaching for him, "you're killing me."

He smiled slowly down at her, memorizing every bit of her sensuality and beauty. "But I'm not even touching you," he said reasonably.

"I've noticed," she retorted. "That's what's killing me."

Lara traced the length of Carson's powerful body with her fingers until she found the rigid evidence of his hunger. She nipped very lightly at his aroused flesh with her fingernails. Blood beat visibly, heavily, in him, telling her the cost of his restraint.

"I have a cure for too-rapid heartbeat," she whispered, tugging softly at him with her fingertips.

"Do you?" Carson asked, smiling crookedly even as his hips moved in sensual response to her touch. "Maybe I should go get your tape recorder or take notes. Medical science needs to know how to slow down—"

Carson's teasing tone changed to a groan as Lara shifted position suddenly, gracefully, and he felt the wild, intimate heat of her mouth loving him. A shudder racked his body.

"Oh, God, baby," he gritted, torn between residual laughter and a desire so hot he could scarcely breathe. "I hate to tell you, but that's not going to slow my heartbeat down one damn bit!"

Lara laughed softly, and that, too, was a wild kind of caress against his erect, very sensitive flesh. With a thick sound Carson reached for her, only to have her slide like sunlight through his fingers. The cool black silk of her hair fanned across his thighs. He reached for her again, wrapping his fingers securely in the ends of her long hair, but instead of pulling her back up his body and into his arms, he found himself utterly captive to the piercing pleasure she was giving him.

With a groan of hunger and passion, Carson released Lara's hair in order to slide his fingers down the curve of her waist and hip, seeking the silky skin of her thighs until he finally caressed the melting softness that waited for him. He felt her hunger, her shivering heat, her welcoming body, and suddenly he knew that he had to be sheathed within her or he would be pulled apart by the violence of his own need.

"Lara," Carson said hoarsely, "I've got to have you."

She heard the urgency in his voice, felt it in the sudden trembling of his body as he lifted her over him. All teasing gone, she came willingly to him, opening her legs to ride his narrow hips as she settled into place on his body. Carson's face was dark and harsh with need, his eyes almost black, his body drawn as taut as a massive bow. His visible need sent a burst of passionate heat through Lara, melting her even as he slid deeply into her softness with a smooth thrust of his hips.

Lara couldn't understand the words Carson said, for they were blurred by the thick, hard driving of his need, but she saw the transformation of his face when release came, the pleasure so intense that it tore him apart in great, shuddering bursts that made him cry out. Then her own transformation came, her own release, and cries of pleasure and love rippled out of her in the endless moments before she collapsed across his broad chest, breathing as hard as he was.

It was a long time before their frantic heartbeats slowed and their breath came at normal intervals. Even then Lara and Carson remained joined, loving each other with gentle kisses and warm hands smoothing over skin still flushed with pleasure. Smiling to herself, Lara put her cheek against Carson's chest and began silently counting his heartbeats.

"See?" she said triumphantly, nuzzling his nipple. "It worked."

A rumbling, purring sound of contentment replaced the rhythm of Carson's heartbeat in Lara's ear. "Sure did," he said deeply. "Better every time. Better and better and better again. I can't wait for the—"

"That's not what I meant," she said, interrupting, laughing gently. "I was talking about your heartbeat. It's way down. Barely sixty-six a minute. See? It worked. I cured you."

Carson laughed aloud and hugged Lara close, wondering how he had ever gotten through the days before she had come back to the Rocking B and to him as warily as a fox tiptoeing through twilight.

"One time doesn't prove anything," he pointed out, nipping sensually at Lara's ear.

"Oh, yeah?"

"Oh, yeah," he said huskily, tracing the curved shadow at the base of her spine until his fingertips found her feminine heat and softness once again. "Didn't you learn anything about the scientific method in school?"

Lara's thoughts scattered with each slow, gliding caress of Carson's fingers between her legs. "Science?" she asked. "You mean like friction generating heat and—" She shivered and gasped as he found and stroked the exquisitely sensitive focus of her desire.

"I mean like repeatability," Carson said, rolling over, taking her with him. "Didn't you know?" he asked, smiling down at Lara with a combination of possession and humor and passion. "That's the basis of the modern scientific method. If you can't repeat an experiment, then you can't draw useful conclusions from the data."

"I never was very good at science," admitted Lara.

"I'll teach you."

"That's kind of you," she said gravely. "Not many men would have the patience to teach— Oh!" Her words fragmented into a soft cry of pleasure.

Carson's hand moved slowly as Lara tried again to speak. More soft cries of pleasure came from her lips.

She saw the heavy running of Carson's blood in the pulse beating in his neck, felt it as he grew inside her with every heartbeat and knew that soon he would fill her to overflowing. The thought was unbearably exciting, as was the slow movement of his hips rocking against her.

"Yeah. *Oh*," Carson said thickly.

He lowered his head and took her mouth as completely as he had taken her body. She took him in the same way, wanting him deeply, heat bursting through her in anticipation of the shimmering ecstasy to come.

This time when their heartbeats finally slowed, they fell asleep in a sweet, hot tangle, not knowing whose skin was being caressed, whose tongue was tasting the slick residue of passion, whose laughter was trembling within the joined peace of their bodies.

Even hours afterward the memory sent exquisite frissons shivering through Lara, distracting her from her task of sorting the Rocking B's photo archives into piles according to her first, second and third choices to illustrate her history. The more she and Carson made love, the more ways she found to please him. Tender or wild, gentle or fierce, he brought her an ecstasy so great that she sometimes wondered if she would survive the sweet violence of her release. She had discovered that she brought Carson an equal ecstasy; that, too, was a shattering sweetness pouring through her veins each time she realized it anew.

Sighing, Lara decided it was just as well that she had missed her chance to catch Donovan in town; her mind was just too scattered to interview a lawyer right now. For the eighth time she looked from the photo in her right hand to the photo in her left. They both showed weathered men riding gaunt horses. Behind them Texas cattle with horns as long as axe handles poured through a narrow gap into a Montana valley that had never before known anything except deer and buffalo. It was the end of one era and the beginning of another, and it had been captured by a man who knew that he had driven his cattle into a place in the history of his country as well as into a lush, ungrazed land.

Lara put the paired photos aside, unable to choose between them. Instead, she thought about tonight, when Carson would be through with his work. After dinner she would give him a back rub and listen as he talked about the small crises and unexpected pleasures that had come to him during the day. When the knots were gone from his neck and shoulders, he would pull her into his lap, lean back against the couch and ask about the progress of her history.

She had discovered that Carson had very acute perceptions on the subject of human needs and the land itself, about the kinds of things that didn't change whether the time span being considered was months or millennia. And, for a man with a pronounced hostility toward the past, Carson had an excellent eye for the photo that told the most about the land, the men and the moment they had been frozen in time by a camera. She had come to value his insights as much as she valued his laughter and the muscular power of his body. Every day she loved him more.

Lara worked steadily, rapidly, sorting through photos. Most went into a reject pile. The next biggest pile consisted of photos that might be suitable for illustrating her history. Off to one side there was a pile she reserved for sharing with Carson. The pictures in that pile showed everything from a tough old bald-faced cow with three calves peeking out from beneath her belly to the Rocking B's old ranch house adrift in a sea of snow and moonlight.

There was a series of wedding pictures, too, each ceremony more elaborate than the last. The same lace scarf had been worn by three generations of Blackridge wives—four, now. The fragile, delicately wrought scarf presently lay in Lara's dresser drawer, her most prized possession after the wedding ring that fitted so smoothly on her hand.

She smiled softly, remembering the morning after they had first made love. Carson had awakened her by putting his hand over her womb and saying that they would be married as soon as possible because he had been too crazy with desire even to think of protecting her last night. Nor would he protect her in the future, unless she wanted it, because the thought of his child growing in her womb was unbearably sweet. But only if she wanted it, too...

Lara sighed and put her hand just below her waist. Oh, yes, she had wanted it. She had wept when her period had finally come nearly three weeks late. Carson had held her so gently, kissing away her tears, telling her that it was just as well—if he were any happier, he would burst like the Roman candles they had seen at the Fourth of July celebration in town. Besides, he had added, kissing her more deeply, he had discovered that he was selfish. He didn't mind keeping her all to himself for a while longer. That way he had it all, the anticipation of a child in the future and the reality of a generous, abandoned lover right now.

A tiny smile tugged at the corner of Lara's mouth as a shivery feeling invaded the pit of her stomach. She loved being Carson's woman, his wife, his lover, the future mother of his children. Someday she hoped that he would realize that she was also his beloved. Sometimes after they had made love, or when she rubbed away the tension that tied his shoulders in knots, or when she woke up and found Carson watching her with eyes that were almost gold—sometimes then she had the feeling that he wanted to tell her something, something that was very difficult for him to say.

Was it *I love you?*

Were those the words Carson seemed to be searching for and unable to find? If so, then she wanted to tell him that it didn't matter whether he talked of love or not. If the words were so difficult, so painful for him to speak, she didn't have to hear them in order for her life to be complete. Hearing his laughter come more often now that they were married, seeing a smile erase the harsh lines from his face when he looked at her, feeling the brush of his fingers over her cheek when he walked by her chair, those things spoke eloquently of his feelings for her. It wasn't necessary to hear the words, too, especially if saying them brought pain rather than pleasure to the man she loved.

"Such a beautiful smile. What are you thinking about, little fox?"

"Carson!" Lara came to her feet in a rush, her face radiant with the unexpected pleasure of seeing Carson in the middle of the afternoon. "I thought you weren't going to be back until dinner. Did you get all the cows moved to the new pasture?"

Carson's arms came around Lara and he lifted her feet off the floor, holding her in a hard, warm hug. "We're just about done. Murchison and Spur are combing out the strays right now. I'm playing hooky," he added, nuzzling Lara's ear and the curve of her neck.

"I'm glad," she said softly, kissing his cheek, combing her fingers through his hair, loving him.

For a moment they rocked slowly in place, absorbing the sweetness of holding and being held. Lara felt her eyes burn suddenly and blinked back tears. He had come like this to her so many times in the past weeks, surprising her with a fragrant wildflower or a colorful, water-polished stone he had plucked from a creek bed.

Once he had come in unexpectedly and taken her up on the low ridge above the ranch. There he had told her to close her eyes and listen. There was a strong west wind that day, blowing through the narrow ravines that twisted down from the high, rugged mountains beyond the ranch. The wind was sweet, warm, wild and had a sound that was both beautiful and so lonely that it had torn at her heart. When she had told Carson how she felt, he had said, *Yes. That's why I brought you here. Together we can share the beauty and hold the loneliness at bay.* And then he had drawn her so close that she couldn't tell whose heartbeat she felt in her blood.

"Do you have a few minutes?" Carson asked. "I've got something I want to show you."

"Of course," said Lara, ruffling the slightly shaggy hair at Carson's neckline with her fingers, enjoying his warmth and the changing textures of skin and hair.

"Good. Let's go before they go back into hiding."

"They?"

"You'll see," Carson said, putting Lara back down on her feet and taking her hand, tugging her toward the door.

On the way out Lara deliberately ignored the litter of pictures and documents scattered across every available surface in the library. She was a little behind schedule on her history, although her faculty advisor had told her to take as much extra time as she needed—as Carson's wife, Lara wasn't likely to be kicked off the ranch for asking questions, looking for boundary markers and being generally underfoot in her quest for the Rocking B's history. Besides, it was much too beautiful to be inside, even with something as fascinating as old photos to sort through. The day was alive, she was alive and Carson's hand felt so warm in hers.

Carson helped Lara into the pickup truck and drove along a winding, rutted ranch road. He drove to a distant corner of the Rocking B, where the pasture had been cycled back into grazing land at the beginning of summer. A few sleek cows stood belly deep in wild-flowers and grasses, searching among the abundant greenery for favorite forage.

Carson parked the truck, lifted Lara out and took her hand in a warm grip. Smiling, he ignored her questions and curious glances. He led her along the path that cat-tle had made to the tiny lake where springwater welled up in clear, sweet ripples. The pond was ringed by a thick growth of reeds and cattails.

Motioning for silence, Carson led Lara up the back side of a small hill that overlooked the pond. The grass had been recently walked on but was already springing back into upright position. At the top of the hill, Carson pulled Lara down into a nest of fragrant grass laced with flowers. Once seated, Lara was all but hidden by the tall greenery. Carson sat behind her, pulled her between his legs so that she could rest against his chest and got out the binoculars he had taken from the truck.

"We're upwind here," he murmured, the words a bare thread of sound, "so we'll have to be quiet. Sound carries real well over water, and she's skittish as hell. I don't blame her, either," he continued, quartering the pond with binoculars. "If I had that many—there she is! Poor baby. She doesn't know whether to strut or hide under a rock."

Lara felt as much as heard the low chuckle vibrating in Carson's chest.

"Here," he murmured, giving Lara the binoculars. "Look just to the left of that small willow. See her?"

The warmth of Carson's breath on Lara's neck distracted her. "See what?" she whispered, adjusting the glasses. "What am I supposed to—Carson!" Lara murmured suddenly, her tone soft yet urgent with excitement. "There's a mother duck out there with so many ducklings around her that she looks like a city under siege!"

Carson rumbled softly, a cross between a chuckle and a purr. "Isn't she something?" he whispered. "When I spotted her, I couldn't wait to bring you here. I've never seen a duck with that many babies."

"And you're right," Lara whispered, laughter curling through her words. "The poor thing doesn't know whether to strut with pride or hide under a rock and have a moment of peace." For a time Lara counted silently, finding and losing ducklings as they wove around their harried mother. As the number rose, Lara spoke softly aloud, hardly able to believe what she was seeing. "...twelve, thirteen, fourteen," she counted slowly, trying to keep track of the darting, bobbing bodies. "Fifteen!" she breathed. "My God. Fifteen of the fluffy little darlings. Maybe some of her luck will rub off on me this month," Lara added softly, smiling to herself.

Carson's expression changed, intensity replacing humor on his face. He closed his eyes and brushed his lips over Lara's hair so delicately that she didn't even feel the caress.

"Are you sure, little fox?" he whispered, kissing Lara's neck with the same aching mixture of emotions as when he had kissed her wedding ring while she slept. "I want you to be happy."

Lara lowered the glasses and leaned back against Carson's warm, broad chest. "I want your baby," she said softly.

She felt the shudder that went through him at her words. She heard his breath catch and felt a small, hot trail of moisture as he pressed his cheek against hers.

"Carson," Lara said softly, her voice shivering with emotion that she had moved him so.

"Before you, no one ever wanted me, really. Not the woman who had me, not the man and woman who adopted me, not the women who lined up hoping to marry a big ranch," Carson said, his voice husky, his arms tight around Lara. "Then you came back and you wanted me despite the way I hurt you four years ago. The thought that you really want my baby, too—"

With a husky sound he gave up trying to speak and simply held her while the soft summer wind whispered through the tall grass around them. Finally his arms loosened, and he kissed her as though she were more precious than life itself.

"I'd better get you back," Carson said reluctantly. "I'm taking up too much of your work time. I know you wanted to have the pictures in to be duplicated last week. And we were late getting up this morning."

He smiled at the memory even as he realized that the longer Lara took with her historical research, the greater the danger that she would put too many pieces together. And the longer he was with her, the more he understood just how much was at stake. Since he had been fifteen, he had understood that, if he wanted to have a home and be part of a real family, he would have to do it himself. Yet the more women he had had, the less possible the dream of a home had seemed, until he had all but forgotten it.

Then Lara had come back, turning life inside out, revealing to him how empty he had been and how richly she filled him. He was still discovering that richness, still growing to meet the promise of her generous spirit. At times he could almost feel old, scarred layers of himself splitting and falling away, allowing room for new thoughts, new hopes, new laughter, new emotions—even the ability to cry.

Lara turned slightly against Carson's chest and smiled up into his eyes. Against the backdrop of lush grass, the green in his eyes eclipsed the amber, reminding her of Long Pool in late afternoon, clear emerald water sparkling with points of deep golden light.

"You have the most incredible eyes," she whispered. "Always changing, always beautiful."

Smiling, Carson bent and smoothed his mustache over Lara's cheek. "If I start telling you about your incredible, beautiful body and the lovely way it changes when I touch you," he said, nuzzling along her jawline, "we'd be lucky to get back to the ranch before the first snow, much less in time for dinner."

"Is that a threat or a promise?" Lara asked softly, turning and catching his lower lip between her teeth for an instant.

"Let's find out," he invited.

Carson saw how tempted Lara was in the seconds before she sighed and stroked his mustache with her fingertips. "I should get those pictures so I can catch Donovan before he goes on his vacation."

Carson was too close to Lara to prevent her feeling the sudden stiffening of his body at the mention of Donovan's name. She saw the instant deepening of the brackets on either side of Carson's mouth as his lips flattened. At that moment she realized that, whenever the lawyer's name came up, Carson changed the subject in one way or another. It was the same when she tried to make or keep various appointments with Donovan—somehow, inevitably, something always came up to prevent her from seeing the lawyer.

"You don't want me to see Donovan, do you?" Lara said quietly.

"No." The word was clipped, cold, as bleak as the flat line of Carson's mouth.

"Why? Surely you can't still be angry about that note he sent after he found out we were married. I'm certain he didn't mean to imply that the reason for our hurried marriage was that I was pregnant," Lara said, smiling crookedly. "He's too much a gentleman of the old school to be so crude."

Carson closed his eyes and fought to hold on to his temper as he thought of the note the old lawyer had sent: *Fast work, boy. Larry knew you real well, didn't he? I presume the heir is soon to follow, ensuring that Larry's progeny will be part of the land forever, world without end, amen.*

Indignation and outrage had crackled in every slashing line of Thackery Donovan's handwriting. Carson had seen it, even if Lara hadn't. He had wanted to kill the old man for even hinting at what it was his moral duty as a lawyer to keep confidential. But Larry's will had been like a burr under old Thack's saddle since the day Larry had walked in and demanded that his will be redrawn. No matter how Thack had fought and shouted about "immoral" or "crazy" or "stupid," Larry hadn't been swayed. It was legal, and that was all that mattered. Larry had known what he wanted. If he couldn't have it, no one else could have what he wanted, either.

World without end, amen.

"Carson?" asked Lara softly.

Abruptly he focused on Lara rather than on the cruel, destructive and indestructible past.

"Thackery Donovan is like Larry," Carson said finally. "If you let him, he'll take all the joy out of life. Thack is part of the past. You and I don't live there anymore." Carson bent and kissed Lara's lips, breathing his warmth into her, breathing her warmth in return. "You're happy now, little fox," he whispered. "We both are. Keep away from Thack, and we'll stay that way." He smiled slowly, teasingly. "Besides, you have enough stuff scattered around the library for six university degrees. What do you need with more junk?"

"There are gaps in the Rocking B's legal record," Lara said, her voice quiet, her eyes intent as she tried to make Carson understand. "The firm of Donovan, Donovan and Donovan can fill those gaps from their files." Then, urgently, she added, "Carson, the past can't hurt us anymore. Some things that happened were sad and bitter, but some things were beautiful, too. It all balances out in the end."

"Don't you believe it," he said flatly. "The past will tear us apart."

Carson's voice was so hard, so certain, that Lara was frightened. She had hoped, as he became happier in his own life, he would have less hostility toward the pageant of history that brought her so much joy. But it hadn't happened that way. If anything, his hostility to their personal past before their marriage had grown greater with every day they were together.

"See?" Carson said, his tone heavy as his thumb traced the downward curve of Lara's mouth. "We were so happy a few moments ago, but now—" He swore softly, savagely. "Tell me what you need. I'll get the damned papers for you. Just stay the hell away from Thackery Donovan!"

Chapter Eleven

LARA PUSHED BACK FROM CARSON'S desk and stood up
very carefully. She had discovered just a few moments
ago that the room had an alarming tendency to revolve
around her if she stood up too fast. She was afraid that
she had finally caught the respiratory flu that had been
making the rounds of the Rocking B. The older hands
had been hit hardest, with Murchison and Willie spending two weeks in bed and two more recovering.
Murchison had gone back to work too soon; the flu had
rebounded and put him back in bed. Spur had been
down for three days, then back to work and then down
again. Carson had run a slight fever for one day, slept
a few more hours than usual that night and been back
in the saddle no worse for wear the next day.

All the men had joked that the flu was a blessing in
disguise: it made them lose their appetite, which was
just as well, because Mose's cooking was worse than

usual. As for Yolanda, her niece had taken her back to Billings for a long-overdue vacation. Now that Lara was caring for Carson, there was no reason for Yolanda not to spend time with her nieces and grandchildren.

Lara had sailed through the flu weeks blithely, cooking for the men who were hungry, setting out aspirin and antibiotics that had been prescribed for the hands who needed them, making sure that there was a steady supply of cool, tempting fruit juices on hand to drink. As man after man fell ill, got well and relapsed into flu again, she had assured the cowboys that her health was a clear-cut case of the superiority of clean living over the kind they obviously favored. They had been too tired to give her more than a halfhearted raspberry in rebuttal.

Seeing them all so listless and pale had squeezed Lara's heart. Instead of working on her history project, she had spent most of her time going from ranch house to bunkhouse, checking on the men, calling the doctor when the fevers went higher than one hundred and three degrees and then driving to town for another round of antibiotics for the latest flu casualty. Dr. Scott had taken to calling her Lara Nightingale.

Only to herself did Lara admit that she was more tired than usual lately and much less interested in food. She had very much hoped that those symptoms signaled the early stages of pregnancy. It had been seven weeks and four days since her last period. She hadn't said anything to Carson yet because the last time her period had been late, it had come after seven weeks and five days. She didn't want to raise his hopes, only to disappoint him again.

But as the room swayed gently around Lara and her skin roughed up with a sudden chill, she bitterly conceded defeat. Flu, not pregnancy, was sapping her normal vitality. Flu, not pregnancy, had taken away her appetite.

"Damn, damn, *damn*," Lara said as hot, unexpected tears spilled down her face.

She wiped them away with a hand that shook. Lately her moods had been unpredictable, which had raised her hopes of pregnancy, but this sudden drop into despair was ridiculous. She had gone to the doctor after her previous period had been so late. Dr. Scott had assured her that her body was fully functioning and that sudden changes in a woman's life—like marriage—could throw off her menstrual cycle. It was nothing to worry about. If she wasn't pregnant after six or eight months of trying, she and Carson should come in for a thorough workup. Until then, he advised, they both should just relax and enjoy the process of conception.

Lara's lips trembled between smiling and crying as she thought that never had a doctor's advice been so enthusiastically followed. The currents of passion flowing between herself and Carson increased in depth and intensity each time they made love. When Carson gave her a certain look or a certain smile, fire shimmered through her. It was the same for him. A look, a touch, and she could see his blood begin to beat heavily, filling him with sensual heat.

Lara shivered suddenly and rubbed her arms. She could use some of Carson's heat right now. It was cold for September. Yet when she went to check the thermometer on the library wall, the mercury was nudging eighty. It wasn't cold for the season. It was hot.

And so was she. Too hot.

As Lara turned away from the thermometer, the library seemed to darken for a moment. She braced herself against the wall until the dizziness passed. Ruefully she conceded that the older hands hadn't been joking when they had called this bug the worst one since the Second World War. The only silver lining to this particular flu cloud was that it didn't have you hanging your head in the toilet until you prayed you would die. This bug just laid you out for a few days or weeks while the world passed by in a fever haze, followed by the kind of exhaustion that made you sweat if you walked across the room.

The bug hit fast and hard. Spur had barely been able to ride in from the range. Lara had suspected that he was making more of his sickness than there was. Now she knew better. Waves of weakness washed over her. She was grateful that all she had to do was get to the library couch. Walking to the bedroom would have been beyond her. As she groped for the couch, she told herself that she would have to apologize to Spur for teasing him about being too sick to ride.

With a sigh Lara tumbled onto the couch and lay there for a moment, trying to get up the strength to pull the afghan off the back of the couch and cover herself. Then she realized that she had already pulled the blanket off and fallen on top of it. To cover herself she would have to roll to her side in order to free the afghan. That would take a lot of energy. She fell asleep before she decided whether moving aside was worth the trouble in order to get warm.

"TAKE CARE OF SOCKS FOR ME, would you, Willie?" asked Carson, handing over the reins. "I want to check on Lara. She looked kind of pale this morning."

"She hasn't been to the bunkhouse since last night," offered Willie, taking the big horse's reins. "'Course, only one of the hands is still down, and Jim-Bob ain't all that sick now."

Carson took the front steps two at a time, smiling in anticipation of seeing Lara's face light up with pleasure when he walked in. For the first few weeks after they had argued over Thackery Donovan, Carson had been worried that Lara would piece together too much of the past from the legal documents he had reluctantly gotten for her, but as far as he knew, she hadn't done more than leaf quickly through the papers, checking dates against a column that contained the cryptic entries referring to the reams of oral history she had typed up.

He had helped her as much as possible, wanting the damn project over and done with so that he could draw a breath without waiting for his newly discovered, unexpectedly beautiful life to blow up in his face. The fear of losing everything was always there, a cold shadow of the past lying beneath the brilliant warmth of the present.

Pausing in the living room, Carson listened intently. No quiet sound of movement came from the kitchen where Lara had taken over Yolanda's duties. No muted click of keys came from the computer he had taught

Lara how to use, saving her hours of time as she worked on her paper. In fact, there were no sounds at all. Frowning, Carson stood without moving, wondering if Lara had gone to the Chandler homestead to work on Cheyenne's notebooks.

At the thought of the homestead, Carson smiled to himself, remembering Lara's look of stunned delight when he had given her the deed to the homestead as a wedding present. He had wanted her to have it. He had wanted her to know beyond doubt that she was as deeply rooted on the Blackridge ranch as anyone who had ever lived there. He had wanted to give her the security of having her own place, her own piece of the earth no matter what happened. And if the worst happened, he prayed that the homestead would keep her from turning her back and simply walking away from the past, the Rocking B and him.

With a silent, savage curse Carson shoved the bleak thought back down in his mind. It wouldn't come to that. Somehow, someway, he would prevent that.

A small sound came from the library, as though a stack of papers had slithered across the floor. In three long strides Carson was across the living room. His boots scuffed softly on the narrow rug in the hall leading to the library. The door was ajar. He pushed it open a bit more and slipped in, waiting to hear the swift intake of Lara's breath when she spotted him standing there.

The only thing Carson heard was the same odd, slithering sound. He walked further into the room. What he saw made his heart turn over. Lara was struggling to sit up on the couch, but even as he watched, she slumped backward. The sound of her clothes rubbing over the leather couch was what he had heard.

"Lara!"

She turned toward his voice. "Carson? I—" Her teeth chattered. "Cold," she said raggedly. "So cold."

"It's all right, little fox," he said, scooping her up off the couch, holding her close to his own warmth. "I'm here. I'll take care of you."

The instant Carson touched Lara, he knew that she was a lot sicker than any of the men had been. She literally burned beneath his touch, yet he could feel the chills shaking her. He wondered how long she had lain on the couch, too weak even to pull the afghan over herself. The thought twisted through him, hurting him as nothing before ever had.

She had been helpless, and he hadn't even known.

Carson carried Lara upstairs and put her under the covers. Pausing only long enough to kick off his boots, he slid in next to her, pulling her close once more. He held her while chills racked her slender body. He stroked her slowly and spoke softly, telling her again and again that she would be all right, he would take care of her, he would warm her and she would sleep and then she would be well again. He doubted that she heard him, but he kept talking, anyway. It helped to keep his own freezing fear at bay.

He had been afraid of losing her, but never like this, having her life slide through his fingers like twilight bleeding into night.

Even as the thought came, Carson told himself he was being foolish. Lara was young, healthy, rippling with laughter and vitality. She simply had the flu. In a few days or weeks she would be well again. She would look up at him and smile, and then she would nuzzle against his mustache, teasing him until he made love to her and she came apart in his arms, crying his name and her love.

She would be all right. She had to be. Anything else was unthinkable.

When the last of the chills finally faded, Lara sighed brokenly and lay without moving in Carson's arms. He waited until he was sure that she was asleep before he eased carefully out of bed, tucking the covers around her to keep her warm. She whimpered softly, restlessly, searching blindly for him even in her fever-ridden sleep.

"I'm here," Carson said quietly, stroking Lara's hair. "Rest, little fox. I'll be right here the whole time."

With his free hand Carson picked up the receiver of the bedside phone, punched in the doctor's number and waited impatiently for Dr. Scott to take the call.

"Another hand down with the flu?" asked the doctor.

"It's Lara. I found her on the couch, too weak to sit up."

"Fever?"

"Like hell itself."

"How high?"

"You tell me. Her teeth are chattering too hard to put in a thermometer. Her skin feels like an oven."

"Nausea?"

"All she said was, 'Cold. So cold.' As soon as the chills stopped, she fell asleep."

The doctor grunted. "How does her breathing sound? Too many of these flu cases are going straight into pneumonia."

Carson's expression became even more bleak. He bent over and listened to Lara for a minute before turning back to the phone.

"Her breathing sounds okay," said Carson. "A little fast, maybe, but she's not having any trouble that I can hear."

"I'll be out in two hours. Keep her warm and quiet. Get her to drink something if you can. If her breathing changes, prop her up in bed and call me right away."

Carson hung up, looked at the clock and then back at Lara lying bundled up in the middle of the bed, her black hair streaming out over the covers. She looked too small, too pale, her fingers fragile against the forest-green bedspread. Gently he picked up her hand, kissed it and tucked it beneath the covers once more. She murmured something and turned toward his touch. He stroked her hair until she sighed and curled up against his thigh, calm again.

He picked up the phone, dialed the barn and told Willie that he was in charge of the Rocking B until Lara was well.

The hours until the doctor came passed in slow motion for Carson. He lay next to Lara, holding her, stroking her hair, listening to each breath as though his life depended on it. She seemed to slip in and out of sleep, never waking enough to focus on her surroundings, never sleeping deeply enough that a sound or a movement wouldn't disturb her. Yet she always seemed to know that he was there. No matter how restless she became, she moved toward rather than away from him. The realization made Carson's hands tremble as he stroked her hair. He kissed Lara gently, repeatedly, feeling emotions seething inside him, pressing against old scars, old boundaries, until they cracked and gave way, letting him breathe again, letting him grow.

Motionless but for his hand stroking Lara, Carson lay beside her. Finally he heard Dr. Scott at the front door. With a last caress Carson got up and went to let the doctor in.

"How's she doing?" asked Dr. Scott.

"Sleeping, kind of. Restless. Hot. A few more chills, but not as bad."

Dr. Scott grunted. "Drink anything?"

Carson shook his head. "Wasn't interested."

The doctor grunted again. He followed Carson through the bedroom door, took one look at Lara's pale cheeks with their scarlet fever banners riding high and bright, and pulled a thermometer out of his bag.

"Wake up, Mrs. Blackridge," he said, shaking Lara's shoulder firmly.

Lara mumbled and stirred. When her eyelids finally opened, her eyes were glazed.

"Put this under your tongue and keep it there."

Lara's eyes closed again, but she kept the thermometer in place while the doctor took her pulse and blood pressure, and listened very carefully to her breathing. He managed to do it all without uncovering more than a fraction of her body at a time. Even so, her skin roughened up with chills. She didn't complain. She seemed more asleep than awake, disoriented by the fever. Dr. Scott removed the thermometer, looked at it and then at Carson.

"You folks using contraceptives?" asked the doctor.

Carson looked startled. "No."

"Thought so. Well, that makes things a wee bit trickier."

"What the hell does that mean?" demanded Carson, fear leaping in his blood.

"Take it easy," Dr. Scott said, lifting his shaggy gray eyebrows at the intensity of Carson's response. "All it means is I have to find out if Lara's pregnant before I treat her. If she is, then we'll have to be real careful about what we give her in the way of medicine. There's always a chance—minor, but still a chance—that the pregnancy might be adversely affected, even terminated, by some medications."

"Listen," Carson said bluntly, "there's a major chance that *you* will be 'adversely affected' if you don't do everything possible for Lara. That's my bottom line, Doctor. My wife. I want her well again. I want to come into a room and see her smile. I want to walk with her at sunset when loons sing on the pond. I want to show her every wildflower and every—"

Abruptly Carson looked away, unable to speak. The sight of Lara lying so pale and still beneath the doctor's ministrations had gone into Carson's heart like a knife. Normally Lara was alert, vibrant, quick to respond to a word or a touch. Yet as he looked at her now, he doubted that she heard or understood much of what was going on around her.

"I hear you, Carson," the doctor said gently. "How long has it been since her last period?"

Carson tried to think, but the image of Lara's pale, still face kept interfering. "Five weeks. No. Seven."

"Probably too soon to tell without tests, but—" Dr. Scott shrugged and set aside the thermometer.

Disturbing the covers as little as possible, he slid his hand beneath the sheet and began to probe gently at Lara's abdomen. He hesitated, probed some more and then pulled the covers aside and started unfastening her jeans. Lara stirred and muttered, shivering. Carson pulled the spread up so that it covered as much of her as possible without interfering with the doctor's examination.

"Carson?" she asked.

Her voice was so thin that it frightened him. "I'm here, little fox," he said, taking her hand. "Dr. Scott wants to examine you before he gives you any medicine."

Carson couldn't tell from Lara's dazed, too-dark eyes whether she understood. All he could be sure of was that she pulled his hand down to her cheek and sighed, taking comfort from his presence.

"I'll be damned," the doctor said finally, pulling the covers back into place. "Feels like she's at least three months along. I'll have to run some tests to be sure, but if I were a betting man, I'd put good money on you being a papa come spring."

"But she had a period," Carson objected. "She can't be—"

Dr. Scott interrupted. "It happens that way with some women. Mrs. Blackridge? Lara? You following this?"

Carson turned and saw tears running down Lara's face and pooling in the upturned curves of her smile. The doctor smiled in return.

"Guess you're tracking well enough," he said. "Was your last period heavy, light, normal?"

"Light." The word was a raspy sigh. "Very...light."

"Any more bleeding since then?"

Slowly Lara shook her head.

"Cramps?"

"No," she whispered.

"Nausea?"

Again she shook her head.

Dr. Scott grunted. "You might be one of the lucky ones." He smiled up at Carson, who was looking stunned. "Cat got your tongue, Carson?"

Slowly Carson bent and kissed Lara's eyelids and her cheeks and the fingers that were intertwined with his. The hand that lifted to stroke his cheek was too hot, trembling with weakness, but no touch had ever moved him more.

"I'm going to give you a shot," Dr. Scott said, pulling a syringe from his traditional black bag. "I'll be leaving some antibiotics in pill form, too. Take them until they're gone. Drink eight ounces of fluid an hour, or I swear I'll give it to you IV. Hear me?"

Lara nodded.

Dr. Scott drew a blood sample, gave Lara a shot and packed up his bag. Carson followed him out into the hall just beyond the bedroom.

"Will she be all right?" Carson asked bluntly.

"She'll be fine. Flu and the third month of pregnancy is a double whammy, but she's strong. As for the baby, it'll be fine, too. Mother Nature has a way of taking care of the fetus first and the woman second."

"That doesn't comfort me," Carson said in a clipped tone.

Dr. Scott laughed. "Yeah, well, get used to it because that's the way it is. As far as Mother Nature is concerned, people are just an egg's way of making more eggs. Reproduction is first. Everything else is second. But don't fret about it. Women have been doing it long enough that they've got it down pretty well by now."

"That's why they go to hospitals to have their babies, right?" retorted Carson. "Don't try to con me, Doctor. I've seen enough cows give birth to know that things go wrong."

"Statistically, it's—"

"Screw statistics!" Carson grated. "Lara isn't a number!"

The doctor sighed. "Been a rough few weeks for you, hasn't it?" he asked mildly. "All the hands sick and then most of them relapsing, work piling up, new marriage to adjust to. Less than that has been known to put an edge on a man's temper."

After a visible effort Carson reined in his emotions. He ran his hand through his hair, took a deep breath and tried to explain. "I want her well again," he said simply. "I...need her."

"Don't you want the baby, too?"

"Hell, yes, I want it. I want it a lot," Carson said, his voice vibrating with intensity. "*But I want Lara more.*"

"No reason you can't have both. I'm being straight with you about that, Carson. Your woman is going to be fine. Now go back in there and let her know you're near and solid even if the rest of the world is all distant and fuzzy."

Carson watched the doctor walk away and told himself that everything was going to be fine. Lara would get well. There was no reason to feel as though the past were poised like an icy winter avalanche, ready to rush forward, burying everything, crushing warmth and life from the present, leaving only memory and loss and a lifetime of regret.

THE FIRST THREE DAYS OF FEVER passed very quickly for Lara and with glacial slowness for Carson. By the fourth day her temperature had returned to normal. By the sixth day she was more than strong enough to be bored lying in bed, but the doctor had wanted her to stay in bed for two more days. She had demanded, wheedled and finally bribed Carson with kisses to bring her research material to work with; even so, he only brought her enough for an hour's work at a time. Two at the most. The rest of the books he gave her were mysteries.

Sighing restlessly, Lara looked out the window. There was a side yard enclosed by tall fences covered with climbing roses, giving total privacy both to the yard and the bedroom itself. The roses were a soft profusion of colors and fragrance, and the grass was a green invitation to come out and lie quietly in the sun. Lara wanted to be out there where thousands of petals trembled in the warm breeze. She wanted to feel sunlight all over her, drawing out the last residue of sickness, leaving her vibrant and burnished with heat. The only thing that kept her in bed was her promise to Carson.

"You look good enough to eat," Carson said, standing in the doorway with a batch of new magazines in his hand.

"Carson!" she said, turning toward him, smiling with surprise and delight. "You're back early."

He smiled and looked at Lara with open appreciation. The rose lace gown he had given her the day before made her skin glow. "Has anyone ever told you what a beautiful smile you have? It lights up a whole room."

Lara watched Carson walking toward her with his powerful body and easy, loose stride and wondered how she had been so lucky to win him when every woman in the state of Montana had been setting traps and laying snares for him since he had turned sixteen.

"Here," Carson said, fanning the magazines across the bedspread. "One of everything."

Lara held out her arms to Carson, ignoring the colorful cascade of magazines. She felt the warmth of his arms sliding around her, the tantalizing brush of his mustache across her lips and the intimate flavor of his kiss.

"Mmmm. Raspberries and cream," he said, slowly releasing her. "My favorite."

"You taste like the wind," she said, smoothing her cheek over his. "Sweet and wild."

Carson's hands tightened on Lara in the instant before he controlled the desire that prowled so hotly within him. He had gone without women before in his life, but it had never affected him with the intensity that going without Lara for the past week had.

"Carson?"

He nuzzled her hair and made a sound that managed to be both a deep purr and a question.

"I want to go to the side yard and lie in the sun. Just those few steps won't hurt me," Lara said quickly, anticipating Carson's objections. "It's hardly much farther than the bathroom and I've been managing that quite easily for the last three—"

The tumble of words stopped as Lara felt herself being lifted into Carson's arms. His long fingers snagged the comforter that lay across the foot of the bed. Within moments Lara found herself lying in the sun, feeling the heat of the ground seep up through the comforter Carson had spread over the grass for her.

"Anything else?" he asked, smiling.

"A hug?"

Carson stretched out beside Lara and gathered her into his arms. For long moments they simply held each other, absorbing the sunlight and the warmth and the husky murmur of bees sliding between soft petals to touch the nectar hidden inside. Slowly Lara's hands crept into the open collar of Carson's shirt, then her fingers softly undid the snaps on his shirt. With a sigh of pleasure, she worked her fingers through the thick, warm hair covering his chest. When she touched the smooth disk of his nipple, it immediately hardened into an erect nub. Desire poured through Lara in a hot, sweet wave.

"Carson," she whispered, seeking his mouth, finding it.

For a few moments Carson allowed himself to enjoy the deep, sensual kiss. Then finally, reluctantly, he captured Lara's caressing hands, kissed them and tucked them back around his neck.

"Carson?"

"Not yet, honey," he said huskily. "You're still weak as a kitten."

"Only compared to you," Lara retorted, kneading the thick muscles of his shoulders. "Dr. Scott said it would be all right."

She felt the sudden stillness of Carson's body.

"When did he say that?"

"I called him this morning," Lara said. "He told me I can 'resume marital relations' anytime I want. I want, Carson."

A tangible shudder of desire went through him. His heartbeat surged, filling him with heat. He fought to control the total response of his body to Lara's invitation. It was no use. A word, a kiss, and he was hard, ready, aching to be sheathed within her loving warmth.

"Are you sure?" Carson whispered. "You were so sick when I found you in the library. It…frightened me a little," he said. "Oh, hell, Lara, it terrified me," he gritted, burying his face in the black silk cloud of her hair. "I don't want to do anything that would hurt you."

"Then you'd better make love to me," she said, threading her fingers deeply into his thick, cool hair, seeking and finding the warmth of his scalp beneath. "I want you so much that it's a kind of hurting."

"Lara," Carson said hoarsely, his arms closing around her with an intensity that he could barely restrain. "My sweet, warm, beautiful woman." Reluctantly he released her and stood up to pull off his clothes. "I'll make it good for you, honey."

"You always make it good for me."

Anticipation shivered through Lara as she watched Carson's powerful body emerge from his clothes. Her breath caught as she saw how aroused he was. When he knelt beside her, she ran her fingertips down his torso to the hard, erect flesh where his blood beat visibly, hotly. When she stroked him, his whole body tightened as though he had brushed against an electrical current. For a few moments he allowed himself to enjoy the sweet torment of her caress before his hands swept down, catching her trembling fingers, removing them from his hungry body.

"It's too soon, baby," he said, his voice thick with passion and regret as he brought himself under control. "You're so weak you're shaking."

Lara made a sound that was caught between a laugh and a sob. She looked up at Carson with eyes that were nearly black with passion.

"I'm shaking because I know what kind of pleasure is waiting for me," she said huskily. "Take me there, Carson. Go there with me."

It was Carson's fingers that trembled this time. He whispered Lara's name as he traced the soft curve of her lower lip. Then he bent over her and tasted the warmth behind her lips so gently that the kiss was like a sigh. She had expected a passionate claiming as sudden and hard as his obvious need for her. The delicate, exquisitely erotic tasting of her mouth made her shiver wildly, for it was a violent contrast to the pulsing heat of him against her thigh.

"Carson," she whispered, feeling the restraint in every ridge of muscle on his back. "You don't have to hold back. I'm—"

Lara's words became a cry of passionate surprise and pleasure as his fingertips slid beneath the silky peignoir and stroked the soft skin behind her knee. Her leg flexed in sensual response, opening her body to his touch. His hands stroked lightly, tracing her thighs, brushing over the midnight hair that concealed so many honeyed secrets.

The silky caress of the peignoir retreating up her body, the whispering touch of Carson's mouth and the tangible warmth of the sunlight pouring over her bare legs made Lara moan. When she felt the brush of Carson's fingers behind her other knee, she drew up that leg as well, giving herself to Carson and the sun. Though he knelt between her legs so closely that she could feel the brushing of his rigid flesh against her softness with each hard beating of his heart, still he did not take what she wanted so much to give.

Lara called Carson's name as flames of need licked over her. The word was a throaty plea, then a gasp as the peignoir slid up over her breasts to reveal the pale, satin skin and the velvety hardness of her nipples.

"Raspberries and cream," Carson said huskily. "I could eat you, little fox. You give yourself to me so sweetly that I—" His voice thickened. "There aren't any words. There's only this."

Carson's tongue touched each nipple and delicately traced the aureole, savored Lara's visible trembling at each touch. He took off the frothy lace peignoir and let it slide from his fingers, wanting nothing between his body and the woman who came to him so perfectly. Slowly, as gently as sunlight itself, he kissed her lips and the hollow of her neck, the creamy swell of her breasts and their deep pink crowns, the shadow pool of her navel and the smooth curves of her thighs. His hands moved over her legs in tantalizing caresses, shifting her subtly with each touch until her legs were drawn up against her body in a gesture of trust and sensual abandon.

At the first touch of his fingertips tracing her layered softness, waves of pleasure radiated through Lara. She opened her eyes and tried to say Carson's name, but all that came out was a broken sound of pleasure as he looked into her eyes and caressed her again. He smiled as he felt her melting at his touch, wanting him. The slow, sweet friction of his palm made her moan. Lara tried to tell Carson that she needed him, but all that came out was a husky sound. A languid fire spread up from his caress, ravishing her as sweetly as his touch. She tried to speak again but forgot the words as she felt him slowly begin to take her. The sensation was so exquisite that she closed her eyes and her body arched helplessly, silently pleading for more of him. He answered her with a small rocking motion that sent showers of pleasure through her. His name came from her lips in a ragged sigh when he finally filled her, only to retreat slowly, leaving her empty once more.

"Carson," she whispered, looking up into male eyes that were dark pools of need and a pleasure so intense that it was nearly pain.

Slowly he came to her again, filling her completely, rocking against her gently, perfectly, teaching her with every sweet movement that passion could be expressed in many ways; and that pleasure could build so subtly, almost secretly, that there was no warning of the ecstasy poised to consume her. Seeing his face taut and his powerful body misted with sweat, feeling him move with such restraint inside her, suddenly made her body unravel in tiny, endless ripples that were so exquisite she wept without knowing it.

Carson held himself tightly within Lara, both sharing and increasing her climax with small, powerful movements of his body. Then he was overtaken even as she had been, and he poured himself into her until he cried out unknowingly, consumed by an ecstasy both fierce and endlessly sweet.

When the last aftershocks of pleasure finally stopped sweeping through their joined bodies, Carson kissed away the tears caught in Lara's black lashes. He rolled onto his side, taking her with him, holding her close. The breeze lifted a corner of the comforter. He caught it and pulled it over Lara, kissing her with tender care. She smiled and curled more closely against him, loving him so much that she was afraid to put it into words because she didn't want him to think that she was asking him to say the words in return.

Finally, with aching tenderness, Lara brushed her lips against Carson's warm, salty skin and relaxed completely in his arms. He returned the kiss as gently as it had been given to him, holding Lara close while she drifted into sleep, holding her and wishing with all his strength that he could absorb her into his very soul, shaking with the force of that wish.

"Little fox," he whispered, "what am I going to do if you leave me?"

There was no answer but the wind lifting Lara's hair across Carson's cheek in a silky caress.

Chapter Twelve

"Mmmm," Lara murmured as Carson slowly released her mouth from his kiss, "I thought I was bribing you into bringing my research papers. Now I wonder who's bribing whom?"

A smile that was both beautiful and oddly haunted transformed Carson's face. Even though Lara had been up and around for a week, fear still clutched at Carson's heart every time he remembered how helpless she had been in the library when he had found her.

"I'm bribing you," he admitted huskily, looking down at Lara as she sat cross-legged on the bed, fully dressed. "I want you to take it easy, even though Dr. Scott said you could go out and brand calves if that's what you wanted to do. Stay here. Be here when I come back."

The urgency beneath Carson's words caught at Lara. "Don't worry about me," she said, taking his hand and bringing it to her lips. "I'm fine, Carson. Good as new. Better," she added, grinning and putting a hand on her slightly rounded stomach. "I'm twice as good. Go on and take care of the ranch. I hate to think of how much work you've put off to take care of me the last two weeks."

"After the fever broke, I enjoyed every bit of it." Carson hesitated, then looked at Lara with eyes that were intent, luminous...oddly haunted. "You've given me so much, Lara," he said simply. "More than I can tell you. If I've been able to give even a small part of it back to you, I'm glad."

The door closed gently behind Carson, leaving Lara alone but not lonely. The echo of Carson's deep voice and the memory of the golden warmth of his eyes as he looked at her made loneliness impossible. Smiling, she reached for the stack of documents that dealt with the legal aspects of the Rocking B's history from 1940 to 1960.

Feeling more vital and alive than she had in years, Lara tackled the last two decades of the Rocking B's history that she needed for her thesis. There were many papers dealing with small loans for seed and fertilizer, loans that were repaid within nine months. Some of the notes amounted to little more than IOUs written by hand on notebook paper. Others were more formal.

One document in particular intrigued Lara. It was dated March 17, 1949, and signed by Larry Blackridge, but it hadn't been drawn up by any of the Donovan lawyers. If the first page was anything to go by, the document seemed to detail the circumstances under which Larry Blackridge would borrow at no interest a large sum of money from Monroe White.

"White," muttered Lara. "White. Have I heard that name before in connection with the Rocking B? A shirt-tail relative of some kind? Must be. Who else would loan money with no collateral and no interest?"

Lara pulled over a notebook and began to read, pen poised to take notes. The more she read, the less sense the document made. Wryly she reminded herself that impenetrable prose was a common problem in legal documents. With a sigh she began the first page all over.

Gradually Lara realized that she was reading a pre-nuptial agreement between Sharon Harrington and Lawrence Blackridge. Monroe White was Sharon's maternal grandfather, a man of enormous wealth. Once the legal language was boiled down, the details emerged in all their emotionless austerity. Sharon, a woman of thirty-four years, was to be wife "in every sense of the word" to Larry, a man of twenty-four years. In return for said marriage, she would bring a dowry of fifteen thousand dollars, which would immediately be given to her husband. In addition, the White family would agree to guarantee loans at no interest for the future development of the Rocking B as long as the marriage remained intact.

The document went on for page after page of all but unreadable fine print, yet the basic meaning was inescapable. Monroe White had purchased a nearly bankrupt rancher for his beloved, regrettably unattractive spinster granddaughter. Larry had married Sharon not out of love but out of desperation; he had been on the verge of losing the ranch that meant more to him than anything else in the world. White had been a shrewd negotiator. Nowhere did the document allow for Larry to divorce Sharon without immediate forfeiture of the Rocking B. If Sharon wanted the divorce, she in turn forfeited all right to the Rocking B, to repayment of past loans and to custody of any children of their union.

Unconsciously Lara sighed as she set aside the sad circumstances underlying Larry's marriage. The document answered one question left over from Lara's own childhood. She now knew why Larry hadn't married the mother of his illegitimate child. He had loved Becky, but he had loved the Rocking B more. As for Sharon... If the rumors Lara had heard all her life were true, in the beginning Sharon had loved Larry Blackridge with a spinster's hopeless passion for a man too young and too handsome to come to her without the lure of money.

And in the end Sharon had hated Larry with all the fury of a woman scorned.

Frowning, Lara returned to the documents. Nothing unexpected turned up until nearly six years later. There was a terse note signed by a doctor at the Mayo Clinic, who bluntly stated that Sharon Harrington Blackridge was sterile beyond the ability of medical science to cure. Three weeks later another legal document appeared. This, too, had not originated in the offices of Donovan, Donovan and Donovan. In exchange for unspecified "expense money," an unnamed minor agreed to turn over her baby for adoption by the Blackridges. Two months later baby John Doe legally became Carson Harrington Blackridge, son and heir of Lawrence and Sharon Blackridge. The day the adoption was registered, the sum of one hundred thousand dollars was transferred to the Rocking B's ranch accounts from the estate of Monroe White.

Tears blurred Lara's eyes for a moment. Behind the stark fiscal transactions were lives that cried out with pain. She knew from her research that the three years preceding Carson's adoption had been devastating for the Rocking B. Falling beef prices, brutal blizzards, disease—all the bad luck that ranchers are subject to had descended simultaneously on the Rocking B. Larry had gone deeper and deeper into debt. In the end he had been forced to choose between his dream of conceiving a blood heir and ownership of the Rocking B itself.

Nowhere in all the massive legalese was there any clause indicating Larry's willingness to love the child he had bought and then adopted; but then, nowhere in the Blackridge history had Lara found any indication that love had been important to Larry. The land was, though. That and blood relationships. In the end, the land had been the stronger obsession.

Without realizing it, Lara rested her hand just below her waist as though to reassure the unborn child that it was wanted, loved and would be cared for with all the understanding she and Carson could command. The baby would never become a pawn in a power struggle between mother and father as Carson had been between Sharon and Larry. The baby would never have to look in a mirror as Carson had done and know that he hadn't been wanted, not really, not as a child to be loved. Sharon had wanted a family. She had bought both the child and Larry's compliance in an adoption that it was obvious he had never wanted. Larry's price had been one hundred thousand dollars.

Sadly Lara put aside the thought of how it must have been for Carson as a child, growing up unwanted by the only father he had ever known. Tears blurred her vision. She forced herself to control them. If she thought about Carson now she would lose all the emotional distance from her subject that a researcher must have. Later she would think about the personal sadness, the irreversible pain. Later she would cry for the lonely boy who had become the man she loved.

Grimly Lara returned to the papers. She almost missed the document that indirectly had shaped her own childhood. It was another loan paper, another transfer of White money to the Rocking B's empty coffers. It was the loan that had made possible the doubling of the Rocking B's boundaries, creating an empire in fact as well as in Larry's dreams. What caught Lara's eye was the document's date—six months to the day before she was born.

The paper contained a clause which stated that Larry would never, in any covert or overt way, acknowledge any but legitimate offspring. If he died before Sharon, the ranch would go in its totality to her and Carson. If she died first, her half would be held in trust for Carson, with Larry acting as administrator. If Larry tried at any time to will, sell, assign, give away or use as collateral for a loan any part of the ranch to anyone except Sharon or Carson Blackridge, all debts owed to the White estate would become immediately due and payable in full.

In effect, if Larry acknowledged Lara as his illegitimate daughter, he would lose the Rocking B. There was no way he could have repaid the huge "loans" the White estate had made to the ranch through the years unless he sold the land itself.

"My God," Lara said softly to herself, setting aside the document with a shaking hand. "How Sharon must have hated Larry, hated my mother, hated me. Sharon held the Rocking B like a sword over Larry's head for almost forty years. He must have hated her in return—and the 'son' she had forced him to accept as an heir when all Larry had ever wanted was a child of his own blood to inherit the ranch that had been Blackridge land since the Civil War."

It eased an old, old hurt to know that Larry hadn't refused to acknowledge Lara because he was in some way ashamed of her. The man who had smiled so indulgently into Becky's camera hadn't scorned the child of that illicit affair. He had been a man caught in a cruel vise. The fact that it had been largely a vise of his own creation didn't make the situation less painful or the outcome any less tortured.

And then a thought came like black lightning, dragging darkness and cold behind. Carson must have hated Becky, hated Lara. They had the one thing he did not have—Larry's approval.

"Oh, Carson," Lara said softly, looking blindly down at the documents scattered across the bed. "How terrible it must have been for you. And how ironic that from such hatred came such beauty for us. If you hadn't wanted to get even with Larry four years ago, you never would have come close enough to me to know me as myself rather than as a living symbol of so much of your unhappiness."

Tears burned in Lara's eyes as she remembered that night four years ago. But they were tears of a different sort, understanding rather than humiliation, shared pain rather than shame.

"The miracle, my love," she whispered, "is that you didn't utterly destroy me four years ago when you had the chance. How hard it must have been for you to walk away from the revenge you had wanted all your life."

Lara closed her eyes and tried not to cry as she realized how close she had come to never knowing Carson as a friend and lover, husband and father of her child. All those sad, tangled lives, a past that had been so cruel that Carson simply refused to discuss it even now, just as he refused to believe in love. She didn't blame him for that. If she had been raised as he had been, watching what "love" had done to Sharon and Becky and Larry, she doubted that she would be strong enough to risk what would certainly seem like the agony of love.

"Someday you'll understand, Carson," she whispered, running her fingers slowly over the thick, smooth surface of the paper in her lap. "The past is behind us, not in front of us. Their sadness isn't ours, nor are their hatreds. We're beyond that. We've found our own battles. And we've won."

Yet even as Lara whispered the words, tears slid silently down her cheeks. The documents she had just read had made the huge book of history turn over a new leaf, bringing her a new understanding of the past and the present. The new knowledge was poignant, even painful. She had a deeper understanding of why Carson sometimes watched her with haunted eyes. He had never been loved. Even now he found it all but impossible to believe in her love, and so he expected it to be taken away without warning.

Let the dead bury the dead, and the living get on with living. The past can't do anything for the present except ruin it.

How many times had Carson said those words to her in one variation or another?

And how many times had she tried to make him understand her love for all the small acts and large emotions of history that had shaped the present?

Carson's hostility to the past was as deeply rooted as Lara's fascination with it. No, that was wrong. His hostility was greater. He feared and hated the past because it had almost destroyed him. He was still fighting it, still trying to climb out from under the cold dead weight of the past and live securely in the warm possibilities of the present.

Lara knew that it wasn't an easy process for Carson. Last night she had awakened to find him sitting up in bed, rigid. His skin had been clammy to her touch. She had been afraid that he was having a relapse of the flu that had made everyone on the Rocking B so miserable, but when she had asked him if he felt all right, he had said only *I dreamed you were gone*. Then he had made love to her with aching intensity, as though he were trying to take her into himself all the way to his soul. Even when they finally slept again, he had held her tightly, as though he still feared waking and finding her gone.

And what had he said this morning as he left her surrounded by the heaped documents of the past? *Stay here. Be here when I come back.*

Lara brushed futilely at the tears that welled more quickly than her hand could carry them away. The understanding of the depth of Carson's past wounding was as painful to her as if she herself had been the one raised without love. She wanted to go to Carson, to tell him that she loved him and would never leave him, to hold him and be held by him in turn. Yet even as the impulse came, she knew that it was more for her own comfort than for Carson's. The hurt was new to her. It wasn't to him. It was as much a part of his life as the Rocking B itself.

"Use your head, not your heart," she told herself, wiping away the last of her tears. "You can't change in a day the lessons that took Carson a lifetime to learn, and it's both stupid and cruel of you to try. You know it's all right to believe in love because you've always been loved. Carson has only allowed himself to be loved by you for a few months. Give him enough time to let love become part of his past as well as his present. Then he'll be able to look at the future without fear. That's how you can heal him. Hold him when he wakes up in the middle of the night. Be there in the morning. Love him."

Gradually Lara's tears dried as she forced herself to stop thinking about Carson and get to work sorting and sticking two decades of Rocking B legal documents into neat piles. When she finished, she labeled and set aside the piles with a feeling of relief. Research had never been an unpleasant chore for her, but these last two decades of the Rocking B's history had simply been too painful for her to enjoy researching them. The worst was over, though. No more basic research had to be done. She could begin to organize her paper.

As a reward for a hard job conscientiously completed, Lara turned to the box of Cheyenne's journals that Carson had brought over from the homestead for her to read. She loved the spare wit and deeply felt descriptions of the land that were the hallmarks of her grandfather's observations on the ranch, people and life. She had read through all Cheyenne's journals except the one dealing with the years of her own life because she hadn't needed those years for her research. Nor had she felt strong enough to deal with her own past before this moment. But after seeing the circumstances that had shaped Carson's life, she turned to her own history as to a healing balm.

Lara lifted the heavy leather-bound book onto her lap and leaned against the bedstead for support. One of the enduring threads of her childhood had been the image of Cheyenne pulling a big leather book from a locked cupboard and going to the kitchen. On the nights when Cheyenne had spent hours writing by lamplight, or when he had carefully fastened photos, letters and other small mementos to the pages, Lara had watched, fascinated.

When she had asked to look at the whole book, her grandfather had always gently refused, saying that he was writing a personal history that shouldn't be read until he had told the last word. After all, there wasn't much point in reading a book without an ending, was there?

Lara had never been able to refute that logic, and, in time, Cheyenne had written the last word.

As soon as Lara opened the book, she confronted her own history staring back at her. There was a picture of her mother at fourteen, standing between two big men. One of them was Cheyenne. One was Larry. She had an arm around each man and her head tilted in laughter. She was giving Larry a sidelong glance that was a compound of mischief and elemental female awareness of an attractive male. Larry was looking at her with an odd expression on his face, as though a stranger stood in the place of the girl he had expected to find. The picture was dated two years before Lara's birth. Beneath the picture was a single line of Cheyenne's elegant writing. The writing was dated the day of Lara's birth.

Sometimes I think it all began that day.

For a moment Lara had to fight an impulse to close the book. She felt like an eavesdropper. The thought brought a bittersweet smile to her mouth. Wasn't eavesdropper just another name for historian? If she could stir through the embers and ashes of strangers' lives, surely she had the courage to stir through her own.

I'm worried about Becky.

There followed a long page of a father's concern over a daughter who was too pretty for his own peace of mind. Nowhere was Larry Blackridge mentioned.

After that there was no entry for several months except those referring to cattle and the land, the small

crises and triumphs of ranching that had remained un-
changed through history. Finally Lara came to a line that
had been written and then underlined later, with a note
added in the margin giving the date of the underlining.

*Larry's wife must be giving him hell. He's been over
here more often than he's been home. Becky's getting
a boot out of cooking for "her men." Larry's getting a
boot out of it, too. Never known him to laugh so much.*

In the margin the date was a year to the day before
Lara had been born.

There was more about the ranch on the following
pages and then a segment where pages had been torn
out. On the frayed remainder of one page was the terse
statement: *Some things are better left unsaid.*

Instinctively Lara knew that the missing pages dealt
with Cheyenne's feelings on learning that his young
daughter was pregnant with Larry Blackridge's child.
Lara closed her eyes for a moment, wishing that her
own birth hadn't caused so much pain for the people
she loved.

She turned the page and saw a cardboard-mounted
picture of a newborn baby, wrinkled and tiny, staring
unblinkingly into the camera. The cardboard had been
glued over a page of Cheyenne's observations on the nature of raising cattle in a cold country. Obviously the
picture had been added later. Across the bottom of the
cardboard were a few lines written in an unfamiliar
hand. As she read, Lara realized that it was her own
mother's handwriting.

*You were born today, daughter. You were born to me
and only to me. You are mine in a way no one else will*

ever be. I will call you Lara, which means "shining," because you are the light cast by my love for Larry. Hello, Lara Chandler, with your rosy cheeks and tiny little fingers. I love you.

Tears welled again behind Lara's eyes. She ran her fingertips over the lines as though through them she could touch the woman who had died before her daughter ever truly knew her. Staring blindly at the page, Lara wished suddenly that she could tell her mother so many things, not the least of which was that Lara had loved her, too.

There were other lines on the cardboard, lines written by Cheyenne.

Found this after Becky's funeral. Figured it was a more fitting way to welcome a child into the world than the poison that spilled out of me when I first found out Becky was pregnant.

Lara smoothed her fingertips lightly over the words. How like Cheyenne to overcome his own bitter disappointment and grow into a larger love. Never once had he made Lara feel like anything but a beloved, welcome addition to his family. Never once had he even hinted that the birth of his granddaughter wasn't every bit as joyous an event as the birth of his own daughter had been.

"You were a rare man, grandfather," whispered Lara. "You gave so much to me. I'm glad that you lived long enough for me to love you in return."

The pages turned beneath Lara's fingers, pages revealing Becky's love for Larry, pages detailing Cheyenne's stoic acceptance of what he could not change. Only rarely did Cheyenne's anger surface, and then only at what he perceived as an injustice toward the one truly innocent party in the whole tangle—Lara.

The Queen Bitch got on her high horse again. Told me I couldn't bring "that bastard" to the Christmas party. I told her I'd see her in hell before I'd hurt my own granddaughter and that, if she didn't want us at the party, she'd better be standing in the doorway with a shotgun and a round in the chamber.

And then a few days later:

Larry apologized for the QB. Said Lara was of course welcome to the Christmas party. I told Larry that if he didn't muzzle that bitch on the subject of Lara, he could find himself another ramrod. I don't blame his wife for hating Becky, but I'm damned if I can see any reason to take it out on Lara. A sweeter child God never made.

The pages turned faster and faster beneath Lara's hands, memories swirling around her, history changing with each new insight, each new understanding, each new point of view. Her mother died in a mountain storm, leaving behind a child who didn't understand why she was alone. Larry's mistress died in a mountain storm, leaving behind a man who became more cruel with the passing of each loveless day. Cheyenne's daughter died in a mountain storm, leaving behind a father who knew only that Becky had loved well but not wisely. An adulteress had died in a mountain storm, leaving behind her lover's wife, a woman whose emotions had twisted and shrunk until nothing was left of her but a single-minded desire for revenge on the man who had never loved her.

And through all the seething years, an adopted boy grew up always beyond the reach of love, always wanting it, never having it, until finally he believed that vengeance, not love, was the only human emotion that endured.

In a strange way Becky's death brought together the two men who had shared her life. When life had troubled either Larry or Cheyenne, they sought each other out, sometimes to talk, often simply to share a silence that demanded nothing, because each man knew that there was too much between them ever to be either described or eased with something as intangible as speech. Each crisis in their lives was bluntly stated in Cheyenne's increasingly frail hand. By the time Lara turned fourteen, Sharon Blackridge had had her first bout of cancer and surgery. When the cancer recurred, Larry came to Cheyenne in the middle of a spring blizzard.

Larry wants me to make sure that Lara doesn't marry anyone until Sharon is dead. I told him that seeing as how Lara is only fourteen, he didn't need to get all in a lather about her love life just yet. He didn't say a word, just looked at me. I knew then that he'd had Becky before she was fifteen.

Came real close to killing him right then. Hadn't felt that way in years. Hope I never do again.

It was a long time before Larry's name was mentioned in the journal. Lara read about the ranch, her grandfather's pride in her grades and his regret that he wasn't rich enough to send her to college. The pages turned and the years with them, and she was working at the café in town.

I'm worried about Lara.

The words went through Lara like a cold wind, echo of Cheyenne's worries years before, when Becky was young.

Heard that Carson was courting her. A good man and a fine cattleman, but lacking tenderness. And she's such a gentle little thing. Considered warning her, but didn't. Everybody's got to measure his own dreams. She's eighteen, and she's had a crush on him since she was thirteen.

Hell, I should go down on my knees and thank God that Carson didn't notice her sooner, like Larry did Becky—or if Carson did notice, he was too damned decent to seduce a child.

Good thing the Queen Bitch is too sick to care about gossip. She'd make life hell for Carson and Lara both.

The entries became more and more sparse, with greater lengths of time separating them, as Cheyenne's health began to decline. Larry's first stroke was noted, as was Cheyenne's own heart attack. Sharon Blackridge's long, slow descent into death was recorded, ending with the day of her funeral.

Lara turned the page, began to read and felt reality dropping away from beneath her feet in an icy, terrifying rush. She read the lines, then read them again, unable to believe, refusing to believe. Yet even as she fought the truth, she felt a page turning over, history shifting inexorably, revealing a new part of the past, a new clue to a truth that tore mercilessly at her soul. She wanted to hurl the book from her, to scream denials, to tear the page out and burn it to ash as bitter as the end of her dreams; but all she did was numbly read the lines again and again, hoping against hope that she was wrong.

First day back from the hospital. Good to be here again, but I came home to die and I know it. It's time and then some. All that holds me here is little Lara. She's such a gentle thing. I pray to God that she'll find a man worthy of her, but I doubt that I'll live to see it. She hasn't so much as looked at a man since she stopped seeing Carson a few years ago. I wonder if—

There was a break in the sentence and in the journal, as though something had interrupted Cheyenne. His next words told Lara what that interruption had been.

Larry came. Told me that he'd finally outfoxed the Queen Bitch. She thought she'd fixed it so that he would never have a child of his own blood inherit the ranch. But as soon as she died, Larry drew up a new will. When Larry dies, Carson has one year to marry Lara. No marriage, no inheritance. And it has to be a real marriage. Carson has two years to get a child or to prove that Lara is sterile.

After a long time Lara forced herself to stop reading and rereading the lines as though she could somehow make the words change by sheer effort of will. She turned the page with a hand so cold that she couldn't feel the heavy texture of the paper. There were no more entries in Cheyenne's journal.

Lara turned back to Cheyenne's last entry, irrationally hoping the words had changed. They hadn't. She closed her eyes, unable to bear the rich sunlight flowing through the windows over the bed. She tried to think constructively, to apply her intelligence to this discovery as she would have to any other new historical fact, but all her thoughts revolved relentlessly around Carson's cruel deception, returning to it again and again, unable to think past it.

An act. All of it. He never wanted me. Not four years ago. Not now. An act. All of it. He never wanted me. Never wanted. Never. Me.

Lara wished that she could cry to ease the ache and burning of her eyes, but no tears come. She felt as though all her strength had vanished in a single terrible instant, leaving her worn and old, unable to cry out in anger or agony or even despair, a stranger in her own body, a stranger in her own life.

She had been so sure of herself and love, so sure that her understanding of reality was valid and Carson's was not.

She had been wrong.

There was a reason Carson had never said he loved her. He didn't. He never would. Four years ago he had sought her out for the sake of revenge on Larry Blackridge, but Carson hadn't been cruel enough to follow through. Four months ago he had sought her out because she was the key to ownership of the Rocking B. That was the "mistake" Carson had referred to when she had asked why he wanted her back. He had let her get away four years ago when he had her roped, thrown and ready for branding. But he hadn't known at the time that Sharon would die and Larry would attach unthinkable terms to the inheritance of the Rocking B.

There was also a reason Carson hadn't tried to protect her from pregnancy. It wasn't because he had been too caught up in the passions of the moment to re-member to guard against conception. It wasn't even be-cause deep down inside himself he had wanted to have a child to raise and love. It was because the sooner she was pregnant, the sooner he was secure in his claim on the Rocking B.

Like Larry, Carson had wanted only the land. Like Larry, Carson had married a woman he didn't love in order to keep the Rocking B.

Lara heard the front door slam and wished suddenly that she had had the sense to flee while she could. Yet even as the thought came, she knew it was too late. The pages of history had already turned, taking her with them, imprisoning her in a world she had understood too late. She was married. She was pregnant.

And she was in love with a man who loved only the land.

Was that how her mother had felt? Caught in a trap of her own making? Pregnant. In love with the wrong man. No place to flee because everywhere she went she would drag the heavy golden chains of her love behind, chains anchoring her to a man who loved the land more than he loved the mother of his child.

History repeating itself generation to generation, a loveless legacy of ambition and power passed from fa-ther to son, world without end, amen. Bitterly Lara thought that maybe the traditional historians were right. Maybe men had always loved the land and the glory more than they had loved the women who made their damned dynasties possible.

World without end, amen.

Chapter Thirteen

"LARA, THAT CANADIAN STORM IS sweeping a few loons down our way," called Carson from the stairway, coming closer with each word. "If the storm holds off, let's go out to the pond and listen to them sing to the rising moon. It's the most beautiful—" Carson's words stopped abruptly when he saw her. "Lara? What's wrong, honey? Are you sick again? Should I call Dr. Scott?"

Eyes closed, Lara made a weary gesture with her right hand. "It's all right, Carson. You don't have to pretend anymore."

Confusion replaced concern on his face. "Pretend? Pretend what?"

"That you care."

"About what? The loons? Honey, you're not making any sense."

"About me." Lara's hand went over her womb. "About us," she whispered.

Carson went very still. "What the hell are you talking about?"

"About the sins of the fathers," Lara said bitterly, feeling a hot, almost violent rush of anger through her blood. She looked at Carson for the first time, and her eyes were black with pain and unwanted knowledge. Her words were tight, formal, as though she had chosen them for a treatise. "About history and land and the inheritance thereof. About men who love the land more than they love anything else, even the women who love them. About Larry and Sharon and Becky. About you and me. About the Rocking B and marriage."

Lara watched Carson's expression become as bleak as her voice. Without a word he came to stand over her. He saw the open journal, spun it around and read the last page. He began to swear tonelessly, the words all the more terrible for their lack of emotion. He turned toward her, reaching out to hold her.

"Lara—" he said hoarsely.

She knew then beyond any doubt that it was true, every word of it, every cruel betrayal. She flinched from Carson's hands. "*Don't*. The act is over. You had your dream. I had mine. Too bad they both couldn't come true."

Carson's hands flashed out and closed on Lara's face, pinning her beneath his glance. "It's not what you think! I wanted you before Larry ever wrote his goddamned will!" Carson forced himself to slow down, to take a deep breath, to cope with the disaster he had foreseen and yet had prayed would never come. "What we have is too good to throw away. When you get past your first anger, you'll see that," he said urgently. "You have to. I won't let you go, little fox."

"Why? You've got all you ever wanted—revenge and the Rocking B. Or was there something in the fine print of Larry's will that Cheyenne missed? Some kind of bizarre minimum time limit for marital relations?" asked Lara, and the bitterness of her words drew her mouth into a thin downward curve.

Carson's eyelids flickered, the only pain he allowed himself to reveal. He had known this might happen, but he had hoped so desperately that whatever they had built together would withstand the blow. Now the cold certainty was growing that he had been wrong. The blow had come too soon. She looked too pale, too remote, as icy and untouchable as a winter moon.

Chills chased over Carson's skin.

"Do you really want to know the fine print?" he asked, his expression bleak.

"I'd be a fool if I didn't. I'm tired of being a fool."

Slowly Carson released Lara from his grasp. "You want revenge, is that it?" he asked, curiosity and something else in his tone, something very like the agony that was clawing at Lara. "I guess I can't blame you for that."

"I want to know the dimensions of the fool's paradise I've been living in," she corrected.

"'Fool's paradise.' Is that how you think of our time together?"

"Spare me the fake sentiment," Lara said, clenching her hands together. "I can take the rest but not that. Not that!"

"Lara," Carson said achingly, reaching toward her again.

When she flinched away, his hands dropped to his side. He closed his eyes. He had anticipated losing her, but he hadn't known how much it would hurt. He hadn't allowed himself to know. He had told himself that she loved him. Surely she would understand that he had wanted her as well as the land. But she didn't. And when he thought about it, he couldn't blame her for that, either. He had gambled on her love being great enough to hold them together, no matter what. He had lost.

Carson's eyes opened slowly. There was nothing to show what he was feeling except the deep brackets on either side of his mouth.

"Cheyenne hit the high points well enough. The rest is simple," Carson said, his voice so controlled that it was toneless. "In the event of a divorce, the Rocking B's title is transferred to our children, with me retained as ranch manager until the day I die, unless I'm the one who sues for divorce. In that case the ranch simply goes to Larry's grandchildren and I drop out of sight as though I'd never been born, never lived on the Rocking B, never—" The words ended in an abrupt silence.

"And if there are no grandchildren?" Lara asked quietly.

Carson went absolutely pale. He tried to speak but could not.

Lara saw his agonized fear that she would end the pregnancy, and beneath her anger pain turned and cried out. *Why couldn't he have loved me just a little? Why do I have to feel his pain even now? Will it ever end? Will that child I'm carrying even now grow up only to break its heart on the cruel realities of the past?*

"Don't worry, Carson," she said tiredly. "You won't lose the Rocking B at this stage in the game. I won't get an abortion just to get even with you. There's been enough cruelty and vindictiveness in the history of the Rocking B. I won't be part of it any longer."

Slowly Lara closed Cheyenne's journal and set it aside. As she did, other answers came to her, other pages of history turning and bringing new understanding of her recent past with Carson Blackridge.

"No wonder you didn't want me going over all the old Blackridge documents," Lara said. "You were afraid I'd find out about the will. When were you going to tell me? After the child was born?" She stared at Carson for a moment and understood. "You weren't going to tell me at all, were you?"

"You were happy," he said simply. "What possible good would have come from making you sad?"

Lara had no answer for that but her own pain radiating through her in waves, threatening to overwhelm her. She couldn't allow that. She had to think. She had to act. She had to decide how she was going to spend the rest of her life.

But no matter how fiercely she tried, nothing came to her mind except pain. She closed her eyes and wished again that she could cry. She felt Carson's hard, warm hands gently circling her face, tilting her up to meet his eyes.

"Has it been so bad being married to me, little fox?"

The tears that Lara couldn't cry raked her throat, all but choking her. "When I thought that you wanted me...that someday you might come to love me." She swallowed, but it didn't help. Her mouth was as dry as her eyes. "Living with you was very beautiful. But now that I know you never wanted me—" A shudder racked her. "Oh, God," she said hoarsely, "why didn't you tell me why you wanted me to come back to the ranch?"

"I've wanted you for years. You were afraid of me. If I'd told you, you would have run again, the way you had been running for years. And by the time you were no longer afraid of me." Carson looked hungrily at Lara's dark, haunted eyes and the pale, beautiful bow of her mouth. "I liked seeing you happy, little fox. I liked what we had together in bed. I liked having you run toward me, smiling."

"Yes," Lara whispered bleakly. "I can believe that. It meant that you had the Rocking B locked up tight."

"That's not—" began Carson.

"Stop it!" she cried suddenly. "The truth is written all over the Rocking B and the Blackridge history!" With an effort Lara controlled herself. "I understand why you did what you did. In time I'll even be able to forgive it. But what I can't forgive is the way you let me fall in love with you all over again. Or was that your final revenge on me for being Larry's bastard?"

There was a long silence. At the end of it, Carson looked drawn, older, alone. "Can you look at these last few months and believe that?" he asked.

"Can I look at that damned will and believe anything else?"

There was another long, taut silence. When Carson finally spoke, it was in a tone that Lara hadn't heard for months, clipped and hard; his eyes were the deep, icy amber of a February dawn. Yet there was a yearning beneath his words that twisted Lara's heart.

"That's why I didn't tell you. You said you loved me, but I knew there wasn't enough love in the world for you to believe that I wanted you with or without Larry's will. So I said nothing. I wanted to heal you and myself and the past. I wanted—" Carson's mouth became a hard, bitter, downward curve. "You weren't the fool, little fox. I was. I knew more about love than you did, and yet I still hoped. I should have known better. Sharon loved Larry, and she made his life pure hell. Larry loved Becky, and he put her through a different kind of hell. You loved me and I—" Carson made a sudden, chopping motion with his hand. "Hell of a thing, love."

Suddenly he turned and walked away. A few moments later Lara heard the sound of the front door closing.

She lay without moving for a long time, trying to think, unable to do anything except hurt. Finally she knew that she couldn't bear being inside the bedroom any longer. She pulled on a light jacket and walked quickly to the only haven left to her, the Chandler homestead.

Yet that, too, had somehow changed. Lara looked around the familiar, worn interior of the homestead and wondered why she should feel a stranger in her own home. She knew every seam, every pit, every gouge in the walls and floor. She knew the faded colors of the throw rugs and the threadbare patterns of the chairs by heart. Each crack and chip in the heavy pottery plates was an old friend, as was the mismatched silverware stacked in wooden drawers whose corners were rounded by use. Every room, every window, every fall of light and shadow in the old house called silently to her, *Remember me?* And the answer was always, *Yes, I remember you.*

Then why did she feel adrift, lost?

Lara's blue-black eyes searched each room as she paced the small house yet again. She had come to the homestead to think because thinking had been impossible at the Blackridge ranch. The things she remembered there were too new, too raw with pain for her to do anything but flinch.

She didn't want to remember the way Carson had looked before he had turned and walked out of the house. He had the ranch. Wasn't that what he had wanted? Land, not love? Then why had he looked so sad and angry? Had she missed some vital page in the history of the past? Had she interpreted the facts of her own personal history mistakenly or too narrowly, with the result that her conclusions outraged truth in the very act of supposedly discovering it?

She had had that kind of distorted focus on reality once before. She had been so sure that Carson had walked out on her four years ago because she was Larry's bastard. So sure...and so wrong. Carson had walked out because he was too decent to seduce a virgin for revenge. That fact hadn't changed with the revelation of Larry's will. That fact remained.

Carson was a decent man.

In school Lara had read scholarly works whose only purpose had been to distort historical facts in the service of the author's own prejudices. She had always felt that those works represented the most distasteful sort of trickery, intellectual lies masquerading as enduring truth. But was she doing that very same thing now? Had she remembered only the most damning incidents from the past four months, and had she interpreted them in only the most damning ways?

Why did the light go out of Carson's eyes when he knew that I had discovered the truth? He had what he wanted. Didn't he?

Didn't he?

There was no answer but the wild cry of a Canadian wind flowing around the mountains, wrapping them in clouds.

Suddenly Lara's own skin seemed too small for her. It was the same for the room, the house itself. She had to be outside. She had to be beneath nothing more than the untamed sky, had to see nothing smaller than the massive thrust of mountains, had to hear nothing but the long cry of the wild wind.

At that instant Lara realized why her mother had always walked out alone during the most violent thunderstorms. In the immense, shattering thunder, no one would hear her scream.

A gust of wind tore the front door of the homestead from Lara's hand. The door banged against the wall, fully open. The door banged again, as though to remind Lara that she had forgotten to close it. She didn't notice. As she hurried out into the yard, she pulled on the mountain parka that she had automatically grabbed from its hook beside the door. Behind her the door banged again, then slammed shut.

Lara scrambled to the top of one of the rolling, grass-covered ridges in back of the homestead and stood for a moment. All around her huge clouds raced and boiled, churned by a muscular wind. Some of the clouds were the color of freshwater pearls. Others were as dark as the mountains whose peaks they concealed. After a glance she hurried on. She knew exactly where she was going. Her mother had taken her there on gentler days, when sunlight rather than thunder poured over the land.

But her mother had also gone there to drink the wild storm winds, and she had gone alone.

Before the first vague forerunners of thunder trembled through the air, Lara reached her destination. A long, rocky spine rose from a grassy ridge. In some places the layered rock had been worn to little more than a jumbled mass of boulders. In other places, a cap of harder rock jutted out over the ridge where softer rock had already been worn away. The result was a low, shallow cave overlooking the valley of the Big Green.

Lara ducked beneath the overhang, sat with her knees pulled up against her chest and waited for the storm to break. And as she waited, thoughts shivered and twisted like clouds called by the raging wind, thoughts escaping her control, reminding her of the very things that she had fled from the Blackridge house in order to forget. She fought the seething memories, throwing back cold truths to take the warmth from a remembered time when she had believed in love. Like the wild wind, the arguments raged in her mind.

Sometimes Carson's hands had trembled when he touched her.

Lust, nothing more. Simply lust. A biological reflex having nothing to do with tenderness and caring and love. He didn't love her.

He had let her fear fade before he touched her. He hadn't pushed her sexually in any way at all. He had kept his promise even when passion had made his whole body hard with need.

If he had pushed, she would have run away and he would have lost the Rocking B.

He had let her undress him. Let her touch him. Had made himself naked and utterly vulnerable to her. Had given himself to her. He had taken all the risks. He hadn't been forced to do that by her fear because her fear had faded with each of his smiles, his deep laughter, his amber eyes approving of her. He could have seduced her much more quickly if he hadn't tied his own hands. After the first weeks she wouldn't have been afraid to make love with him. He must have known that. Yet he had held back. He had kept his word. He had let her come to him.

Lara sat very still, waiting, but there was no cold refutation to take away the warmth of that memory. If seduction had been Carson's only goal, he had acted foolishly by being so restrained. Carson wasn't a foolish man. Therefore, seduction hadn't been his only goal.

With that realization came another memory. It shook Lara like the wind, just as it had shaken her that night in the library when Carson had looked at her with such agony and regret in his eyes for having hurt her years ago: *Oh, God, little fox. There are times when I wish I could crawl out of my skin and die.*

Lara shuddered violently and made a broken sound that was swallowed up by the long howl of the wind. She remembered something else that he had said: *Love is a lie, a trick played on the unwary.* She had been easy prey. She had walked into his arms as trustingly as though he had never betrayed her in the past. But he hadn't betrayed her years ago. Not really. He had stopped short of the cruel, unforgivable act of seduction and revenge.

And then came the cold, undeniable refutation of warmth and companionship. In the end he *had* tricked her. He hadn't told her about Larry's will.

Wind howled and moaned through the valley, bringing an icy foretaste of the storm to come. Thunder rolled in the distance, a vibration more sensed than heard. Below her, scattered at the edge of the wide green valley, was the Blackridge ranch and the Chandler homestead. Her home.

Even as the sight of home reassured Lara at some deep level of her mind, she realized that Carson had never had that kind of reassurance. But he had wanted it. He had needed it. A home. A place that was his own after a lifetime of being told that he didn't belong on the Rocking B because he wasn't a child of Larry's body. How would Lara have felt if she hadn't had the certain knowledge that the Chandler homestead waited for her when the storms of life threatened to tear her apart? How had Carson survived without the silent, enduring presence of home and love to give him strength?

No wonder he had hungered deeply for the Rocking B. It represented the security he had wanted and never gotten from life. With Larry's death the ranch should have become Carson's. He had earned it. It should finally have become the home where he belonged beyond argument or the ability of man to alter. And the ranch had belonged to him—until Larry's will was opened, and Carson was told that, if he wanted the ranch, he had to seduce Lara into marriage and motherhood.

Silently Lara asked herself if she really expected Carson at that point to risk everything he had ever wanted on the goodwill and sympathetic understanding of a girl whom he had hurt so badly that even four years later she ran from the slightest chance of meeting him face-to-face.

And then she remembered that Carson had been trying to see her or lure her to the ranch for more than a year. He had called her faculty advisor and suggested the topic of the Rocking B history while Sharon and Larry Blackridge were still alive. Carson couldn't have known about Larry's will at the time. The will hadn't been drawn up until Sharon died.

I've wanted you for years, dreamed of you until I woke up sweating and tied in knots.

That was why he had tried to get her to the ranch. Lust. Just lust.

Yet even as the cold thought came, Lara found herself unable to believe it. Lust was too simple to explain the complex emotions Carson had shown her. Did a man in the grip of wild lust take such tender care to arouse and then wholly satisfy an inexperienced partner? Did a man who knew only lust sit by a woman's bedside for days while she lay in the grip of a fever that had nothing to do with sex? Did lust drive a man to break his workday and take a woman up to a remote pond—not for a quickie in the grass but to count baby ducks? Did lust make a man cry at the thought of a woman wanting his child?

No.

Then a cold thought came, threatening the warm memories. A man who was worried about getting a woman pregnant and keeping her content might do those things. Marriage was only the first step in securing the Rocking B. The ranch wouldn't be within Carson's control until a child was born.

Lara shivered suddenly, though the wind rarely reached beneath the sheltering overhang. She couldn't believe that Carson was so cold, so calculating, that he would plan and carry out an intricate campaign of gentleness and sharing simply to assure himself of his hold on Lara and the ranch. She just didn't believe it. She didn't know why, but—

She frowned suddenly, reaching back to the blurred time of fever for a memory that was eluding her. She stared out across the land as though the answer were there rather than in her own memory. As sudden lightning stitched across the darkening sky, words came to her, Dr. Scott's and Carson's voices echoing in what Lara had thought was a fever dream but realized now was reality.

I want Lara well. I…need her.

Don't you want the baby, too?

Hell, yes, I want it. But I want Lara more.

Carson couldn't have known that she would hear and remember those words. They couldn't have been the result of calculation rather than emotion. He wanted her more than he wanted the baby that would give him control of the Rocking B.

Yet she had believed that he wanted the land more than anything else.

What if Carson wanted what the ranch represented rather than the land itself? A home. A place to live that was his own. A place where he would be welcomed when he was worn and hungry and cold. A place where he could go to sleep at night and know that someone would smile on seeing him in the morning. A place where he was accepted no matter who his parents were or were not, a place where he was loved whether or not he was perfect in every way.

I'm not perfect. Remember that, and try to forgive me when I fail you.

Had he failed her?

"He doesn't love me!"

Lara didn't know that she had cried out until she heard her own words echoing back from the overhang. "Love me. Love me. Me. Me." She put her head in her hands and trembled, but her thoughts drove on relentlessly, searching out another page of reality, a different understanding.

Did the fact that Carson didn't love her prove that he had failed her? How would her life have been different or more complete if Carson had loved her? Would he have been a more thoughtful, passionate lover? Would he have taken better care of her when she was sick? Would he have given her small caresses as he passed her chair at night? Would he have surprised her with wildflowers and shiny river stones and a mother duck with a raft of fluffy babies? Would he have fought tears at the realization of how badly he had hurt her four years ago? Would the light have drained out of his eyes when her bitterness poured over him, slicing through his hopes of home and happiness until he—

"Stop!" Lara cried out, as though it were something other than her own words battering her. "Oh, stop—"

But it didn't stop. Ruthlessly Lara's memories and intelligence worked together, pages turning, reality slowly shifting, presenting a new view of its complex truths. Understanding raked through her, forcing her to look at Carson and herself, forcing her to realize that truth came from looking at what a person did rather than what he said or did not say. Carson hadn't said he loved her, *but he had treated her as though she were the most precious thing on earth to him.*

If that wasn't love, what was?

And she, who had cried out her love for Carson, had stripped him of his dreams in a single, bitter torrent of words.

Was that an act of love?

And where was he now, the man she loved? Was he out walking in the storm because he couldn't bear to go back to the pain and emptiness of a house that was no longer a home?

With a choked cry Lara scrambled out from beneath the shelter of the overhang. Instantly the wind swirled around her, flicking tiny whips of ice-tipped rain across her cheeks. She didn't feel it any more than she heard the sudden massive thunder rolling off the peaks. All she heard was the echo of her own questions and the shattering reverberations of her answers.

At first Lara thought that the shout came only from her own need, her own dream. Then it came again, tumbled by the wind, Carson's voice calling her name. She turned and saw a wall of blue-black storm racing toward her from the northwest. Lightning arced in an incandescent dance between cloud and earth. An avalanche of thunder came, shaking the land. Carson rode swiftly toward her in front of the storm, spurring his horse across the land at a speed that made her heart stop with fear. She called his name, knowing that he couldn't hear her, unable to help herself from crying out.

Within minutes Carson brought the horse to a plunging halt in front of Lara. He paused only long enough to swing her up into the saddle in front of him before he put his spurs to the big horse again. It responded with the eagerness of an animal that knew it was finally heading for the shelter of the barn with a storm in violent pursuit.

As the horse raced up to the Rocking B's ranch yard, Willie hurried out of the barn and grabbed the bridle. Cold rain pelted down, mixed with stinging hail. Thunder cracked over the land, burying everything in an endlessly breaking wave of sound. Willie said something, but the words were utterly lost. Carson understood anyway. He kicked out of the stirrups, grabbed Lara and raced for the house as Willie ran with the horse toward the barn.

Lightning came again, strike after strike of white light that bleached color from the land. The bang of the ranch house door was lost beneath hammer blows of thunder so immense that the ear registered only an eerie silence. Cloud and earth slammed together in a massive avalanche of hail.

Lara clung to Carson, trembling as the storm battered the house with stunning violence. All she could think of was that Carson could have been caught out there without shelter, looking for her, and she would have been safe beneath the rock overhang and he wouldn't have known. The pieces of ice that were even now scouring the land could have scoured his unprotected body. He could have been thrown, the horse could have fallen, he could have been hurt and then he would have lain helpless in the ice and wind until he died.

That was what had happened to her mother—an icy trail, a fall, a cold too great for human warmth to overcome.

Lara looked up into Carson's eyes, wanting to ask him to forgive her for not understanding him better, wanting to tell him that she loved him, wanting to say everything at once. The drumming of hail buried her words. It was the same for him. She saw his lips moving, saw the burning intensity of his eyes and heard nothing at all.

She came up on tiptoe, straining toward him, even as her fingers searched through his thick dark hair, pulling him toward her. His lips were cold from the wind and so were hers. She knew that the heat of him burned beneath, and she knew that she had to reach it, had to touch the hot rush of his life. She felt herself being lifted suddenly as his arms came around her with crushing force. She was holding him the same way, as though she could become part of him if she just held him tightly enough. His kiss was a promise both wild and sweet, a sharing that needed no words.

Around them the storm raced by, taking with it both thunder and ice, leaving silence behind.

"I'm sorry—"

"—forgive me."

"I should have trusted—"

"—my love. I love you. I love—"

The sudden words glittered in the silence, fragments of overlapping thought and need, and neither he nor she knew who spoke which words, who apologized and who forgave. Their words, like their love, belonged to both of them equally.

Epilogue

"CARSON? IS THAT YOU? ARE YOU finished already?"
Lara asked.

She looked away from the computer screen, smiling
with anticipation and love at Carson as he came into
the library, wondering if he had brought something special to share with her. Last week it had been a river stone
that looked as though tiny, creamy flowers bloomed
within a gray-green matrix. Two weeks ago it had been
an evergreen bough perfectly spangled with rain.

And once, in autumn, he had taken her to lie within
his arms and listen to a loon's tremulous call while
night condensed around them.

"Just something I want you to see," Carson said,
bending down and kissing the nape of Lara's neck. "Do
you have time?"

She turned and put her hand on his cheek. "For you?
Always."

Carson turned and caught Lara's palm against his mouth, silently cherishing her. Then he pulled her to her feet, smiling as she trusted herself to his strength without hesitation.

"How's it coming?" he asked, looking at the computer.

"Much better. You did a wonderful job of matching the men's memories with the Blackridge daguerreotypes," she said, putting her arms around Carson's neck. "Have I thanked you for that?"

"Every day you're with me, every time you smile, but don't let that stop you," Carson murmured, bending down to her lips. "I love the way you thank me. I love thanking you in return."

Gently Carson pulled Lara against him, savoring the soft heat of her mouth, the generosity of her response and the firm, pregnant curve of her body pressed against him. Finally, reluctantly, he released her.

"If we don't get going, the next storm will move in and there won't be anything to show you until spring," he said.

Refusing to answer questions, Carson bundled Lara into a parka and tucked her into the pickup. He drove until he was at the base of a long, low fold of land. The shape of the ridge tickled Lara's memory. Together they climbed the gentle rise. Summer's lush grass had been cured by frost and woven into a dense, tawny mat by autumn rain and wind. Soon the storms of winter would come, pulling a thick white blanket over the land, protecting it while it slept and dreamed, resting in preparation for the sweet violence of spring.

"Close your eyes."

Obediently Lara closed her eyes. She felt the world tilt as Carson lifted her into his arms. Smiling, she hid her face against his warm sheepskin collar, telling him without words that she wouldn't peek. After a time the world shifted again as Carson carefully set her back on her feet.

"Now?" she asked.

Without answering, Carson stepped behind Lara, put his arms around her and pulled her into the sheltering warmth of his body as wind stirred over the open land.

"Now," he said.

Lara looked. Before her the Rocking B's pastures lay on either side of the Big Green's shimmering curves. A scattering of cattle grazed, and a rider wove through them. Except for the fences, little had changed since the first Blackridge had ridden into the valley, gathered a handful of stones and begun to build a new life.

And that was what Carson had brought Lara to see. In front of her, no more than an arm's length away, was the tumbled mound of native stone that had marked the first boundary of the westering dream that had shaped a family, a state and a nation.

"You found it!" Excitement rippled in Lara's words. "This is where it all began, the Blackridge dream and the Chandlers', all those long years ago. I can touch the very same stones, see the same valley, stand on the same ridgetop—and it's all here, everything!"

Lara turned in Carson's arms, giving him a radiant smile. His hand slid inside her parka, and he spread his fingers wide over her rounded body. Beneath his palm he felt their child stir as though impatient to be born and to walk upon the land as his ancestors had before him and as his own children would in their own time. Carson never tired of feeling that mysterious, eager life beneath his hand, of knowing that his child was growing within Lara.

"Yes," Carson said huskily, brushing his lips across hers. "It's all here, everything, right in my arms, and its name is love. I love you, Lara."

He felt the tremor that went through her as he lifted her into his arms. The kiss they shared was like the wind sweeping over the land, sweet and wild, touching everything, joining the past and the present into a future that would be as beautiful and enduring as history and the land itself.